AN UNOFFICIAL GRAPHIC NOVEL
FOR MINECRAFTERS

REDSTONE JUNIOR HIGH

CURSE OF THE SAND WITCHES

BOOK 5

CARA J. STEVENS

ART BY MITCHELL CREEDEN

SKY PONY PRESS
NEW YORK·

This book is not authorized or sponsored by Microsoft Corp., Mojang AB, Notch Development AB or Scholastic Inc., or any other person or entity owning or controlling rights in the Minecraft name, trademark, or copyrights.

This book is not authorized or sponsored by Microsoft Corp., Mojang AB, Notch Development AB or Scholastic Inc., or any other person or entity owning or controlling rights in the Minecraft name, trademark, or copyrights.

Sky Pony Press books may be purchased in bulk at special discounts for sales promotion, corporate gifts, fund-raising, or educational purposes. Special editions can also be created to specifications. For details, contact the Special Sales Department, Sky Pony Press, 307 West 36th Street, 11th Floor, New York, NY 10018 or info@skyhorsepublishing.com.

Minecraft® is a registered trademark of Notch Development AB.
The Minecraft game is copyright © Mojang AB.

Visit our website at www.skyponypress.com.

10 9 8 7 6 5 4 3 2 1

Library of Congress Cataloging-in- Publication Data is available on file.

Cover design by Brian Peterson

Print ISBN: 978-1-5107-4109-6
Ebook ISBN: 978-1-5107-4128-7

Printed in China

REDSTONE JUNIOR HIGH

MEET THE

PIXEL: A girl with an unusual way with animals and other creatures.

SKY: A redstone expert who is also one of Pixel's best friends at school.

UMA: A fellow student at Redstone Junior High who can sense how people and mobs are feeling.

CHARACTERS

MR. Z: A teacher with a dark past.

PRINCIPAL REDSTONE: The head of Redstone Junior High.

TINA: Pixel's nemesis.

VIOLET: A student with amazing enchantment and conjuring skills.

ALPHA, ZEB, AND DEBBIE: Tina's battle-ready friends from Combat School.

INTRODUCTION

If you have played Minecraft, then you know all about Minecraft worlds. They're made of blocks you can mine, creatures you can interact with, and lands you can visit. Deep in the heart of one of these worlds is an extraordinary school with students who have been handpicked from across the landscape for their unique abilities.

The school is Redstone Junior High. When our story opens, it is autumn. The students and teachers at Redstone Junior High are once again repairing the school after the latest invasion and battle. Now that classes are back in session, the kids are hard at work learning how to create redstone contraptions, build, farm, and survive in the wild. This is our heroes' final year, and the work just got a lot tougher.

Pixel and her friends take every opportunity to rest and relax in their secret beach hideaway. Unfortunately, they soon discover they are not alone. Two sand witches are watching them from the shadows, secretly planning a takeover of the school. To top it all off, the principal has been acting even more strangely than usual.

As school gets more challenging, Pixel and her friends retreat to the beach hideout more often to escape and practice their skills. But when strange things begin to happen there, the group suspects that there are sinister forces at work. Will they find out what's haunting them before their principal goes insane and their school falls into the wrong hands?

PROLOGUE

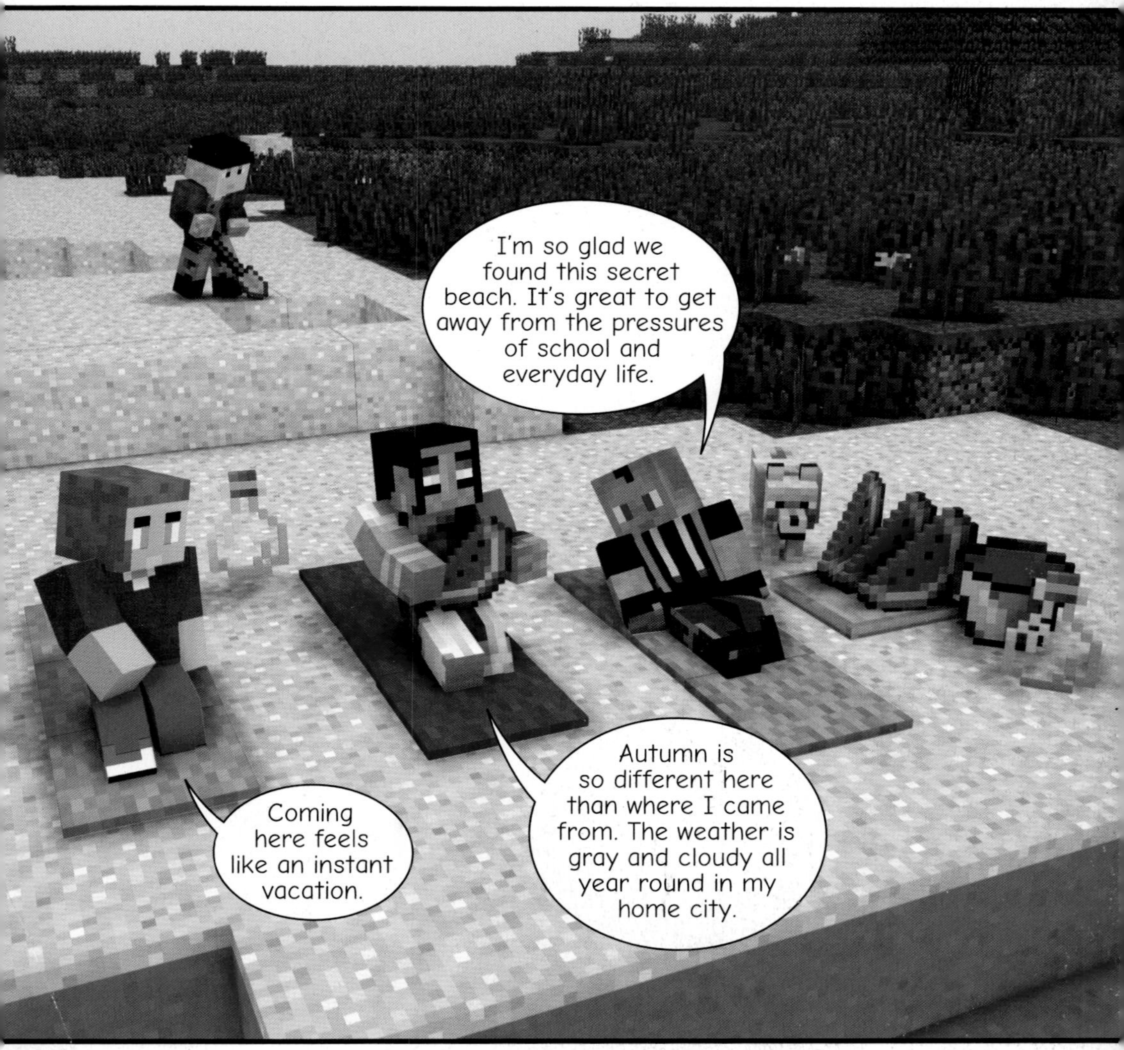
I'm so glad we found this secret beach. It's great to get away from the pressures of school and everyday life.
Coming here feels like an instant vacation.
Autumn is so different here than where I came from. The weather is gray and cloudy all year round in my home city.

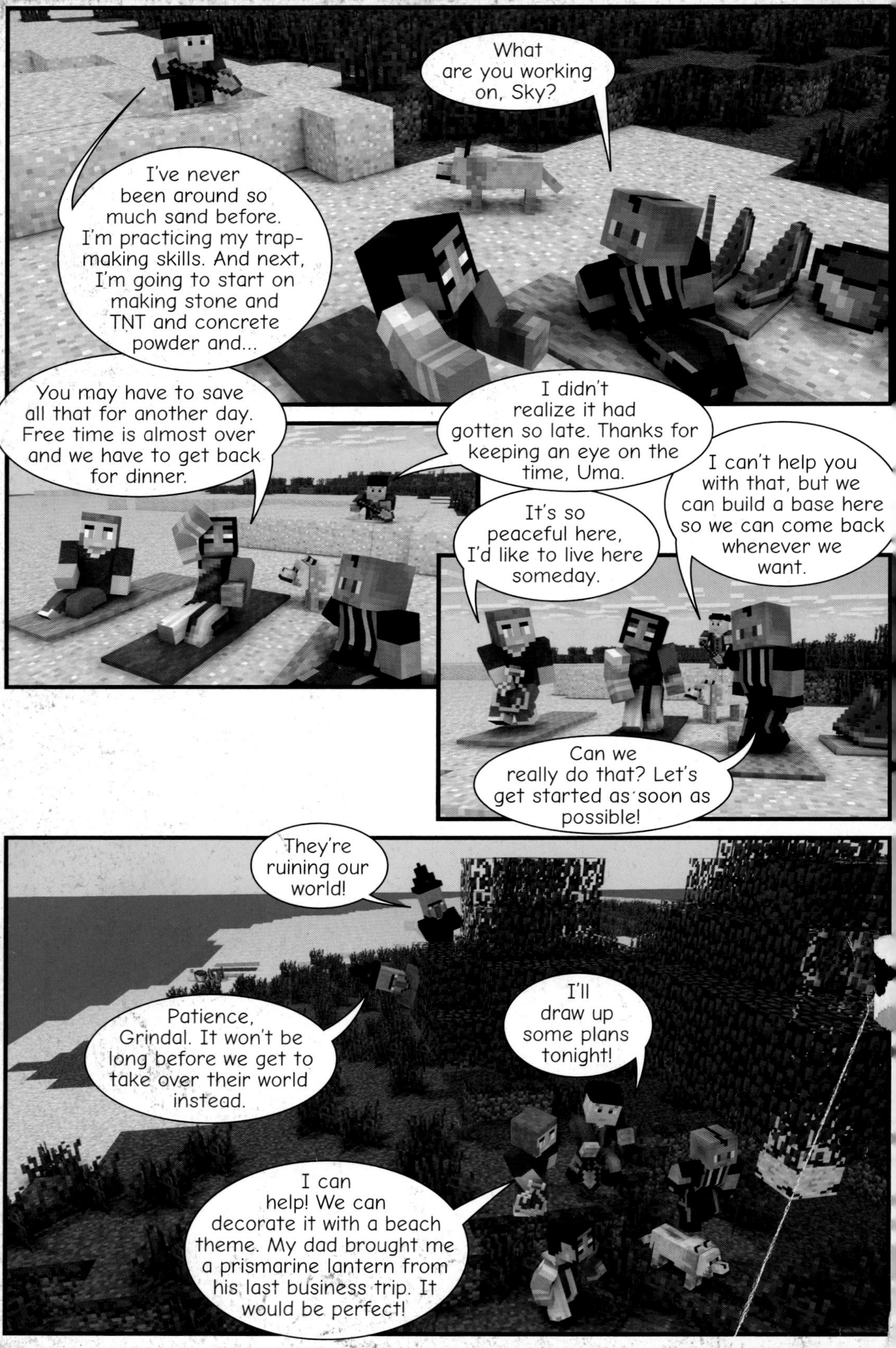
What are you working on, Sky?
I've never been around so much sand before. I'm practicing my trap-making skills. And next, I'm going to start on making stone and TNT and concrete powder and...
You may have to save all that for another day. Free time is almost over and we have to get back for dinner.
I didn't realize it had gotten so late. Thanks for keeping an eye on the time, Uma.
It's so peaceful here, I'd like to live here someday.
I can't help you with that, but we can build a base here so we can come back whenever we want.
Can we really do that? Let's get started as soon as possible!
They're ruining our world!
Patience, Grindal. It won't be long before we get to take over their world instead.
I'll draw up some plans tonight!
I can help! We can decorate it with a beach theme. My dad brought me a prismarine lantern from his last business trip. It would be perfect!

CHAPTER 1

LESSON
LEARNED

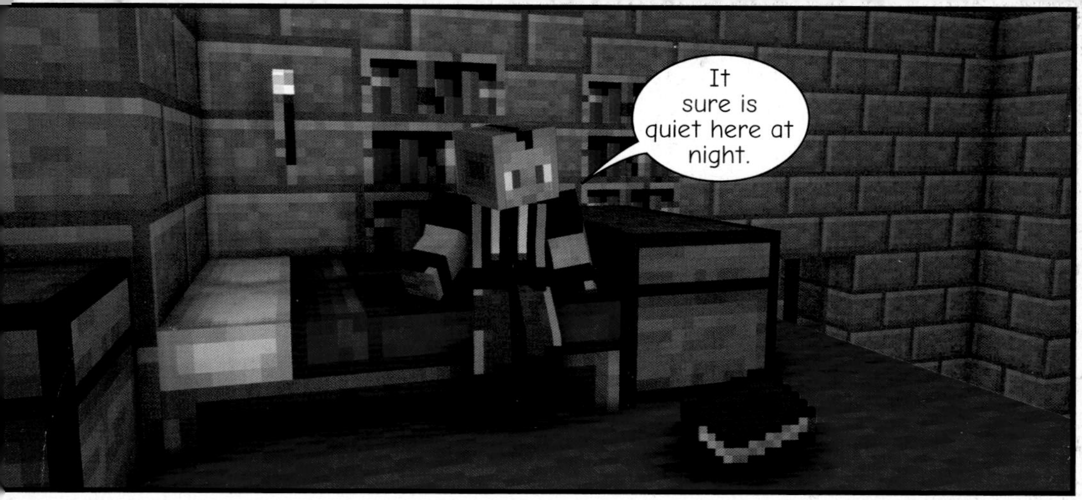
It sure is quiet here at night.

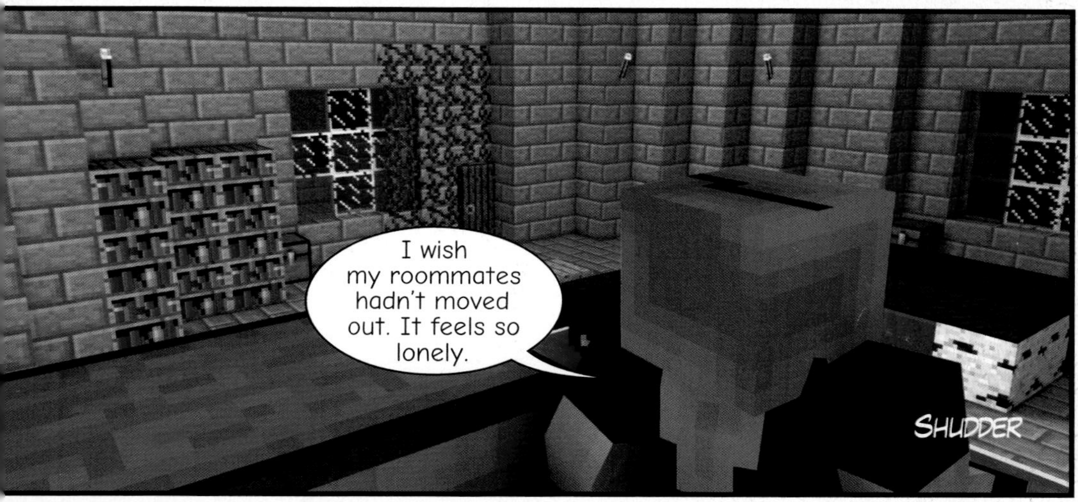
I wish my roommates hadn't moved out. It feels so lonely.
SHUDDER

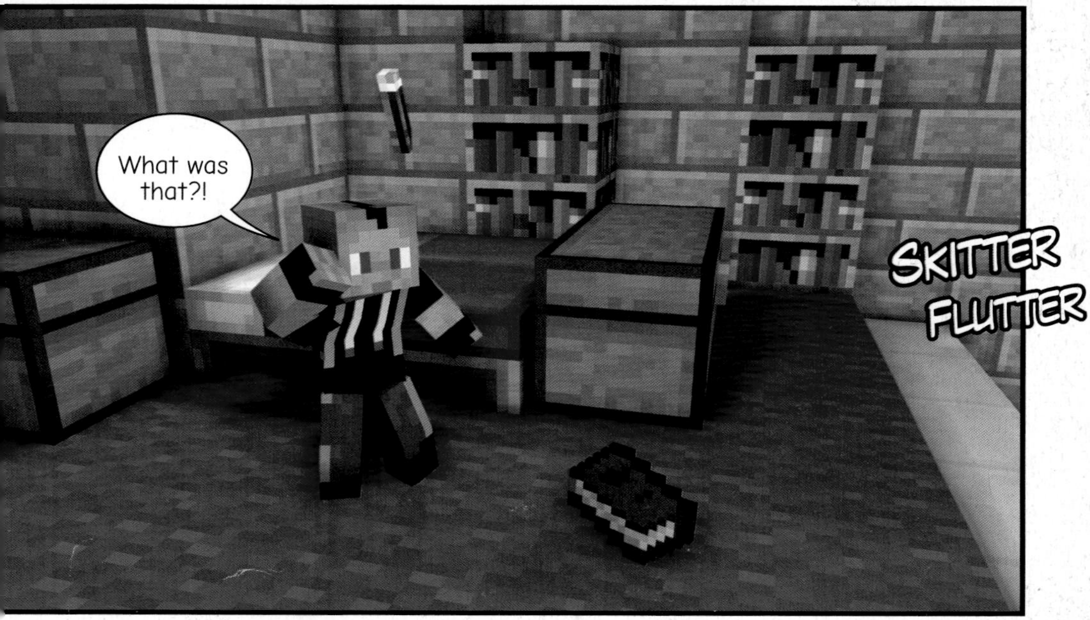
What was that?!
SKITTER
FLUTTER

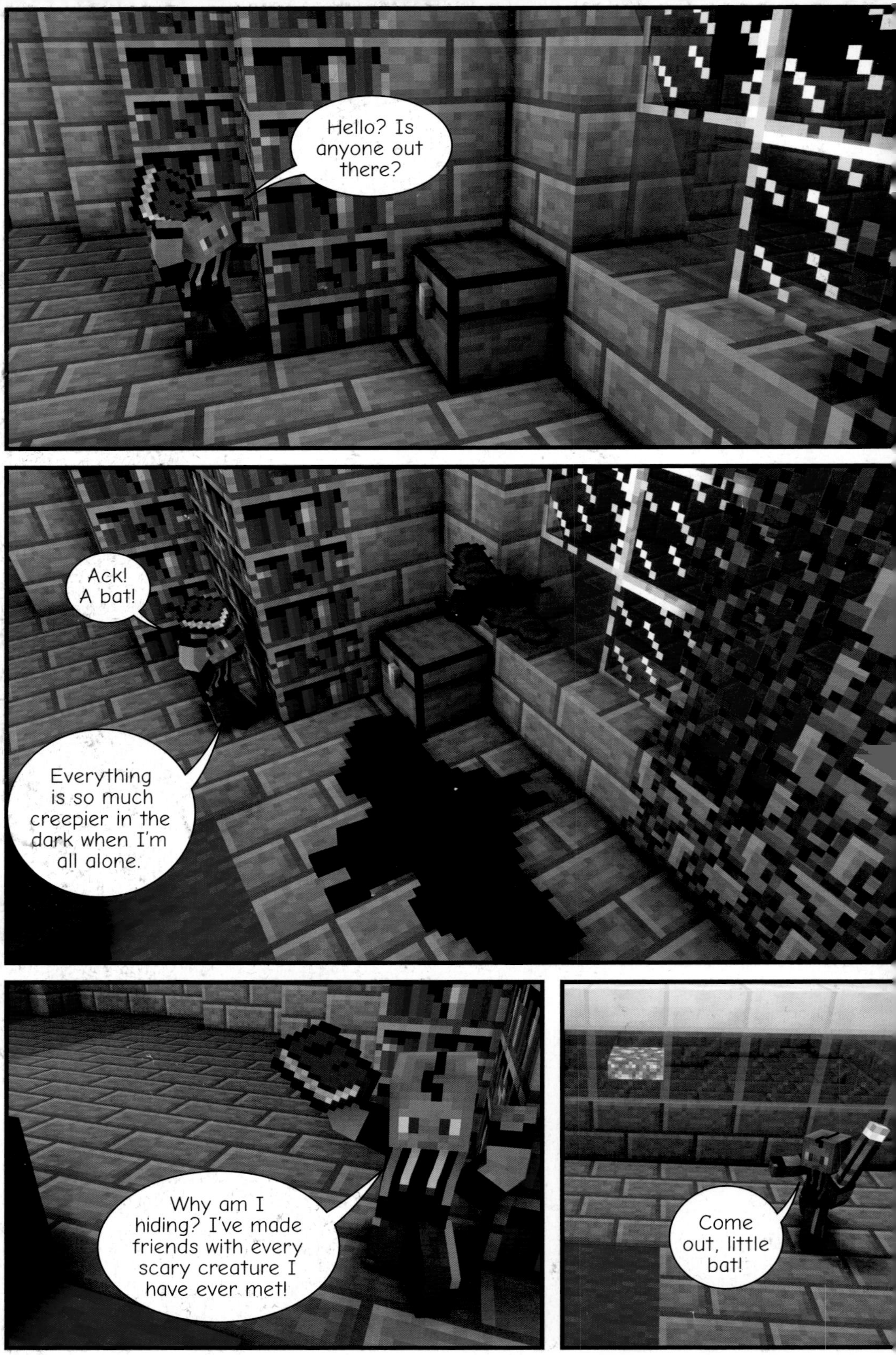
Hello? Is anyone out there?
Ack! A bat!
Everything is so much creepier in the dark when I'm all alone.
Why am I hiding? I've made friends with every scary creature I have ever met!
Come out, little bat!

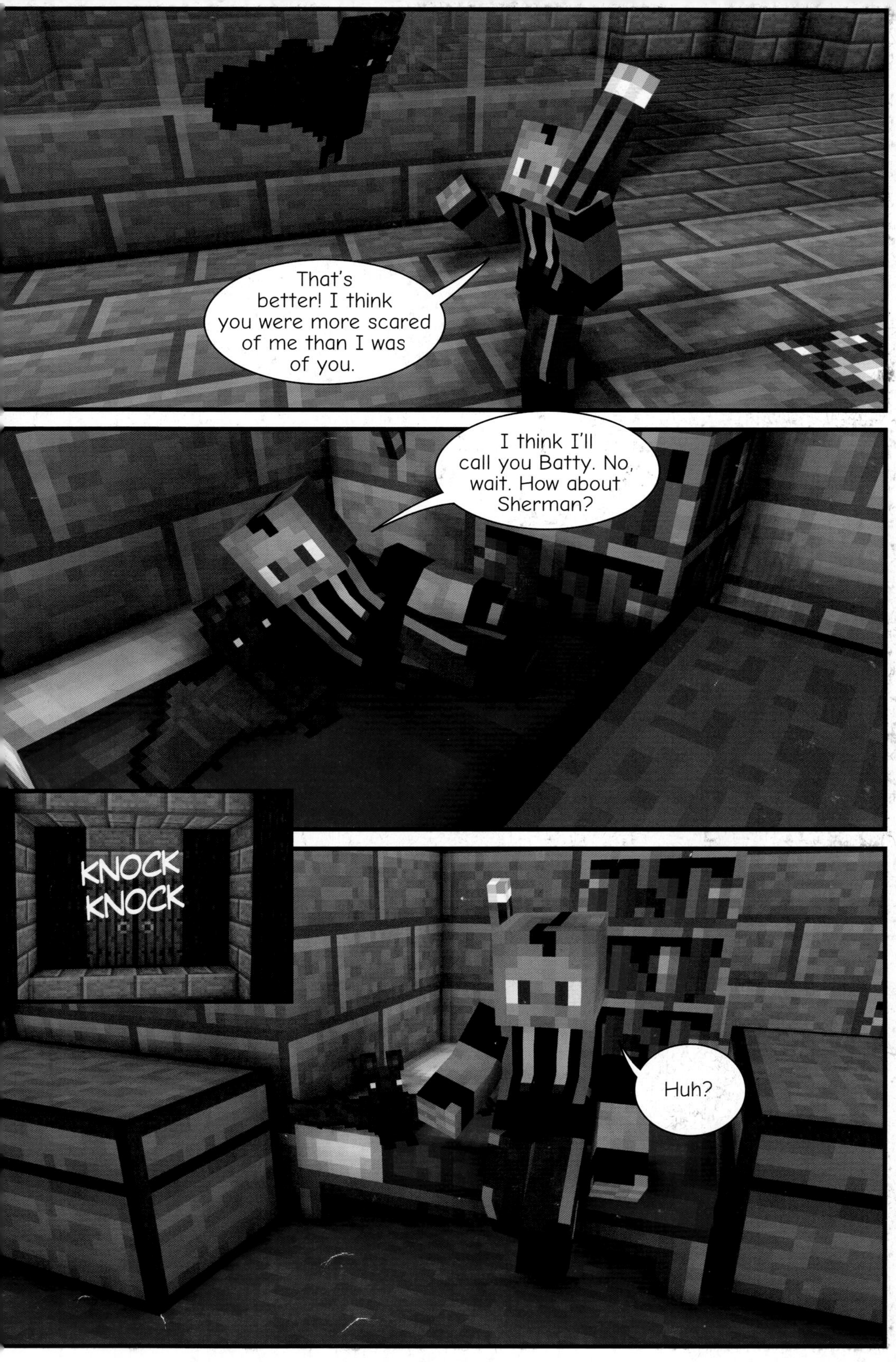
That's better! I think you were more scared of me than I was of you.
I think I'll call you Batty. No, wait. How about Sherman?
KNOCK KNOCK
Huh?

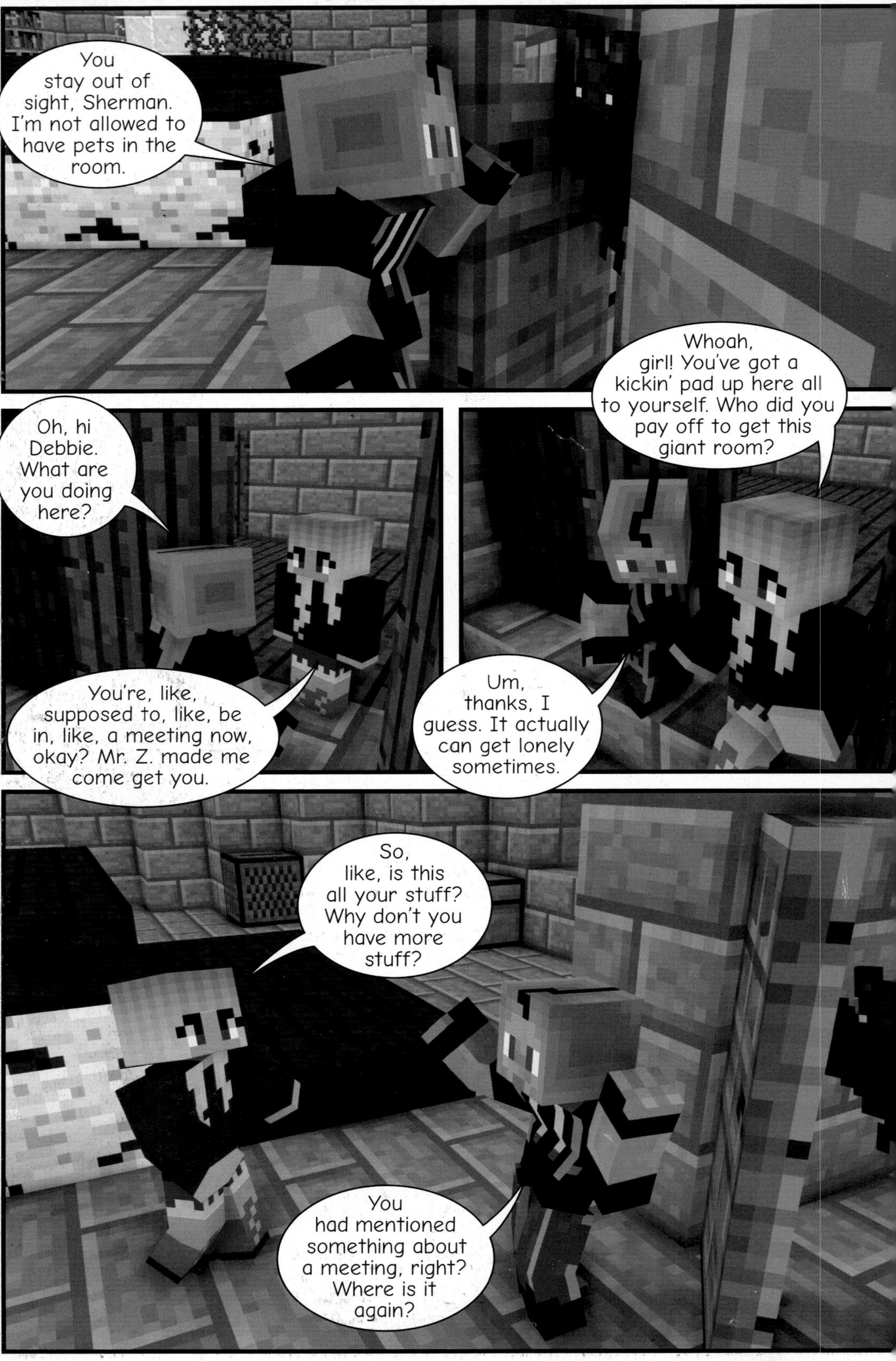
You stay out of sight, Sherman. I'm not allowed to have pets in the room.
Oh, hi Debbie. What are you doing here?
You're, like, supposed to, like, be in, like, a meeting now, okay? Mr. Z. made me come get you.
Whoah, girl! You've got a kickin' pad up here all to yourself. Who did you pay off to get this giant room?
Um, thanks, I guess. It actually can get lonely sometimes.
So, like, is this all your stuff? Why don't you have more stuff?
You had mentioned something about a meeting, right? Where is it again?

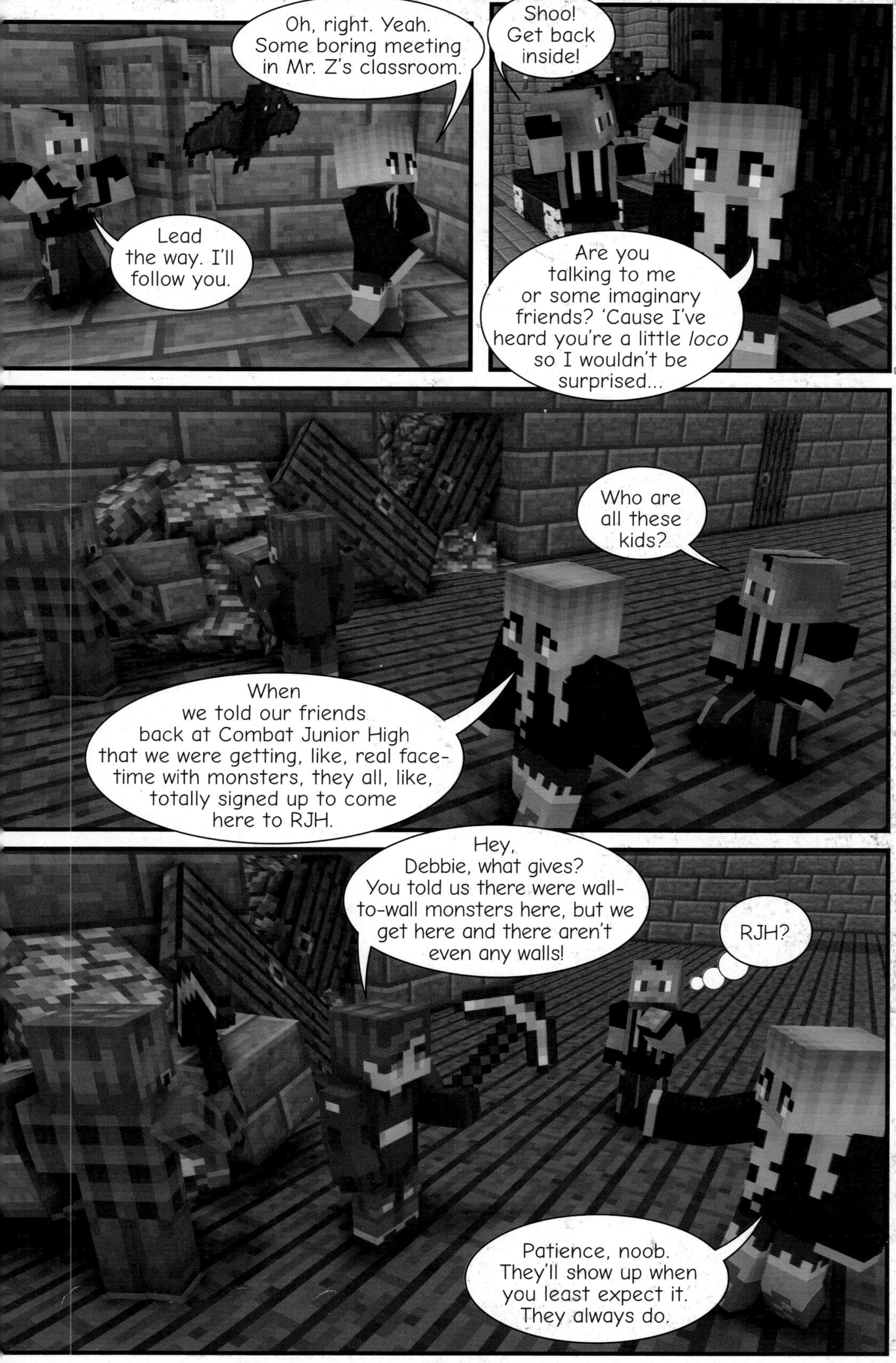
Oh, right. Yeah. Some boring meeting in Mr. Z's classroom.
Lead the way. I'll follow you.
Shoo! Get back inside!
Are you talking to me or some imaginary friends? 'Cause I've heard you're a little *loco* so I wouldn't be surprised...
Who are all these kids?
When we told our friends back at Combat Junior High that we were getting, like, real face-time with monsters, they all, like, totally signed up to come here to RJH.
Hey, Debbie, what gives? You told us there were wall-to-wall monsters here, but we get here and there aren't even any walls!
RJH?
Patience, noob. They'll show up when you least expect it. They always do.

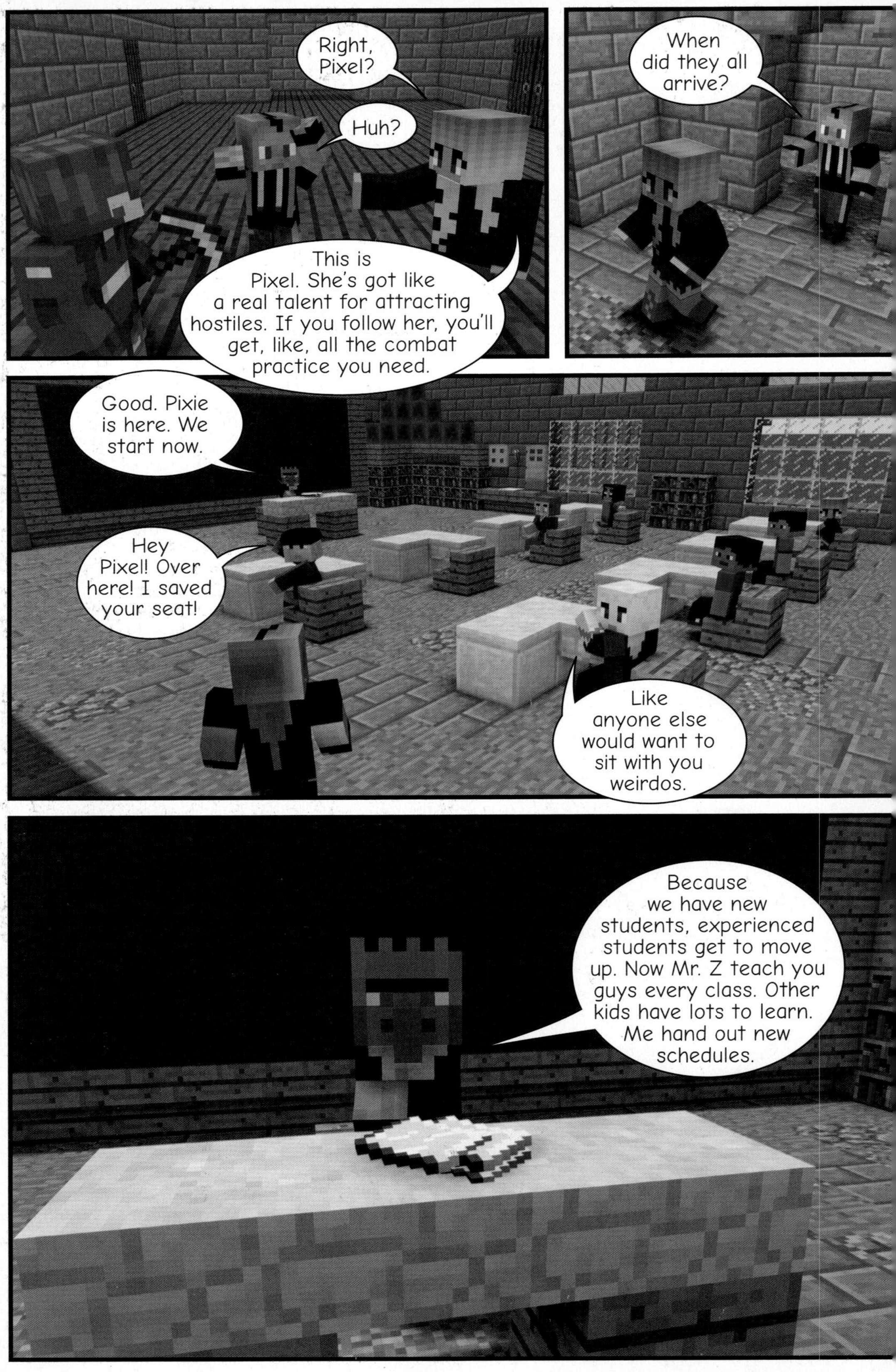
Right, Pixel?
Huh?
This is Pixel. She's got like a real talent for attracting hostiles. If you follow her, you'll get, like, all the combat practice you need.
When did they all arrive?
Good. Pixie is here. We start now.
Hey Pixel! Over here! I saved your seat!
Like anyone else would want to sit with you weirdos.
Because we have new students, experienced students get to move up. Now Mr. Z teach you guys every class. Other kids have lots to learn. Me hand out new schedules.

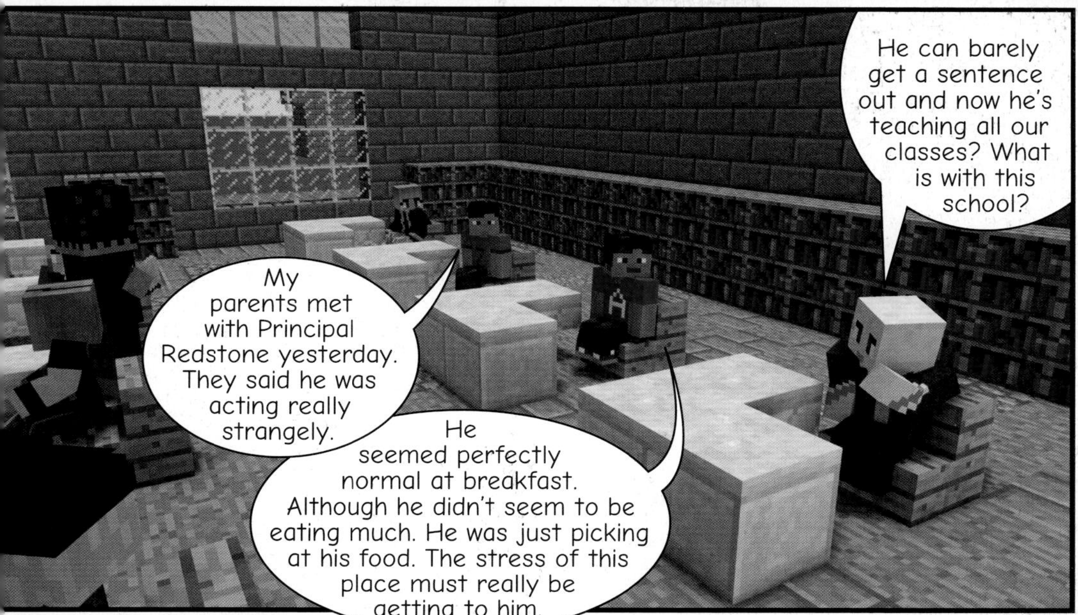
He can barely get a sentence out and now he's teaching all our classes? What is with this school?
My parents met with Principal Redstone yesterday. They said he was acting really strangely.
He seemed perfectly normal at breakfast. Although he didn't seem to be eating much. He was just picking at his food. The stress of this place must really be getting to him.

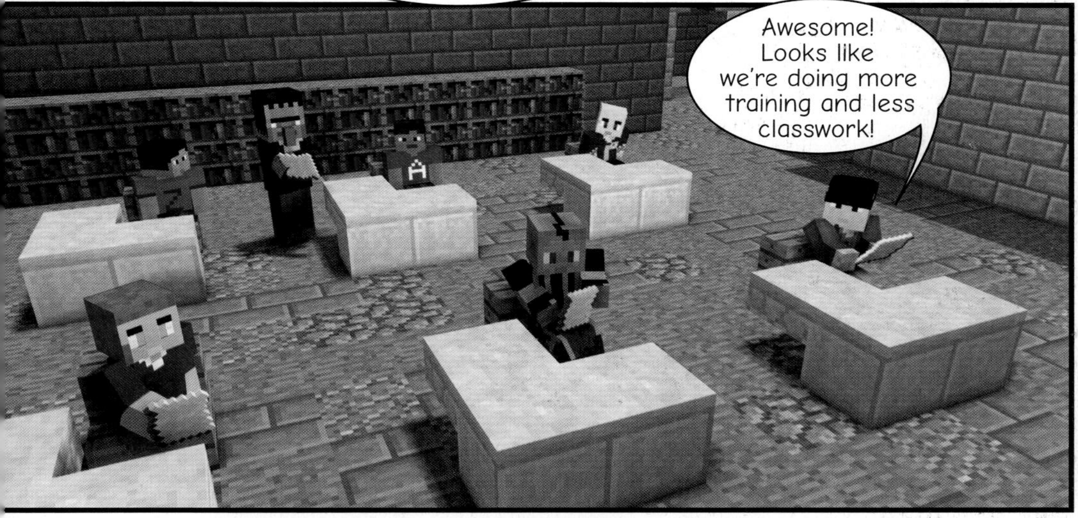
Awesome! Looks like we're doing more training and less classwork!

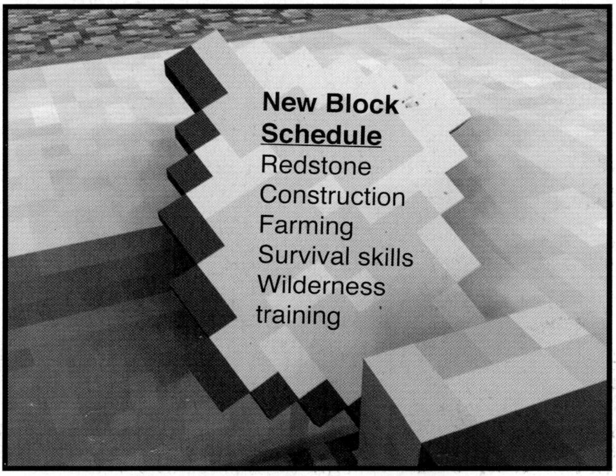
New Block
Schedule
Redstone
Construction
Farming
Survival skills
Wilderness training

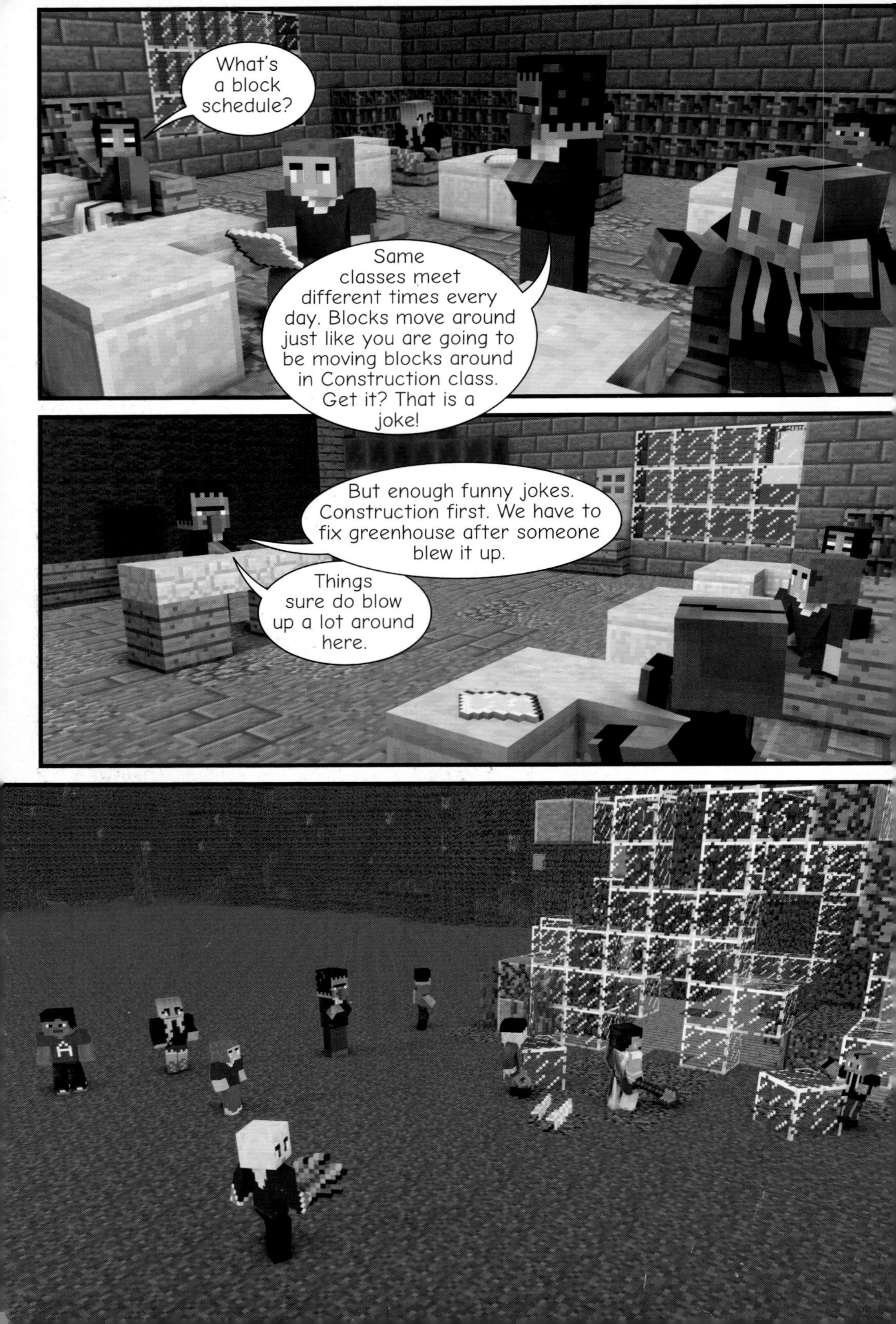
What's a block schedule?
Same classes meet different times every day. Blocks move around just like you are going to be moving blocks around in Construction class. Get it? That is a joke!
But enough funny jokes. Construction first. We have to fix greenhouse after someone blew it up.
Things sure do blow up a lot around here.

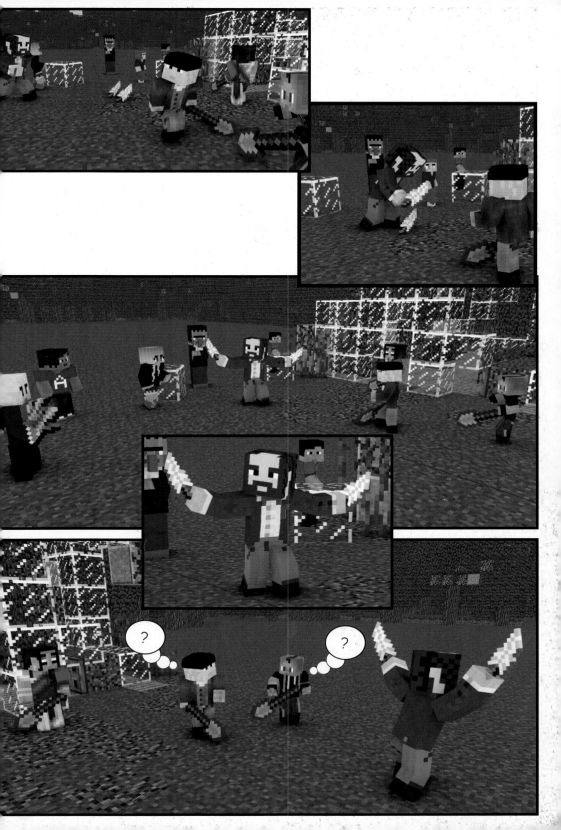

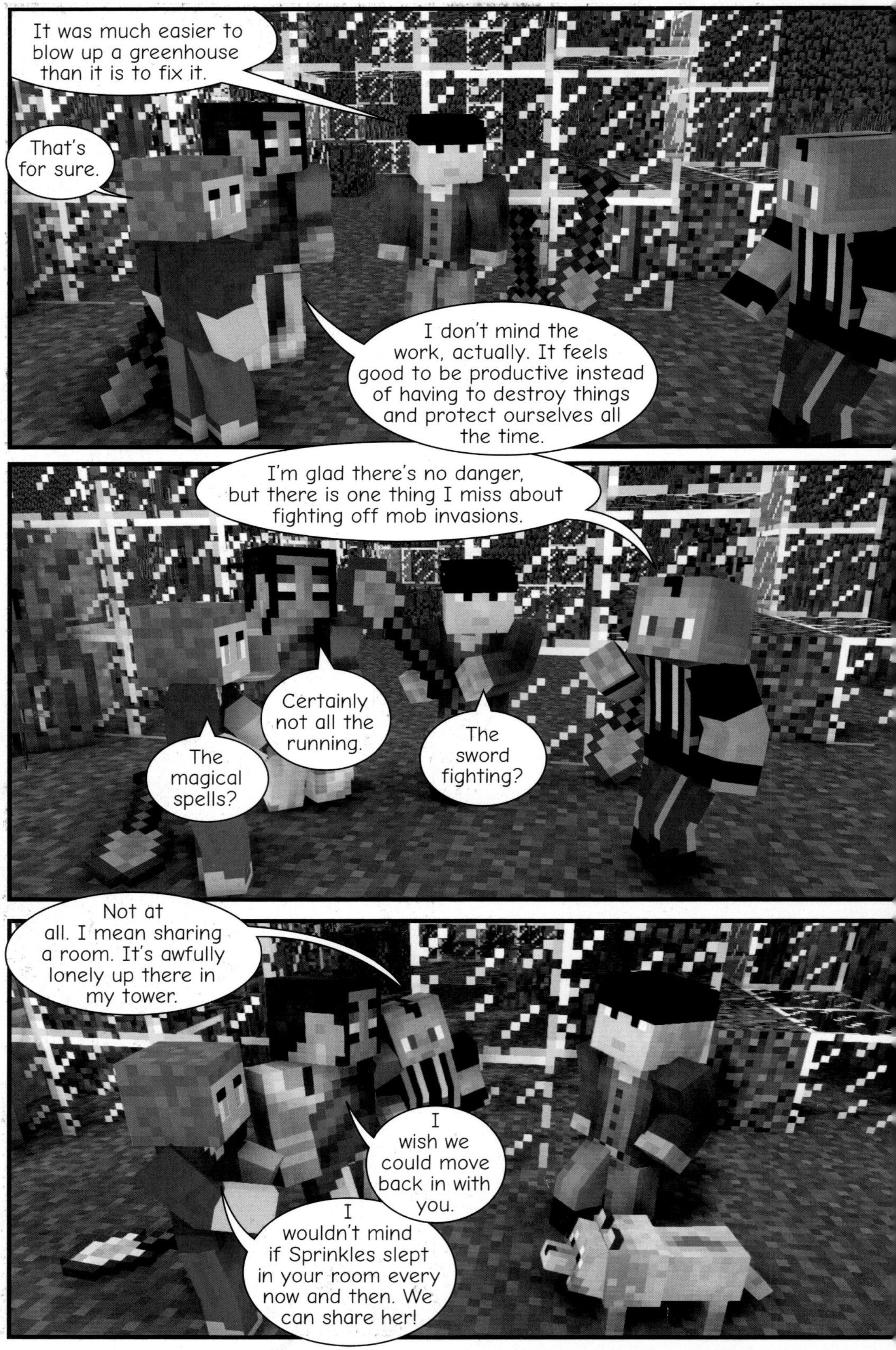
It was much easier to blow up a greenhouse than it is to fix it.
That's for sure.
I don't mind the work, actually. It feels good to be productive instead of having to destroy things and protect ourselves all the time.
I'm glad there's no danger, but there is one thing I miss about fighting off mob invasions.
The magical spells?
Certainly not all the running.
The sword fighting?
Not at all. I mean sharing a room. It's awfully lonely up there in my tower.
I wish we could move back in with you.
I wouldn't mind if Sprinkles slept in your room every now and then. We can share her!

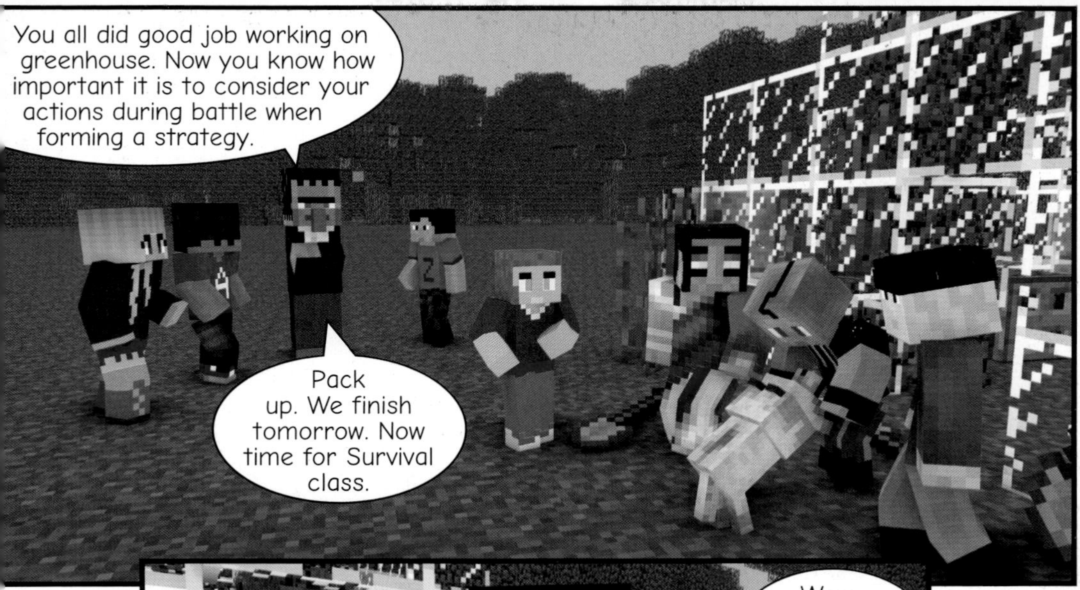
You all did good job working on greenhouse. Now you know how important it is to consider your actions during battle when forming a strategy.
Pack up. We finish tomorrow. Now time for Survival class.

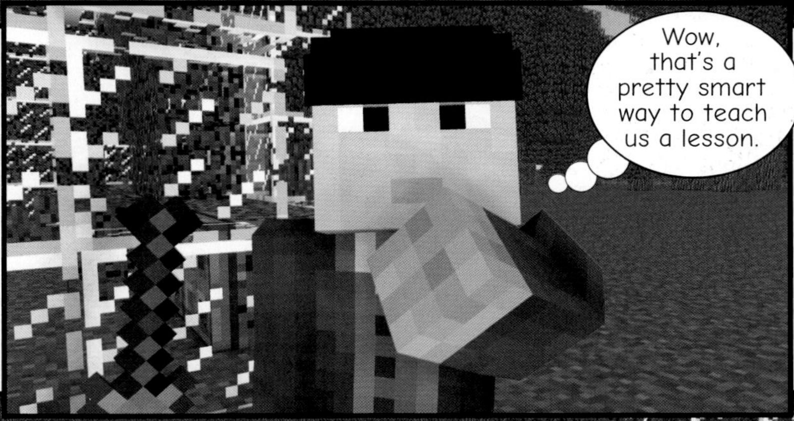
Wow, that's a pretty smart way to teach us a lesson.

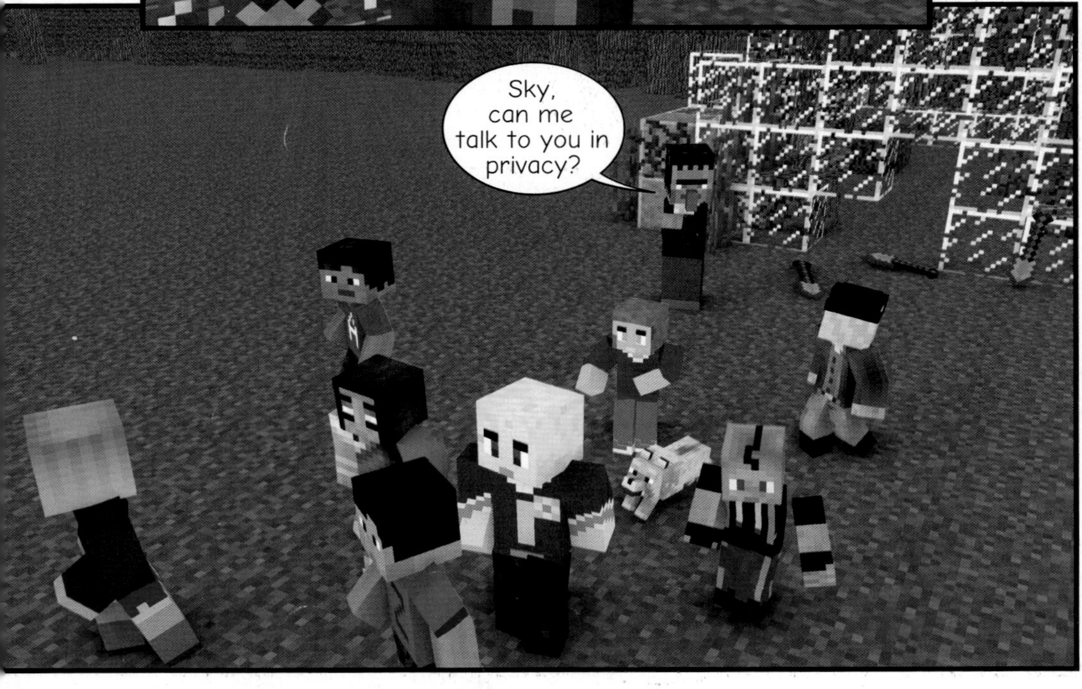
Sky, can me talk to you in privacy?

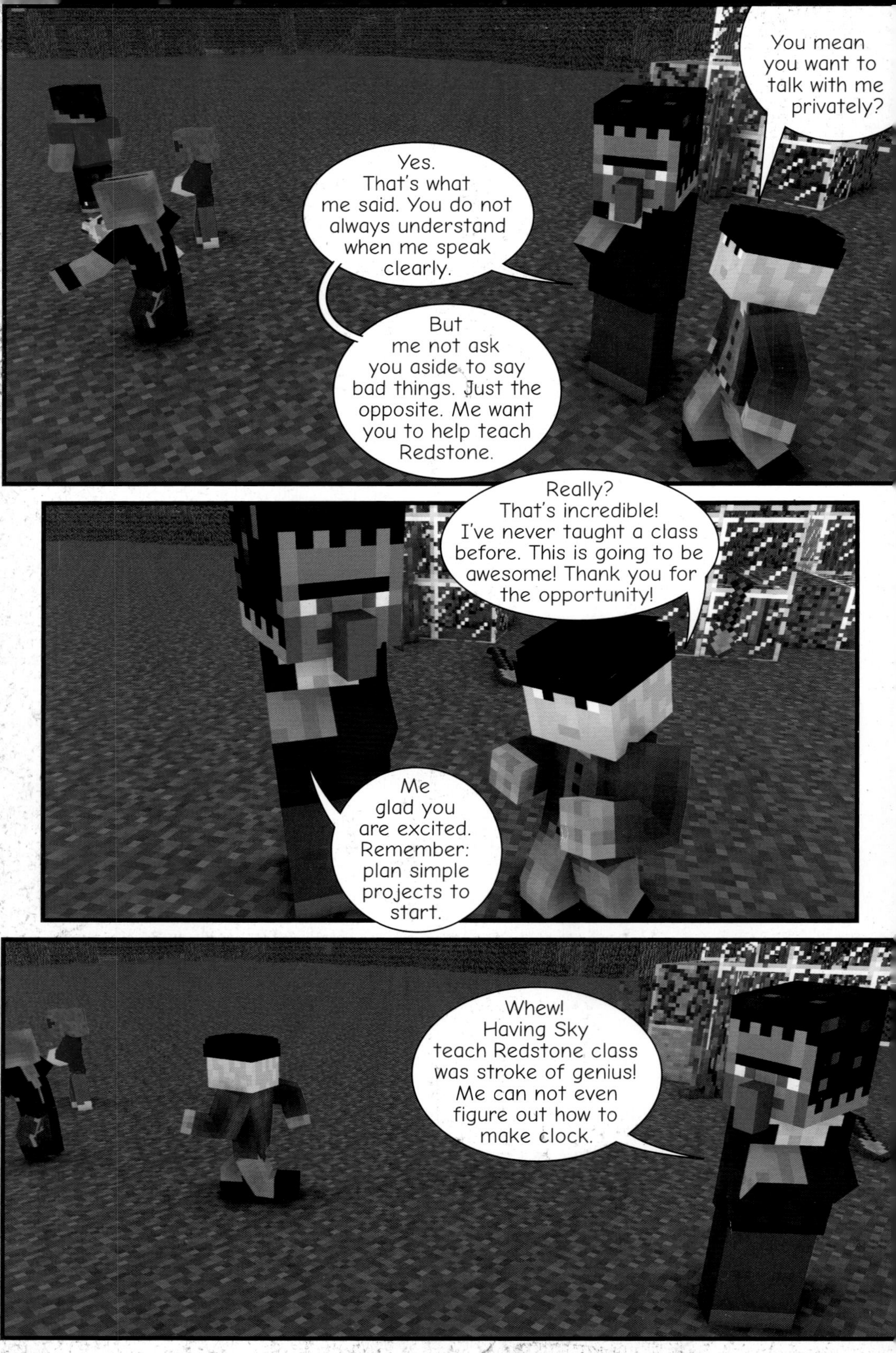
You mean you want to talk with me privately?
Yes. That's what me said. You do not always understand when me speak clearly.
But me not ask you aside to say bad things. Just the opposite. Me want you to help teach Redstone.
Really? That's incredible! I've never taught a class before. This is going to be awesome! Thank you for the opportunity!
Me glad you are excited. Remember: plan simple projects to start.
Whew! Having Sky teach Redstone class was stroke of genius! Me can not even figure out how to make clock.

CHAPTER 2

SURVIVAL SKILLS

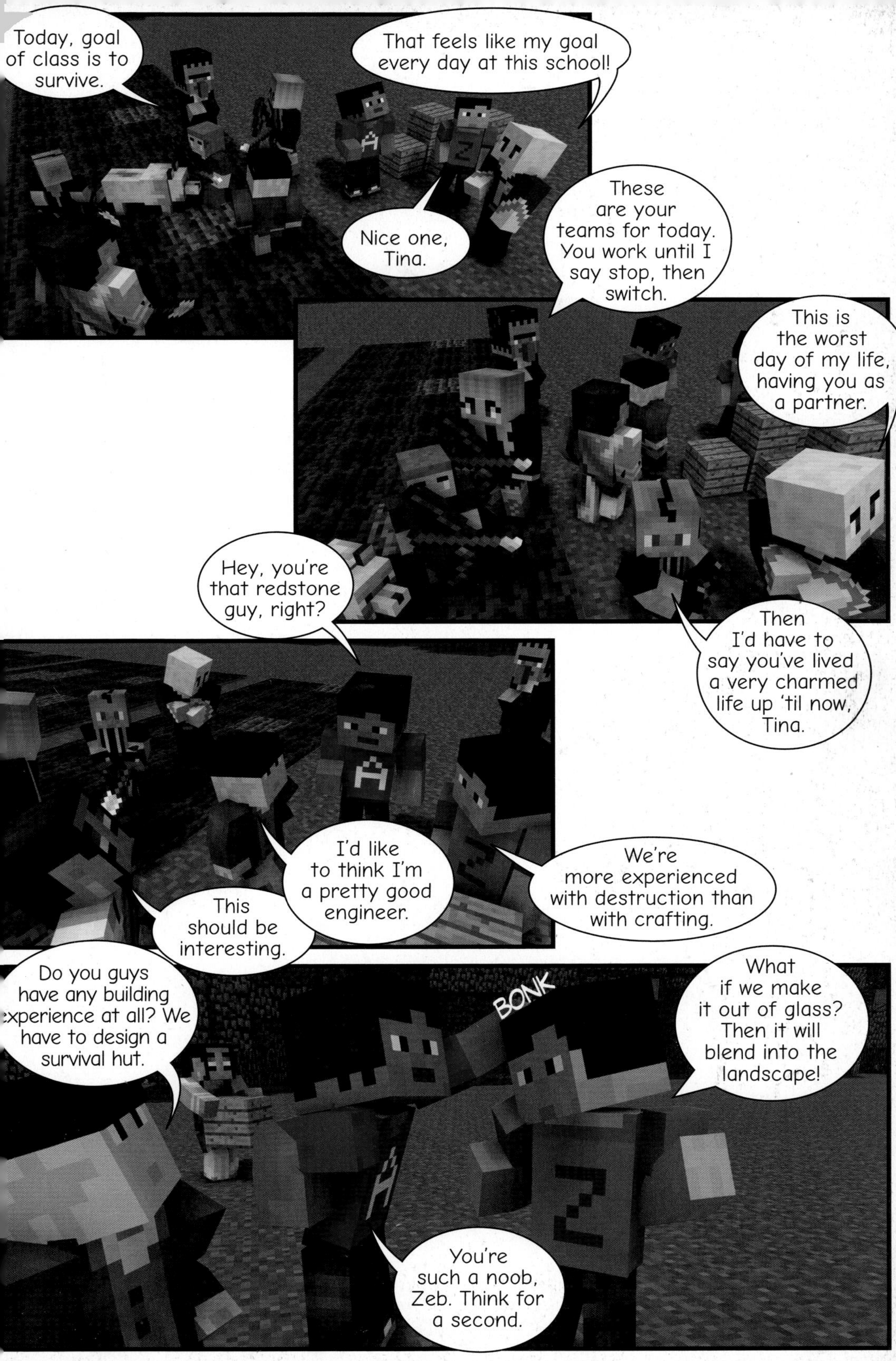

Today, goal of class is to survive.
That feels like my goal every day at this school!
Nice one, Tina.
These are your teams for today. You work until I say stop, then switch.
This is the worst day of my life, having you as a partner.
Then I'd have to say you've lived a very charmed life up 'til now, Tina.
Hey, you're that redstone guy, right?
I'd like to think I'm a pretty good engineer.
This should be interesting.
We're more experienced with destruction than with crafting.
Do you guys have any building xperience at all? We have to design a survival hut.
BONK
What if we make it out of glass? Then it will blend into the landscape!
You're such a noob, Zeb. Think for a second.

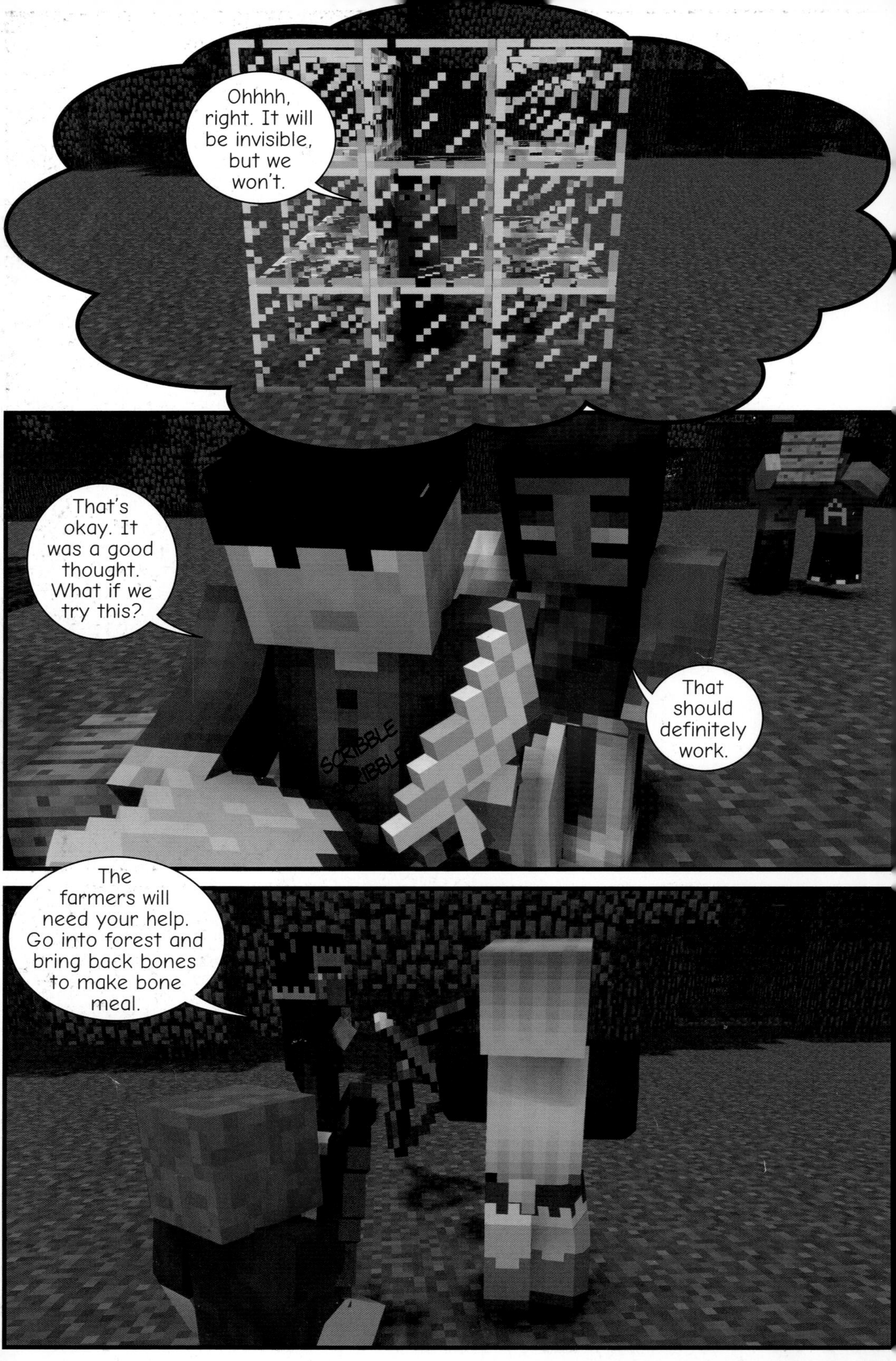
Ohhhh, right. It will be invisible, but we won't.
That's okay. It was a good thought. What if we try this?
SCRIBBLE SCRIBBLE
That should definitely work.
The farmers will need your help. Go into forest and bring back bones to make bone meal.

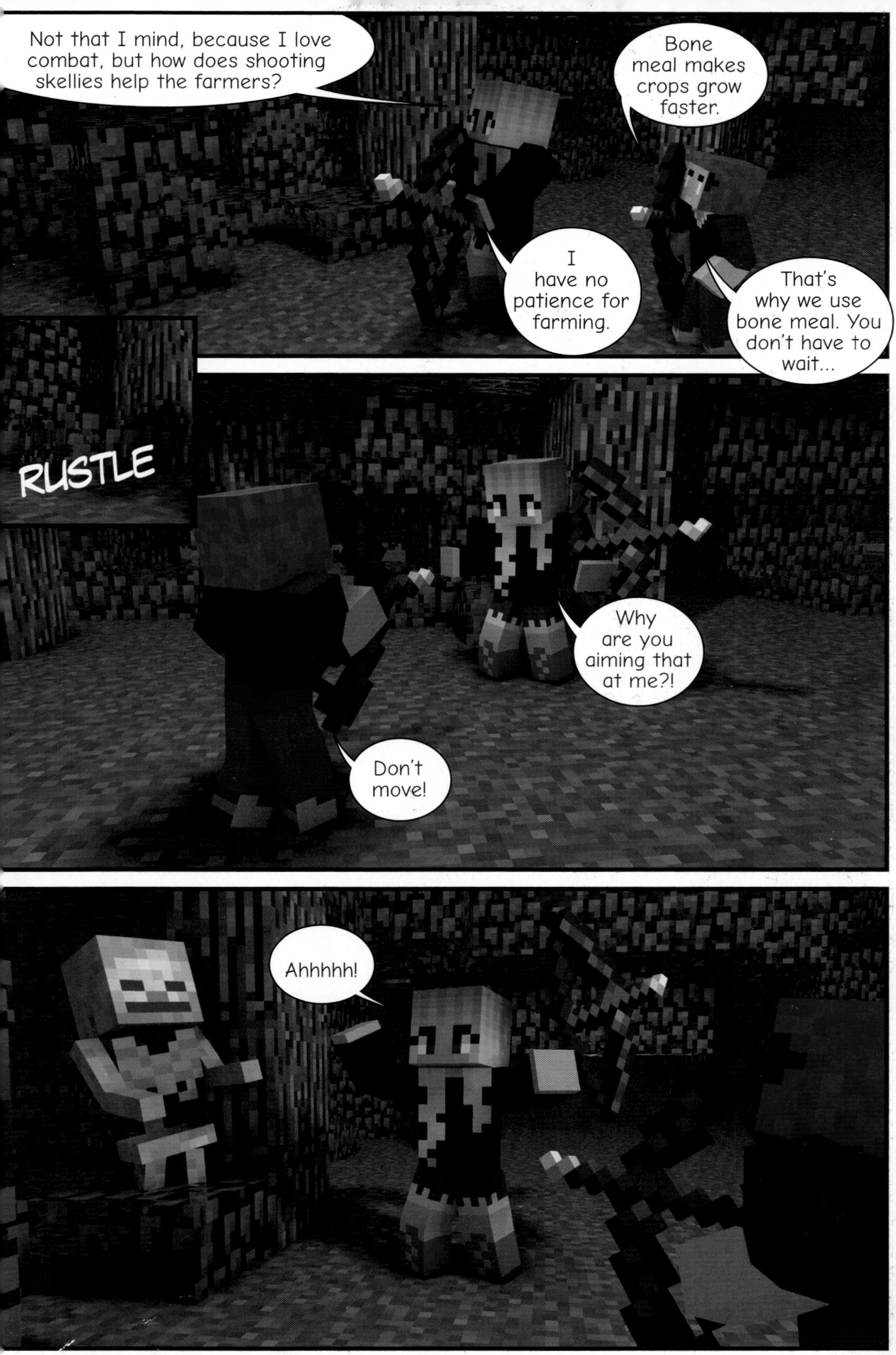
Not that I mind, because I love combat, but how does shooting skellies help the farmers?
Bone meal makes crops grow faster.
I have no patience for farming.
That's why we use bone meal. You don't have to wait...
RUSTLE
Why are you aiming that at me?!
Don't move!
Ahhhhh!

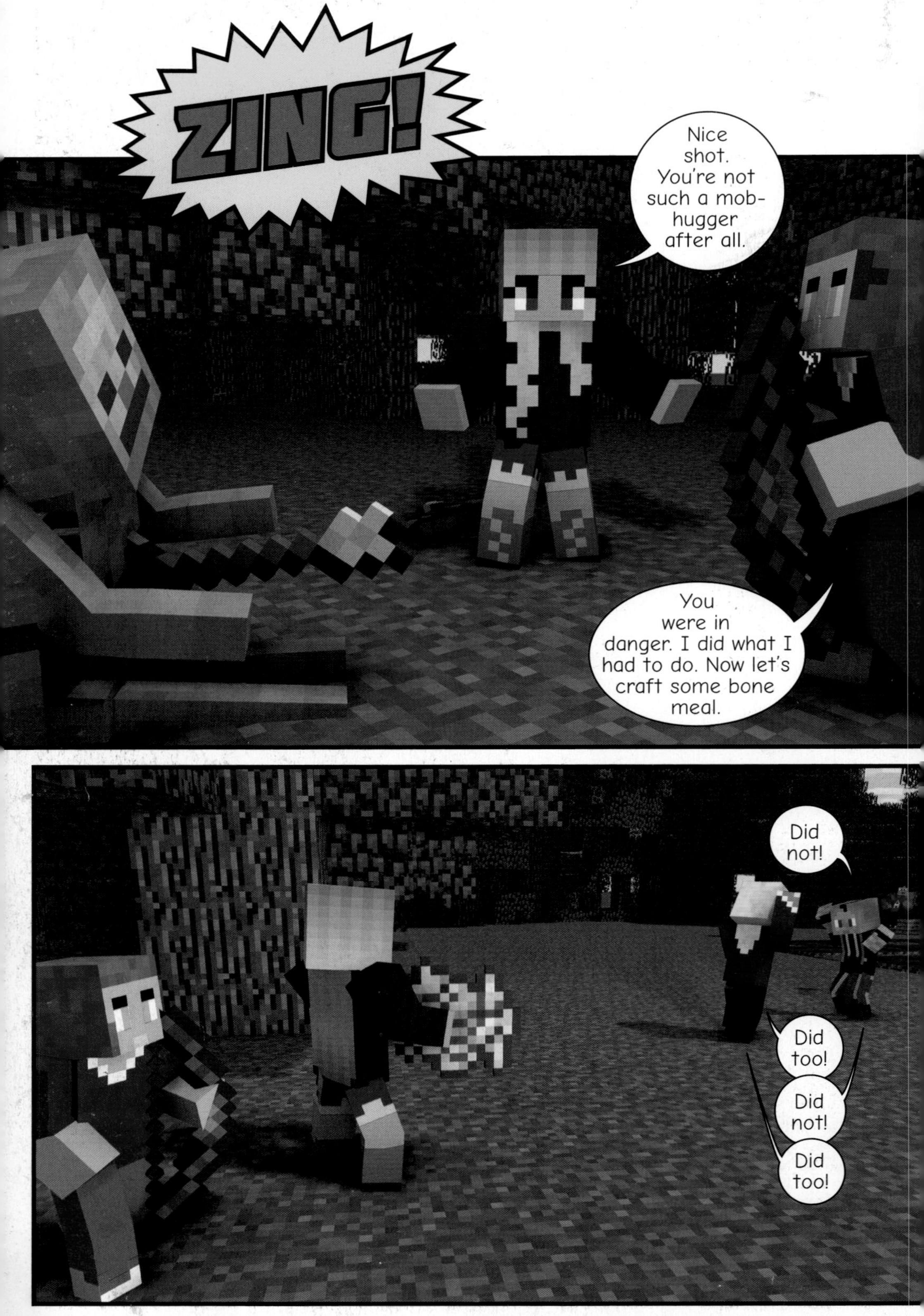
ZING!
Nice shot. You're not such a mob-hugger after all.
You were in danger. I did what I had to do. Now let's craft some bone meal.
Did not!
Did too!
Did not!
Did too!

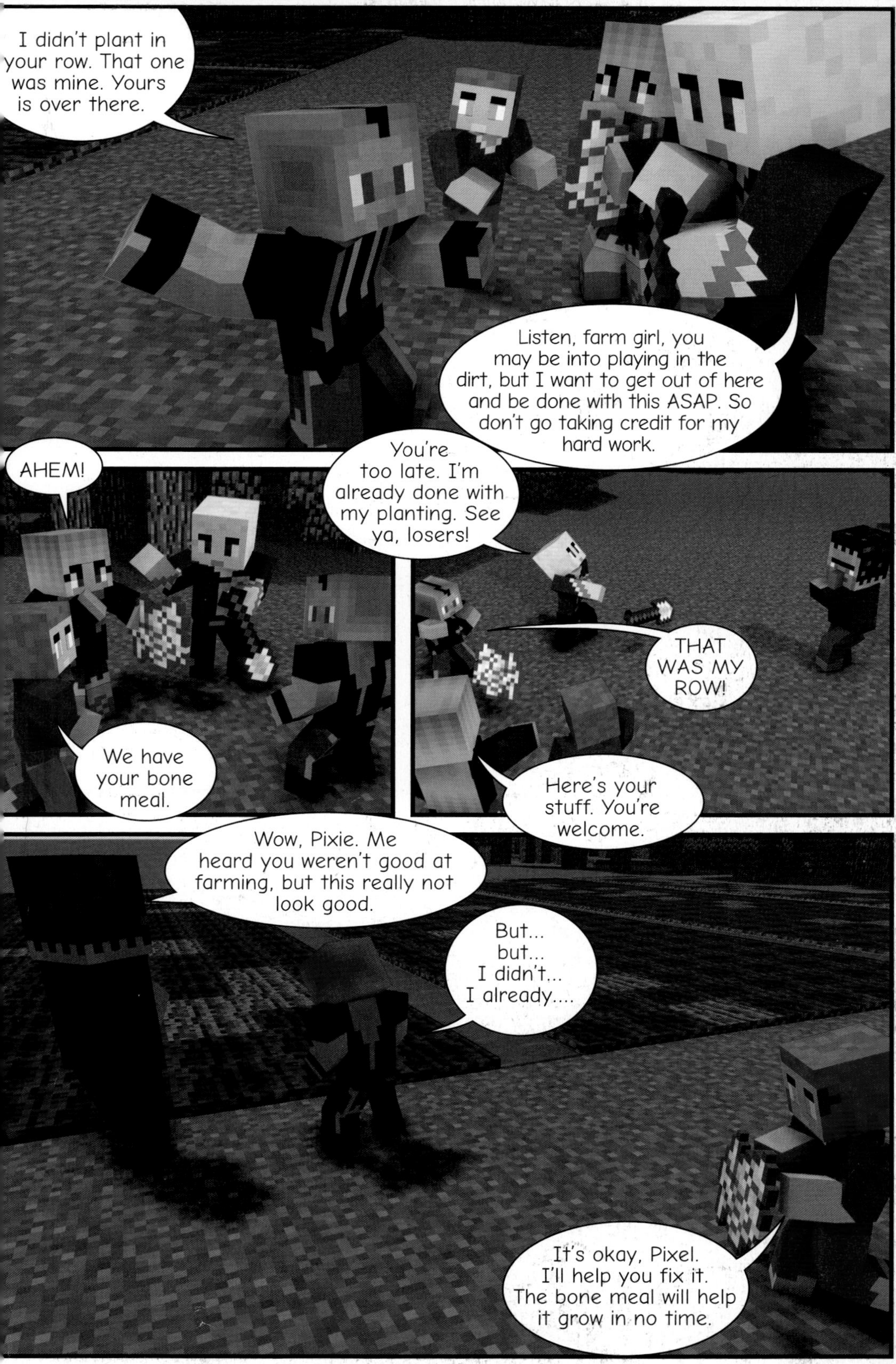
I didn't plant in your row. That one was mine. Yours is over there.
Listen, farm girl, you may be into playing in the dirt, but I want to get out of here and be done with this ASAP. So don't go taking credit for my hard work.
AHEM!
You're too late. I'm already done with my planting. See ya, losers!
We have your bone meal.
THAT WAS MY ROW!
Here's your stuff. You're welcome.
Wow, Pixie. Me heard you weren't good at farming, but this really not look good.
But... but... I didn't... I already....
It's okay, Pixel. I'll help you fix it. The bone meal will help it grow in no time.

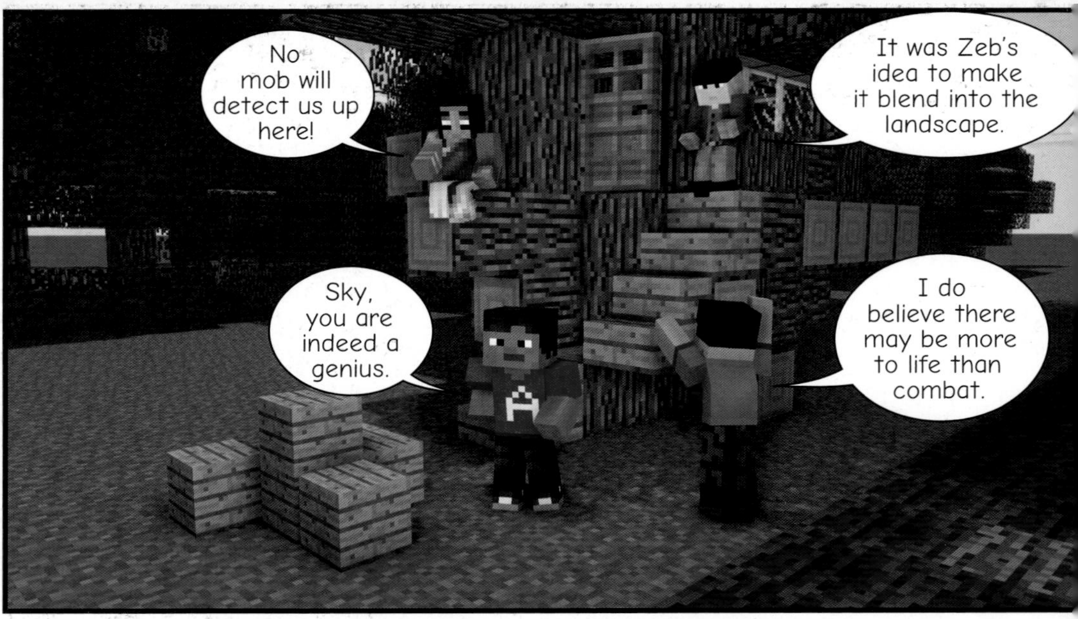
No mob will detect us up here!
It was Zeb's idea to make it blend into the landscape.
Sky, you are indeed a genius.
I do believe there may be more to life than combat.

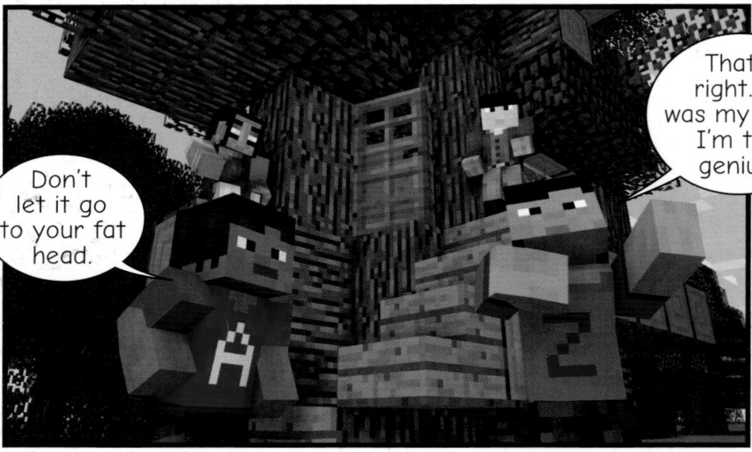
Don't let it go to your fat head.
That's right. It was my idea. I'm the genius!

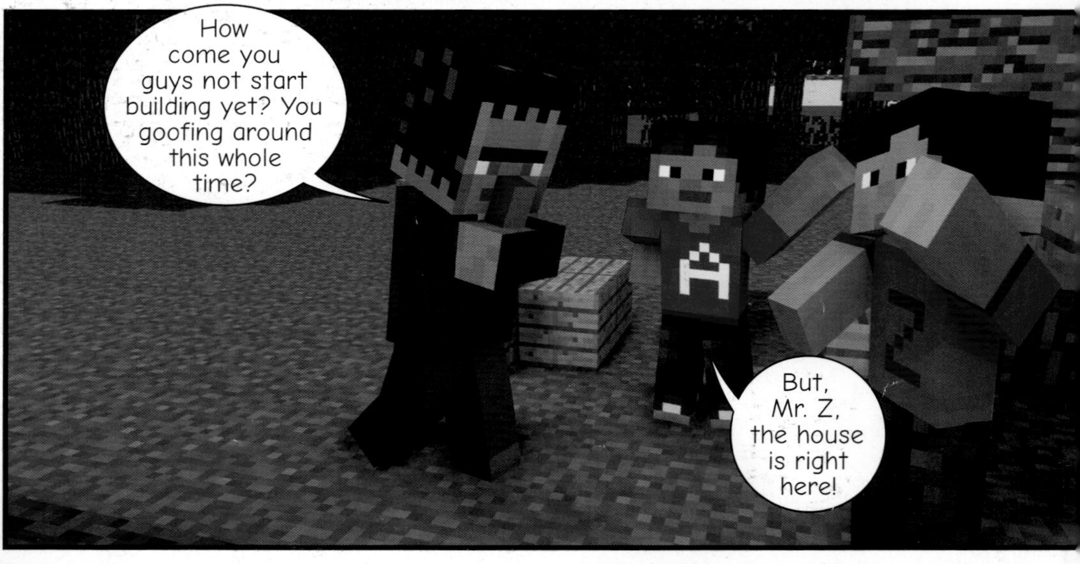
How come you guys not start building yet? You goofing around this whole time?
But, Mr. Z, the house is right here!

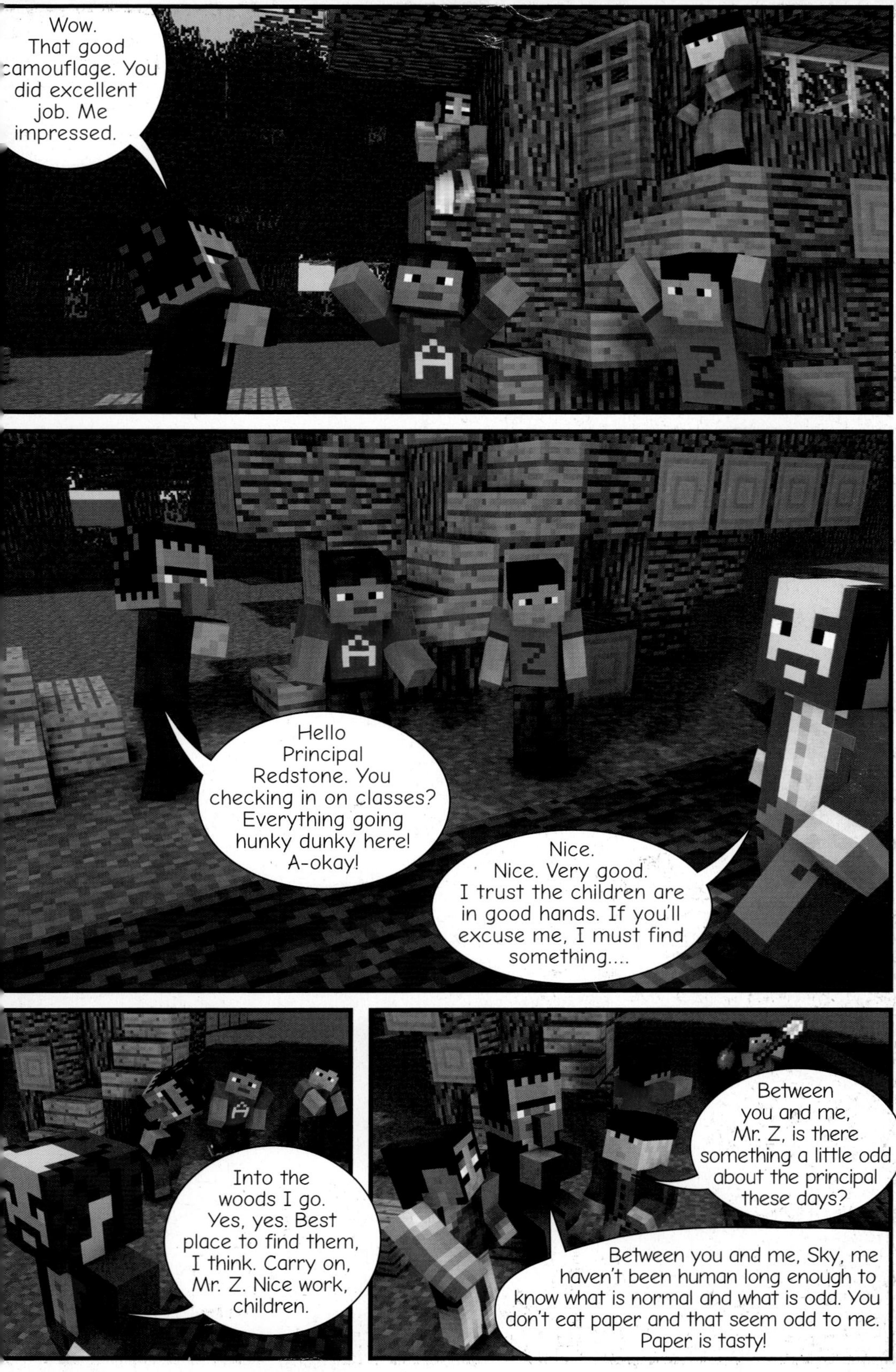

Wow. That good camouflage. You did excellent job. Me impressed.
Hello Principal Redstone. You checking in on classes? Everything going hunky dunky here! A-okay!
Nice. Nice. Very good. I trust the children are in good hands. If you'll excuse me, I must find something....
Into the woods I go. Yes, yes. Best place to find them, I think. Carry on, Mr. Z. Nice work, children.
Between you and me, Mr. Z, is there something a little odd about the principal these days?
Between you and me, Sky, me haven't been human long enough to know what is normal and what is odd. You don't eat paper and that seem odd to me. Paper is tasty!

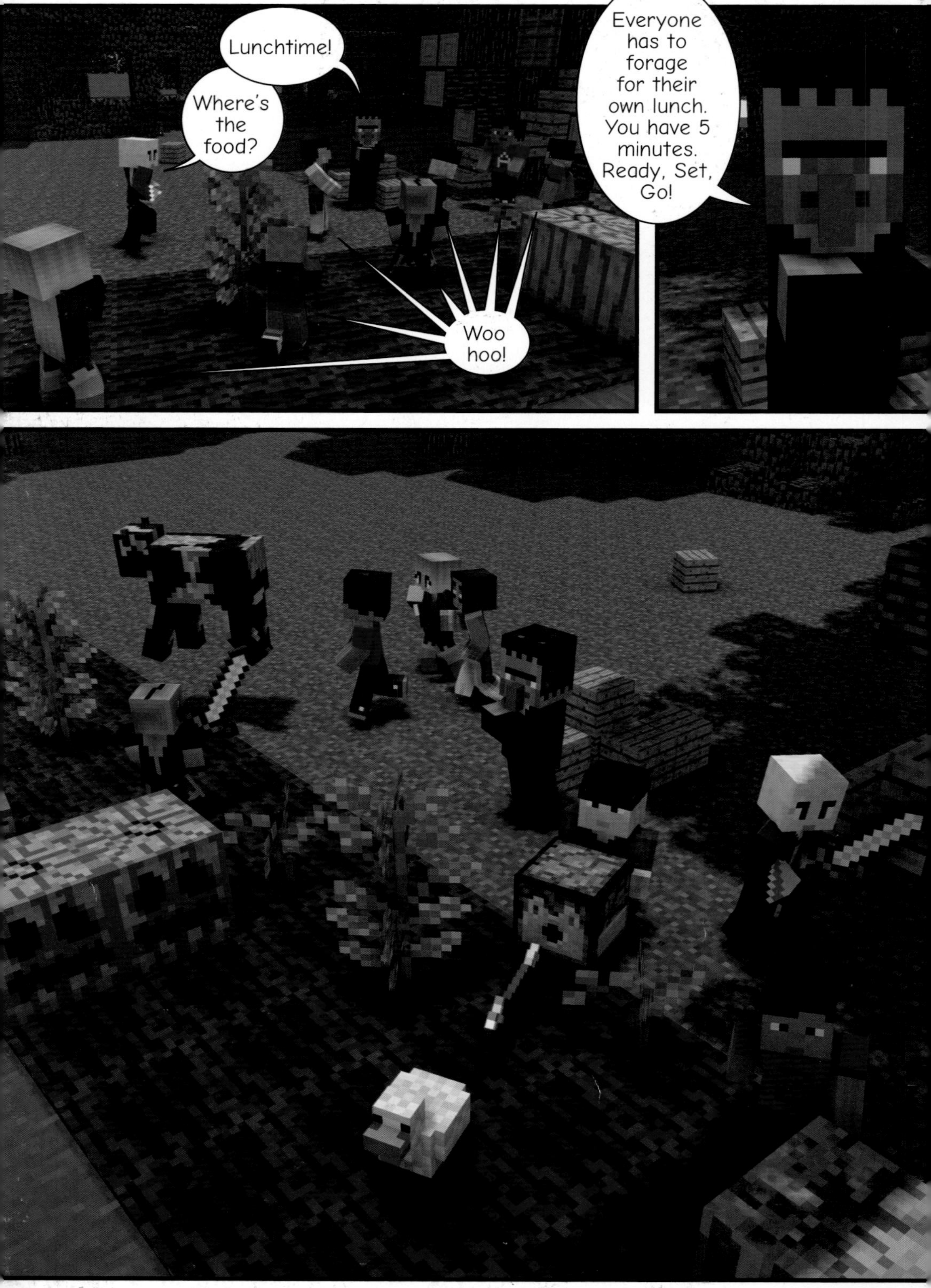

Lunchtime!
Where's the food?
Woo hoo!
Everyone has to forage for their own lunch. You have 5 minutes. Ready, Set, Go!

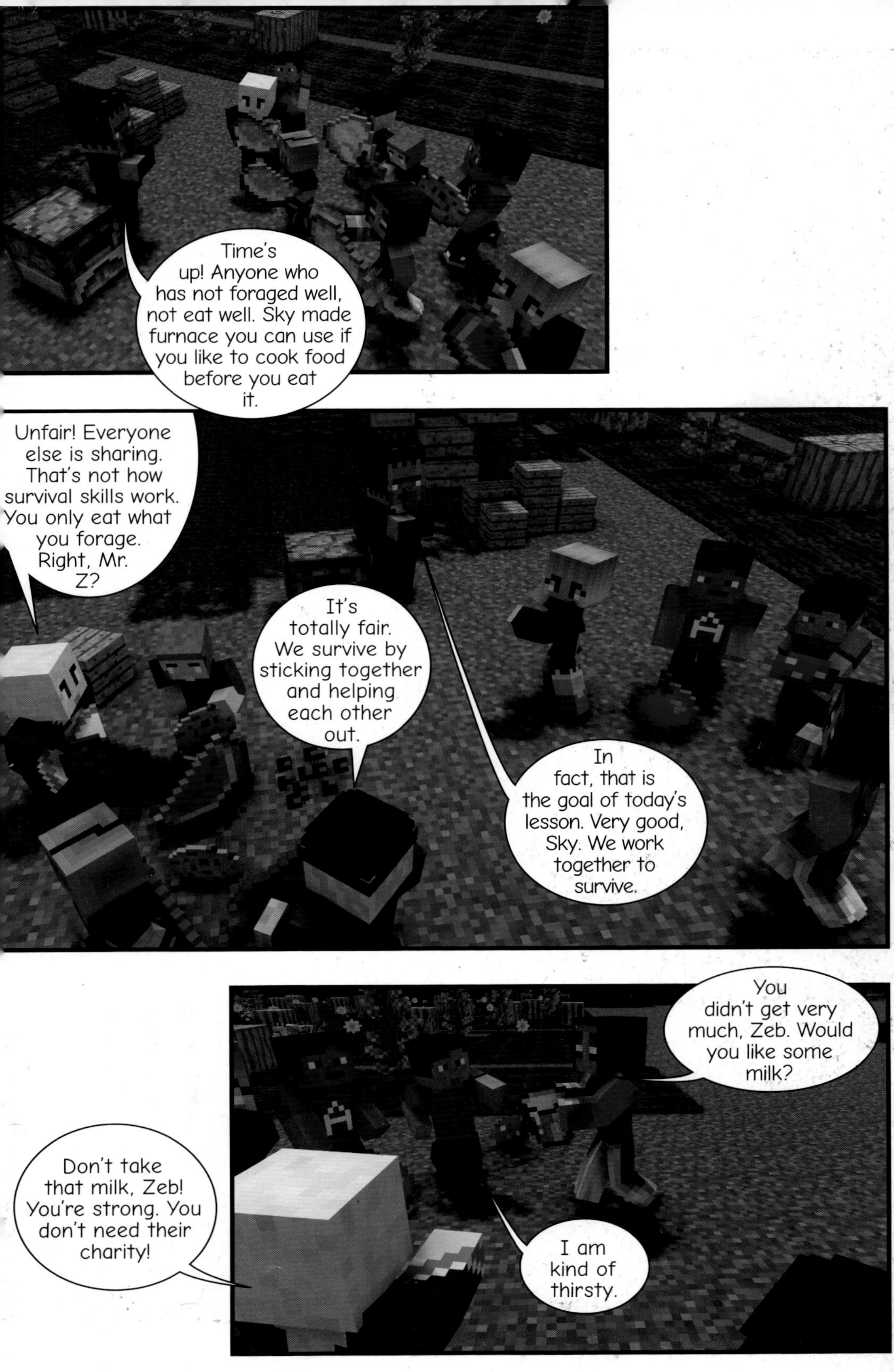

Time's up! Anyone who has not foraged well, not eat well. Sky made furnace you can use if you like to cook food before you eat it.
Unfair! Everyone else is sharing. That's not how survival skills work. You only eat what you forage. Right, Mr. Z?
It's totally fair. We survive by sticking together and helping each other out.
In fact, that is the goal of today's lesson. Very good, Sky. We work together to survive.
You didn't get very much, Zeb. Would you like some milk?
Don't take that milk, Zeb! You're strong. You don't need their charity!
I am kind of thirsty.

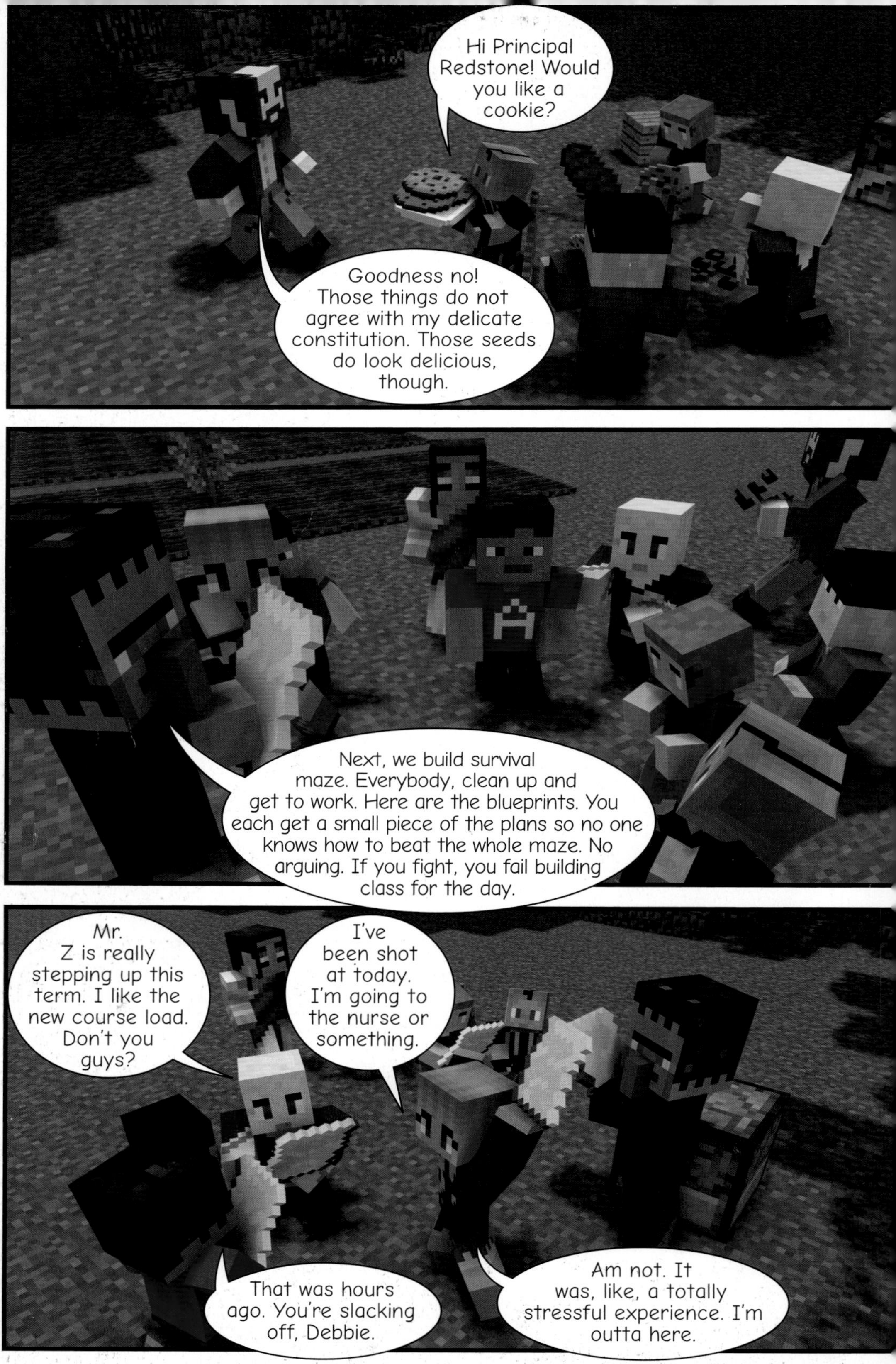
Hi Principal Redstone! Would you like a cookie?
Goodness no! Those things do not agree with my delicate constitution. Those seeds do look delicious, though.
Next, we build survival maze. Everybody, clean up and get to work. Here are the blueprints. You each get a small piece of the plans so no one knows how to beat the whole maze. No arguing. If you fight, you fail building class for the day.
Mr. Z is really stepping up this term. I like the new course load. Don't you guys?
I've been shot at today. I'm going to the nurse or something.
That was hours ago. You're slacking off, Debbie.
Am not. It was, like, a totally stressful experience. I'm outta here.

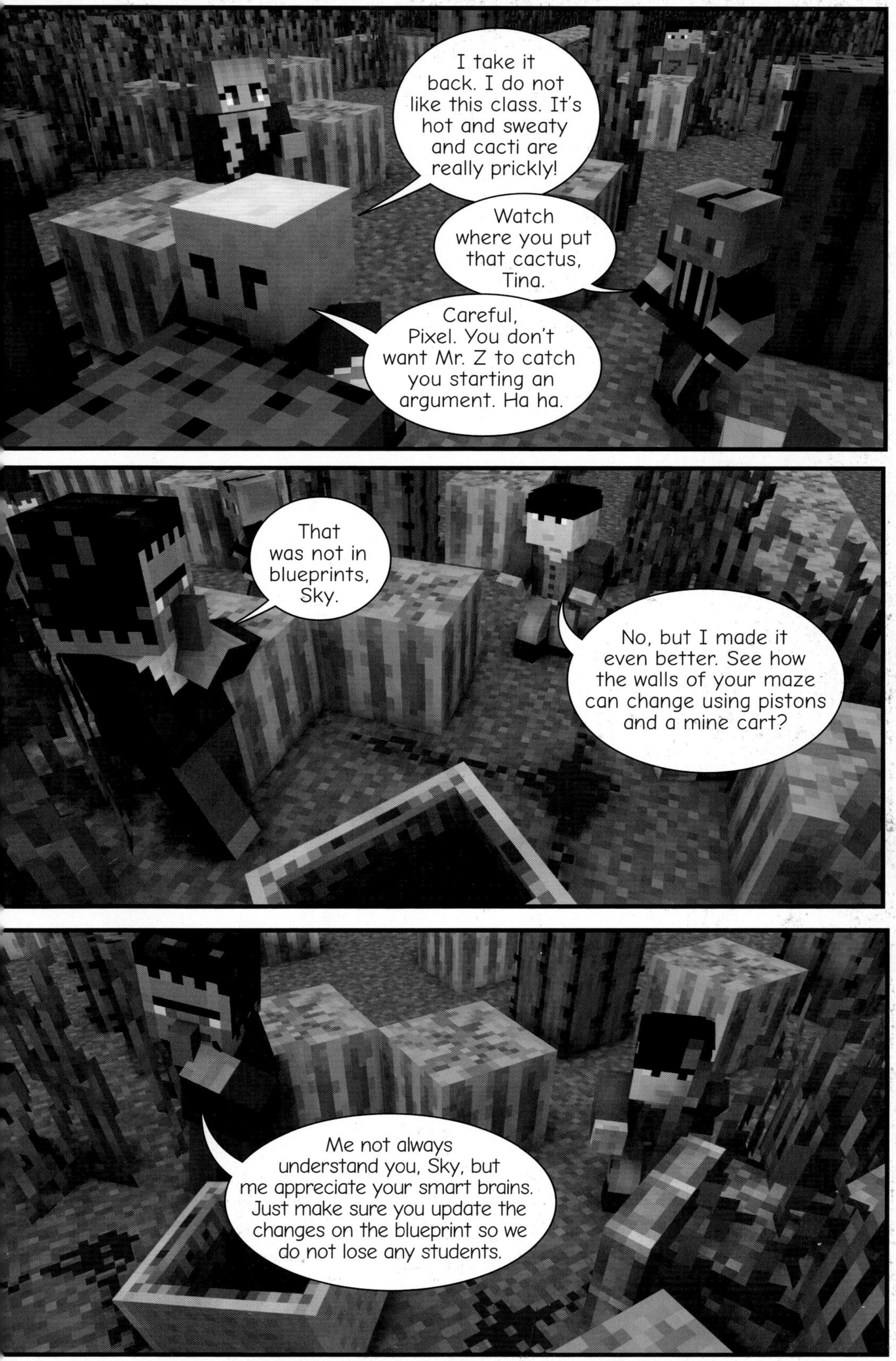
I take it back. I do not like this class. It's hot and sweaty and cacti are really prickly!
Watch where you put that cactus, Tina.
Careful, Pixel. You don't want Mr. Z to catch you starting an argument. Ha ha.
That was not in blueprints, Sky.
No, but I made it even better. See how the walls of your maze can change using pistons and a mine cart?
Me not always understand you, Sky, but me appreciate your smart brains. Just make sure you update the changes on the blueprint so we do not lose any students.

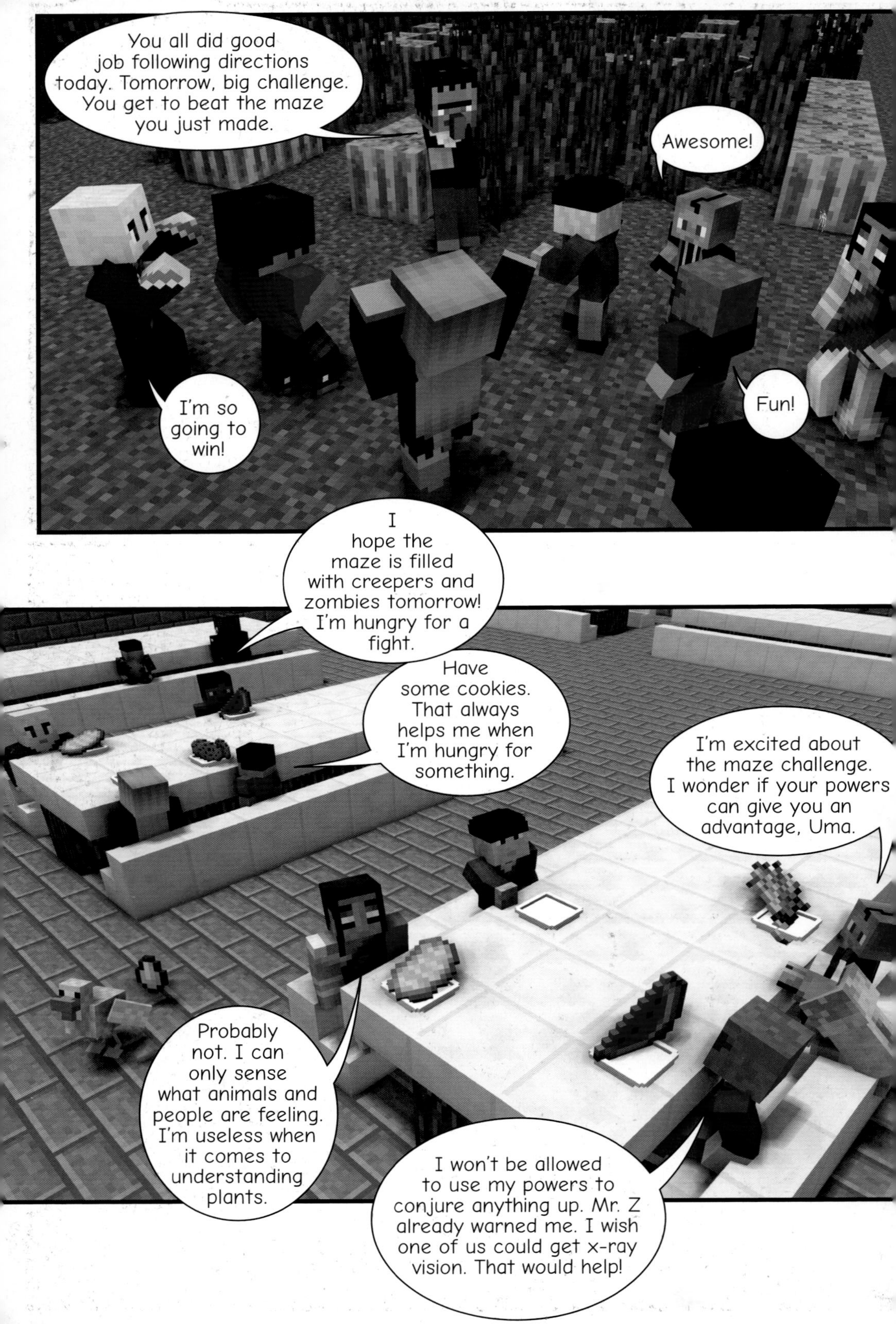

You all did good job following directions today. Tomorrow, big challenge. You get to beat the maze you just made.
Awesome!
I'm so going to win!
Fun!
I hope the maze is filled with creepers and zombies tomorrow! I'm hungry for a fight.
Have some cookies. That always helps me when I'm hungry for something.
I'm excited about the maze challenge. I wonder if your powers can give you an advantage, Uma.
Probably not. I can only sense what animals and people are feeling. I'm useless when it comes to understanding plants.
I won't be allowed to use my powers to conjure anything up. Mr. Z already warned me. I wish one of us could get x-ray vision. That would help!

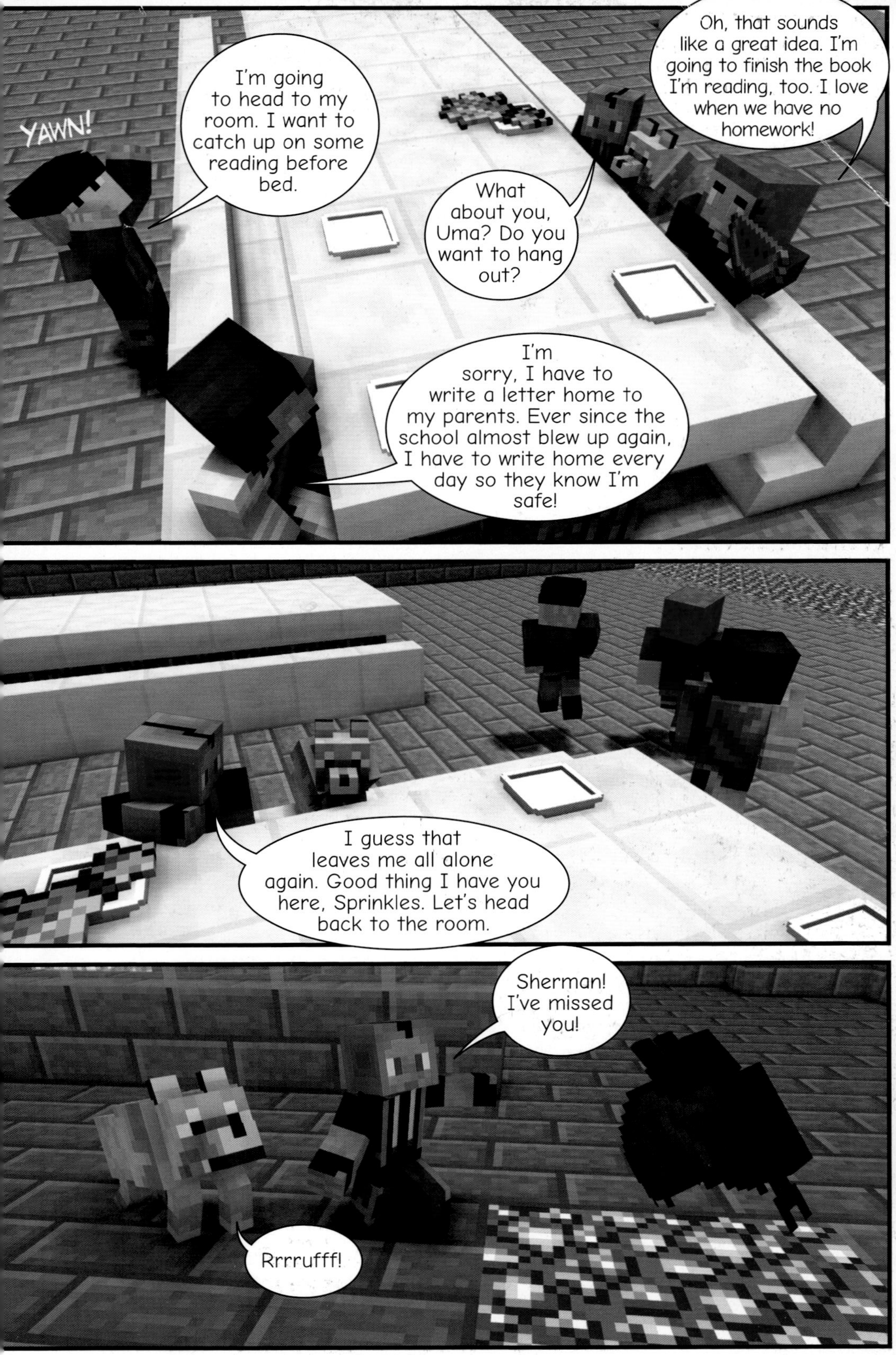
YAWN!
I'm going to head to my room. I want to catch up on some reading before bed.
Oh, that sounds like a great idea. I'm going to finish the book I'm reading, too. I love when we have no homework!
What about you, Uma? Do you want to hang out?
I'm sorry, I have to write a letter home to my parents. Ever since the school almost blew up again, I have to write home every day so they know I'm safe!
I guess that leaves me all alone again. Good thing I have you here, Sprinkles. Let's head back to the room.
Sherman! I've missed you!
Rrrrufff!

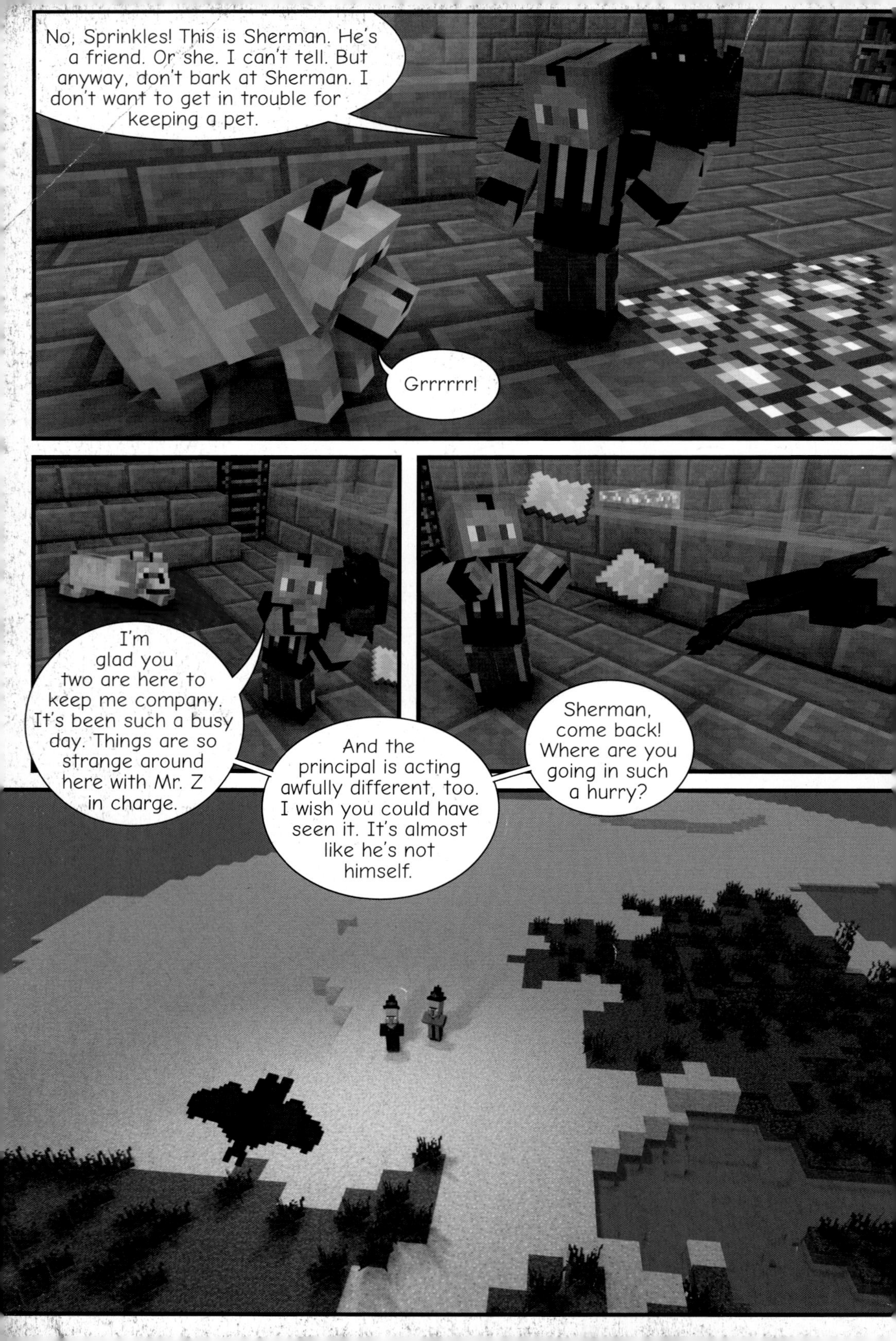
No, Sprinkles! This is Sherman. He's a friend. Or she. I can't tell. But anyway, don't bark at Sherman. I don't want to get in trouble for keeping a pet.
Grrrrrr!
I'm glad you two are here to keep me company. It's been such a busy day. Things are so strange around here with Mr. Z in charge.
And the principal is acting awfully different, too. I wish you could have seen it. It's almost like he's not himself.
Sherman, come back! Where are you going in such a hurry?

CHAPTER 3

THE
IMPOSSIBLE
MAZE

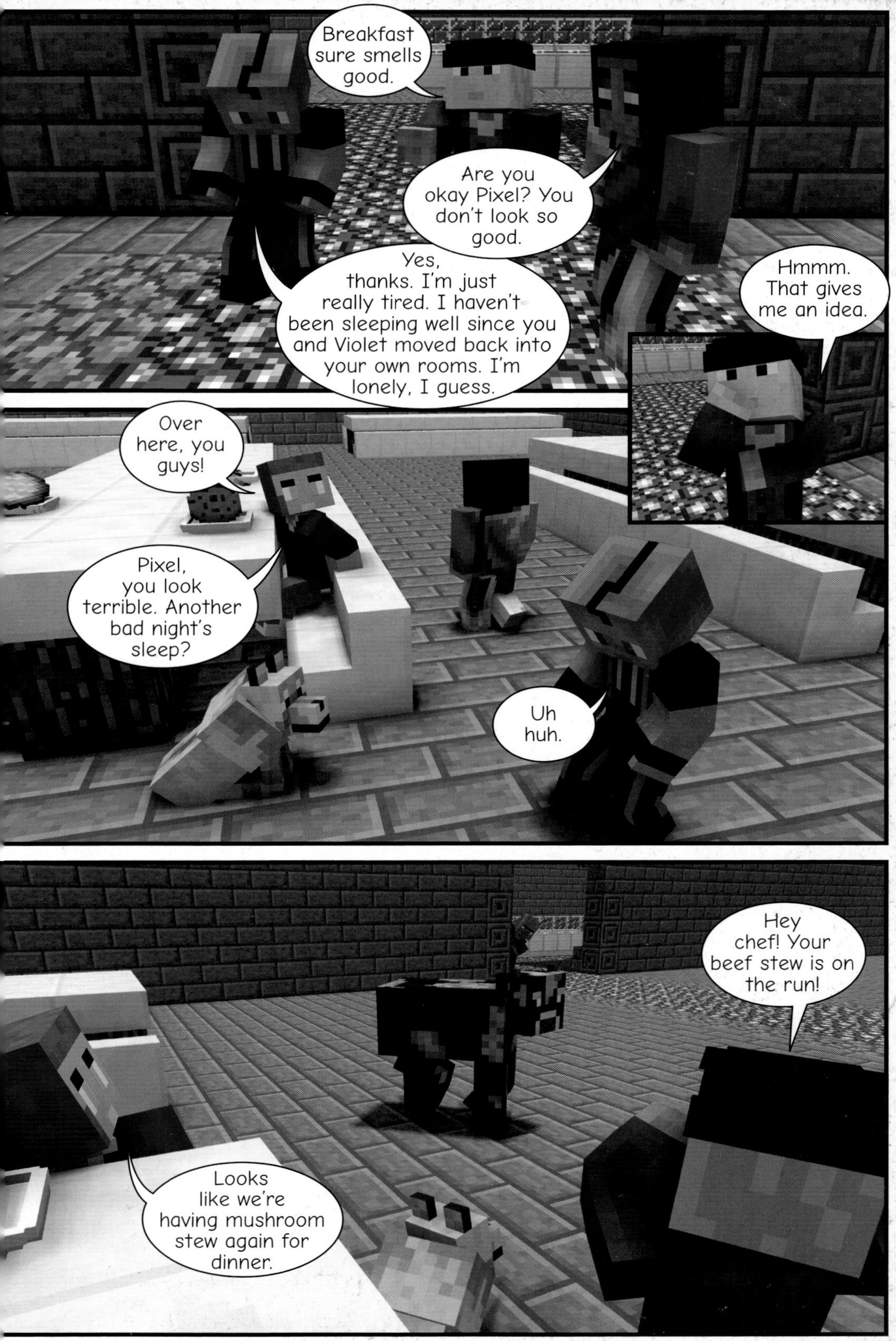
Breakfast sure smells good.
Are you okay Pixel? You don't look so good.
Yes, thanks. I'm just really tired. I haven't been sleeping well since you and Violet moved back into your own rooms. I'm lonely, I guess.
Hmmm. That gives me an idea.
Over here, you guys!
Pixel, you look terrible. Another bad night's sleep?
Uh huh.
Hey chef! Your beef stew is on the run!
Looks like we're having mushroom stew again for dinner.

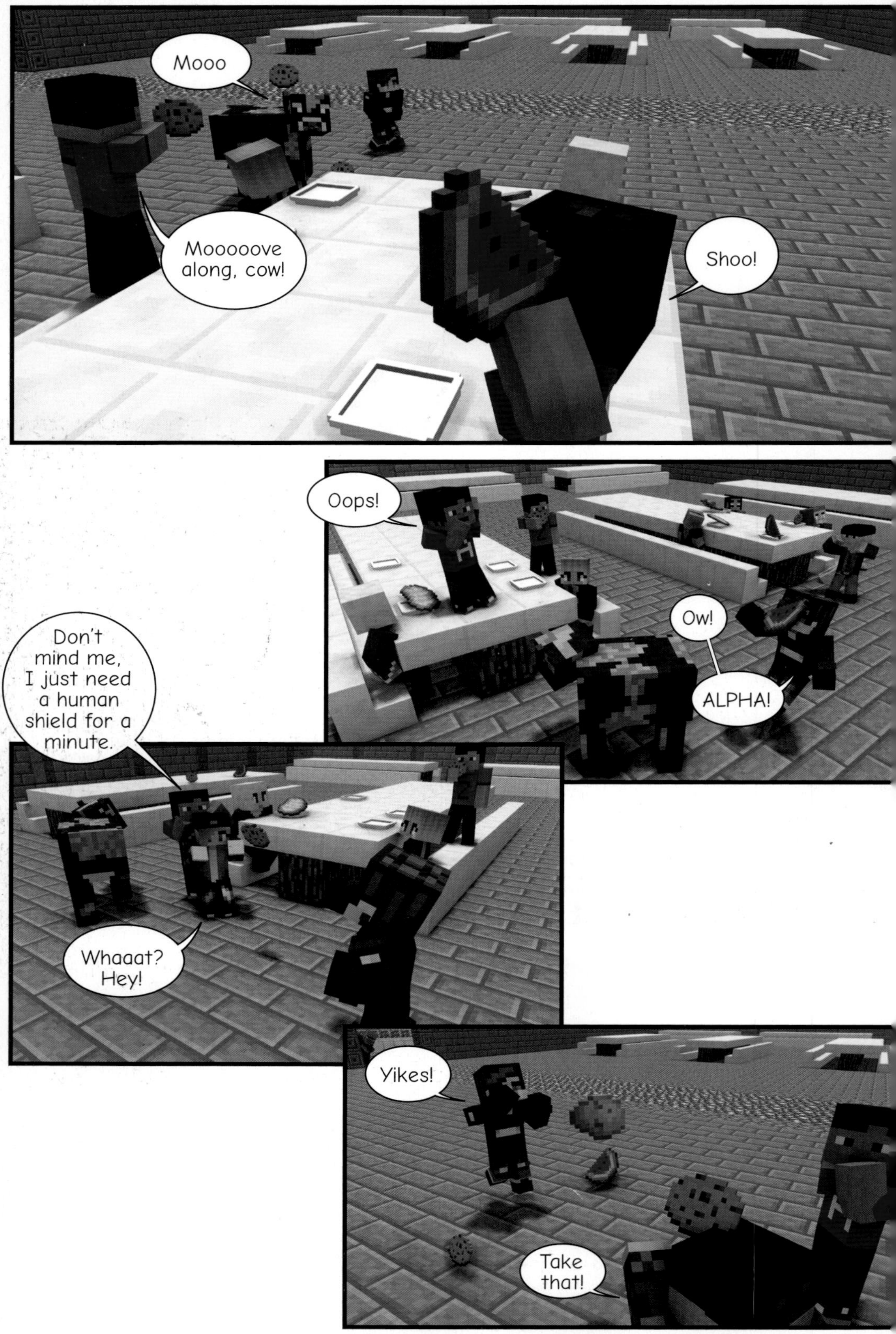
Mooo
Moooooove along, cow!
Shoo!
Oops!
Ow!
ALPHA!
Don't mind me, I just need a human shield for a minute.
Whaaat? Hey!
Yikes!
Take that!

FOOD

FIGHT!

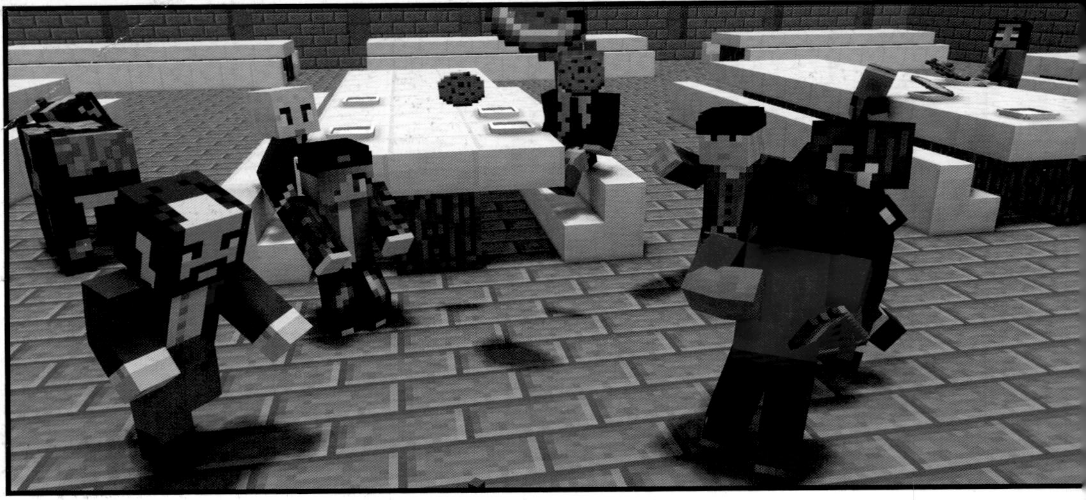

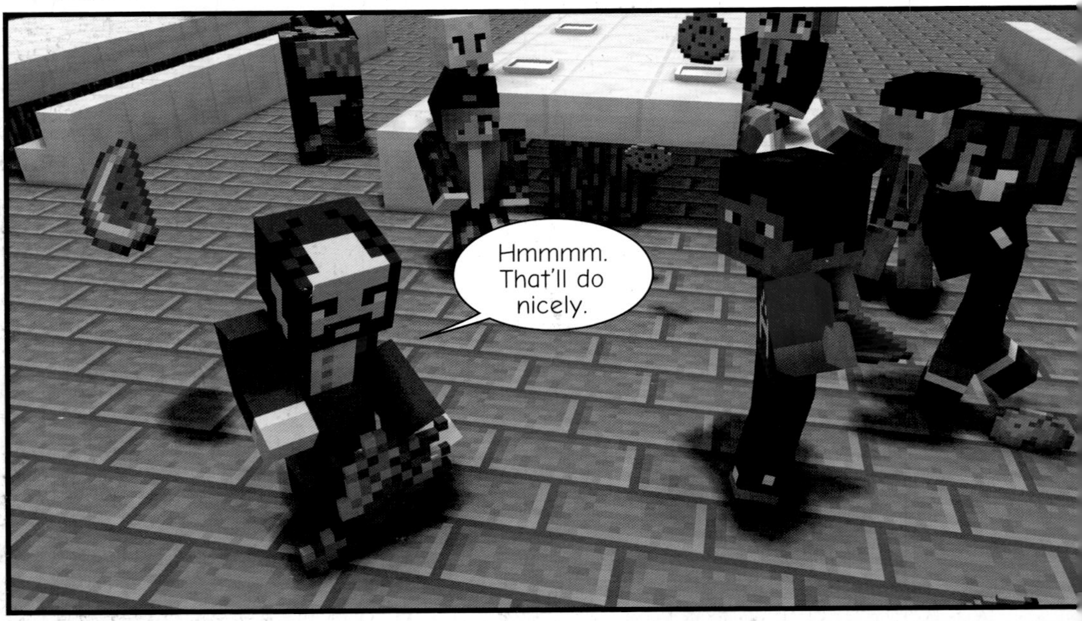
Hmmmm. That'll do nicely.

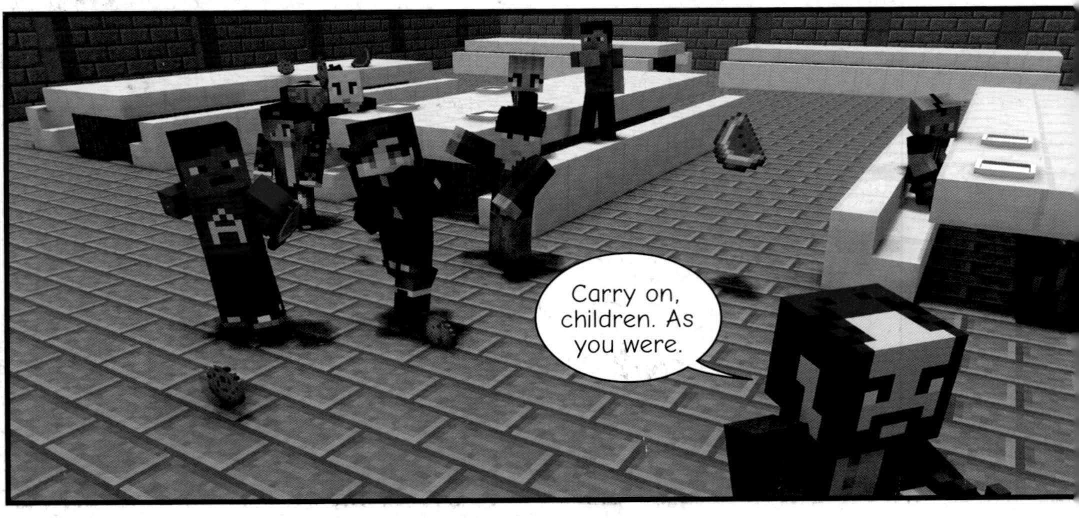
Carry on, children. As you were.

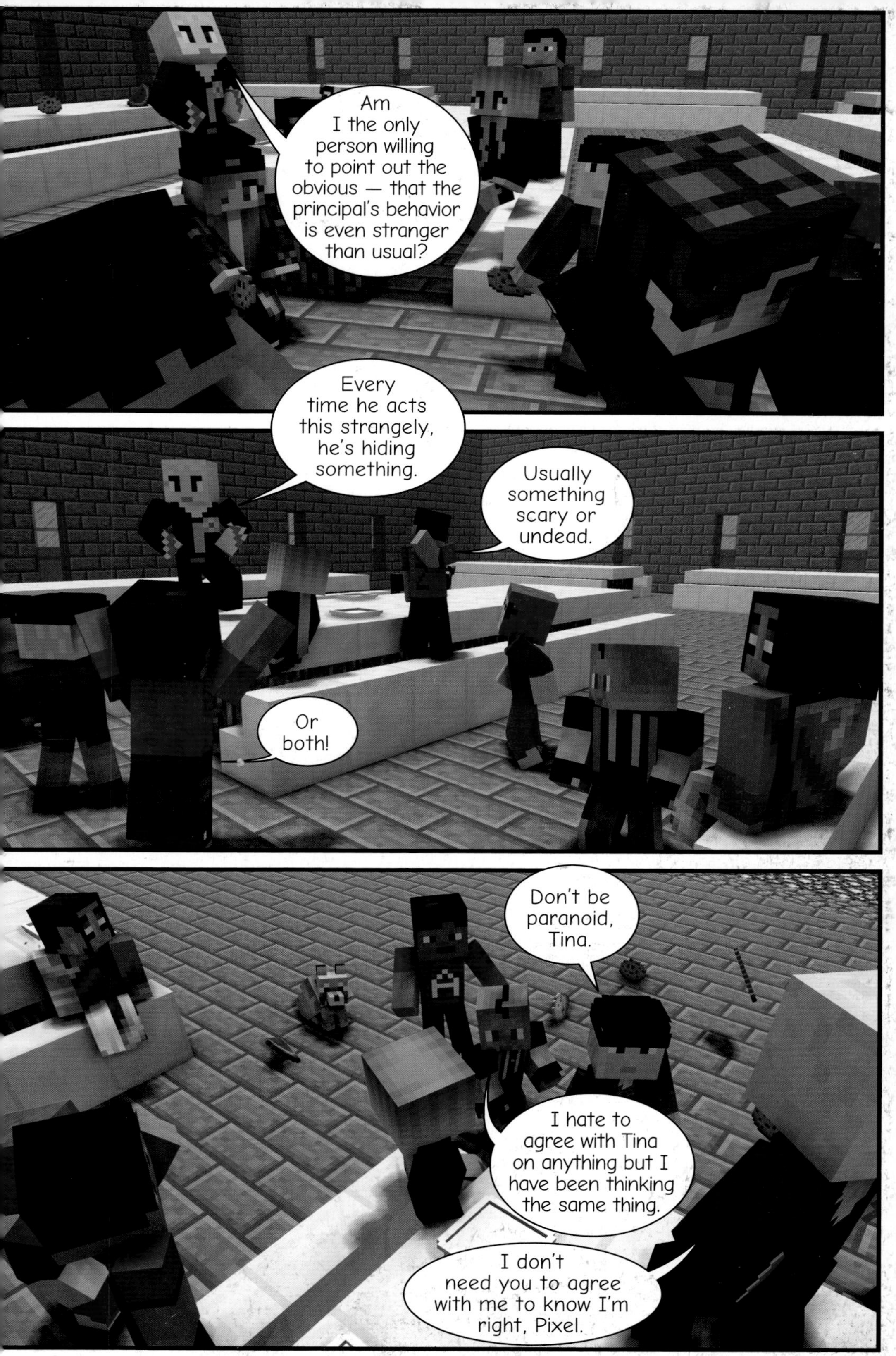
Am I the only person willing to point out the obvious — that the principal's behavior is even stranger than usual?
Every time he acts this strangely, he's hiding something.
Usually something scary or undead.
Or both!
Don't be paranoid, Tina.
I hate to agree with Tina on anything but I have been thinking the same thing.
I don't need you to agree with me to know I'm right, Pixel.

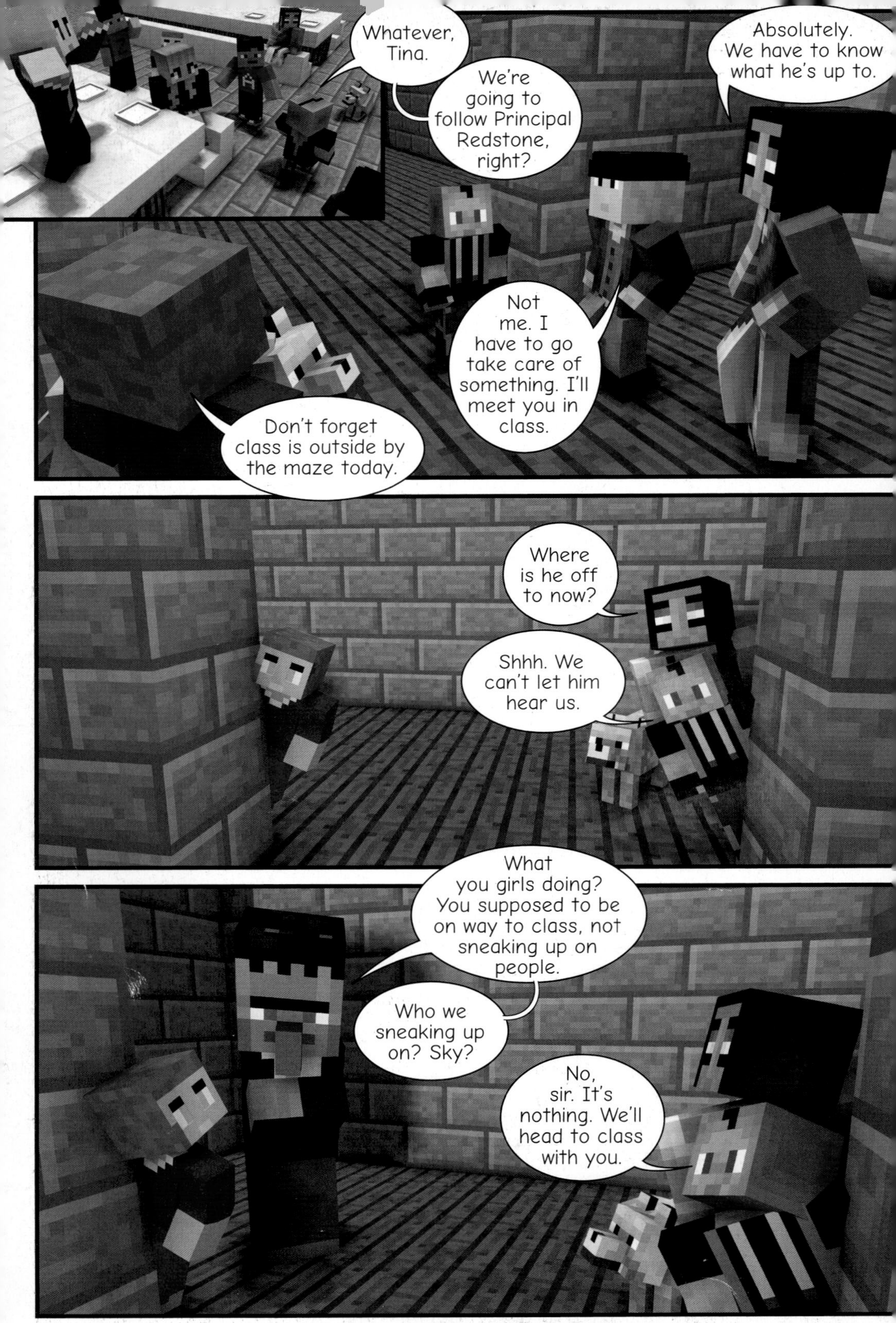
Whatever, Tina.
We're going to follow Principal Redstone, right?
Absolutely. We have to know what he's up to.
Not me. I have to go take care of something. I'll meet you in class.
Don't forget class is outside by the maze today.
Where is he off to now?
Shhh. We can't let him hear us.
What you girls doing? You supposed to be on way to class, not sneaking up on people.
Who we sneaking up on? Sky?
No, sir. It's nothing. We'll head to class with you.

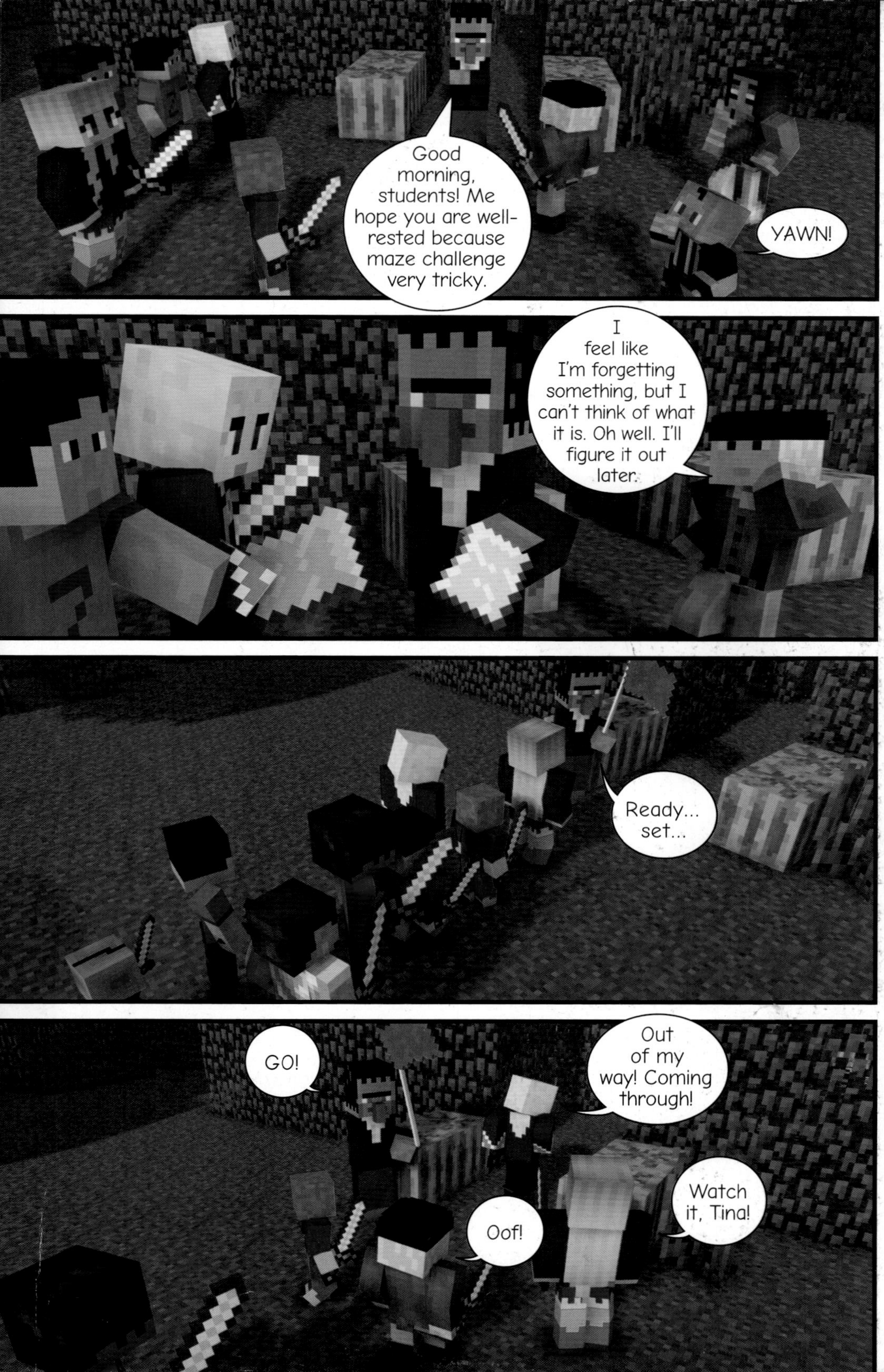
Good morning, students! Me hope you are well-rested because maze challenge very tricky.
YAWN!
I feel like I'm forgetting something, but I can't think of what it is. Oh well. I'll figure it out later.
Ready... set...
GO!
Out of my way! Coming through!
Oof!
Watch it, Tina!

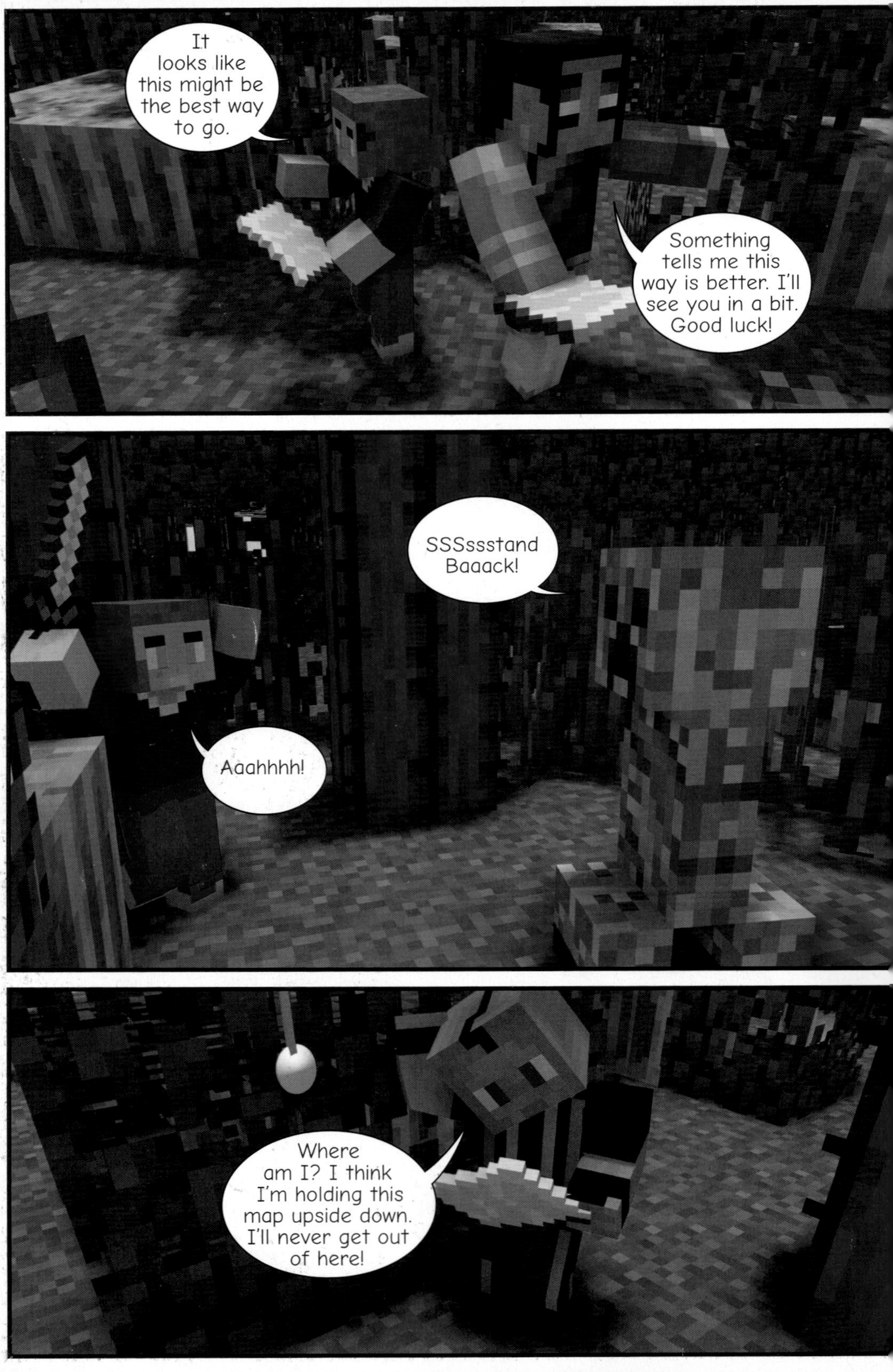
It looks like this might be the best way to go.
Something tells me this way is better. I'll see you in a bit. Good luck!
SSSssstand Baaack!
Aaahhhh!
Where am I? I think I'm holding this map upside down. I'll never get out of here!

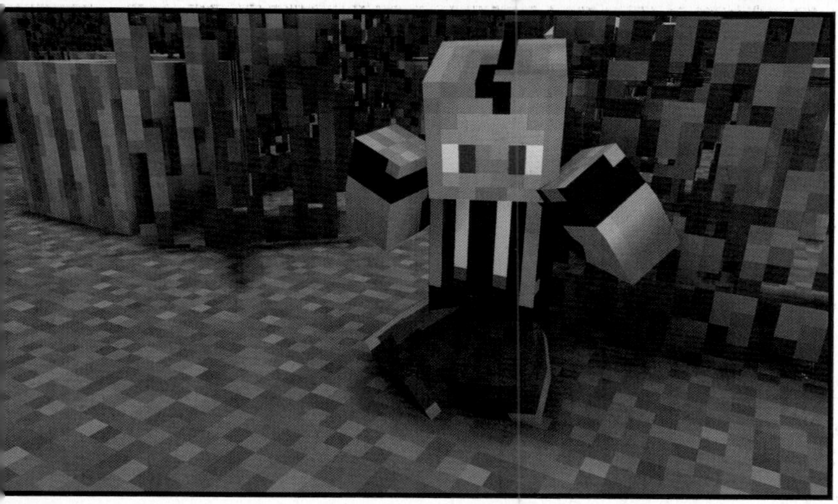

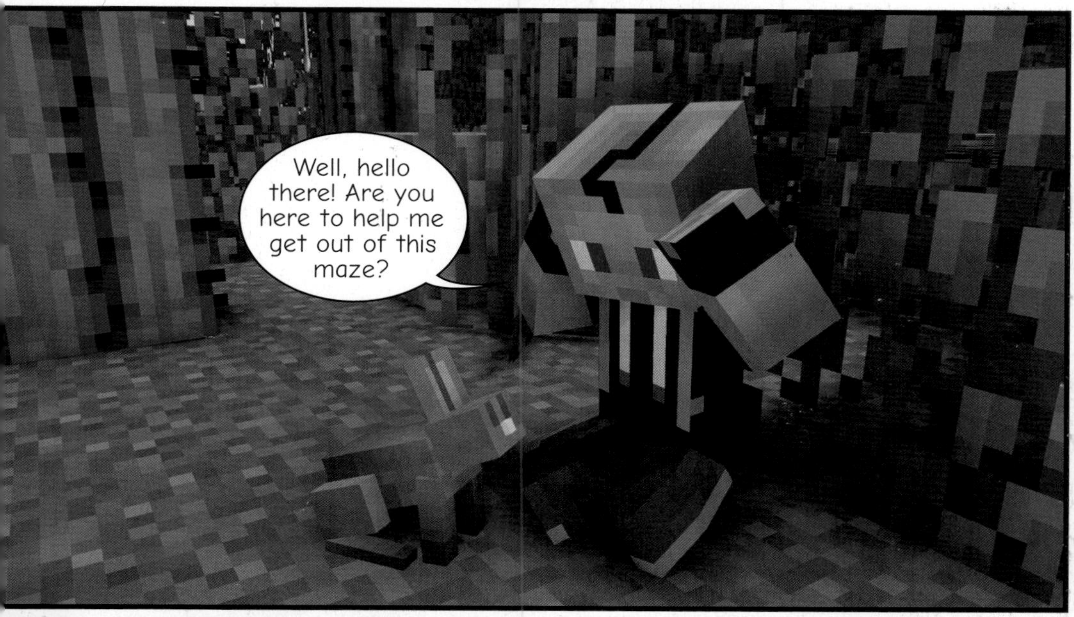
Well, hello there! Are you here to help me get out of this maze?

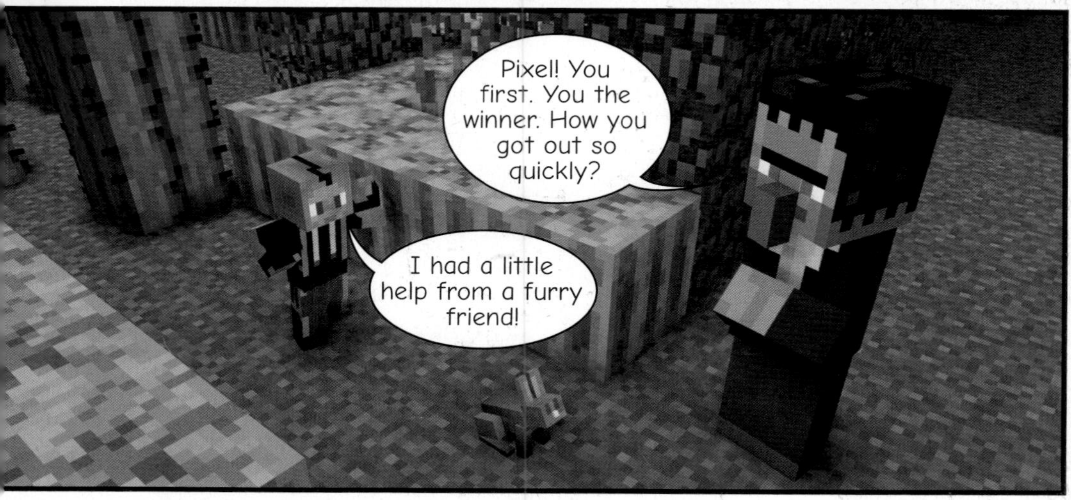
Pixel! You first. You the winner. How you got out so quickly?
I had a little help from a furry friend!

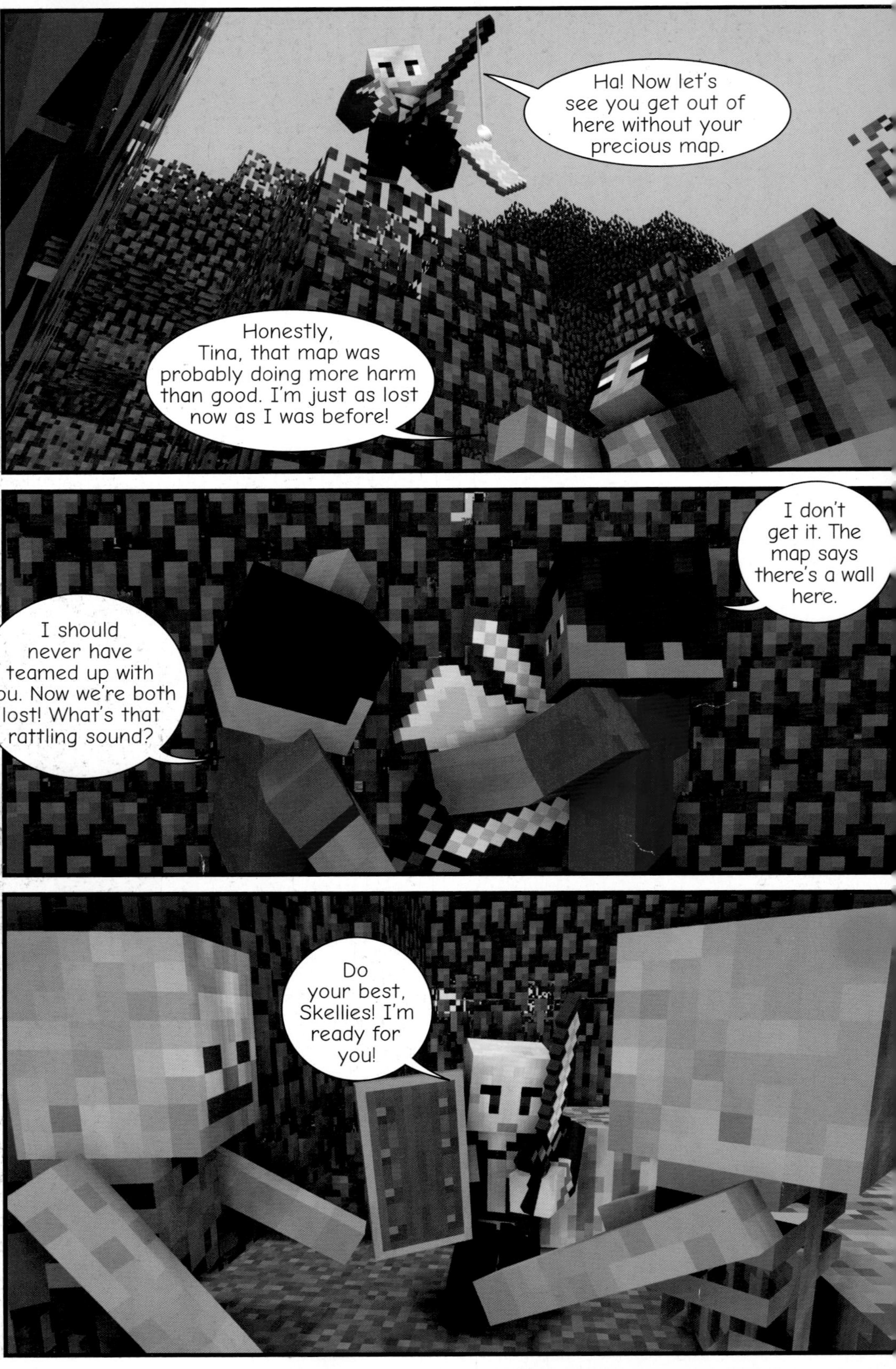
Ha! Now let's see you get out of here without your precious map.
Honestly, Tina, that map was probably doing more harm than good. I'm just as lost now as I was before!
I don't get it. The map says there's a wall here.
I should never have teamed up with you. Now we're both lost! What's that rattling sound?
Do your best, Skellies! I'm ready for you!

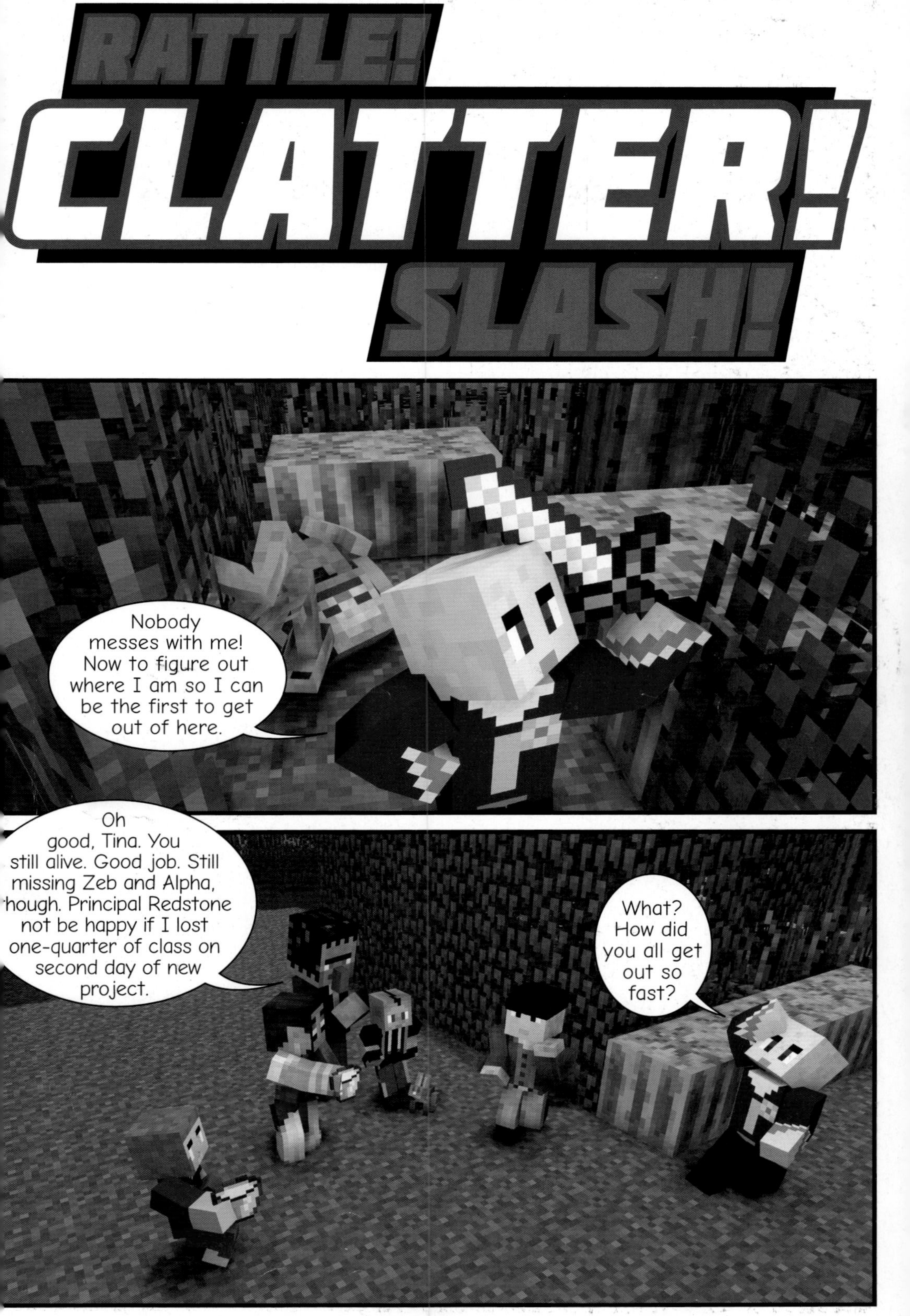
RATTLE!
CLATTER!
SLASH!
Nobody messes with me! Now to figure out where I am so I can be the first to get out of here.
Oh good, Tina. You still alive. Good job. Still missing Zeb and Alpha, hough. Principal Redstone not be happy if I lost one-quarter of class on second day of new project.
What? How did you all get out so fast?

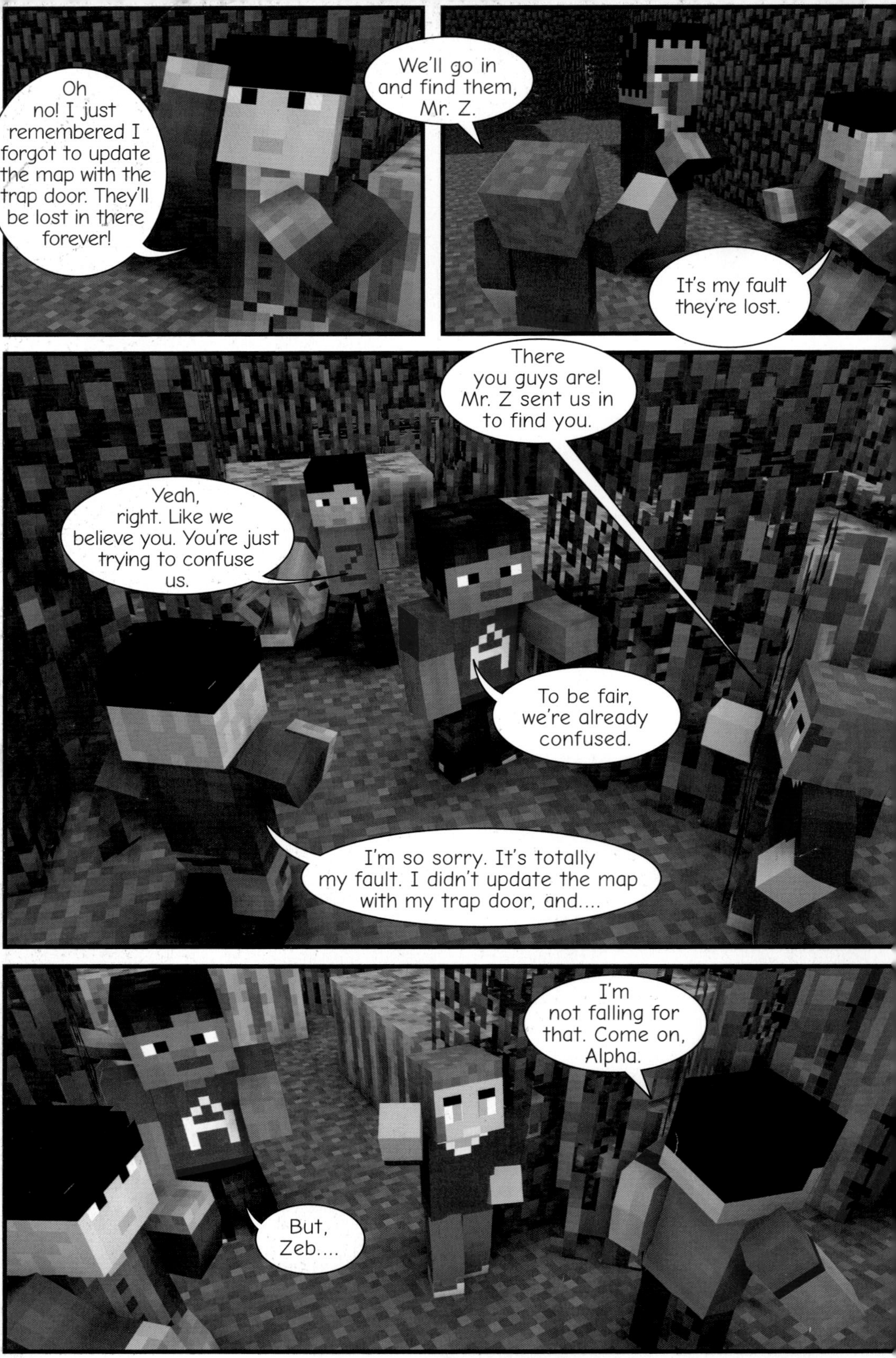
Oh no! I just remembered I forgot to update the map with the trap door. They'll be lost in there forever!
We'll go in and find them, Mr. Z.
It's my fault they're lost.
There you guys are! Mr. Z sent us in to find you.
Yeah, right. Like we believe you. You're just trying to confuse us.
To be fair, we're already confused.
I'm so sorry. It's totally my fault. I didn't update the map with my trap door, and....
I'm not falling for that. Come on, Alpha.
But, Zeb....

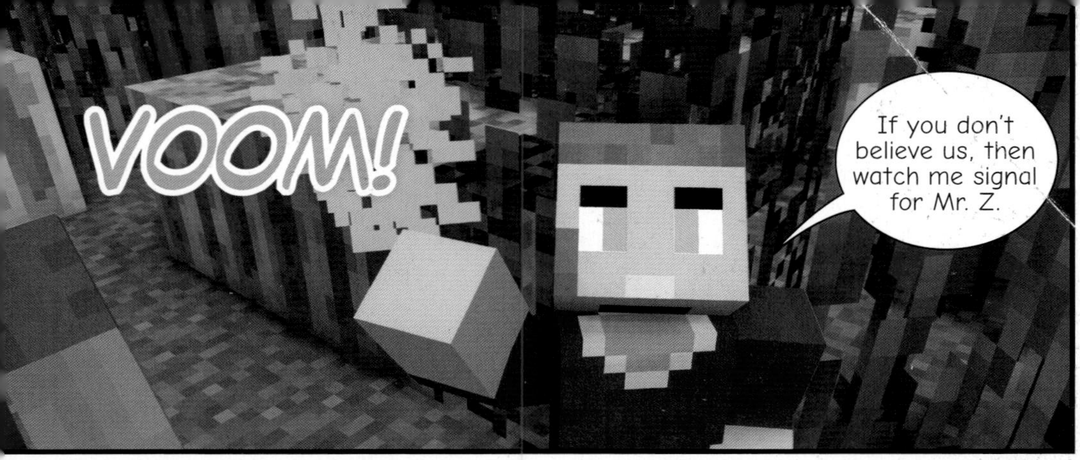
VOOM!
If you don't believe us, then watch me signal for Mr. Z.

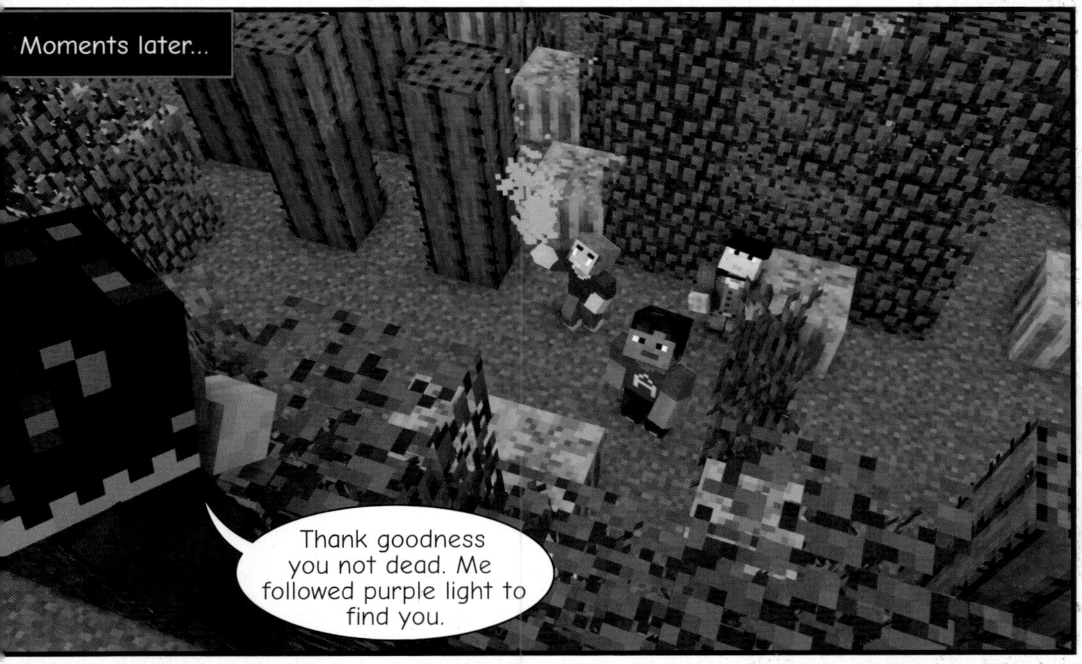
Moments later...
Thank goodness you not dead. Me followed purple light to find you.

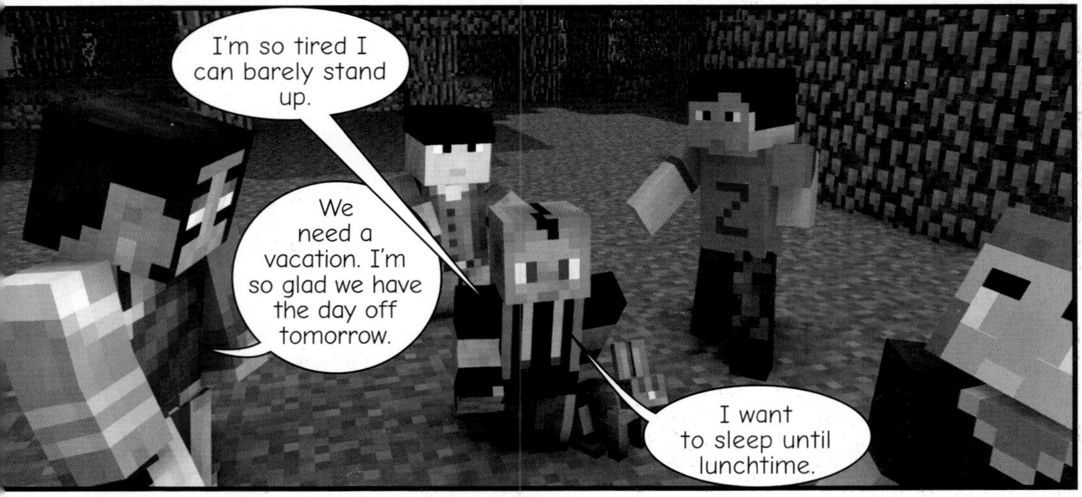
I'm so tired I can barely stand up.
We need a vacation. I'm so glad we have the day off tomorrow.
I want to sleep until lunchtime.

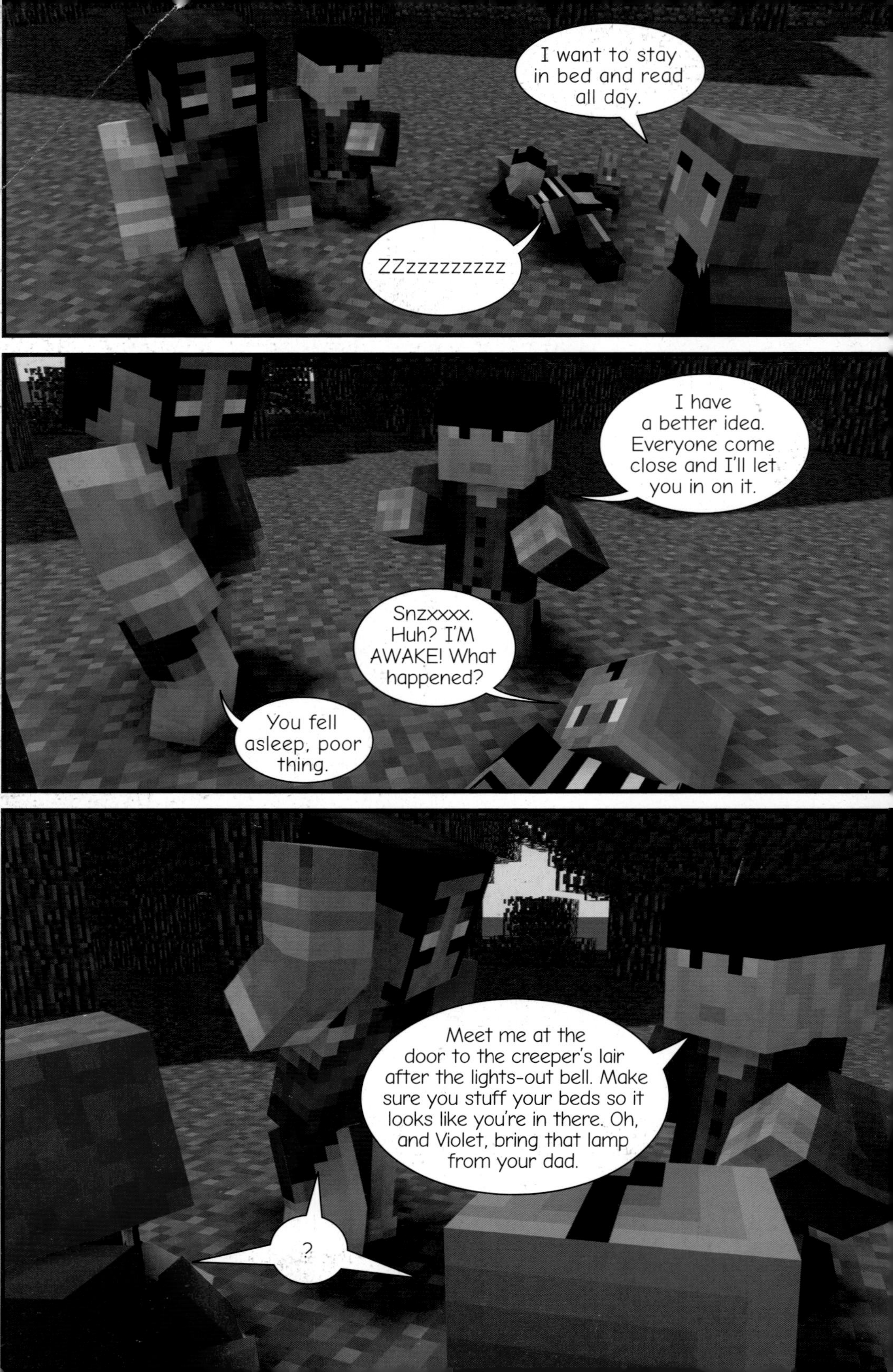
I want to stay in bed and read all day.
ZZzzzzzzzzz
I have a better idea. Everyone come close and I'll let you in on it.
Snzxxxx. Huh? I'M AWAKE! What happened?
You fell asleep, poor thing.
Meet me at the door to the creeper's lair after the lights-out bell. Make sure you stuff your beds so it looks like you're in there. Oh, and Violet, bring that lamp from your dad.
?

CHAPTER 4

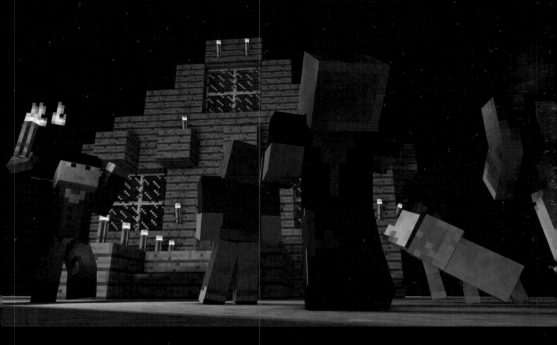

A MIDNIGHT VOYAGE

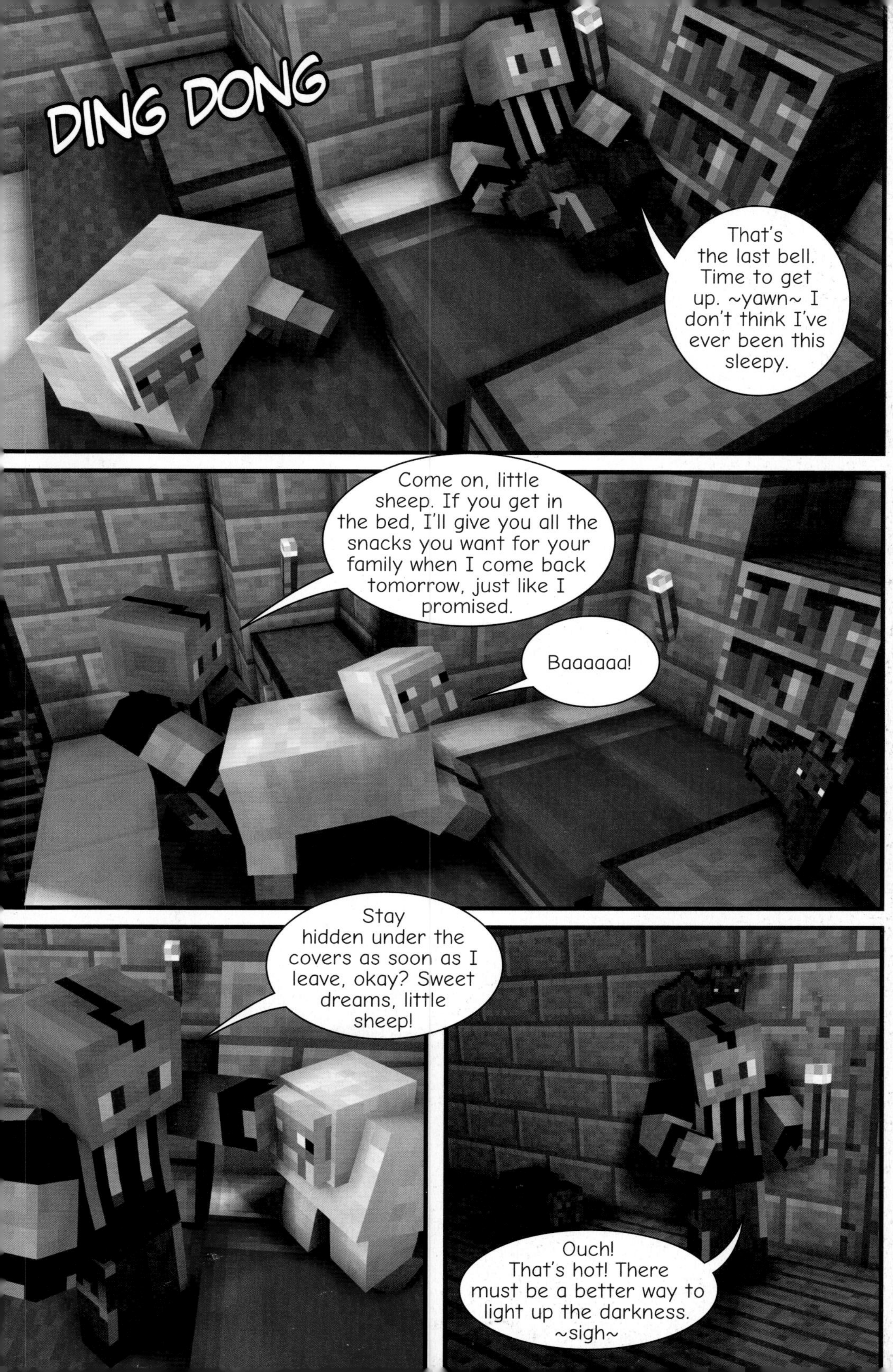
DING DONG
That's the last bell. Time to get up. ~yawn~ I don't think I've ever been this sleepy.
Come on, little sheep. If you get in the bed, I'll give you all the snacks you want for your family when I come back tomorrow, just like I promised.
Baaaaaa!
Stay hidden under the covers as soon as I leave, okay? Sweet dreams, little sheep!
Ouch! That's hot! There must be a better way to light up the darkness. ~sigh~

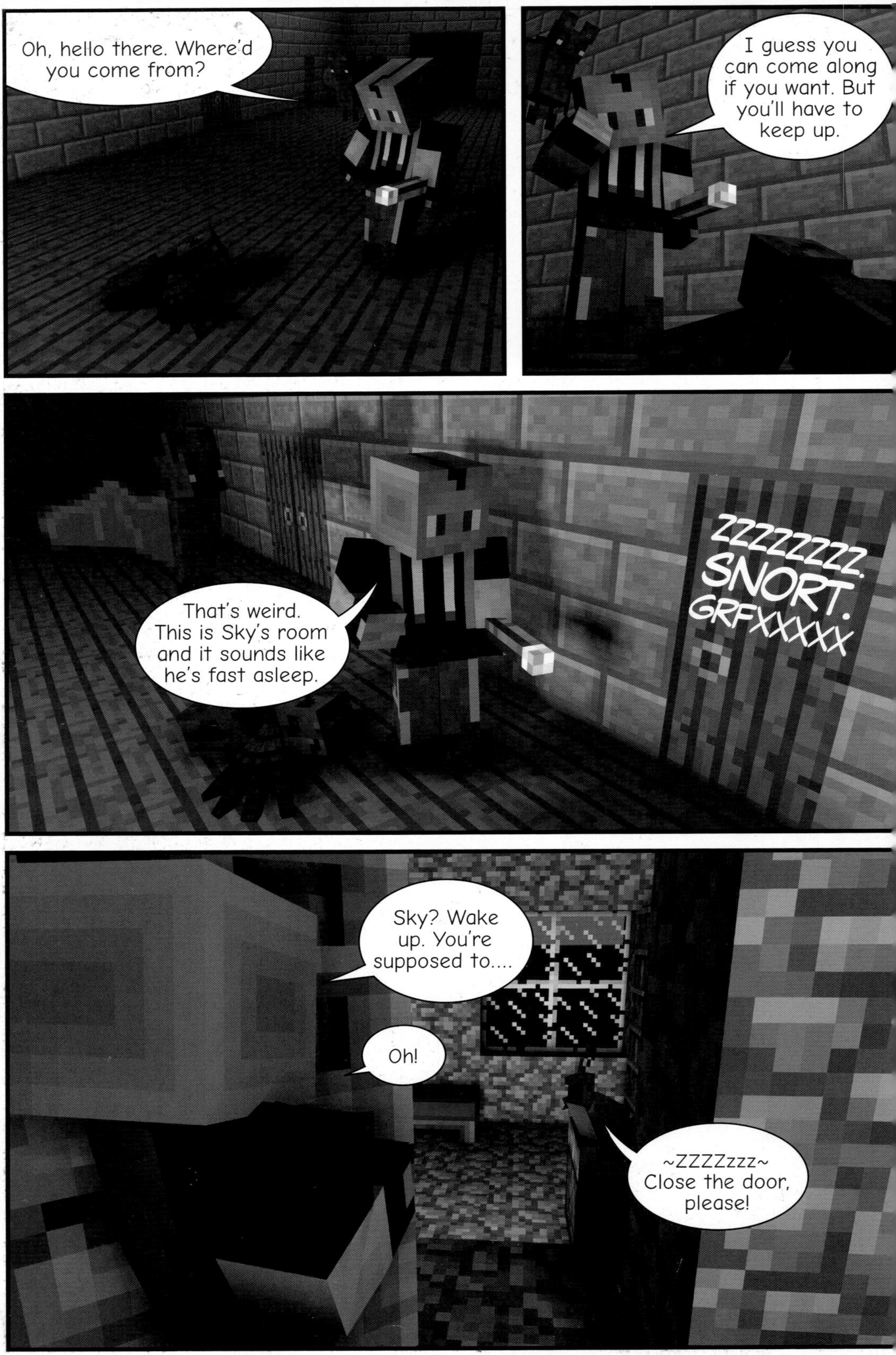
Oh, hello there. Where'd you come from?
I guess you can come along if you want. But you'll have to keep up.
That's weird. This is Sky's room and it sounds like he's fast asleep.
ZZZZZZZZ. SNORT. GRFXXXXX
Sky? Wake up. You're supposed to....
Oh!
~ZZZZzzz~ Close the door, please!

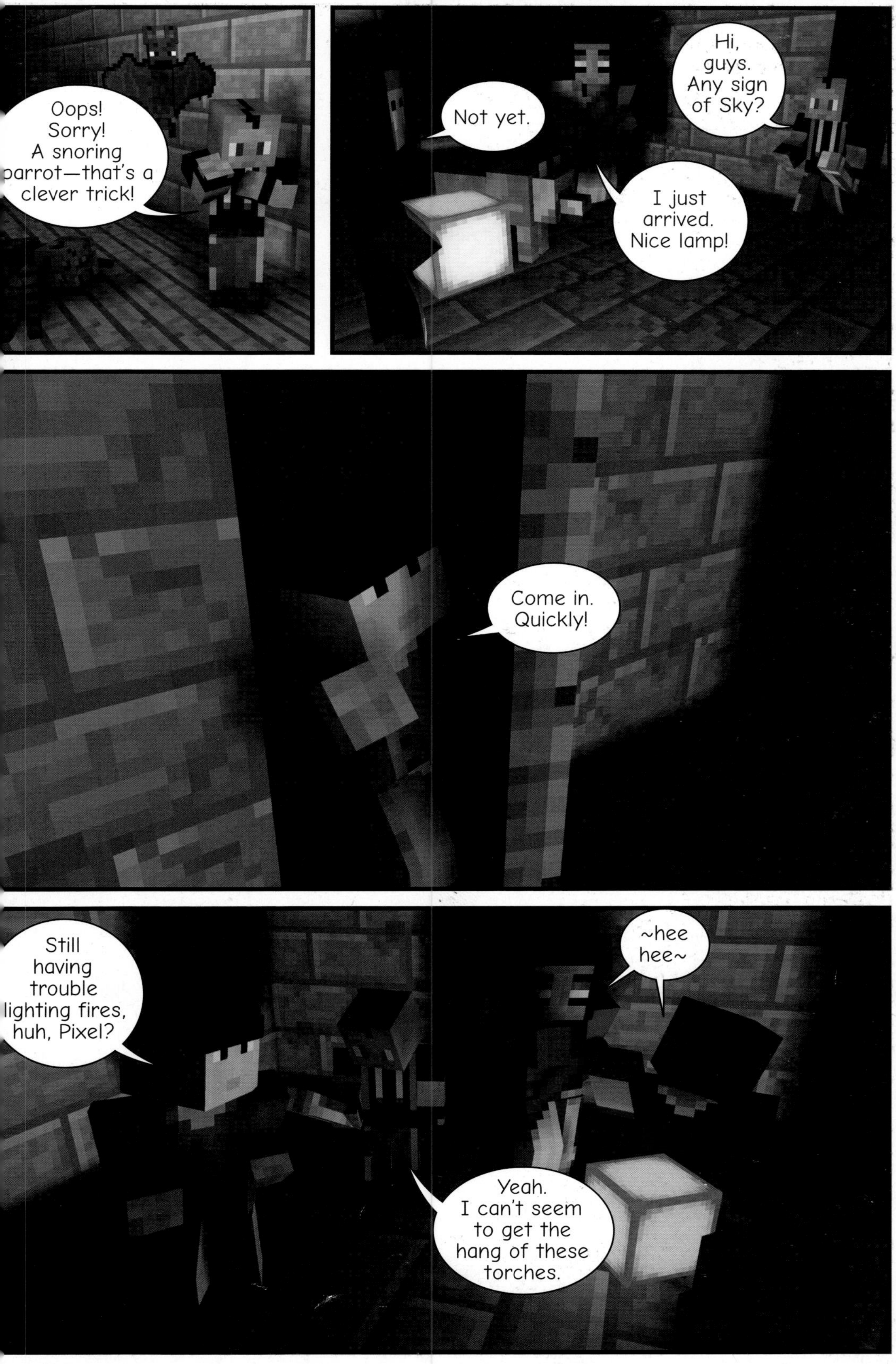
Oops! Sorry! A snoring parrot—that's a clever trick!
Hi, guys. Any sign of Sky?
Not yet.
I just arrived. Nice lamp!
Come in. Quickly!
Still having trouble lighting fires, huh, Pixel?
~hee hee~
Yeah. I can't seem to get the hang of these torches.

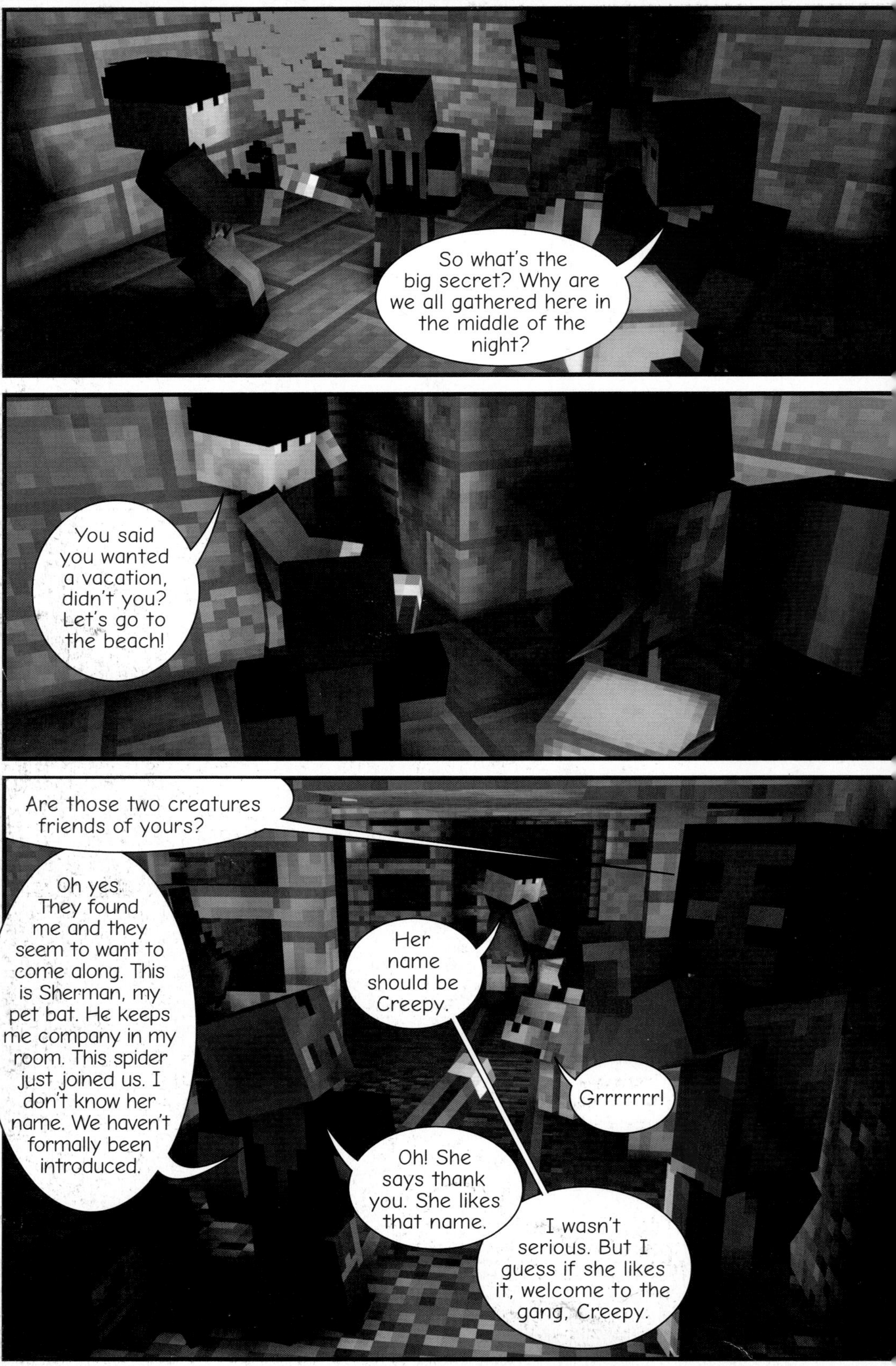
So what's the big secret? Why are we all gathered here in the middle of the night?
You said you wanted a vacation, didn't you? Let's go to the beach!
Are those two creatures friends of yours?
Oh yes. They found me and they seem to want to come along. This is Sherman, my pet bat. He keeps me company in my room. This spider just joined us. I don't know her name. We haven't formally been introduced.
Her name should be Creepy.
Grrrrrrr!
Oh! She says thank you. She likes that name.
I wasn't serious. But I guess if she likes it, welcome to the gang, Creepy.

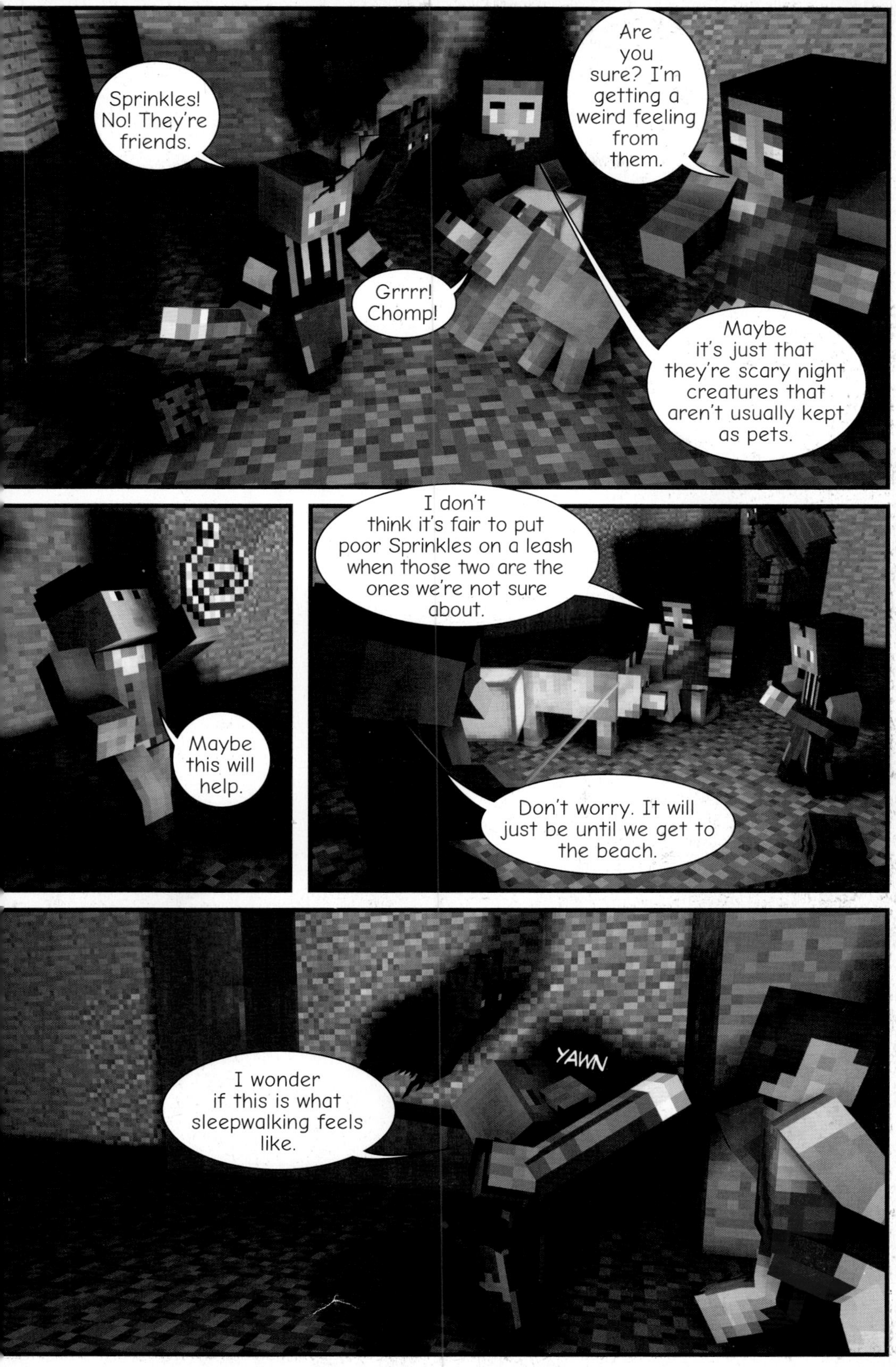
Sprinkles! No! They're friends.
Are you sure? I'm getting a weird feeling from them.
Grrrr! Chomp!
Maybe it's just that they're scary night creatures that aren't usually kept as pets.
Maybe this will help.
I don't think it's fair to put poor Sprinkles on a leash when those two are the ones we're not sure about.
Don't worry. It will just be until we get to the beach.
YAWN
I wonder if this is what sleepwalking feels like.

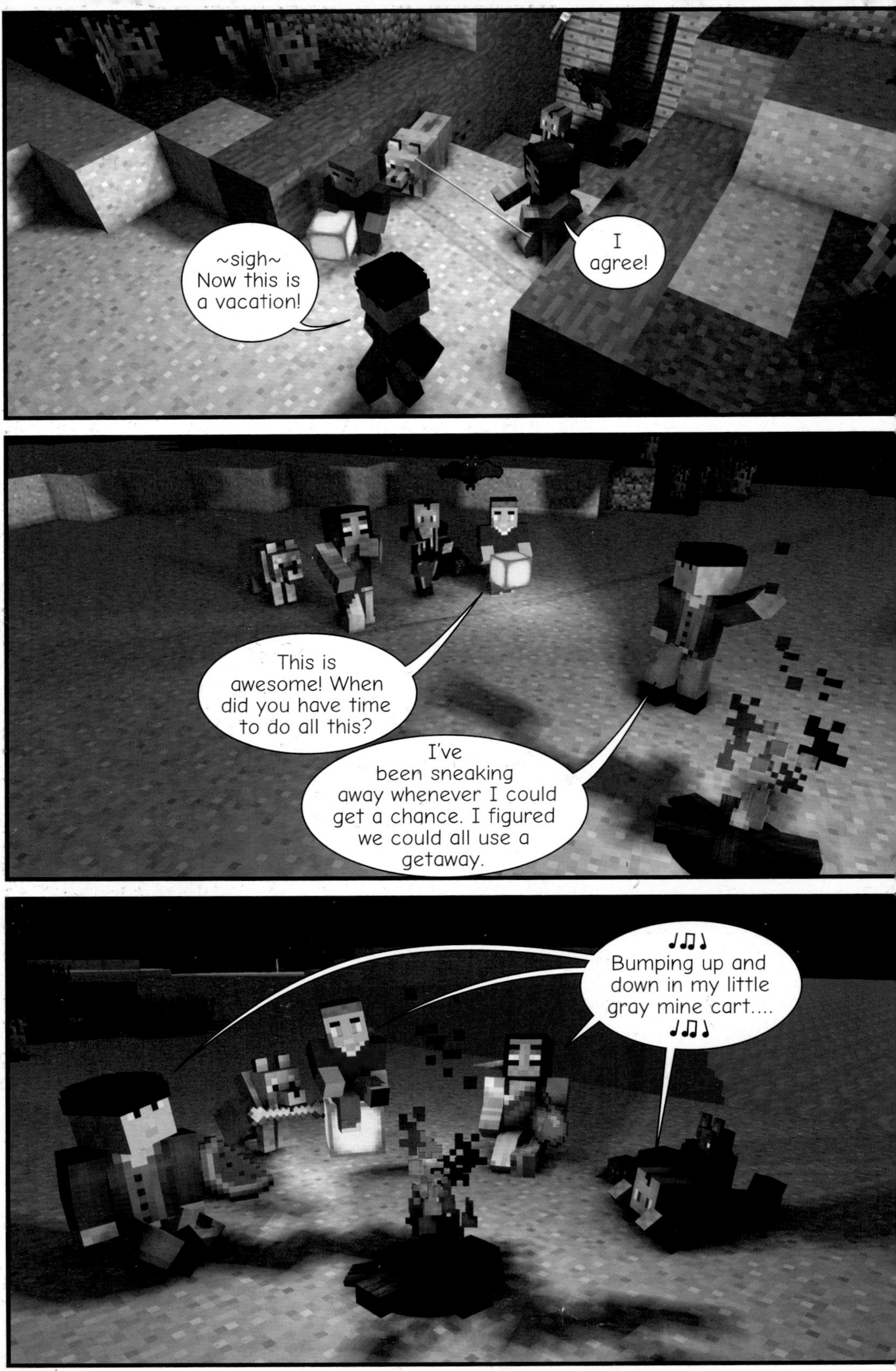
~sigh~ Now this is a vacation!
I agree!
This is awesome! When did you have time to do all this?
I've been sneaking away whenever I could get a chance. I figured we could all use a getaway.
♩♫♩ Bumping up and down in my little gray mine cart.... ♩♫♩

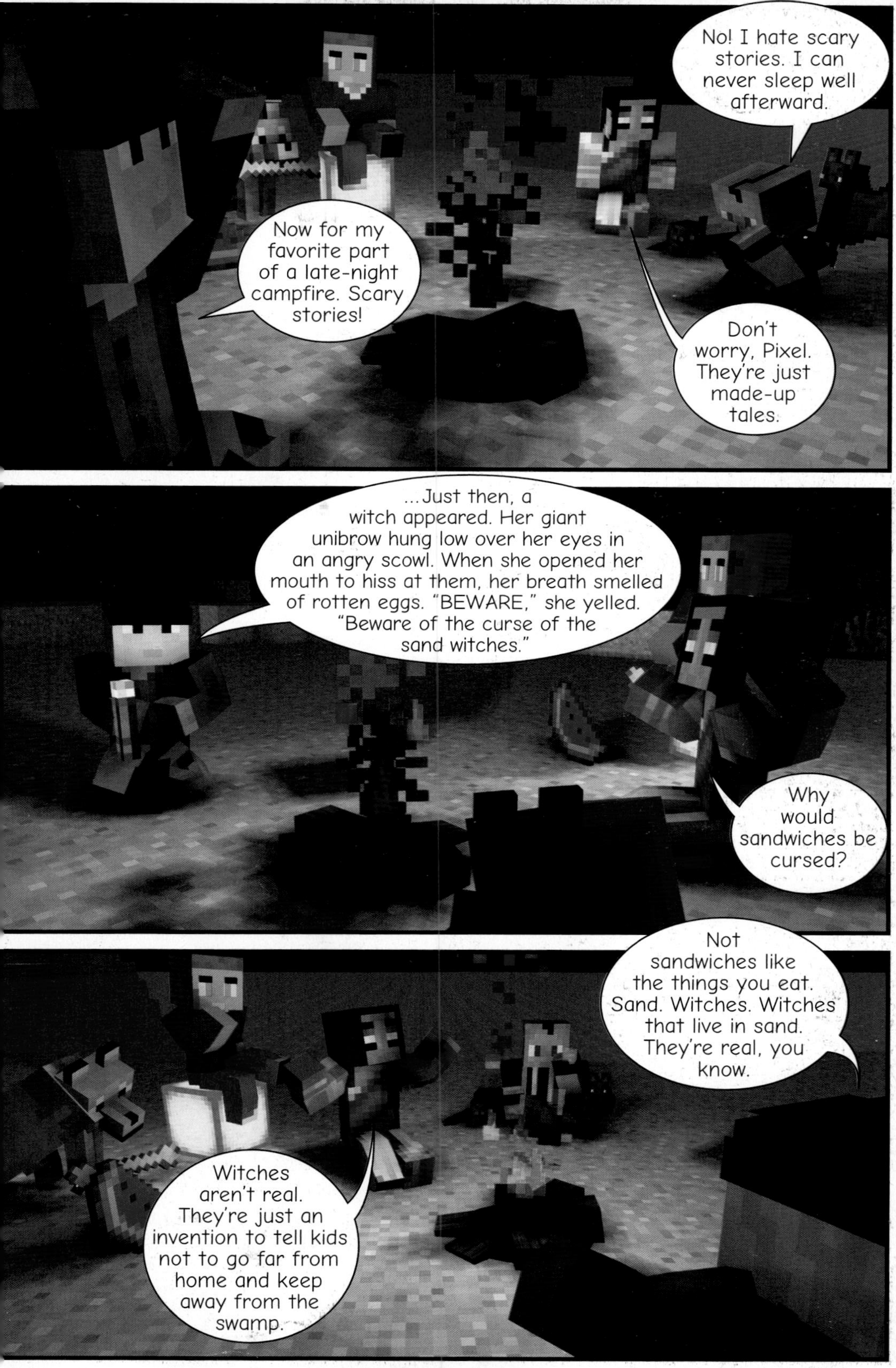
Now for my favorite part of a late-night campfire. Scary stories!
No! I hate scary stories. I can never sleep well afterward.
Don't worry, Pixel. They're just made-up tales.
...Just then, a witch appeared. Her giant unibrow hung low over her eyes in an angry scowl. When she opened her mouth to hiss at them, her breath smelled of rotten eggs. "BEWARE," she yelled. "Beware of the curse of the sand witches."
Why would sandwiches be cursed?
Not sandwiches like the things you eat. Sand. Witches. Witches that live in sand. They're real, you know.
Witches aren't real. They're just an invention to tell kids not to go far from home and keep away from the swamp.

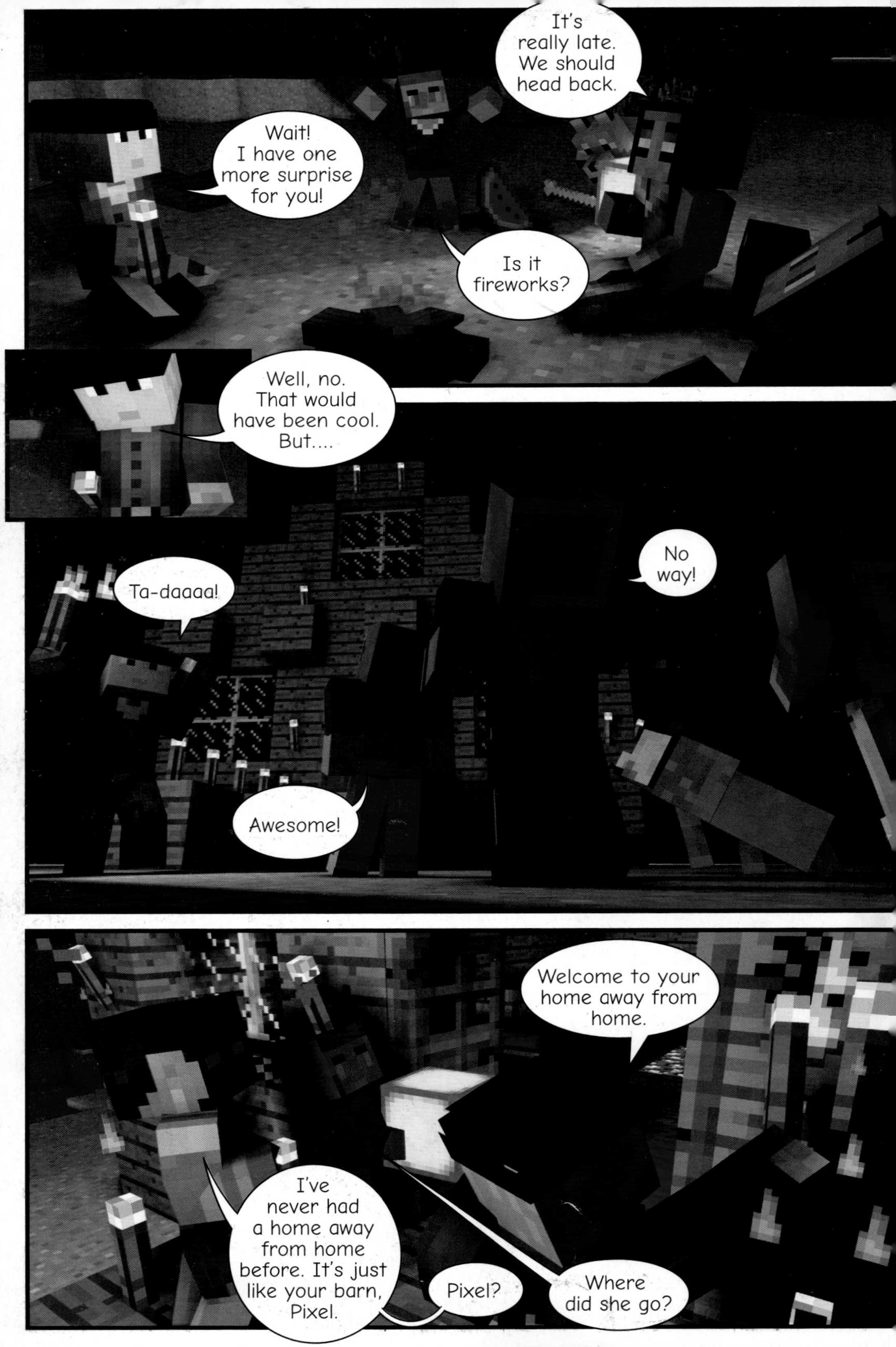
It's really late. We should head back.
Wait! I have one more surprise for you!
Is it fireworks?
Well, no. That would have been cool. But....
Ta-daaaa!
No way!
Awesome!
Welcome to your home away from home.
I've never had a home away from home before. It's just like your barn, Pixel.
Pixel?
Where did she go?

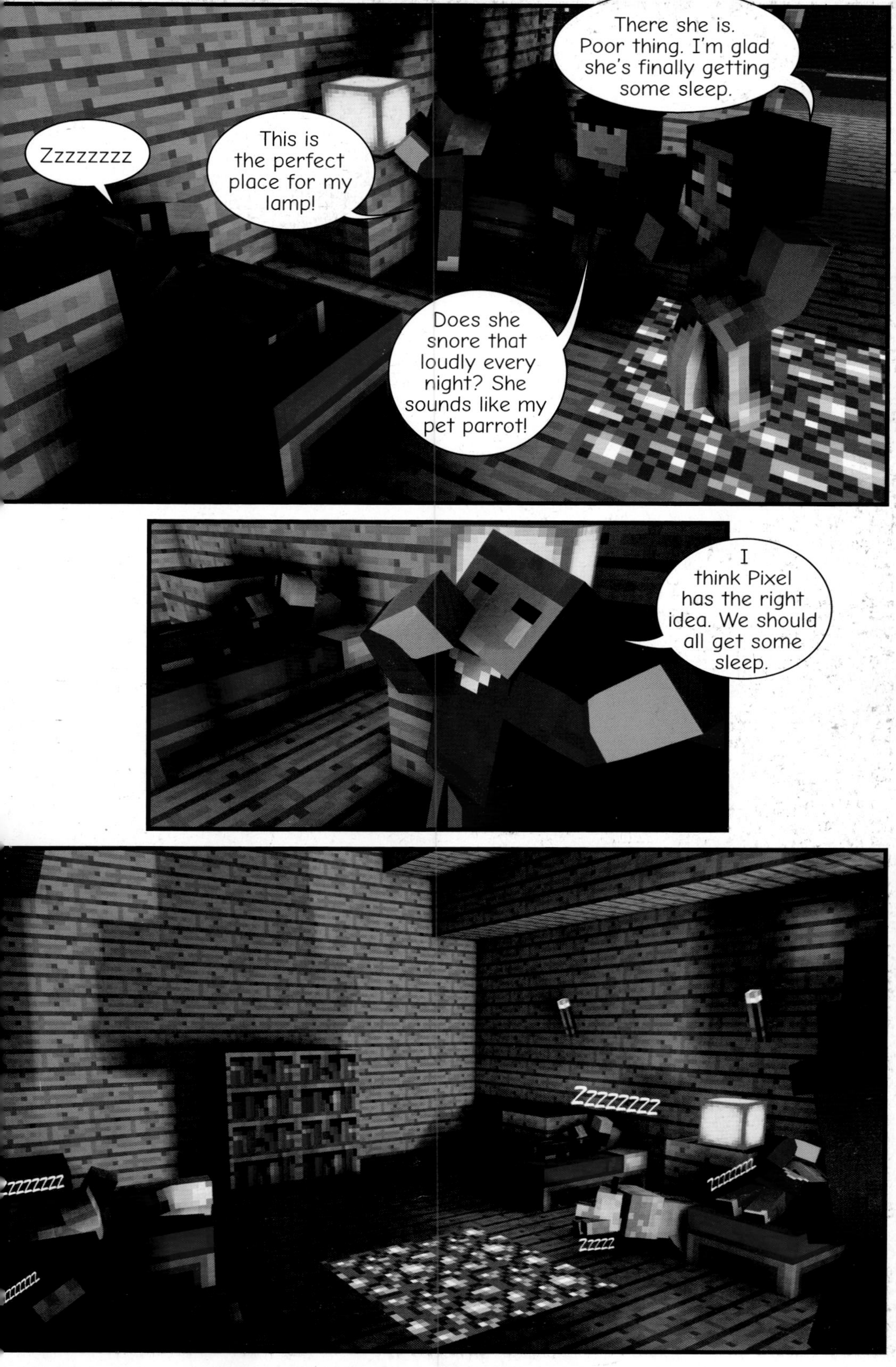
Zzzzzzzz
This is the perfect place for my lamp!
There she is. Poor thing. I'm glad she's finally getting some sleep.
Does she snore that loudly every night? She sounds like my pet parrot!
I think Pixel has the right idea. We should all get some sleep.
ZZZZZZZZ
ZZZZZZZZ
ZZZZZ

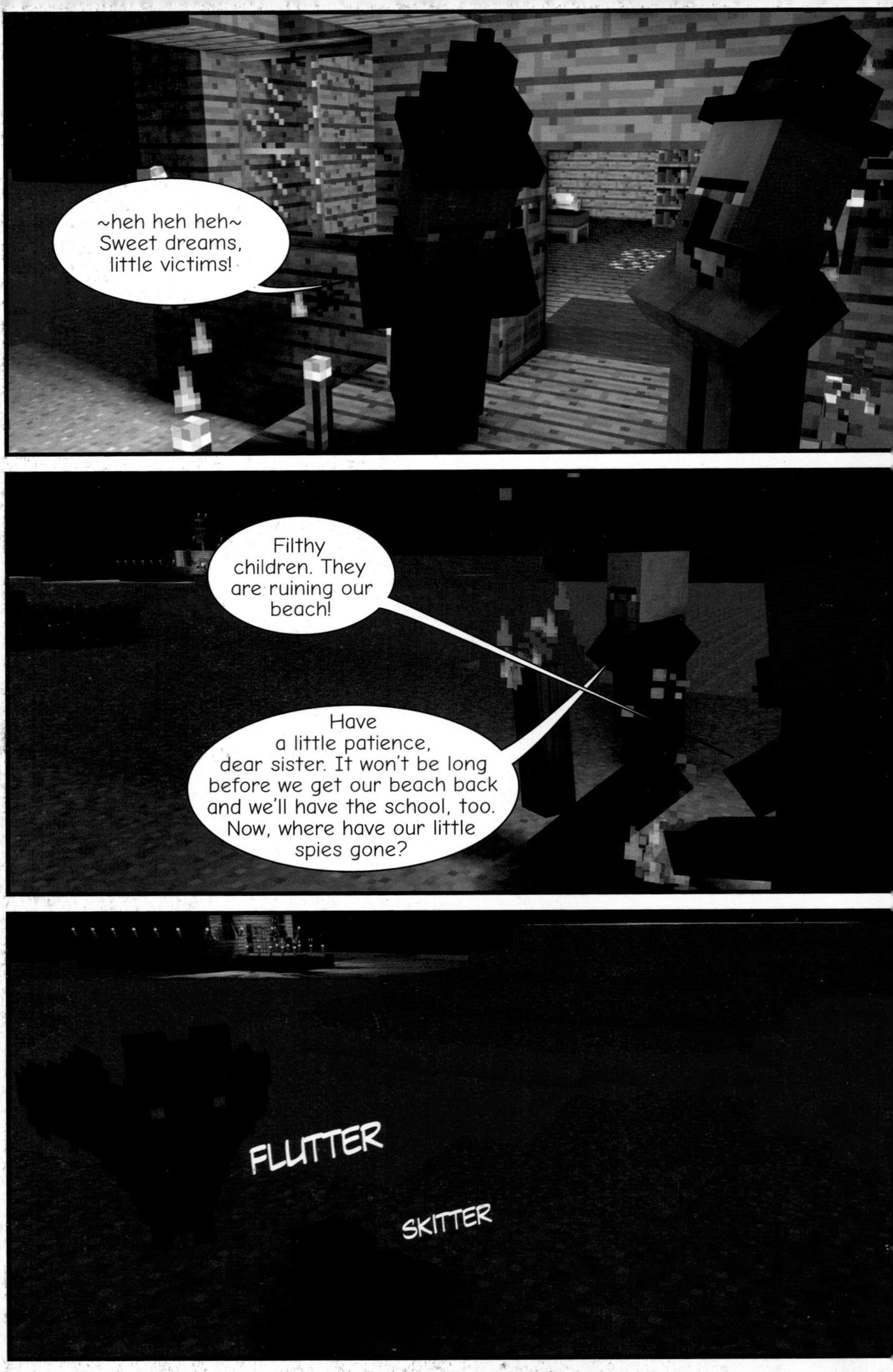
~heh heh heh~ Sweet dreams, little victims!
Filthy children. They are ruining our beach!
Have a little patience, dear sister. It won't be long before we get our beach back and we'll have the school, too. Now, where have our little spies gone?
FLUTTER
SKITTER

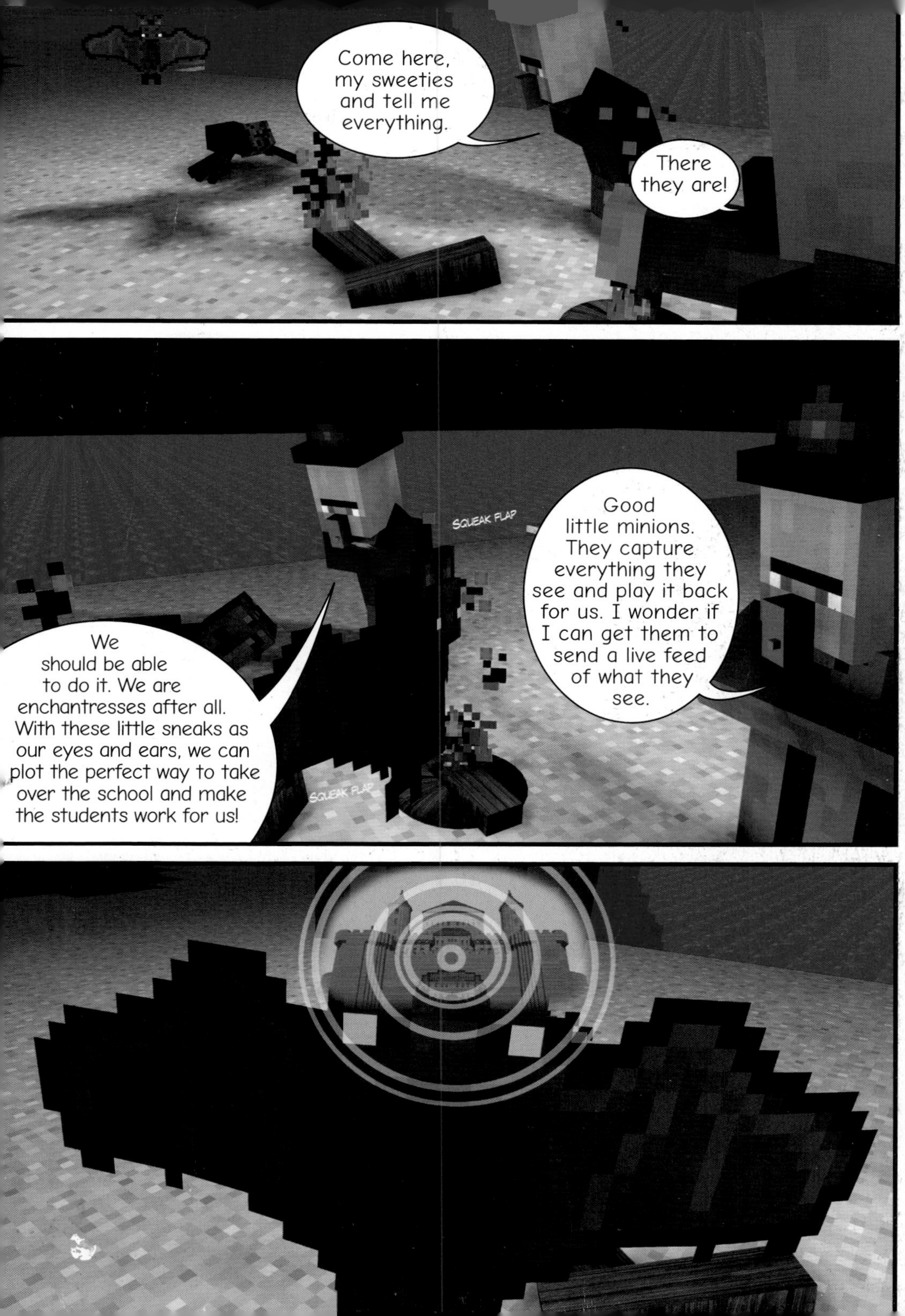

Come here, my sweeties and tell me everything.
There they are!
SQUEAK FLAP
Good little minions. They capture everything they see and play it back for us. I wonder if I can get them to send a live feed of what they see.
We should be able to do it. We are enchantresses after all. With these little sneaks as our eyes and ears, we can plot the perfect way to take over the school and make the students work for us!
SQUEAK FLAP

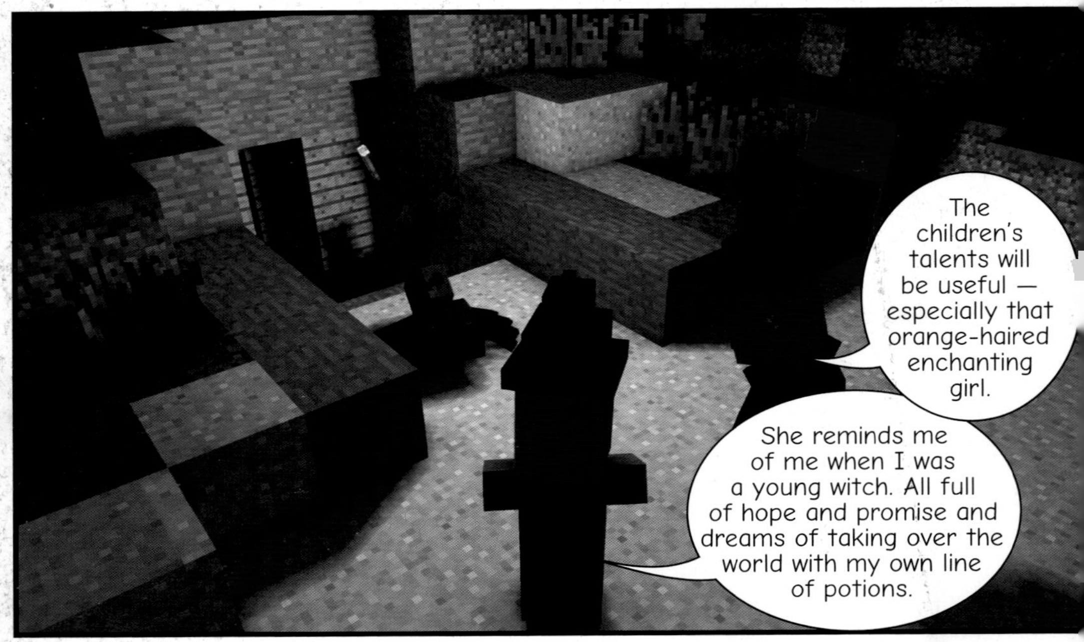
The children's talents will be useful — especially that orange-haired enchanting girl.
She reminds me of me when I was a young witch. All full of hope and promise and dreams of taking over the world with my own line of potions.

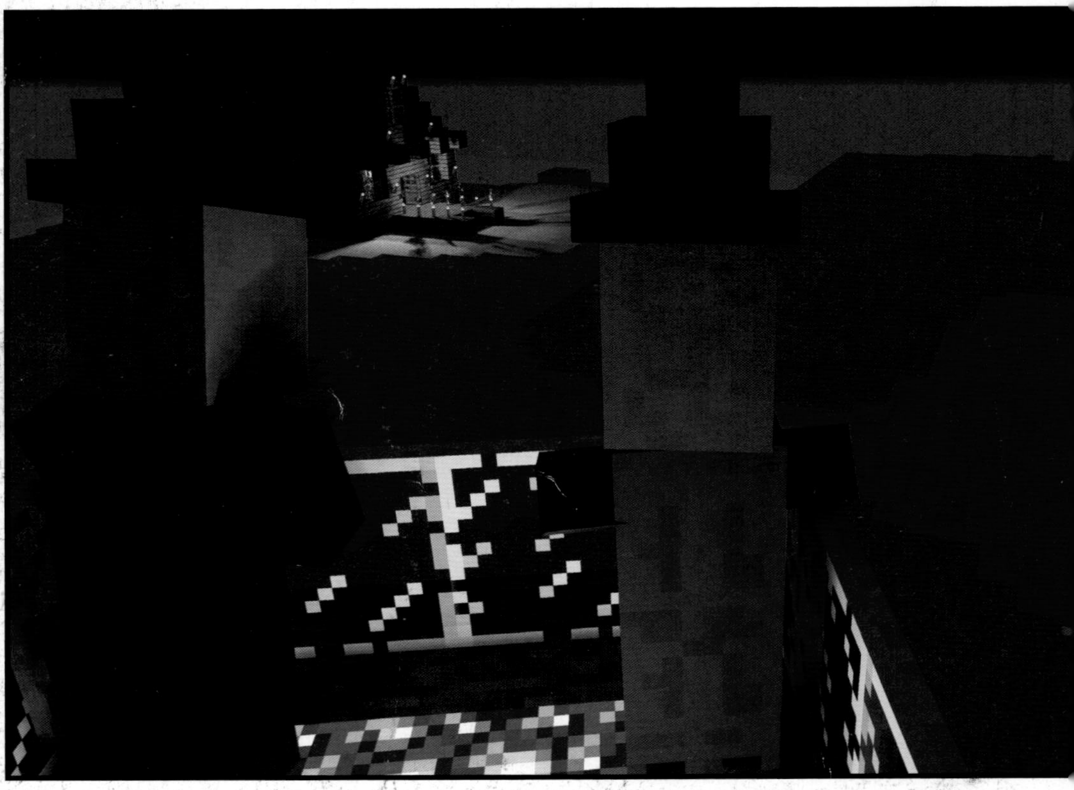

CHAPTER 5

A NECESSARY VACATION

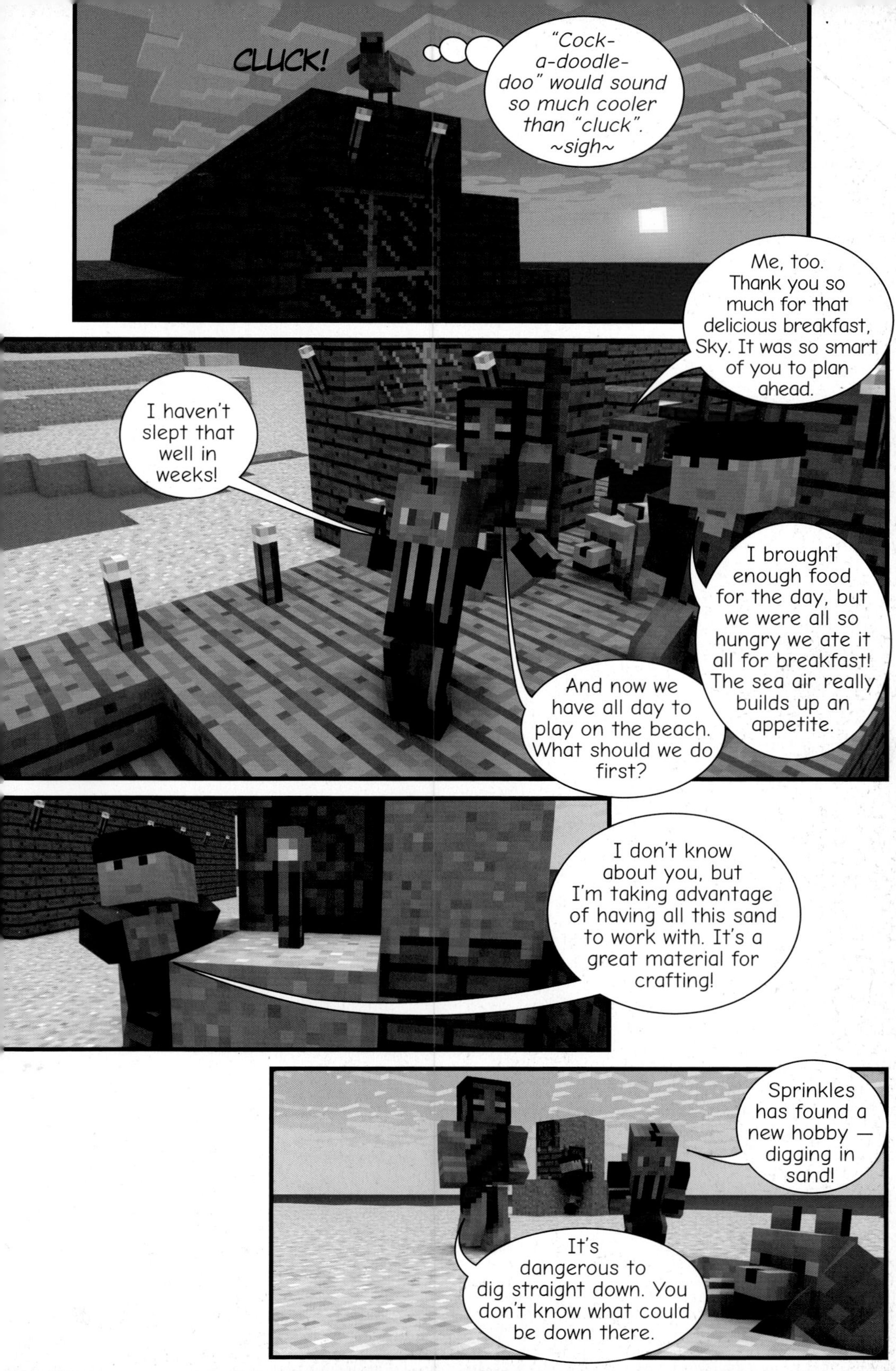
CLUCK!
"Cock-a-doodle-doo" would sound so much cooler than "cluck". ~sigh~
I haven't slept that well in weeks!
Me, too. Thank you so much for that delicious breakfast, Sky. It was so smart of you to plan ahead.
I brought enough food for the day, but we were all so hungry we ate it all for breakfast! The sea air really builds up an appetite.
And now we have all day to play on the beach. What should we do first?
I don't know about you, but I'm taking advantage of having all this sand to work with. It's a great material for crafting!
Sprinkles has found a new hobby — digging in sand!
It's dangerous to dig straight down. You don't know what could be down there.

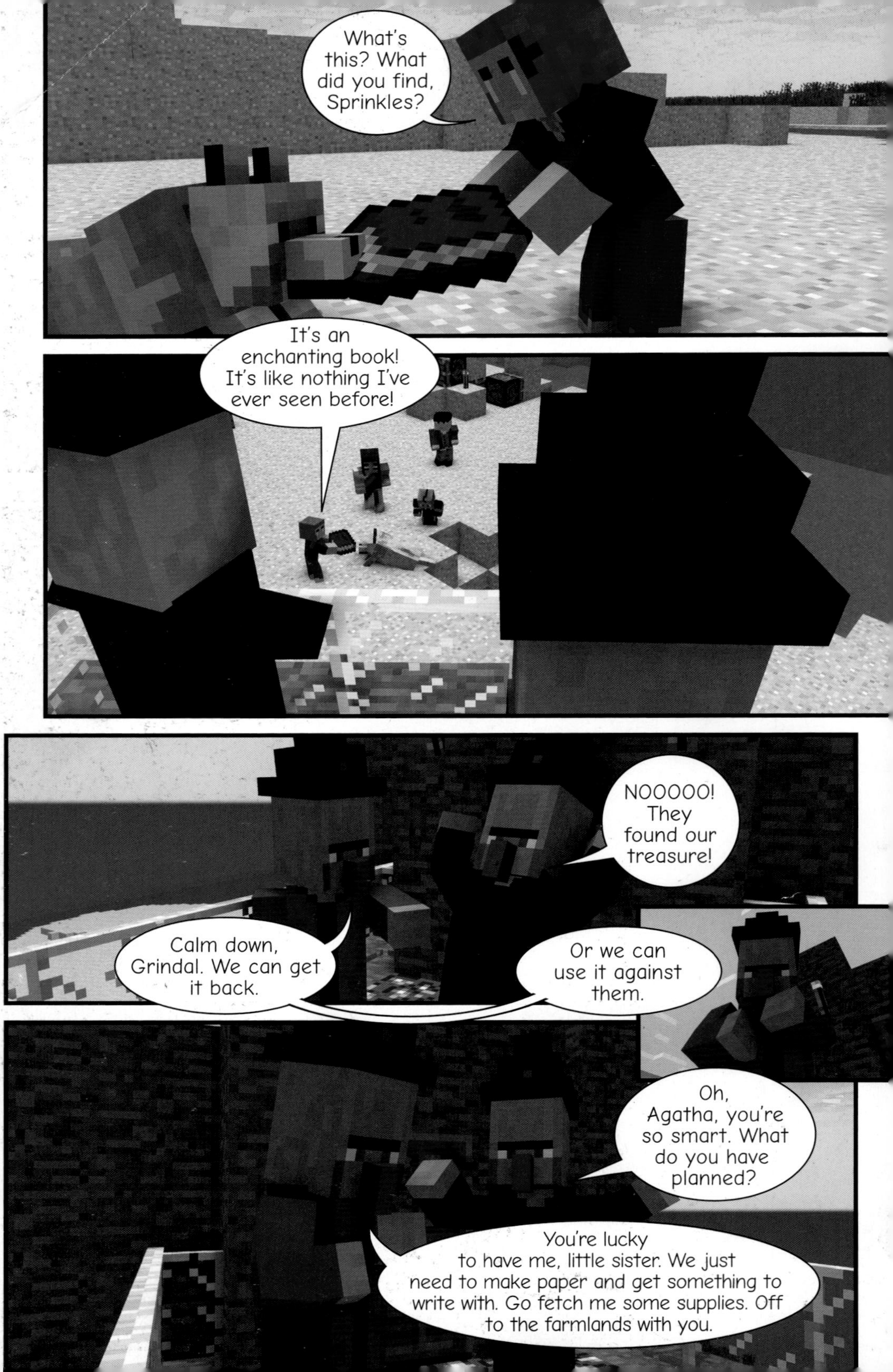
What's this? What did you find, Sprinkles?
It's an enchanting book! It's like nothing I've ever seen before!
NOOOOO! They found our treasure!
Calm down, Grindal. We can get it back.
Or we can use it against them.
Oh, Agatha, you're so smart. What do you have planned?
You're lucky to have me, little sister. We just need to make paper and get something to write with. Go fetch me some supplies. Off to the farmlands with you.

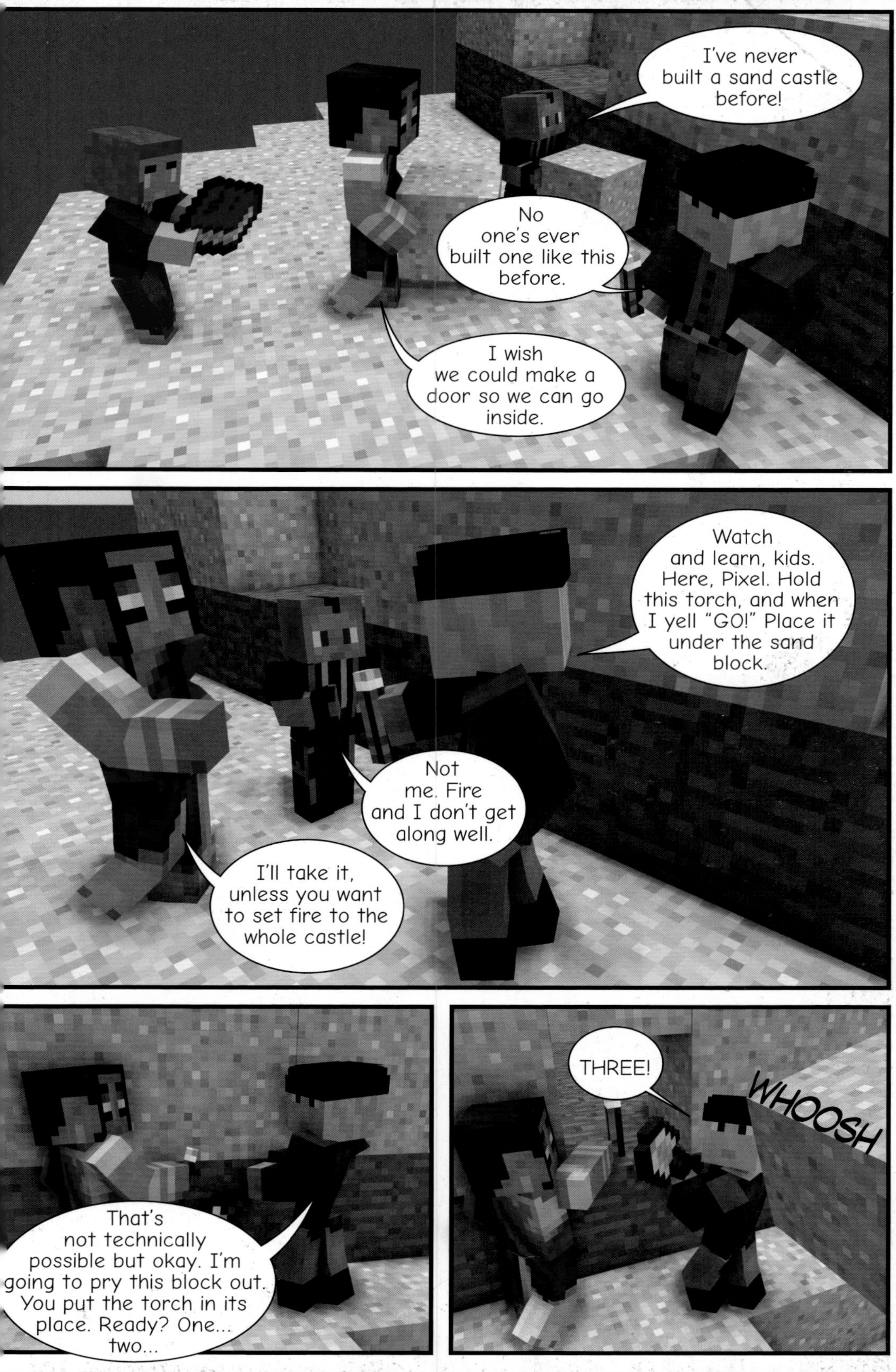
I've never built a sand castle before!
No one's ever built one like this before.
I wish we could make a door so we can go inside.
Watch and learn, kids. Here, Pixel. Hold this torch, and when I yell "GO!" Place it under the sand block.
Not me. Fire and I don't get along well.
I'll take it, unless you want to set fire to the whole castle!
That's not technically possible but okay. I'm going to pry this block out. You put the torch in its place. Ready? One... two...
THREE!
WHOOSH

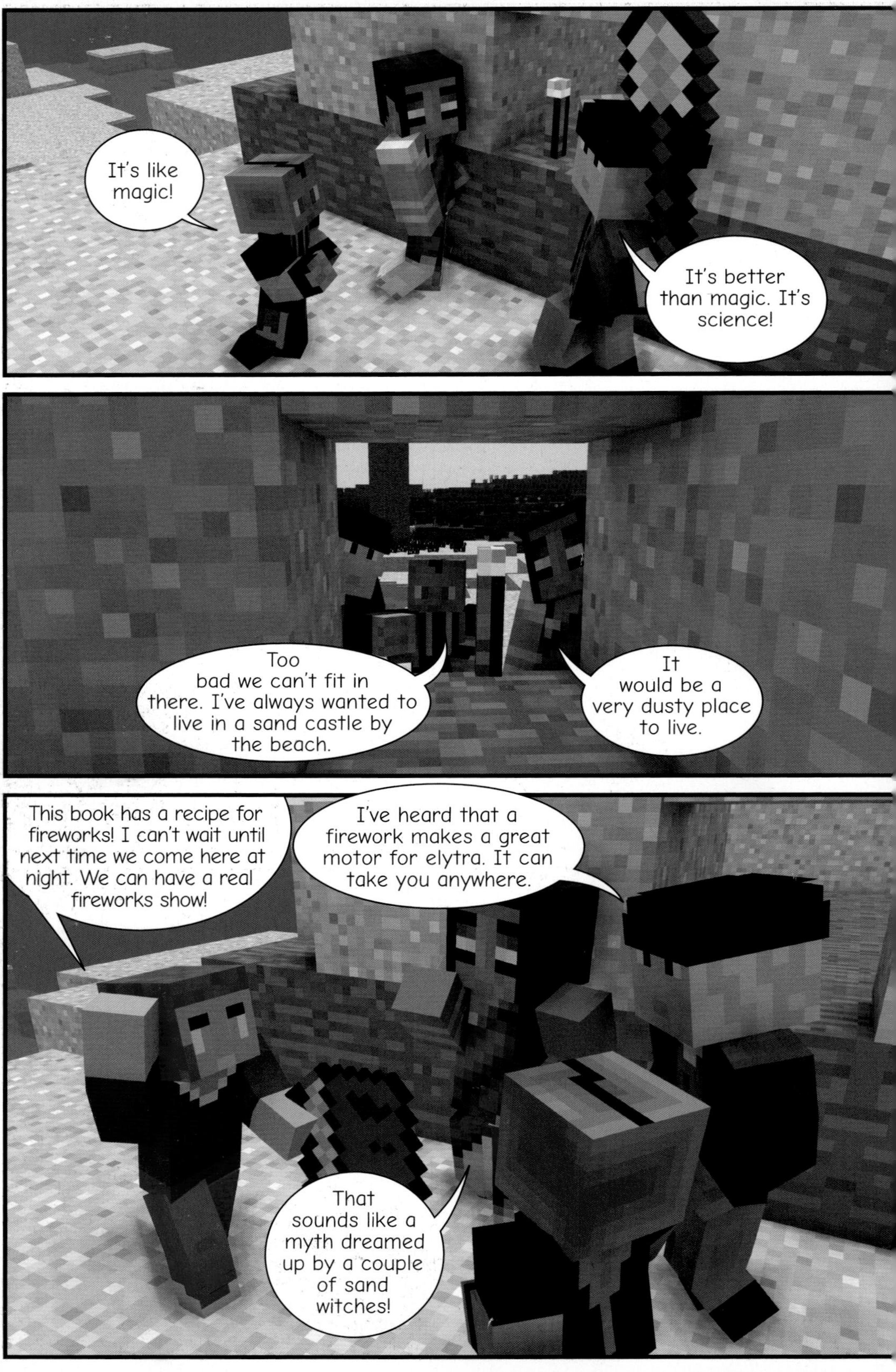
It's like magic!
It's better than magic. It's science!
Too bad we can't fit in there. I've always wanted to live in a sand castle by the beach.
It would be a very dusty place to live.
This book has a recipe for fireworks! I can't wait until next time we come here at night. We can have a real fireworks show!
I've heard that a firework makes a great motor for elytra. It can take you anywhere.
That sounds like a myth dreamed up by a couple of sand witches!

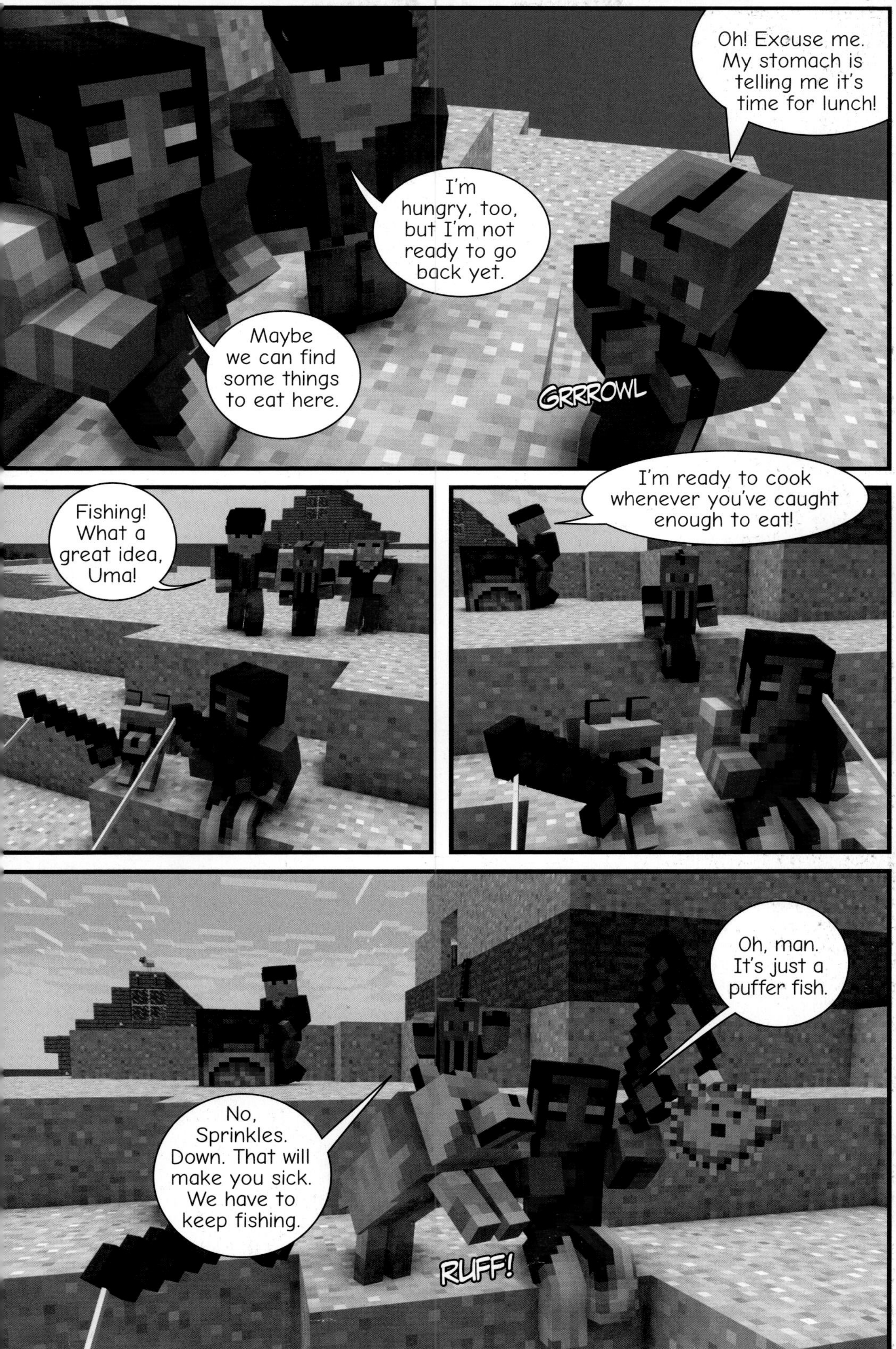
Oh! Excuse me. My stomach is telling me it's time for lunch!
I'm hungry, too, but I'm not ready to go back yet.
Maybe we can find some things to eat here.
GRRROWL
Fishing! What a great idea, Uma!
I'm ready to cook whenever you've caught enough to eat!
Oh, man. It's just a puffer fish.
No, Sprinkles. Down. That will make you sick. We have to keep fishing.
RUFF!

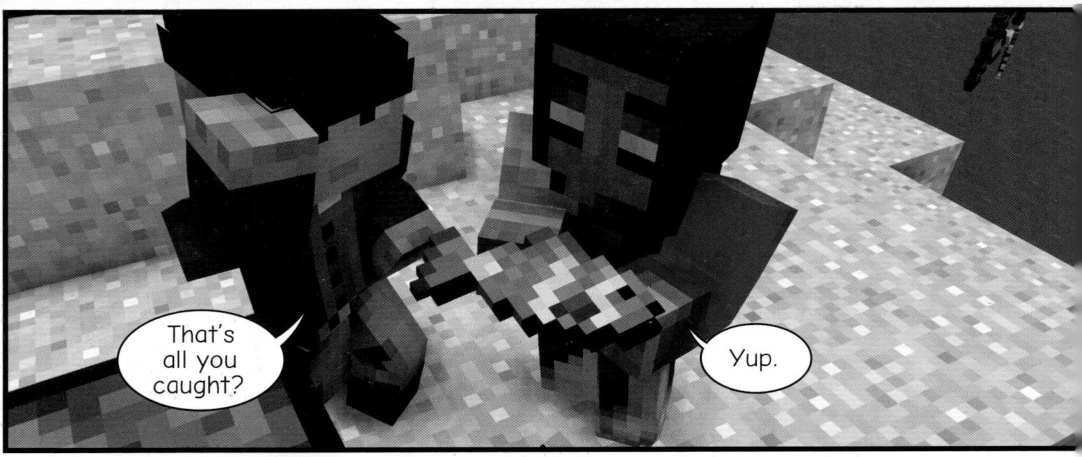
That's all you caught?
Yup.

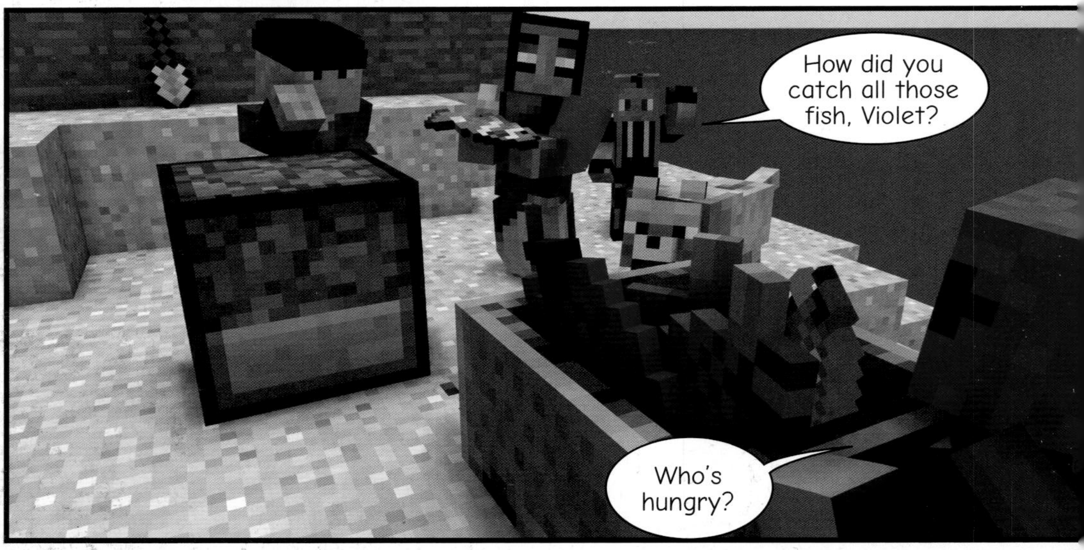
How did you catch all those fish, Violet?
Who's hungry?

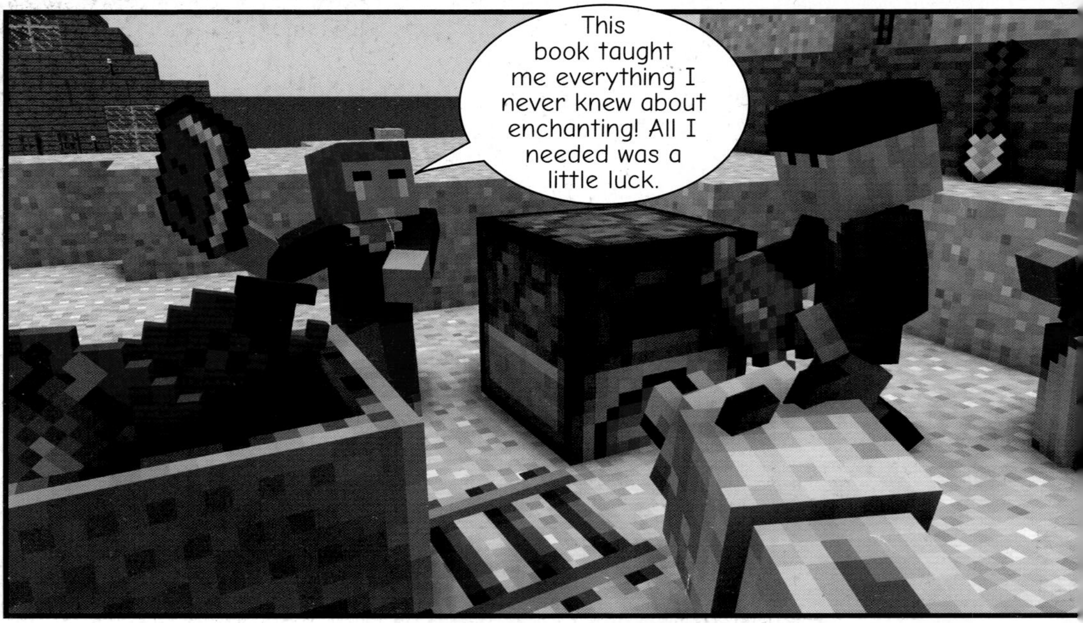
This book taught me everything I never knew about enchanting! All I needed was a little luck.

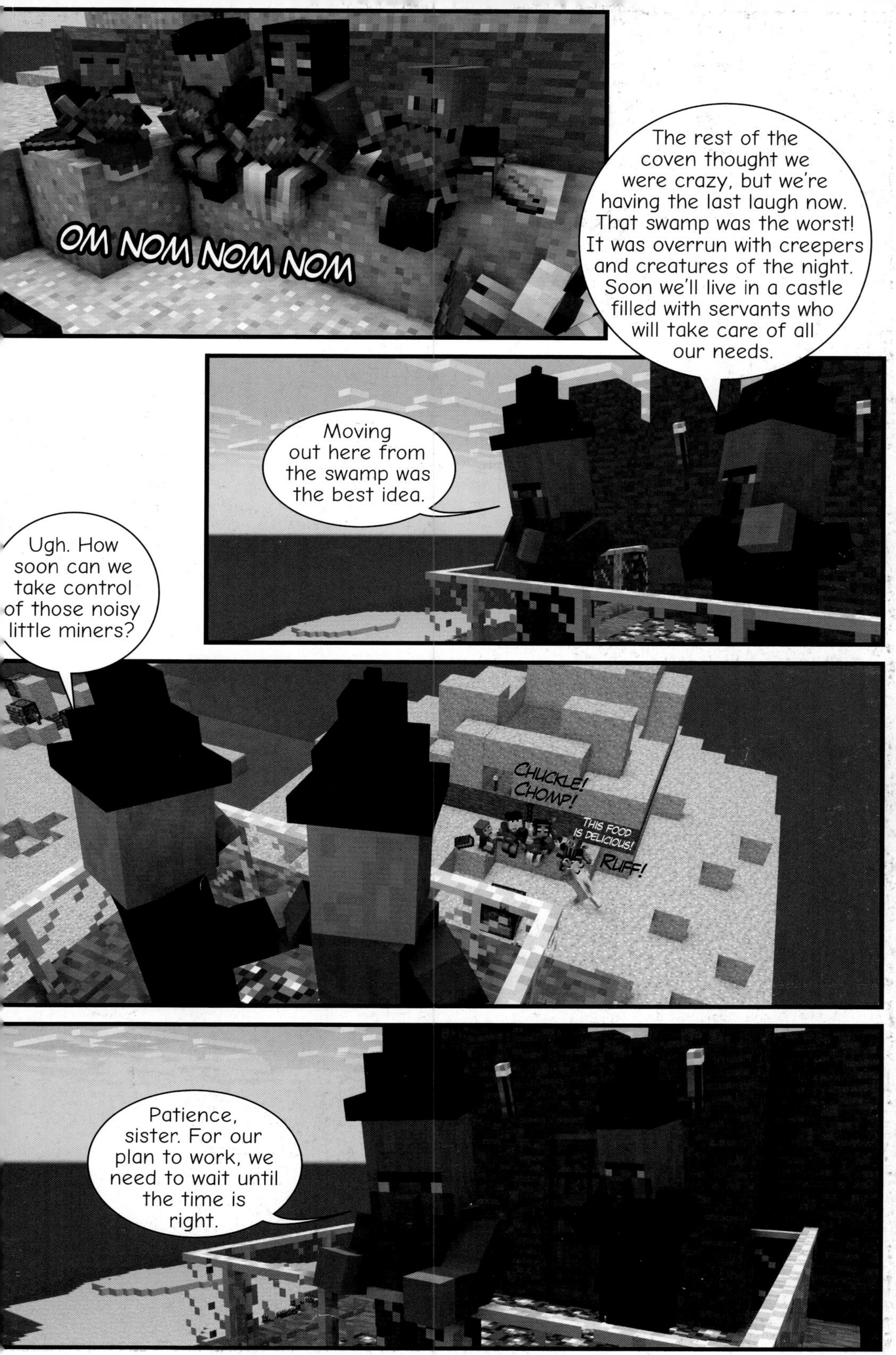
OM NOM NOM NOM
The rest of the coven thought we were crazy, but we're having the last laugh now. That swamp was the worst! It was overrun with creepers and creatures of the night. Soon we'll live in a castle filled with servants who will take care of all our needs.
Moving out here from the swamp was the best idea.
Ugh. How soon can we take control of those noisy little miners?
CHUCKLE! CHOMP!
THIS FOOD IS DELICIOUS!
RUFF!
Patience, sister. For our plan to work, we need to wait until the time is right.

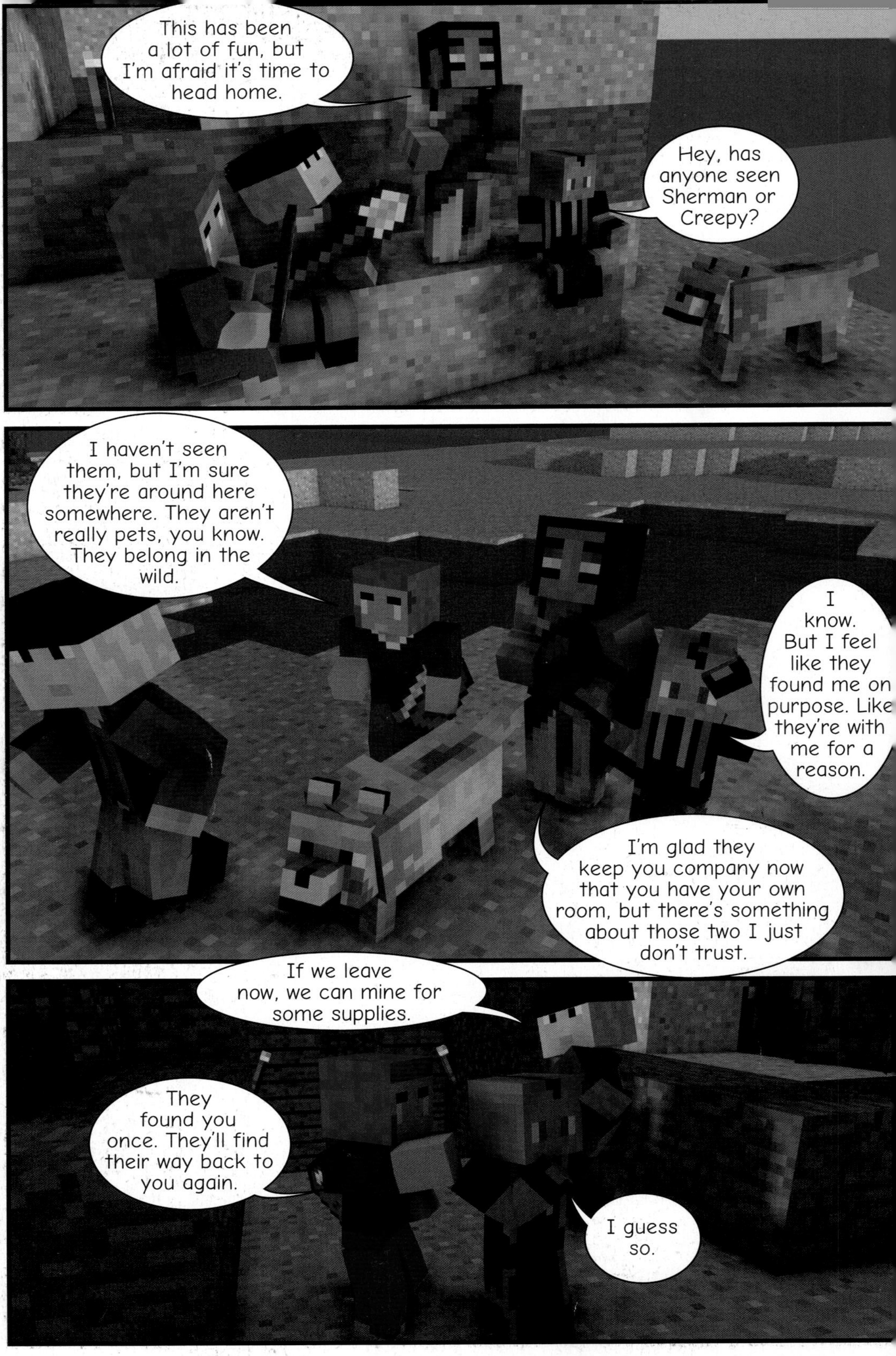
This has been a lot of fun, but I'm afraid it's time to head home.
Hey, has anyone seen Sherman or Creepy?
I haven't seen them, but I'm sure they're around here somewhere. They aren't really pets, you know. They belong in the wild.
I know. But I feel like they found me on purpose. Like they're with me for a reason.
I'm glad they keep you company now that you have your own room, but there's something about those two I just don't trust.
If we leave now, we can mine for some supplies.
They found you once. They'll find their way back to you again.
I guess so.

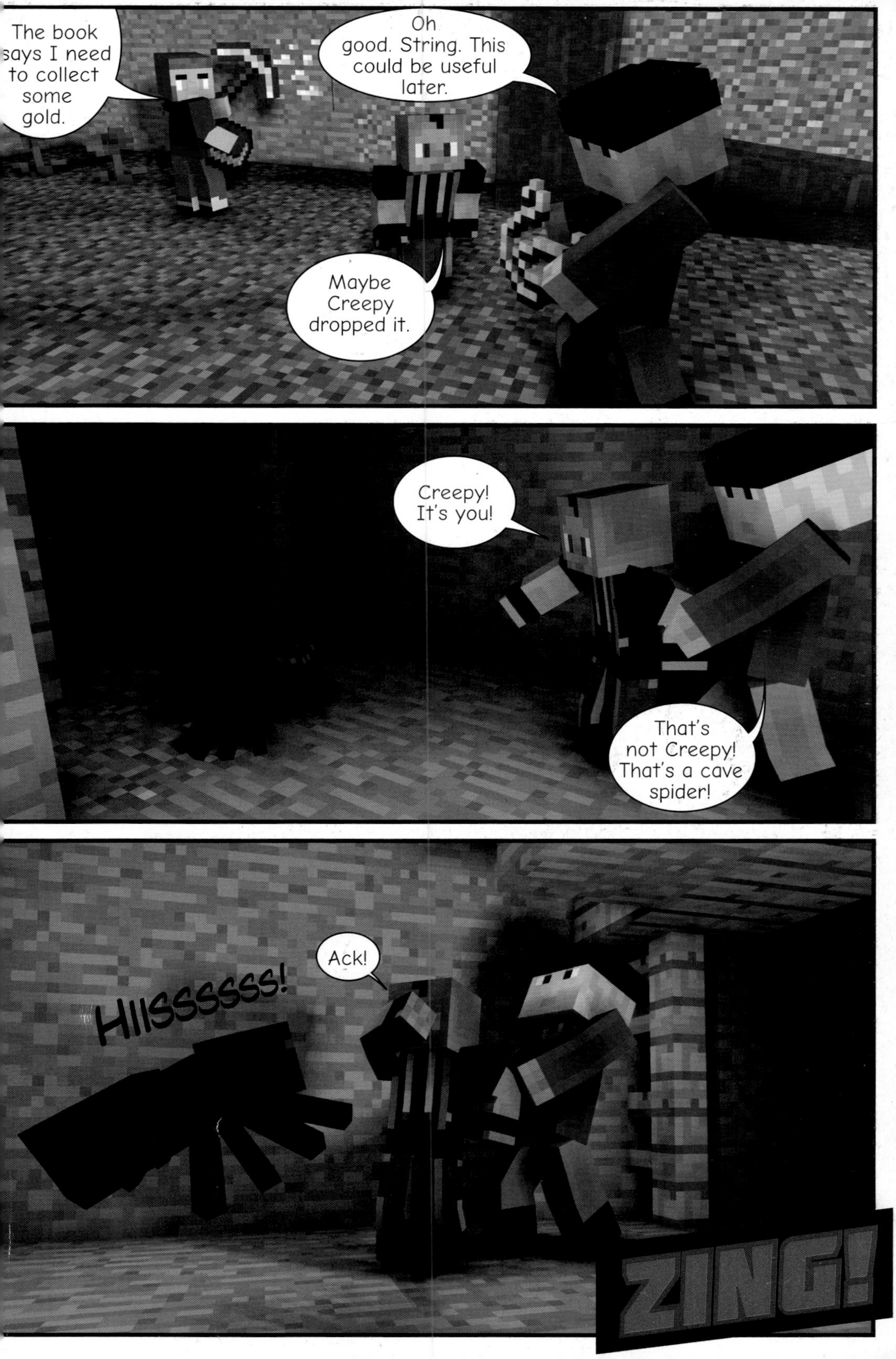
The book says I need to collect some gold.
Oh good. String. This could be useful later.
Maybe Creepy dropped it.
Creepy! It's you!
That's not Creepy! That's a cave spider!
HIISSSSSS!
Ack!
ZING!

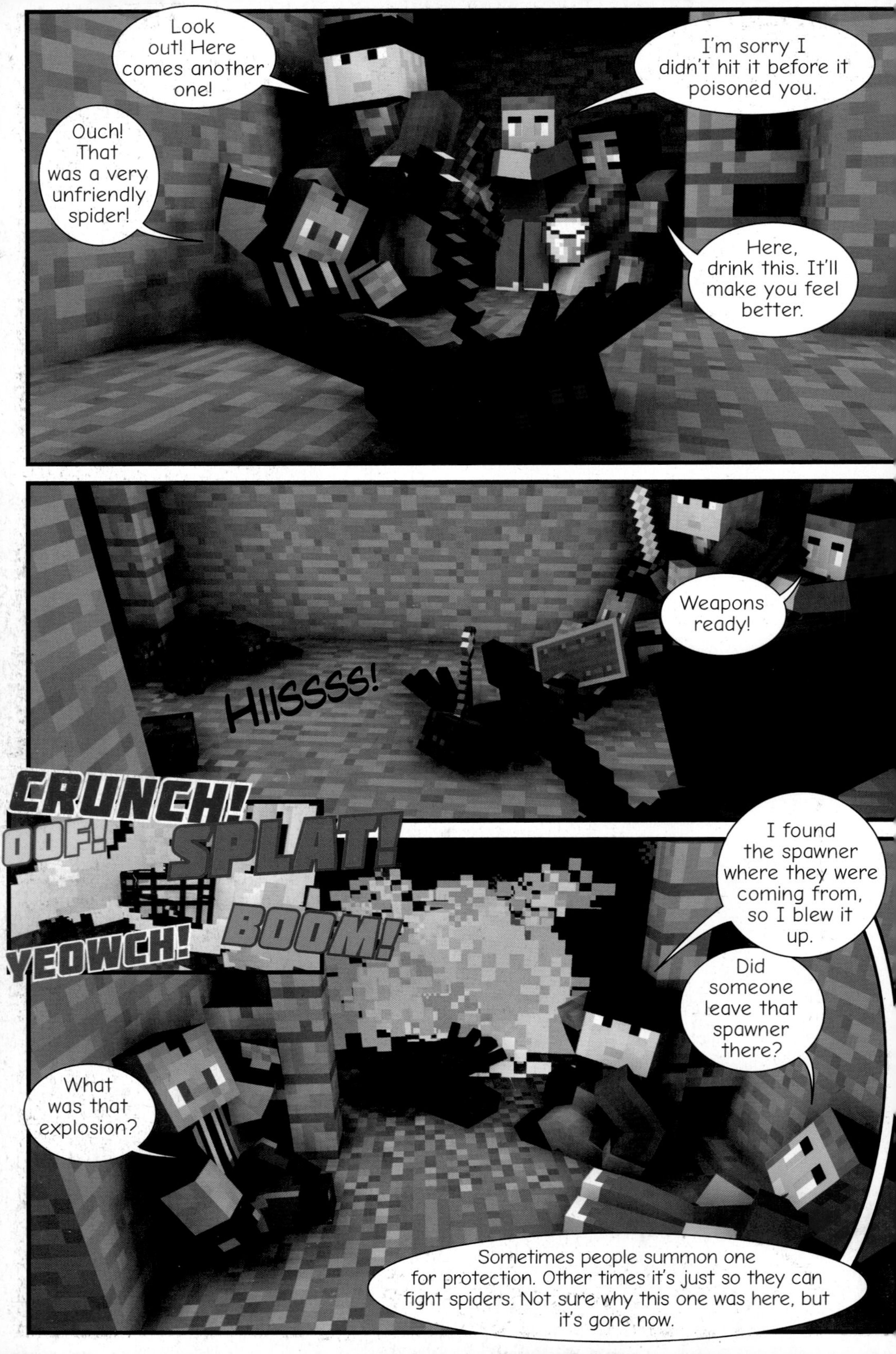

Look out! Here comes another one!
Ouch! That was a very unfriendly spider!
I'm sorry I didn't hit it before it poisoned you.
Here, drink this. It'll make you feel better.
Weapons ready!
HIISSSS!
CRUNCH!
OOF!
SPLAT!
BOOM!
YEOWCH!
I found the spawner where they were coming from, so I blew it up.
What was that explosion?
Did someone leave that spawner there?
Sometimes people summon one for protection. Other times it's just so they can fight spiders. Not sure why this one was here, but it's gone now.

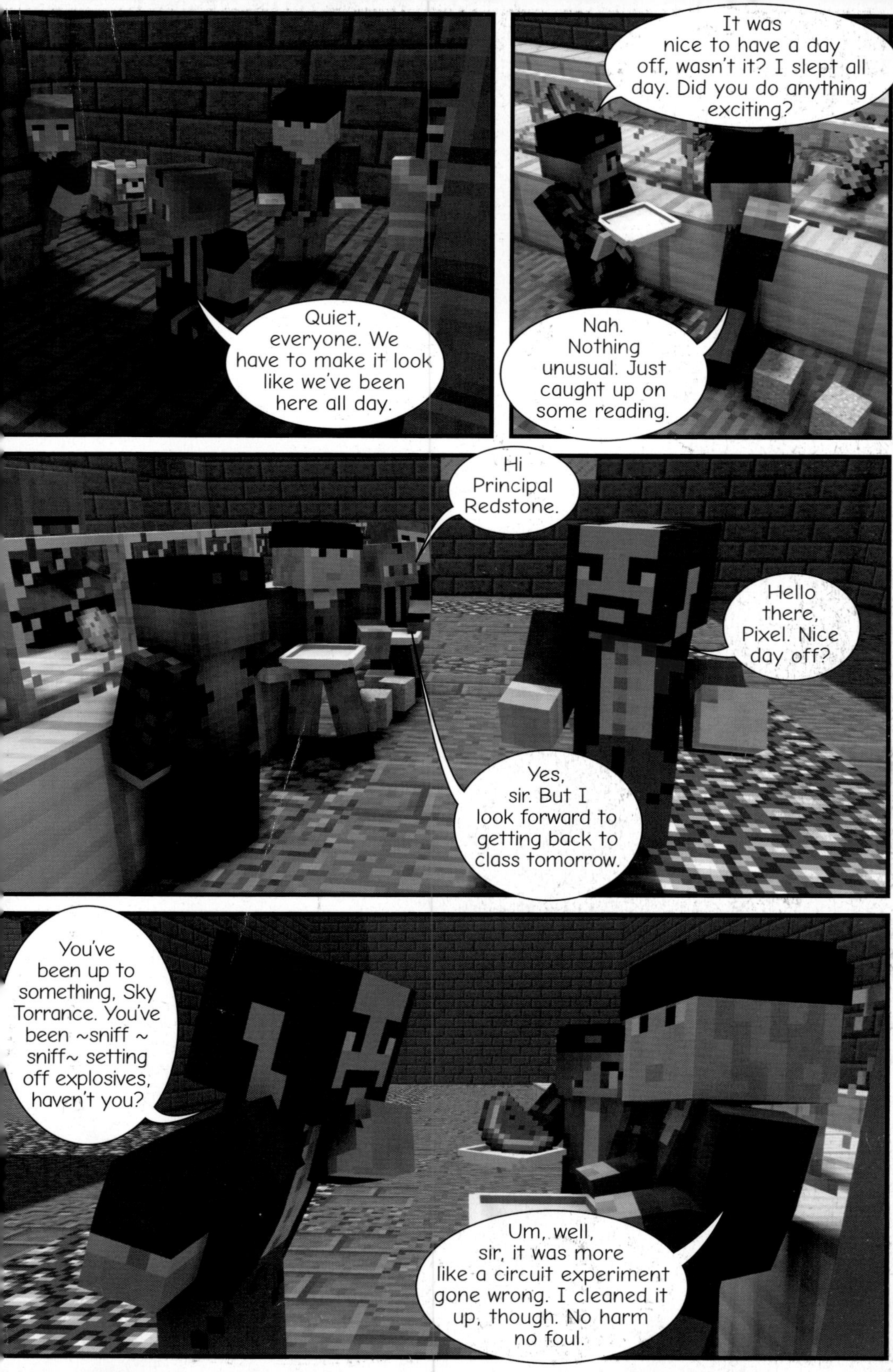
Quiet, everyone. We have to make it look like we've been here all day.
It was nice to have a day off, wasn't it? I slept all day. Did you do anything exciting?
Nah. Nothing unusual. Just caught up on some reading.
Hi Principal Redstone.
Hello there, Pixel. Nice day off?
Yes, sir. But I look forward to getting back to class tomorrow.
You've been up to something, Sky Torrance. You've been ~sniff ~ sniff~ setting off explosives, haven't you?
Um, well, sir, it was more like a circuit experiment gone wrong. I cleaned it up, though. No harm no foul.

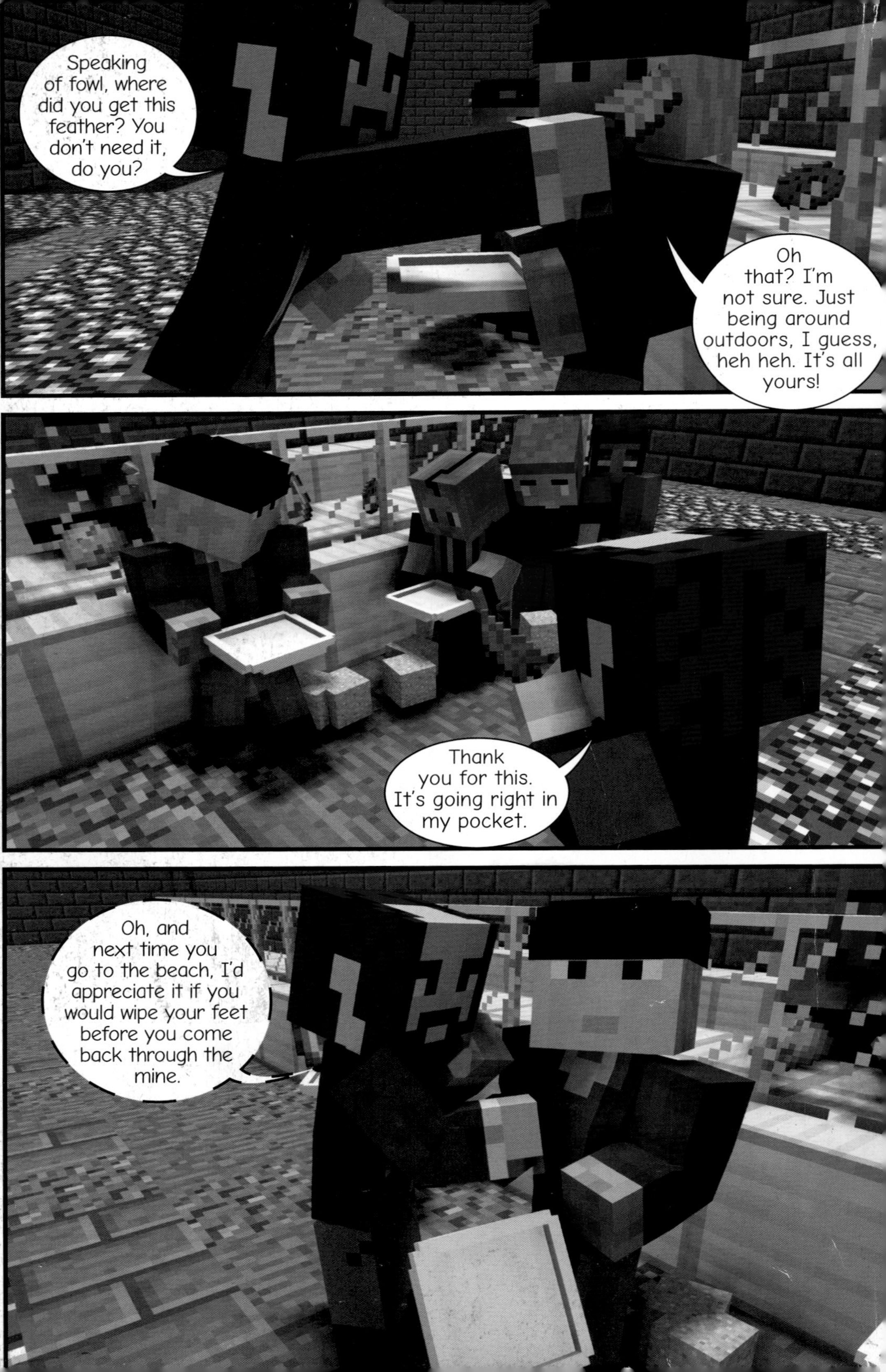
Speaking of fowl, where did you get this feather? You don't need it, do you?
Oh that? I'm not sure. Just being around outdoors, I guess, heh heh. It's all yours!
Thank you for this. It's going right in my pocket.
Oh, and next time you go to the beach, I'd appreciate it if you would wipe your feet before you come back through the mine.

CHAPTER 6

THE HAUNTED HIDEAWAY

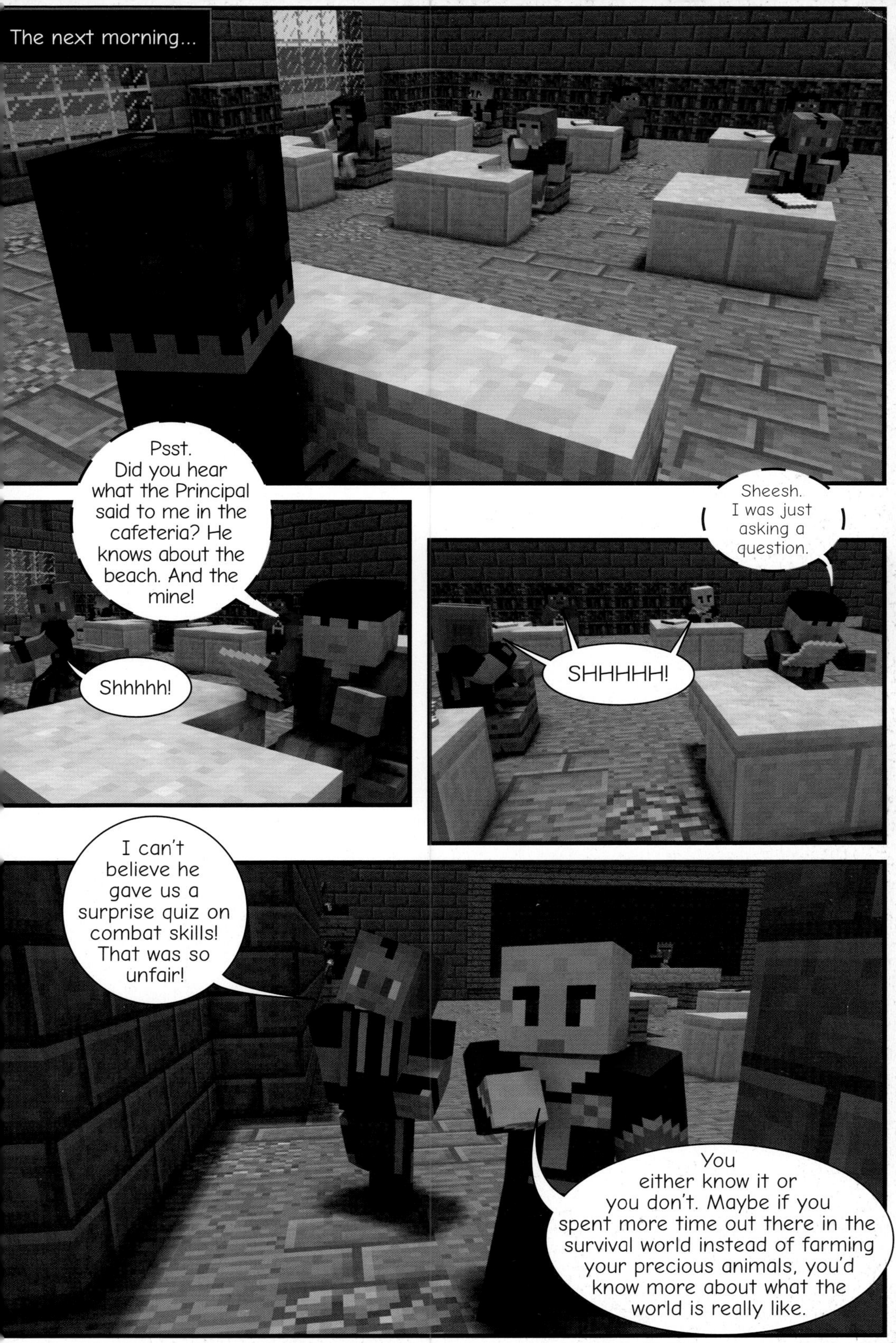
The next morning...
Psst. Did you hear what the Principal said to me in the cafeteria? He knows about the beach. And the mine!
Shhhhh!
Sheesh. I was just asking a question.
SHHHHH!
I can't believe he gave us a surprise quiz on combat skills! That was so unfair!
You either know it or you don't. Maybe if you spent more time out there in the survival world instead of farming your precious animals, you'd know more about what the world is really like.

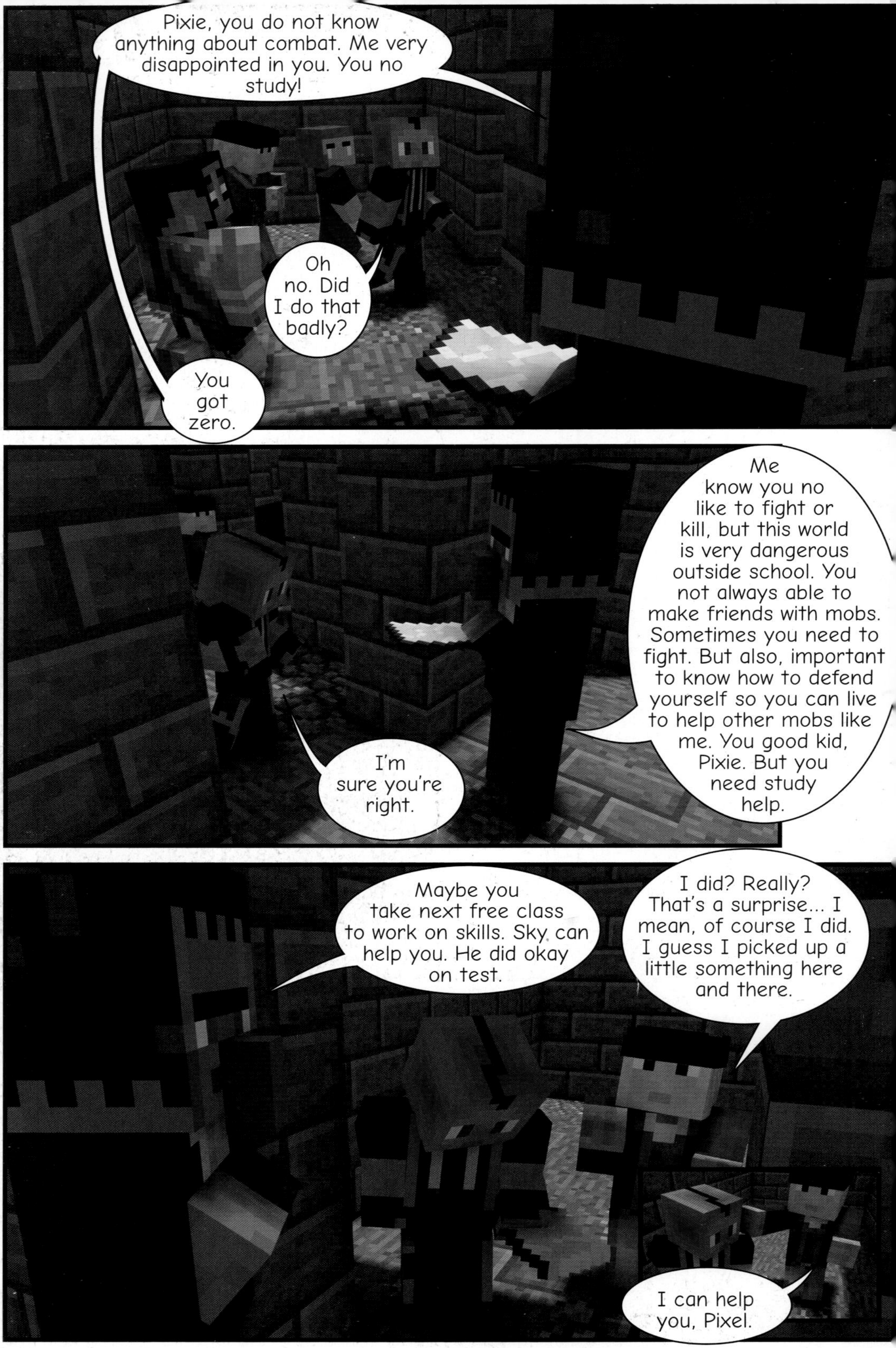
Pixie, you do not know anything about combat. Me very disappointed in you. You no study!
Oh no. Did I do that badly?
You got zero.
Me know you no like to fight or kill, but this world is very dangerous outside school. You not always able to make friends with mobs. Sometimes you need to fight. But also, important to know how to defend yourself so you can live to help other mobs like me. You good kid, Pixie. But you need study help.
I'm sure you're right.
Maybe you take next free class to work on skills. Sky can help you. He did okay on test.
I did? Really? That's a surprise... I mean, of course I did. I guess I picked up a little something here and there.
I can help you, Pixel.

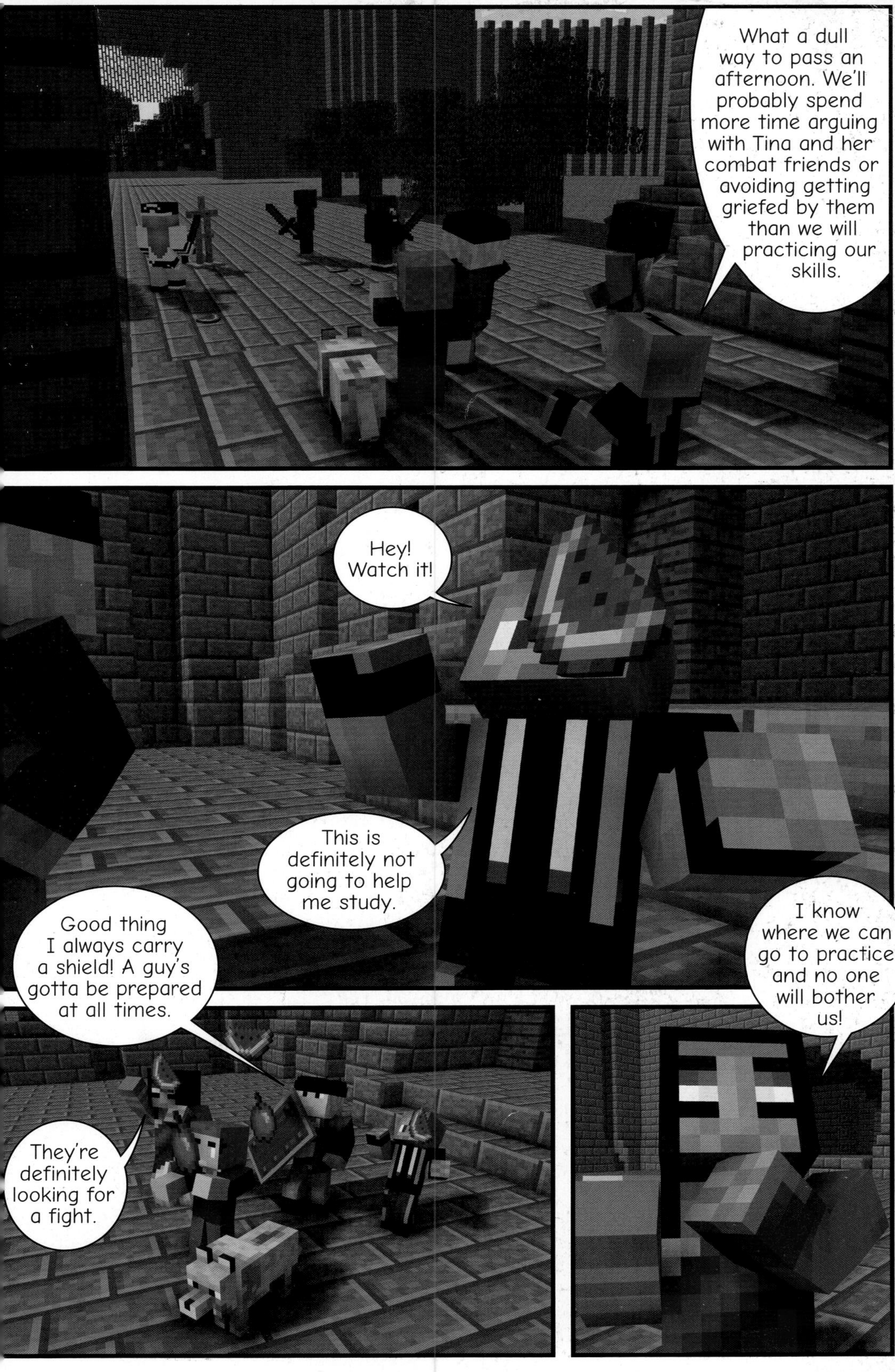
What a dull way to pass an afternoon. We'll probably spend more time arguing with Tina and her combat friends or avoiding getting griefed by them than we will practicing our skills.
Hey! Watch it!
This is definitely not going to help me study.
Good thing I always carry a shield! A guy's gotta be prepared at all times.
They're definitely looking for a fight.
I know where we can go to practice and no one will bother us!

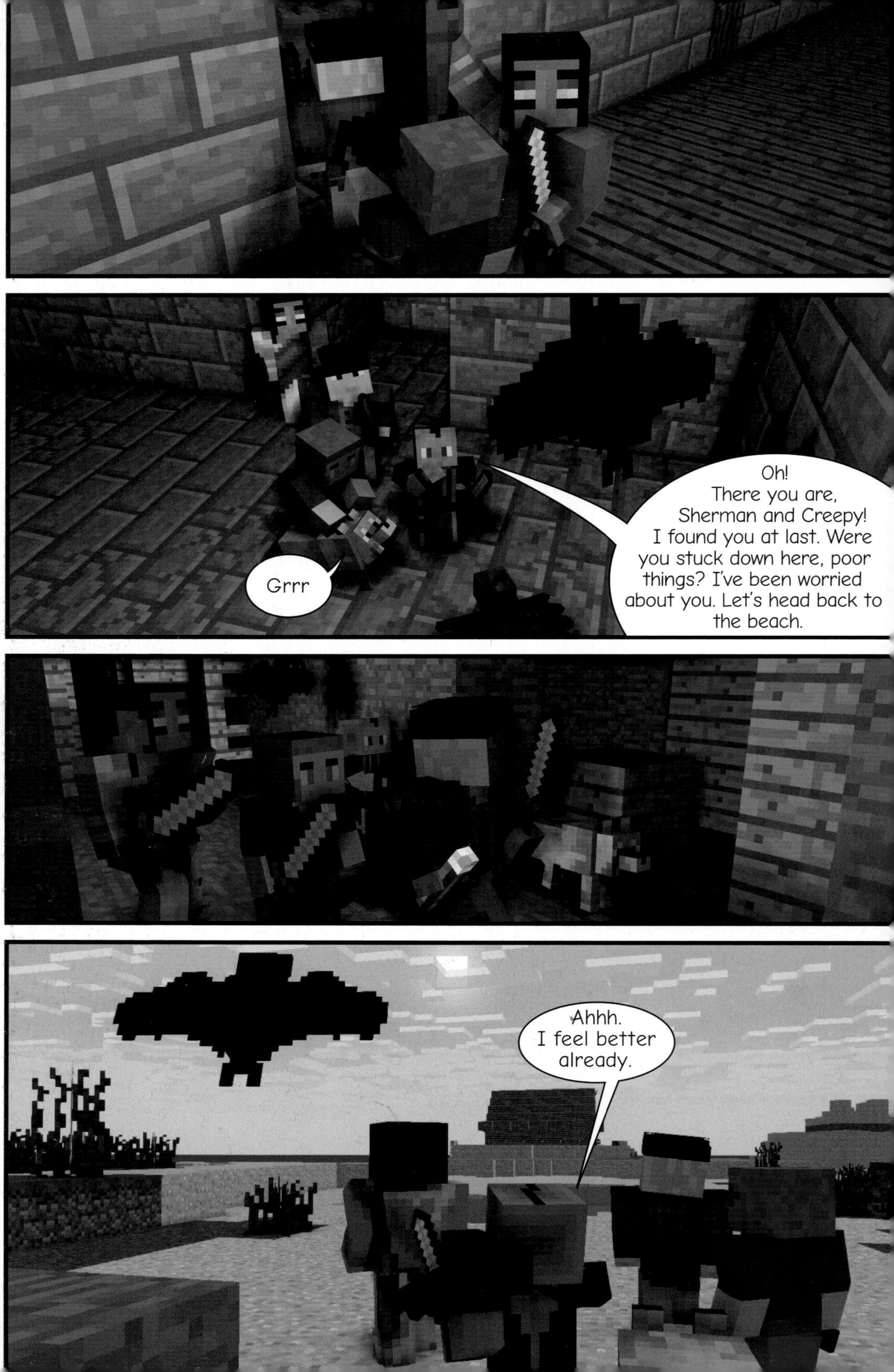
Grrr
Oh! There you are, Sherman and Creepy! I found you at last. Were you stuck down here, poor things? I've been worried about you. Let's head back to the beach.
Ahhh. I feel better already.

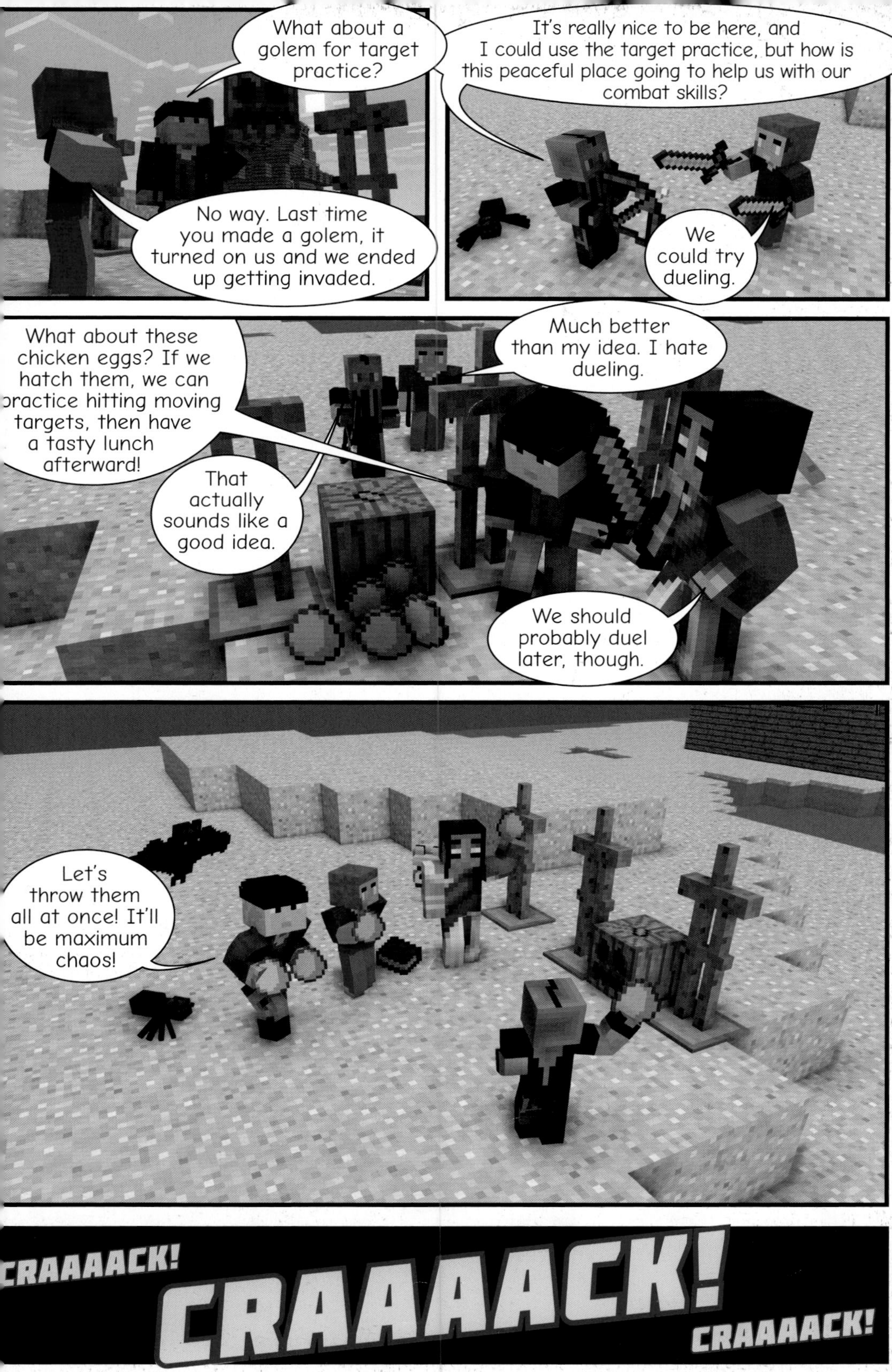
What about a golem for target practice?
No way. Last time you made a golem, it turned on us and we ended up getting invaded.
It's really nice to be here, and I could use the target practice, but how is this peaceful place going to help us with our combat skills?
We could try dueling.
What about these chicken eggs? If we hatch them, we can practice hitting moving targets, then have a tasty lunch afterward!
That actually sounds like a good idea.
Much better than my idea. I hate dueling.
We should probably duel later, though.
Let's throw them all at once! It'll be maximum chaos!
CRAAAACK!
CRAAAACK!
CRAAAACK!

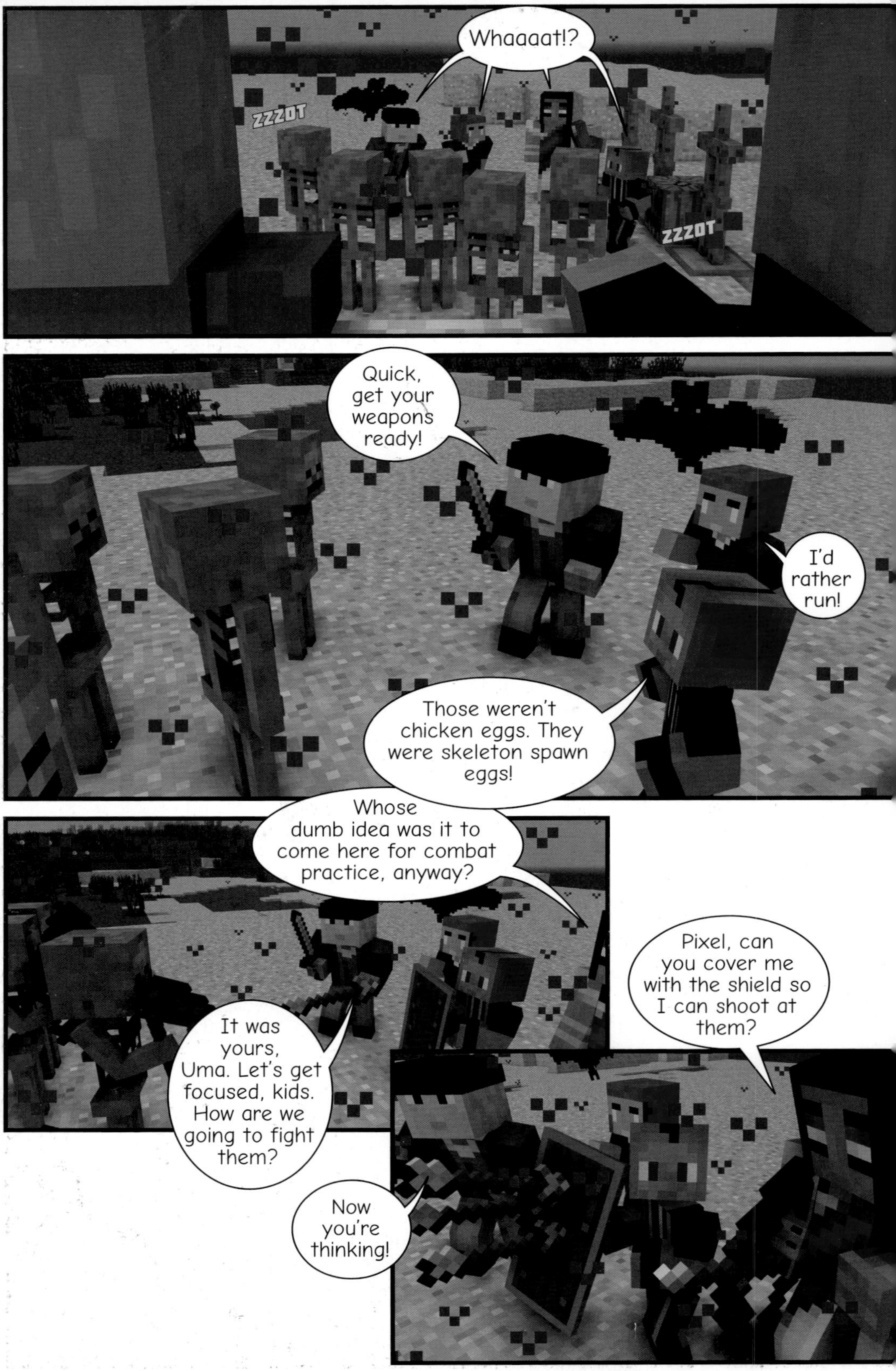
Whaaaat!?
ZZZOT
ZZZOT
Quick, get your weapons ready!
I'd rather run!
Those weren't chicken eggs. They were skeleton spawn eggs!
Whose dumb idea was it to come here for combat practice, anyway?
It was yours, Uma. Let's get focused, kids. How are we going to fight them?
Pixel, can you cover me with the shield so I can shoot at them?
Now you're thinking!

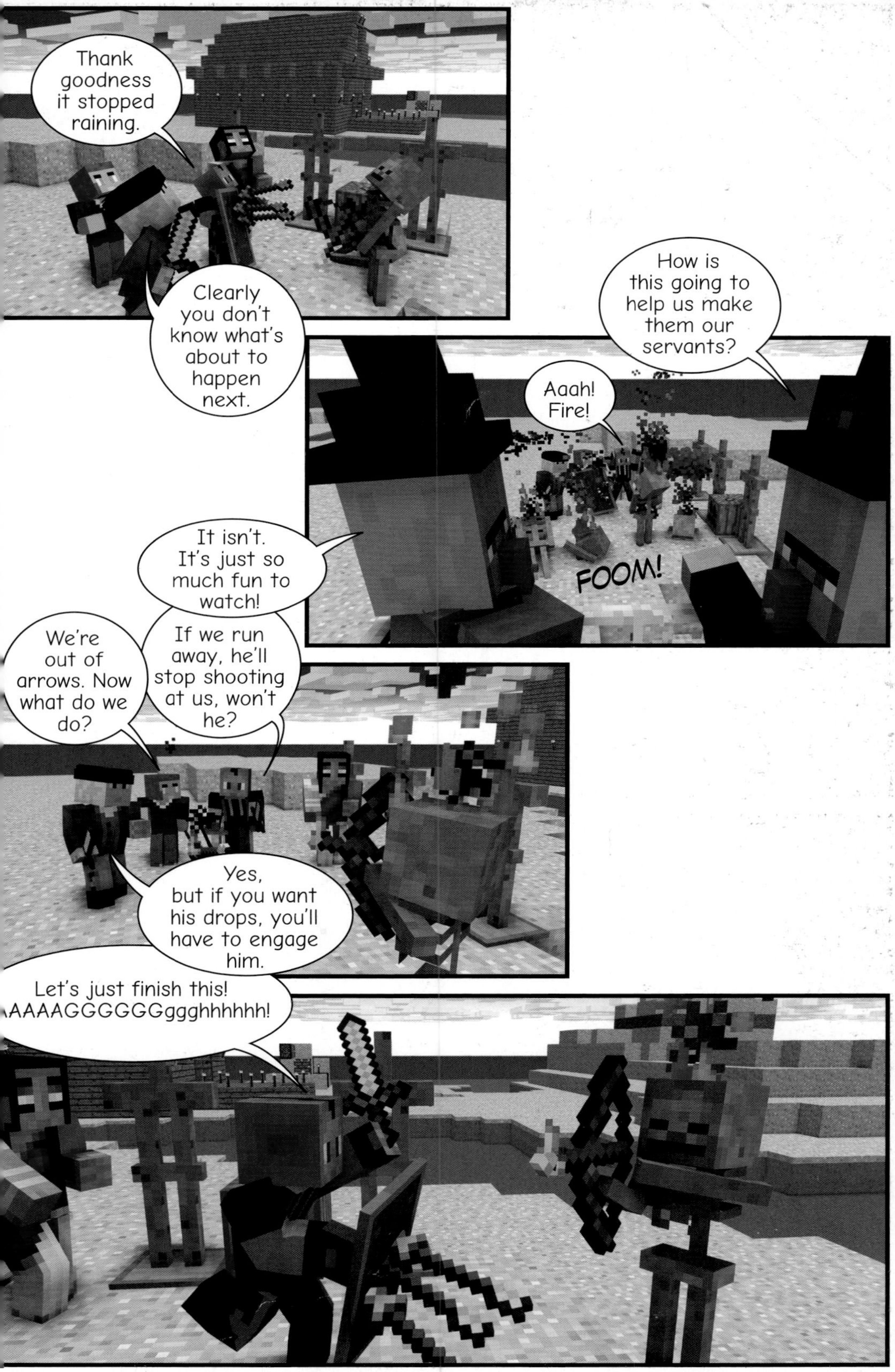
Thank goodness it stopped raining.
Clearly you don't know what's about to happen next.
How is this going to help us make them our servants?
Aaah! Fire!
FOOM!
It isn't. It's just so much fun to watch!
We're out of arrows. Now what do we do?
If we run away, he'll stop shooting at us, won't he?
Yes, but if you want his drops, you'll have to engage him.
Let's just finish this! AAAAGGGGGGggghhhhhh!

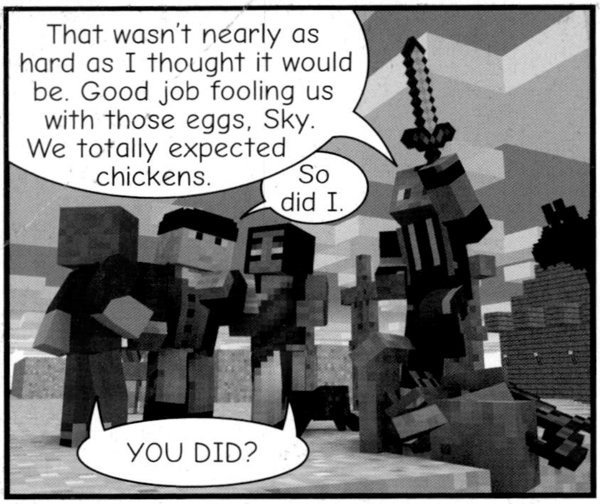
That wasn't nearly as hard as I thought it would be. Good job fooling us with those eggs, Sky. We totally expected chickens.
So did I.
YOU DID?

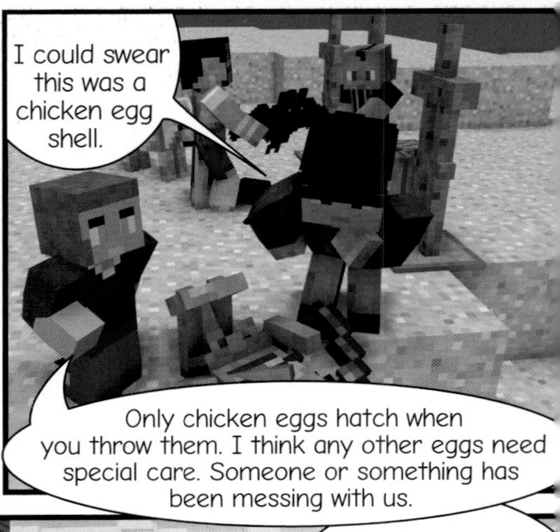
I could swear this was a chicken egg shell.
Only chicken eggs hatch when you throw them. I think any other eggs need special care. Someone or something has been messing with us.

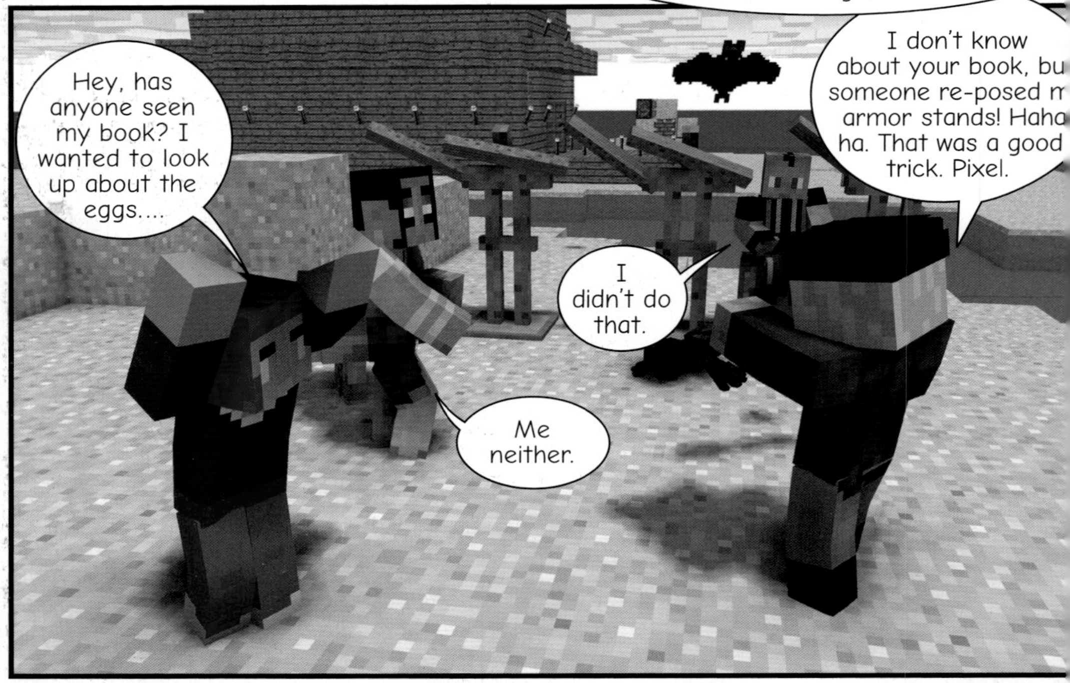
Hey, has anyone seen my book? I wanted to look up about the eggs....
I don't know about your book, bu someone re-posed m armor stands! Haha ha. That was a good trick. Pixel.
I didn't do that.
Me neither.

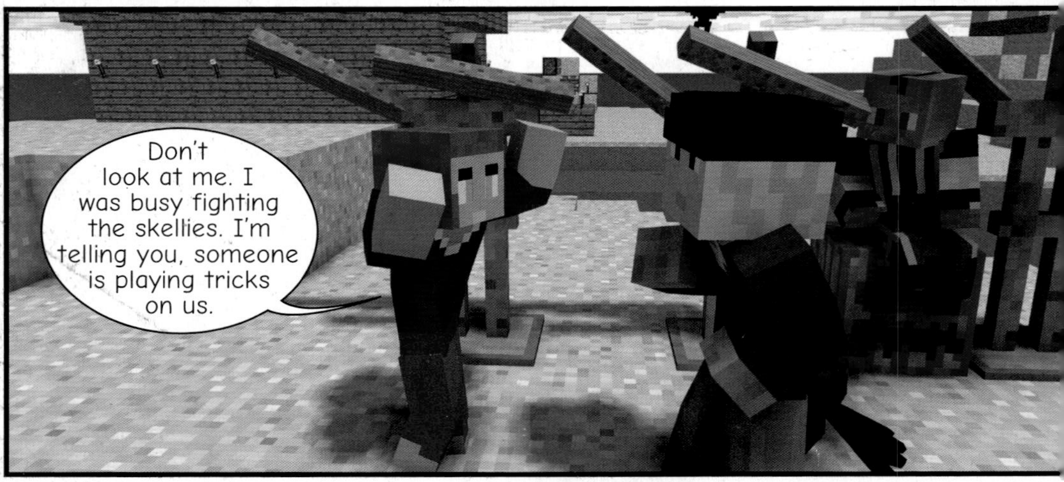
Don't look at me. I was busy fighting the skellies. I'm telling you, someone is playing tricks on us.

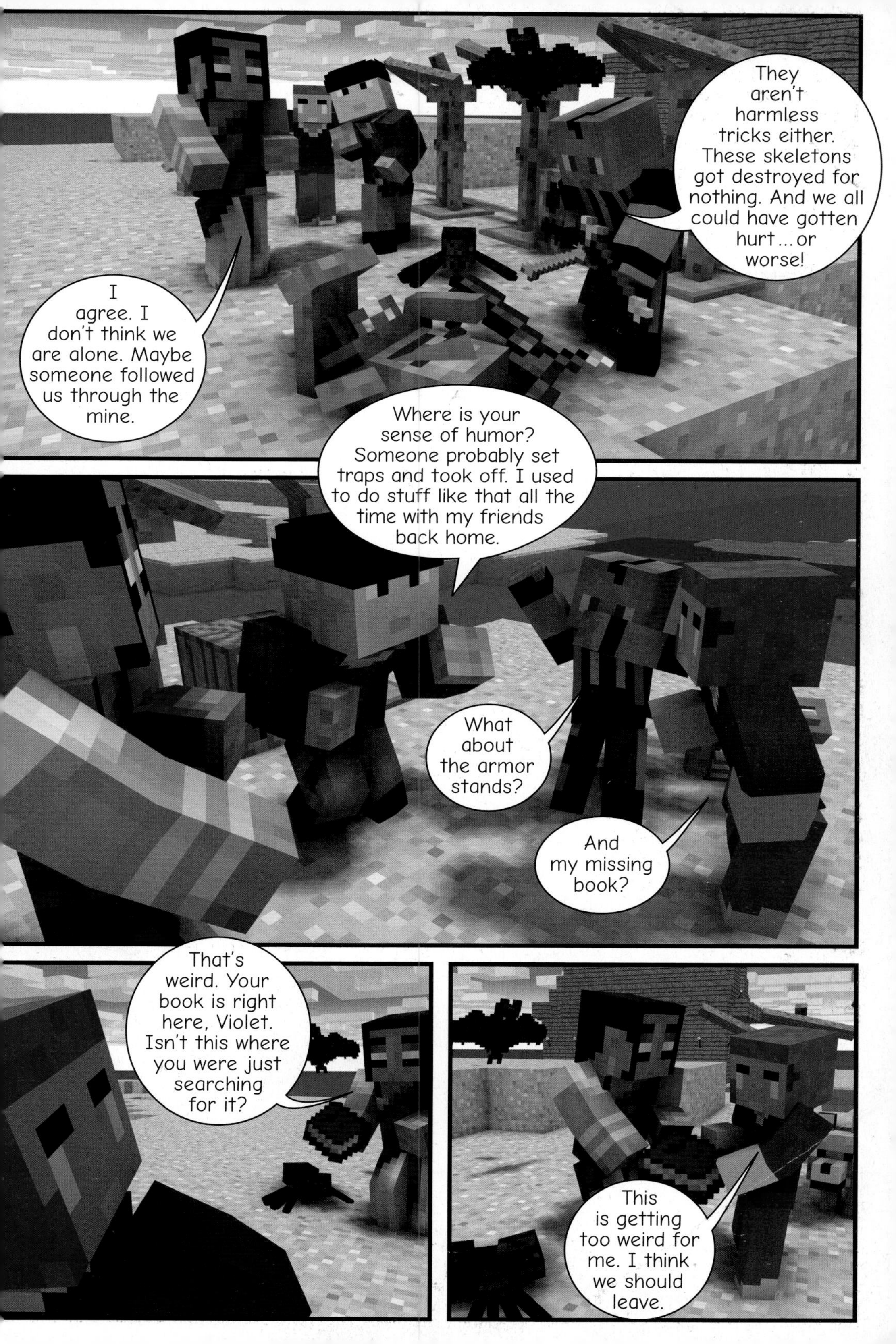

They aren't harmless tricks either. These skeletons got destroyed for nothing. And we all could have gotten hurt...or worse!
I agree. I don't think we are alone. Maybe someone followed us through the mine.
Where is your sense of humor? Someone probably set traps and took off. I used to do stuff like that all the time with my friends back home.
What about the armor stands?
And my missing book?
That's weird. Your book is right here, Violet. Isn't this where you were just searching for it?
This is getting too weird for me. I think we should leave.

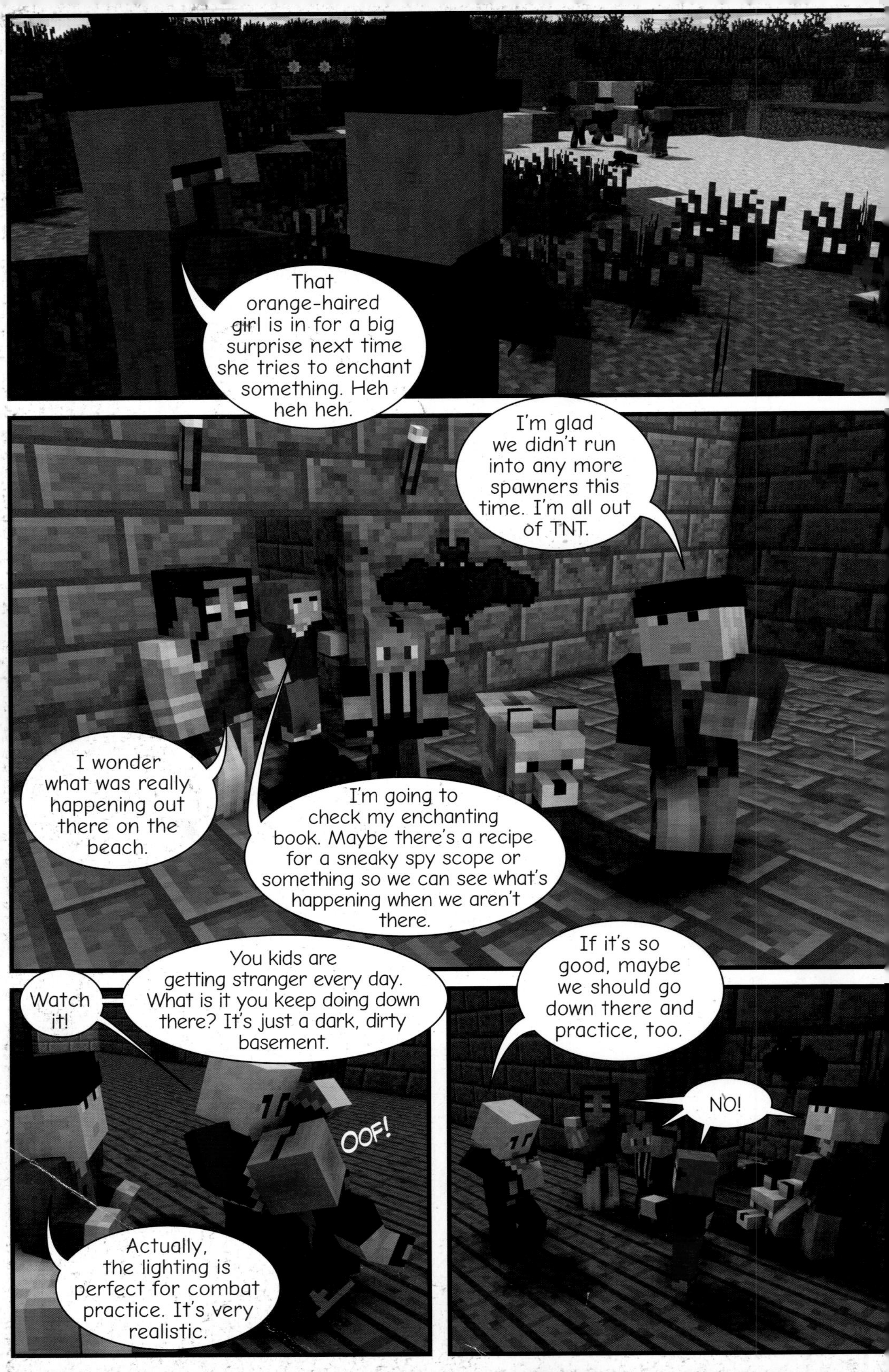
That orange-haired girl is in for a big surprise next time she tries to enchant something. Heh heh heh.
I'm glad we didn't run into any more spawners this time. I'm all out of TNT.
I wonder what was really happening out there on the beach.
I'm going to check my enchanting book. Maybe there's a recipe for a sneaky spy scope or something so we can see what's happening when we aren't there.
Watch it!
You kids are getting stranger every day. What is it you keep doing down there? It's just a dark, dirty basement.
OOF!
Actually, the lighting is perfect for combat practice. It's very realistic.
If it's so good, maybe we should go down there and practice, too.
NO!

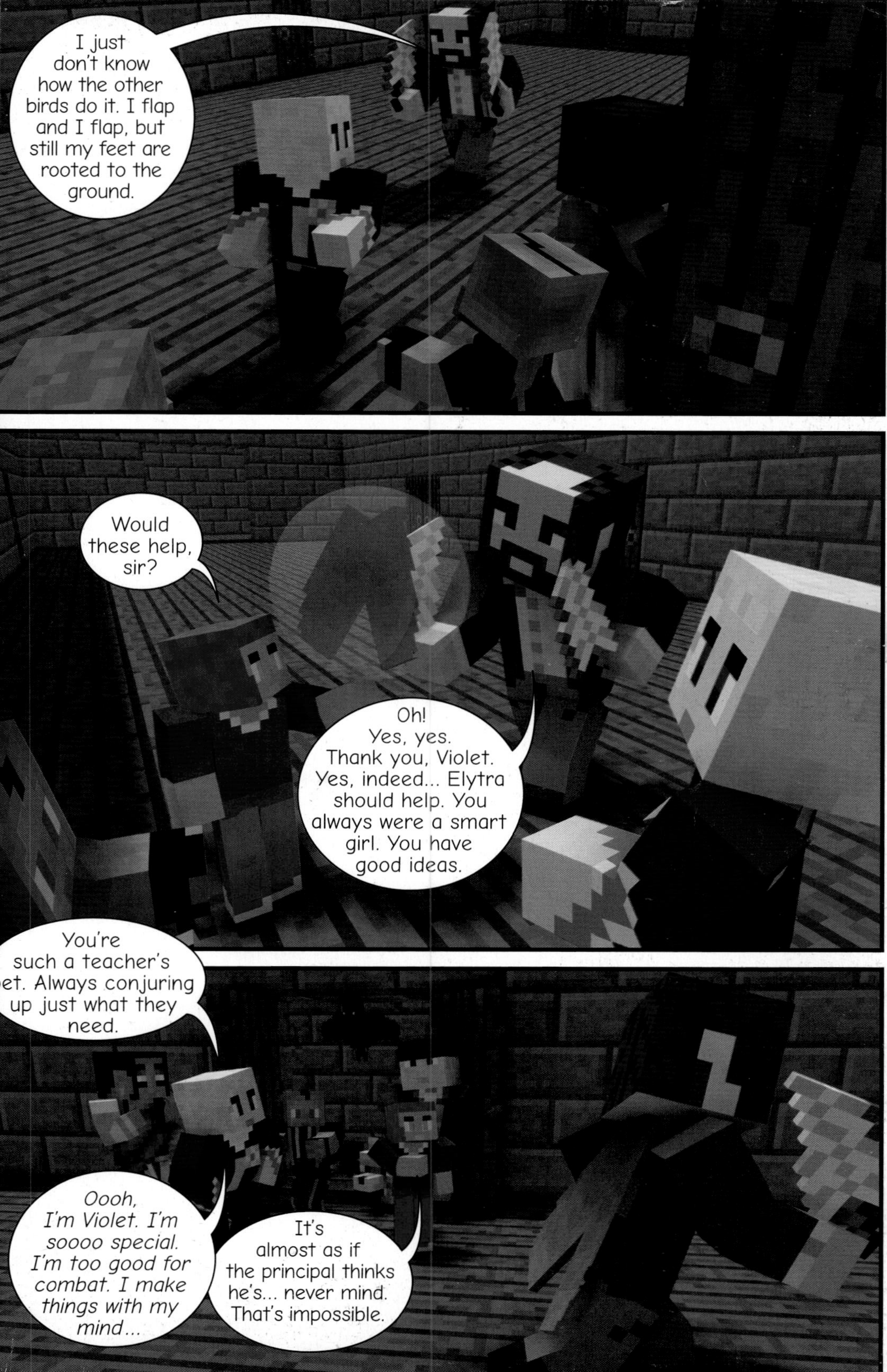

I just don't know how the other birds do it. I flap and I flap, but still my feet are rooted to the ground.
Would these help, sir?
Oh! Yes, yes. Thank you, Violet. Yes, indeed... Elytra should help. You always were a smart girl. You have good ideas.
You're such a teacher's pet. Always conjuring up just what they need.
Oooh, I'm Violet. I'm soooo special. I'm too good for combat. I make things with my mind...
It's almost as if the principal thinks he's... never mind. That's impossible.

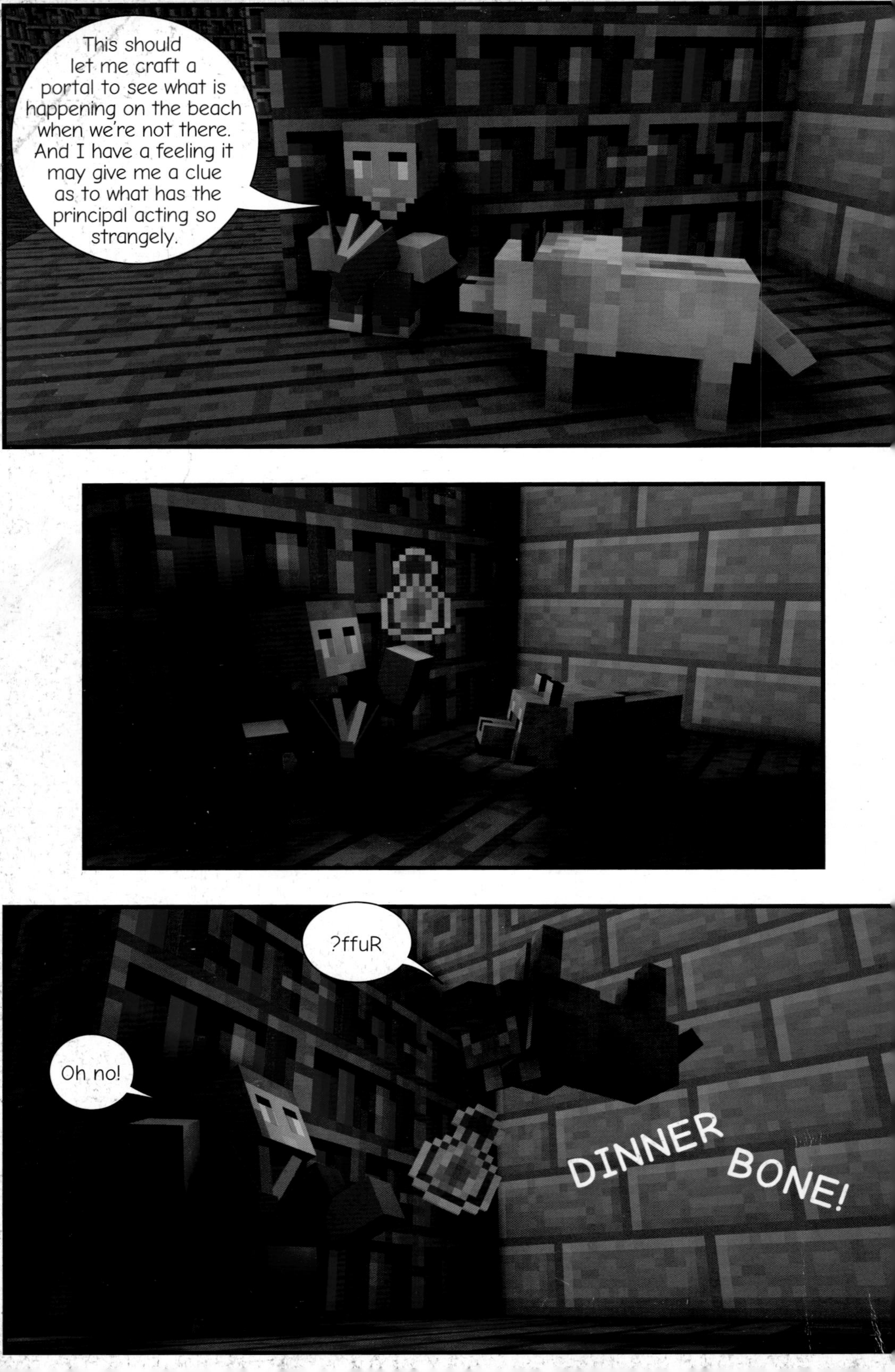
This should let me craft a portal to see what is happening on the beach when we're not there. And I have a feeling it may give me a clue as to what has the principal acting so strangely.
?ffuR
Oh no!
DINNER BONE!

CHAPTER 7

SECRETS
AND SPIES

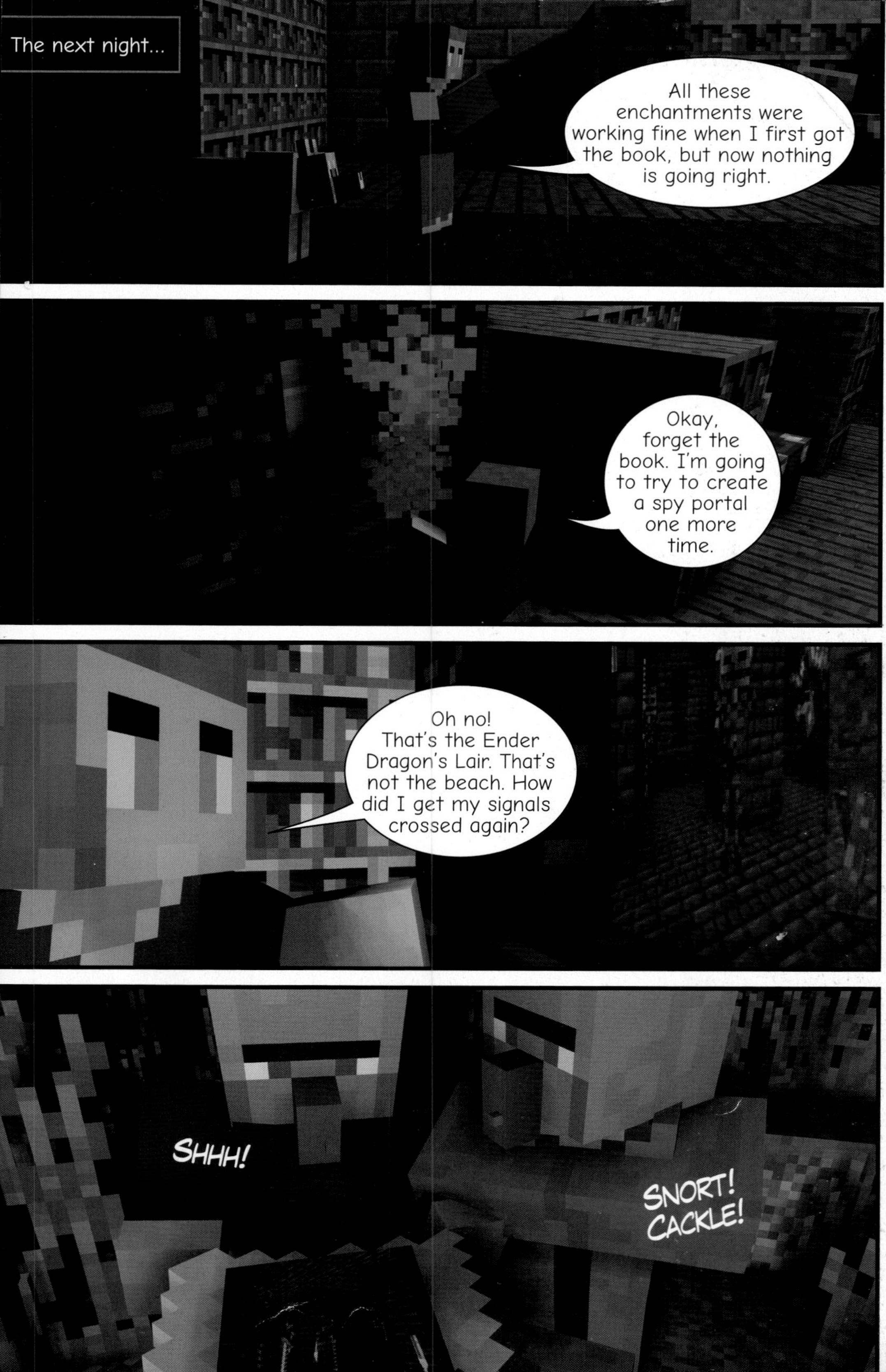

The next night...
All these enchantments were working fine when I first got the book, but now nothing is going right.
Okay, forget the book. I'm going to try to create a spy portal one more time.
Oh no! That's the Ender Dragon's Lair. That's not the beach. How did I get my signals crossed again?
SHHH!
SNORT! CACKLE!

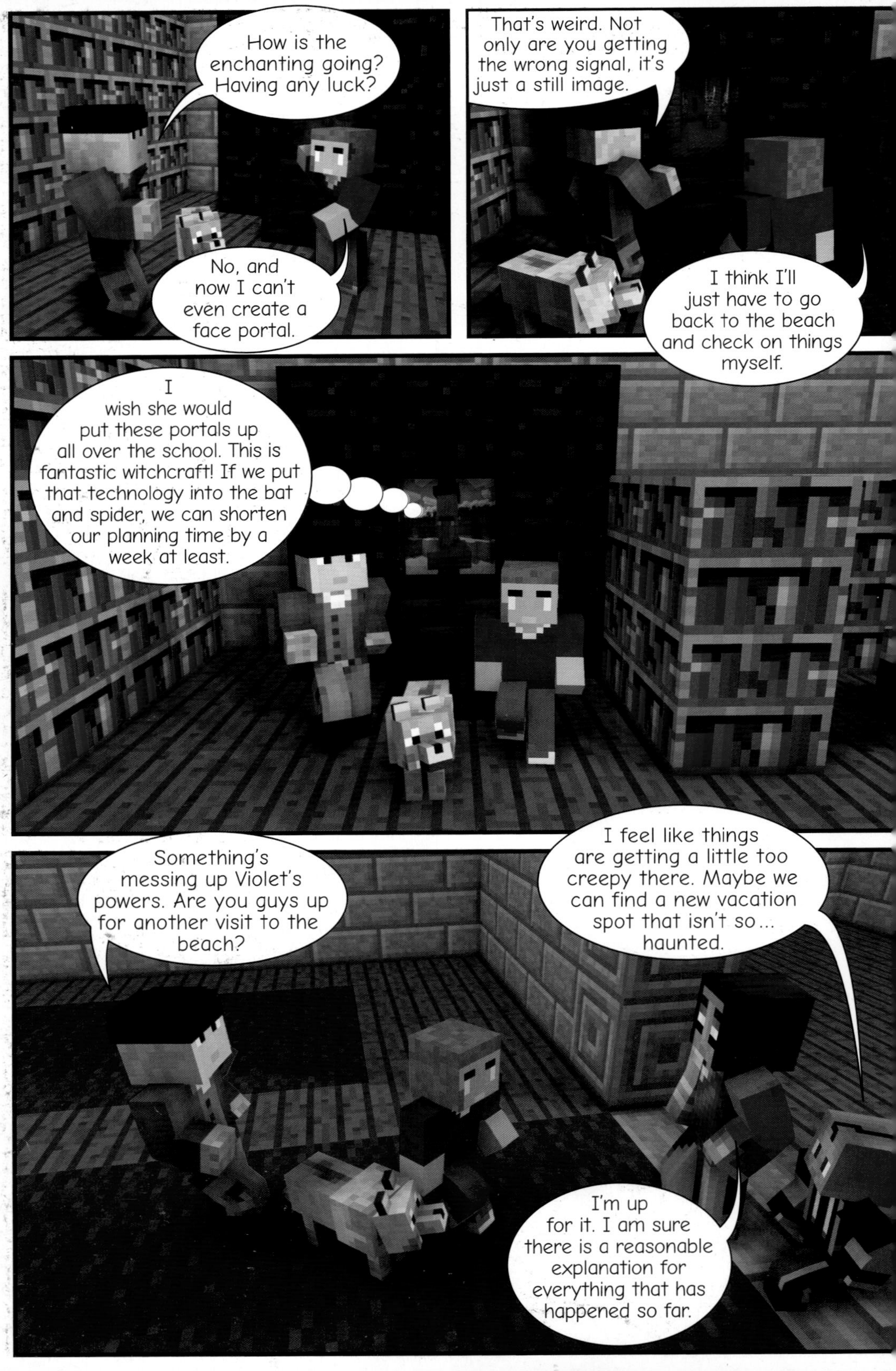
How is the enchanting going? Having any luck?
No, and now I can't even create a face portal.
That's weird. Not only are you getting the wrong signal, it's just a still image.
I think I'll just have to go back to the beach and check on things myself.
I wish she would put these portals up all over the school. This is fantastic witchcraft! If we put that technology into the bat and spider, we can shorten our planning time by a week at least.
Something's messing up Violet's powers. Are you guys up for another visit to the beach?
I feel like things are getting a little too creepy there. Maybe we can find a new vacation spot that isn't so... haunted.
I'm up for it. I am sure there is a reasonable explanation for everything that has happened so far.

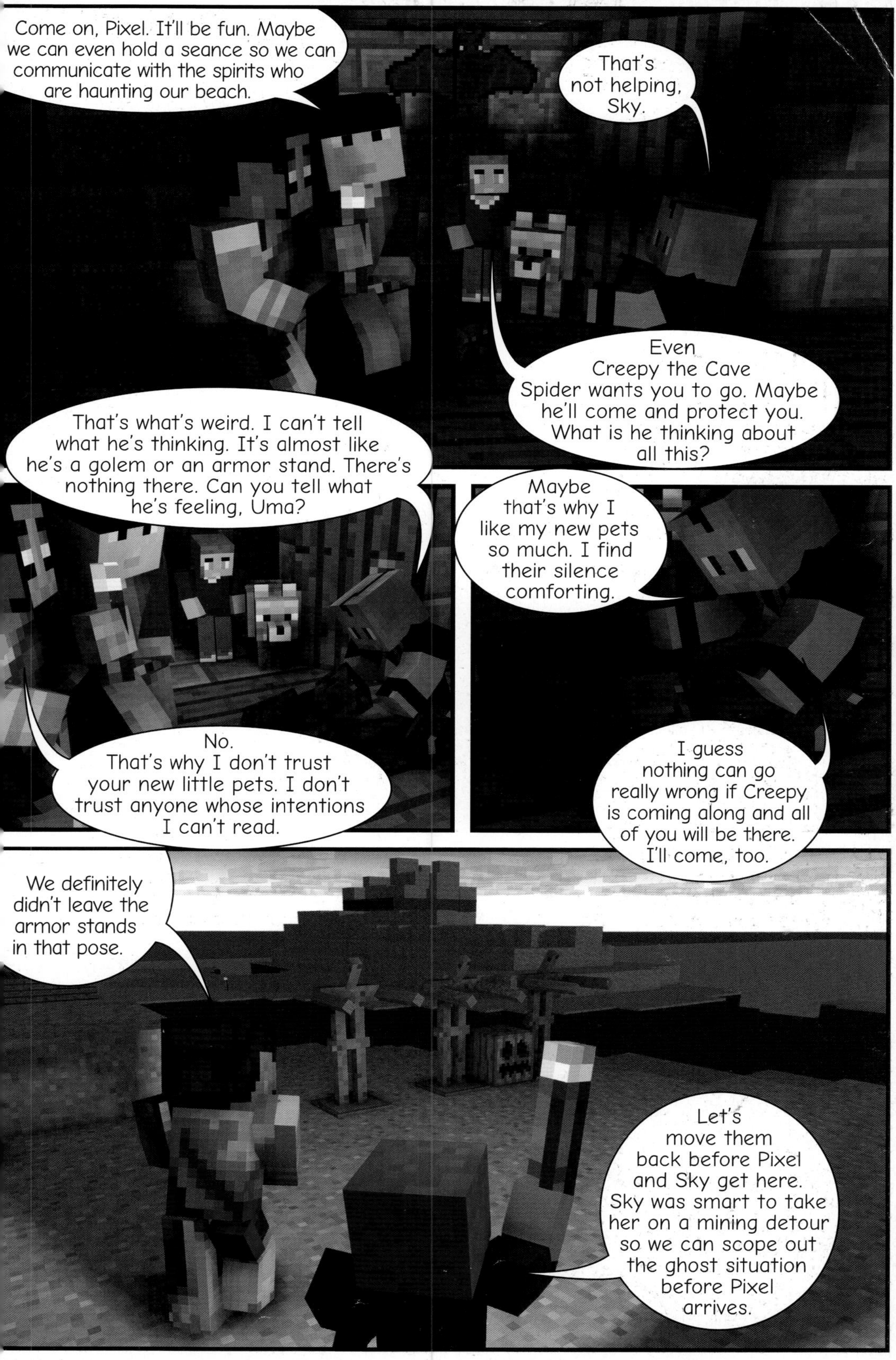
Come on, Pixel. It'll be fun. Maybe we can even hold a seance so we can communicate with the spirits who are haunting our beach.
That's not helping, Sky.
Even Creepy the Cave Spider wants you to go. Maybe he'll come and protect you. What is he thinking about all this?
That's what's weird. I can't tell what he's thinking. It's almost like he's a golem or an armor stand. There's nothing there. Can you tell what he's feeling, Uma?
No. That's why I don't trust your new little pets. I don't trust anyone whose intentions I can't read.
Maybe that's why I like my new pets so much. I find their silence comforting.
I guess nothing can go really wrong if Creepy is coming along and all of you will be there. I'll come, too.
We definitely didn't leave the armor stands in that pose.
Let's move them back before Pixel and Sky get here. Sky was smart to take her on a mining detour so we can scope out the ghost situation before Pixel arrives.

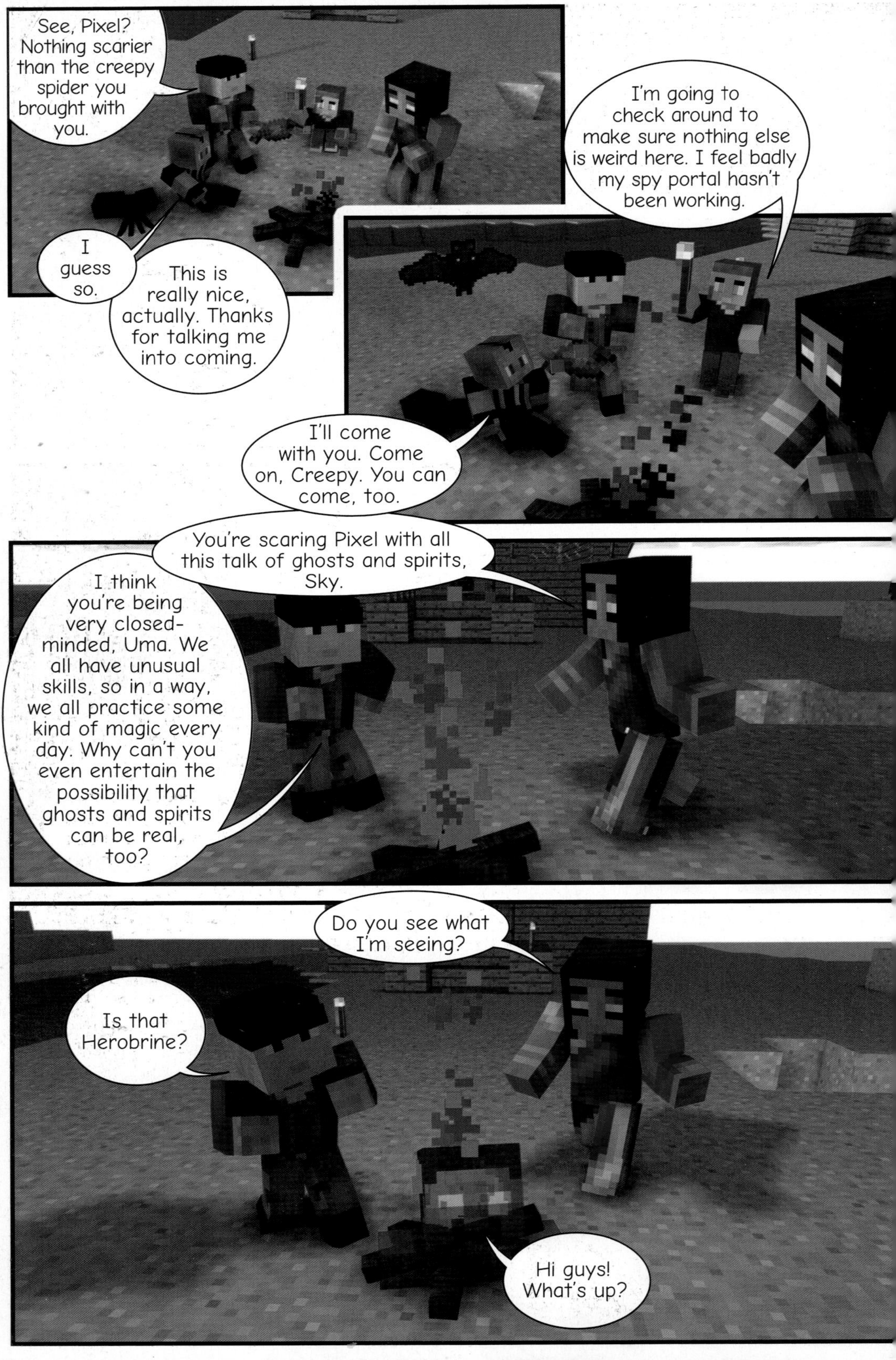
See, Pixel? Nothing scarier than the creepy spider you brought with you.
I guess so.
This is really nice, actually. Thanks for talking me into coming.
I'm going to check around to make sure nothing else is weird here. I feel badly my spy portal hasn't been working.
I'll come with you. Come on, Creepy. You can come, too.
You're scaring Pixel with all this talk of ghosts and spirits, Sky.
I think you're being very closed-minded, Uma. We all have unusual skills, so in a way, we all practice some kind of magic every day. Why can't you even entertain the possibility that ghosts and spirits can be real, too?
Do you see what I'm seeing?
Is that Herobrine?
Hi guys! What's up?

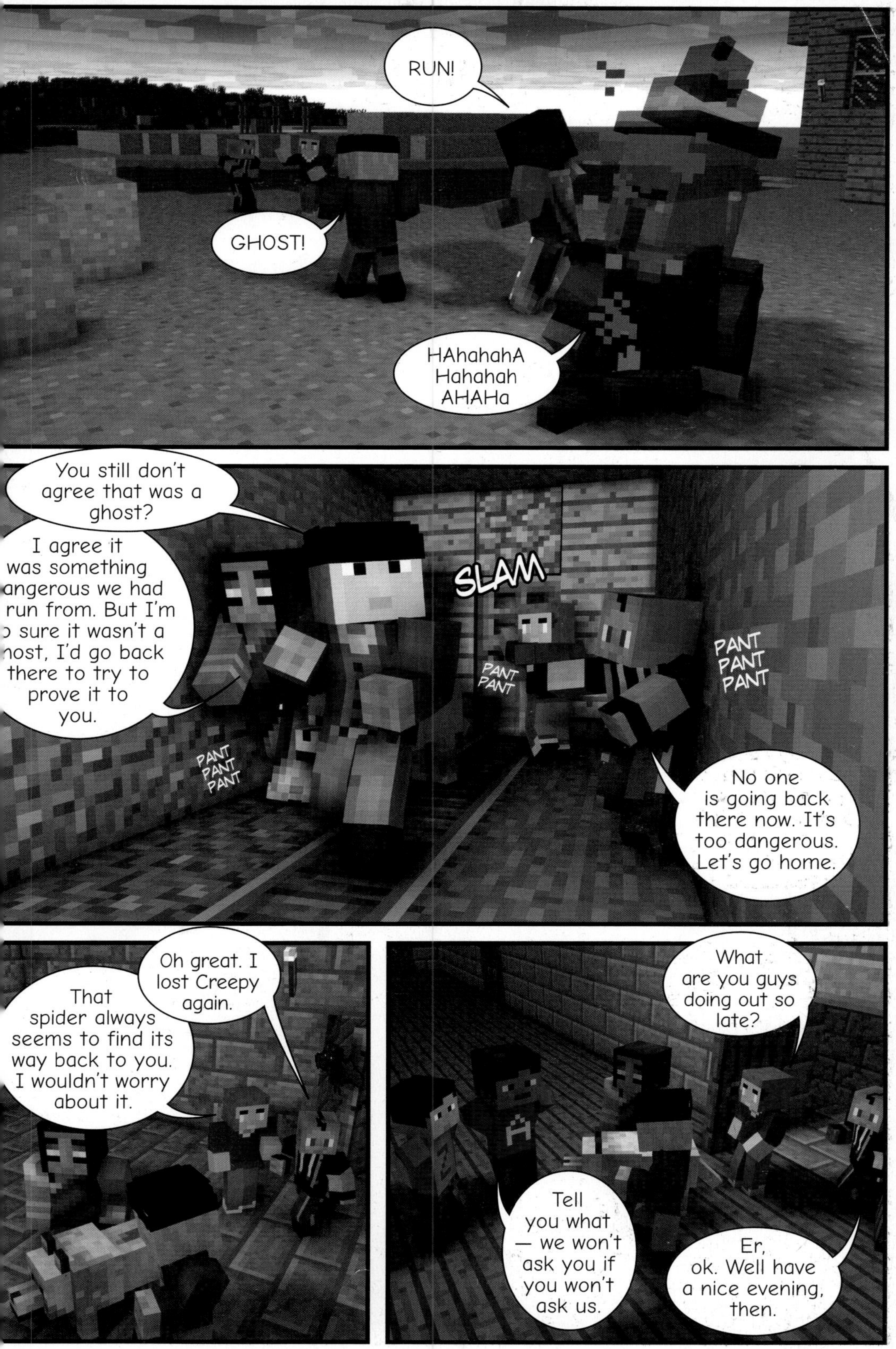
RUN!
GHOST!
HAhahahA Hahahah AHAHa
You still don't agree that was a ghost?
I agree it was something angerous we had run from. But I'm o sure it wasn't a nost, I'd go back there to try to prove it to you.
SLAM
PANT PANT
PANT PANT PANT
PANT PANT PANT
No one is going back there now. It's too dangerous. Let's go home.
Oh great. I lost Creepy again.
That spider always seems to find its way back to you. I wouldn't worry about it.
What are you guys doing out so late?
Tell you what — we won't ask you if you won't ask us.
Er, ok. Well have a nice evening, then.

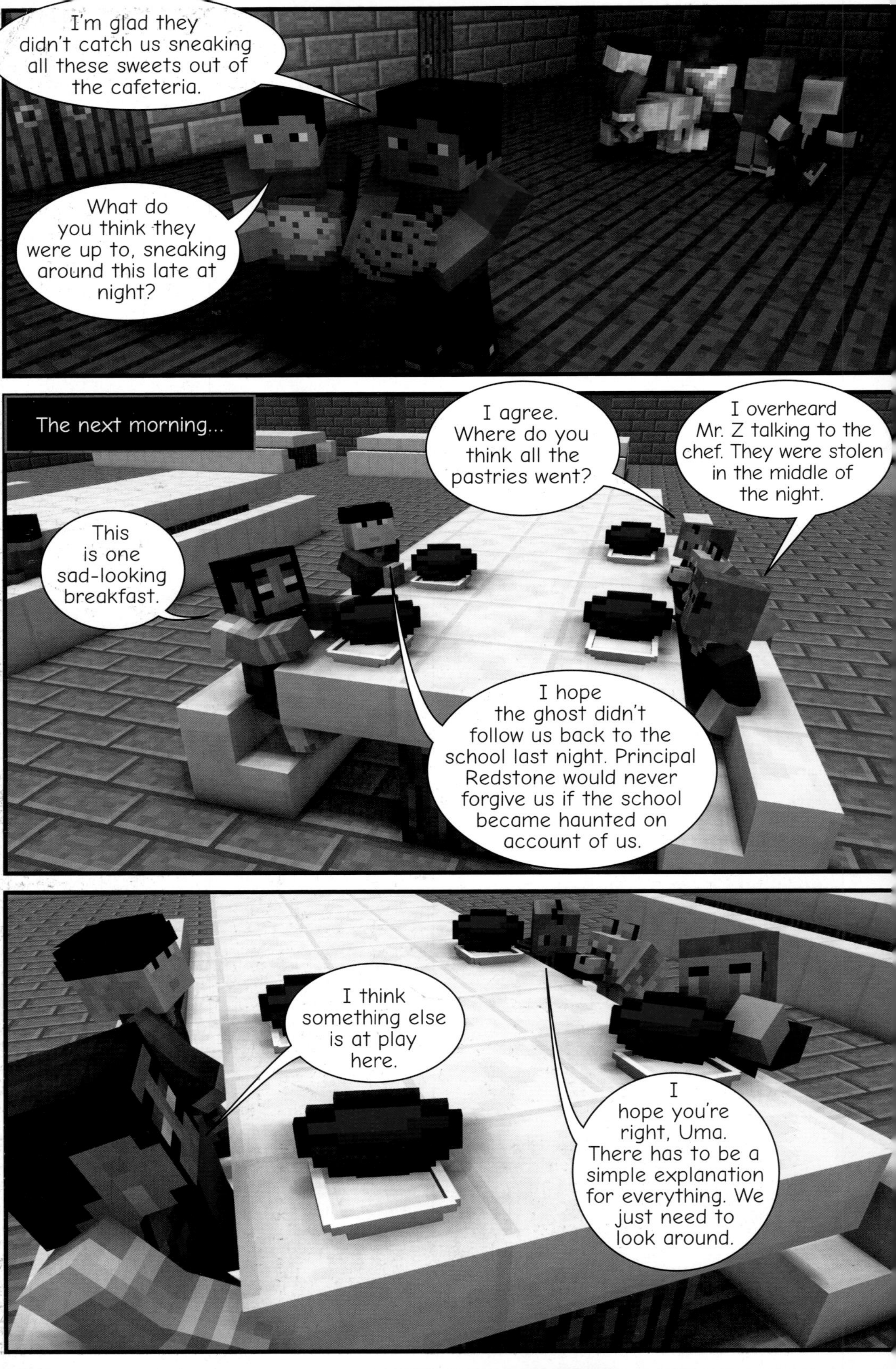
I'm glad they didn't catch us sneaking all these sweets out of the cafeteria.
What do you think they were up to, sneaking around this late at night?
The next morning...
This is one sad-looking breakfast.
I agree. Where do you think all the pastries went?
I overheard Mr. Z talking to the chef. They were stolen in the middle of the night.
I hope the ghost didn't follow us back to the school last night. Principal Redstone would never forgive us if the school became haunted on account of us.
I think something else is at play here.
I hope you're right, Uma. There has to be a simple explanation for everything. We just need to look around.

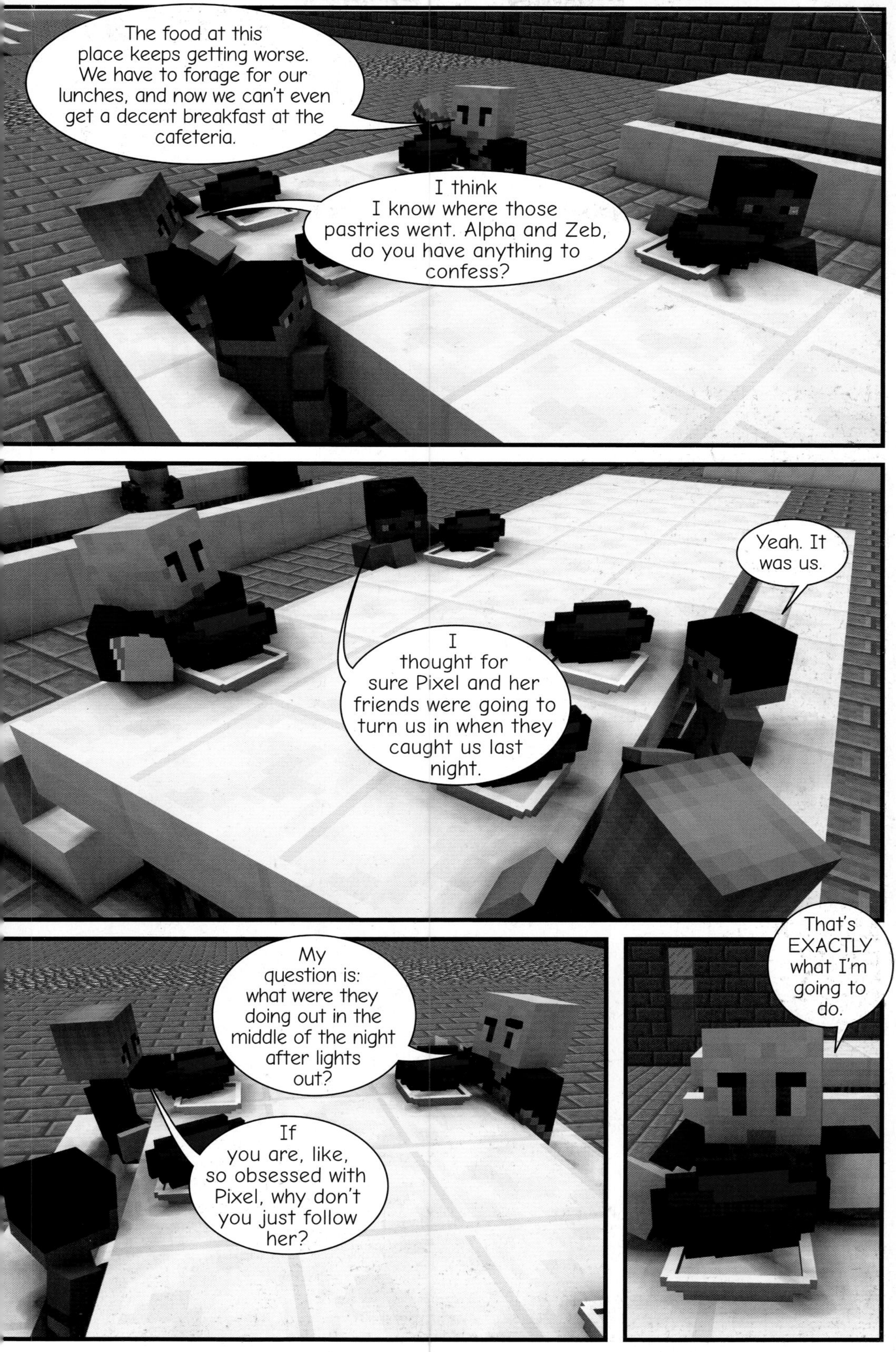
The food at this place keeps getting worse. We have to forage for our lunches, and now we can't even get a decent breakfast at the cafeteria.
I think I know where those pastries went. Alpha and Zeb, do you have anything to confess?
Yeah. It was us.
I thought for sure Pixel and her friends were going to turn us in when they caught us last night.
My question is: what were they doing out in the middle of the night after lights out?
If you are, like, so obsessed with Pixel, why don't you just follow her?
That's EXACTLY what I'm going to do.

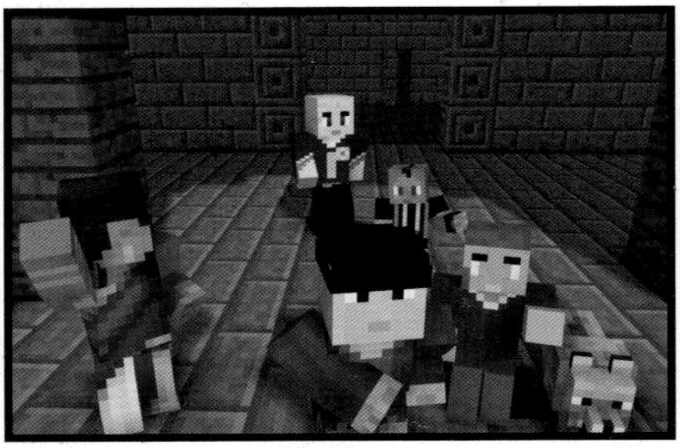

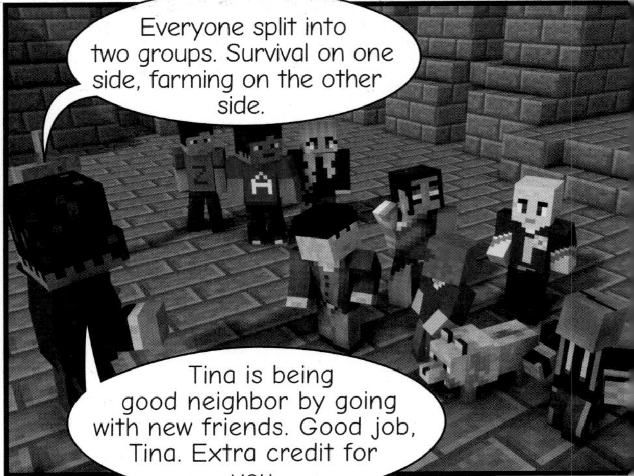
Everyone split into two groups. Survival on one side, farming on the other side.
Tina is being good neighbor by going with new friends. Good job, Tina. Extra credit for you.

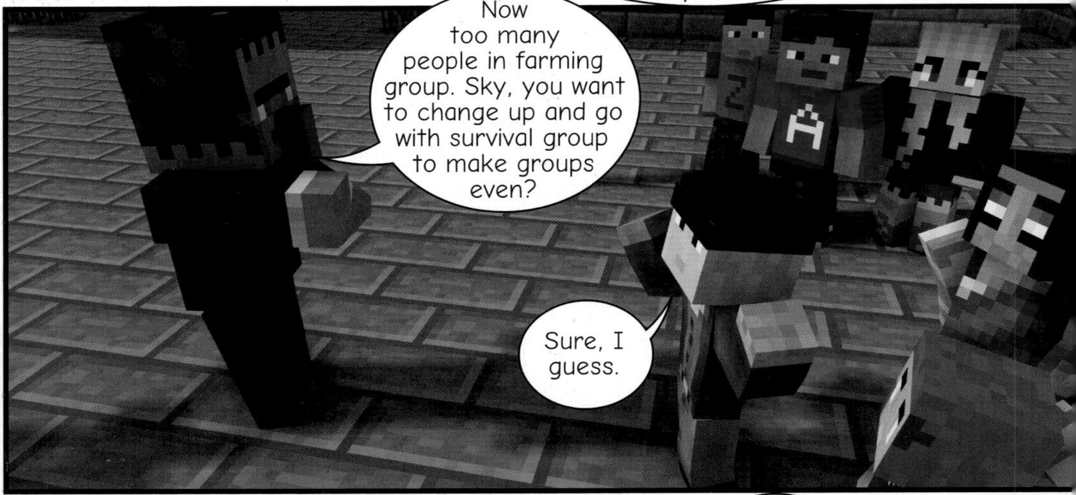
Now too many people in farming group. Sky, you want to change up and go with survival group to make groups even?
Sure, I guess.

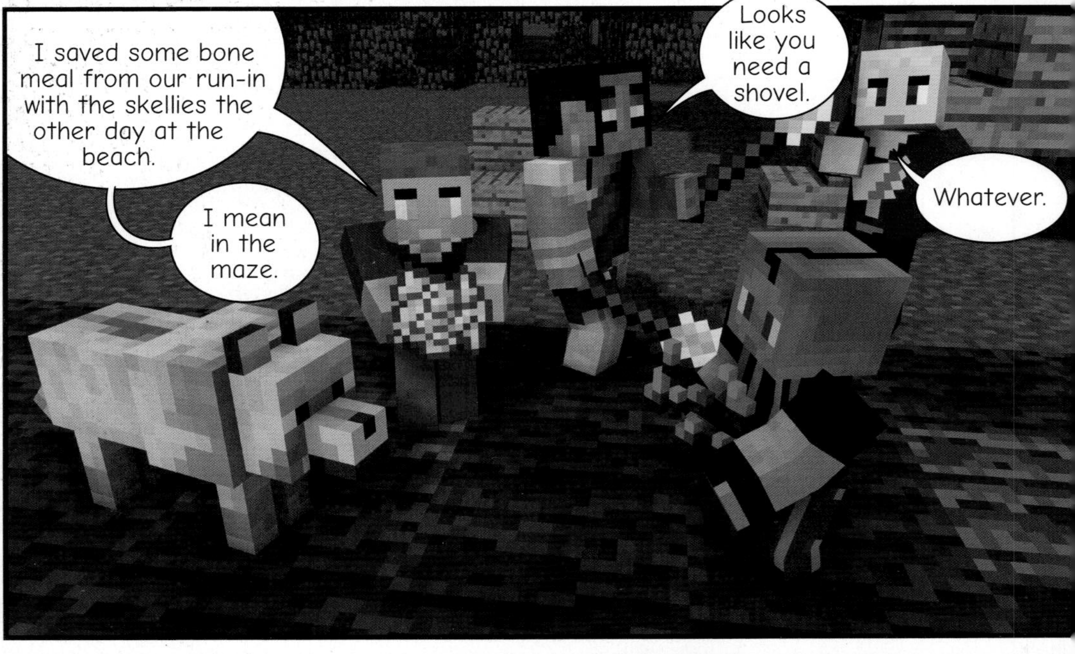
I saved some bone meal from our run-in with the skellies the other day at the beach.
I mean in the maze.
Looks like you need a shovel.
Whatever.

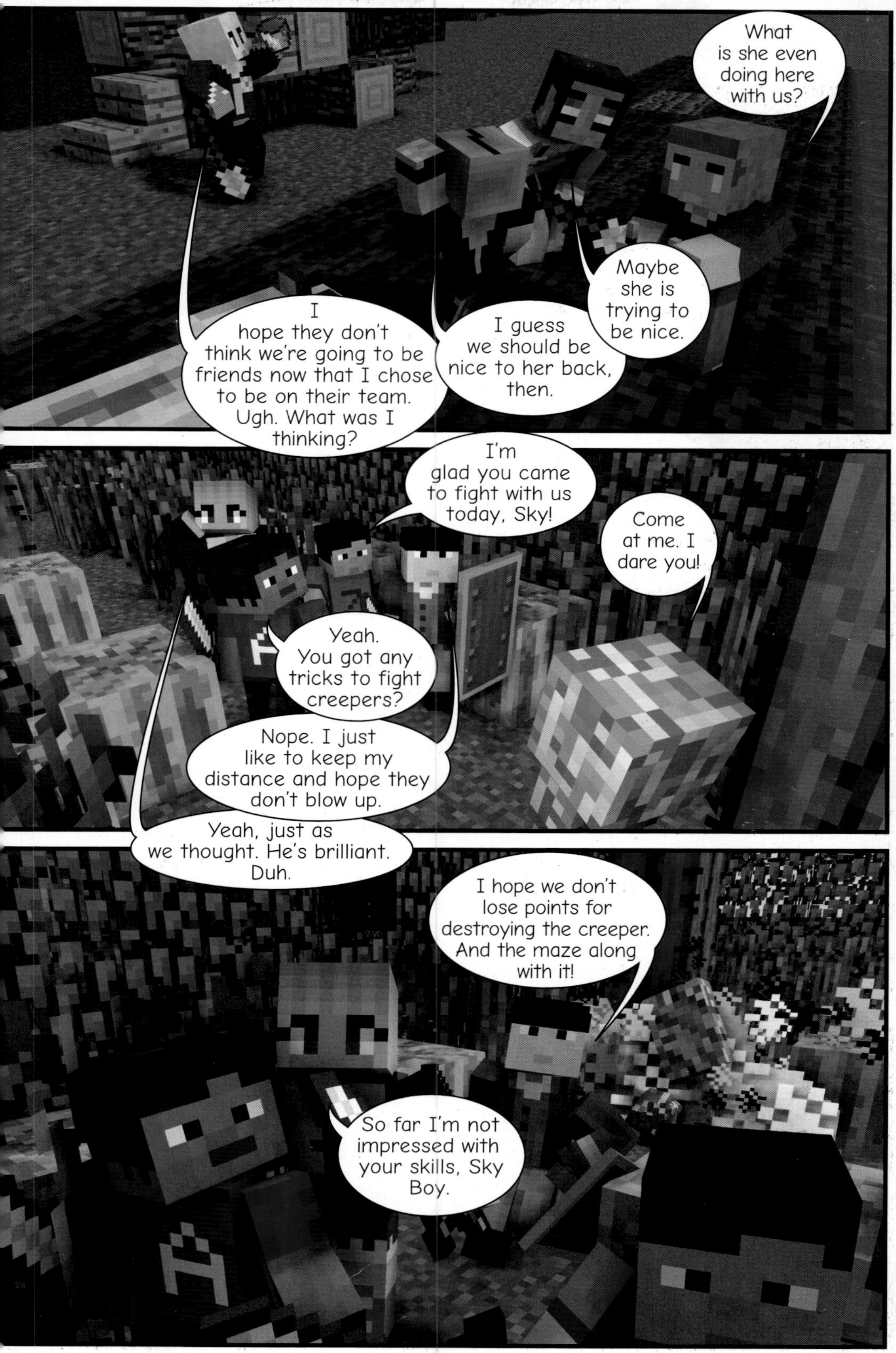
What is she even doing here with us?
Maybe she is trying to be nice.
I guess we should be nice to her back, then.
I hope they don't think we're going to be friends now that I chose to be on their team. Ugh. What was I thinking?
I'm glad you came to fight with us today, Sky!
Come at me. I dare you!
Yeah. You got any tricks to fight creepers?
Nope. I just like to keep my distance and hope they don't blow up.
Yeah, just as we thought. He's brilliant. Duh.
I hope we don't lose points for destroying the creeper. And the maze along with it!
So far I'm not impressed with your skills, Sky Boy.

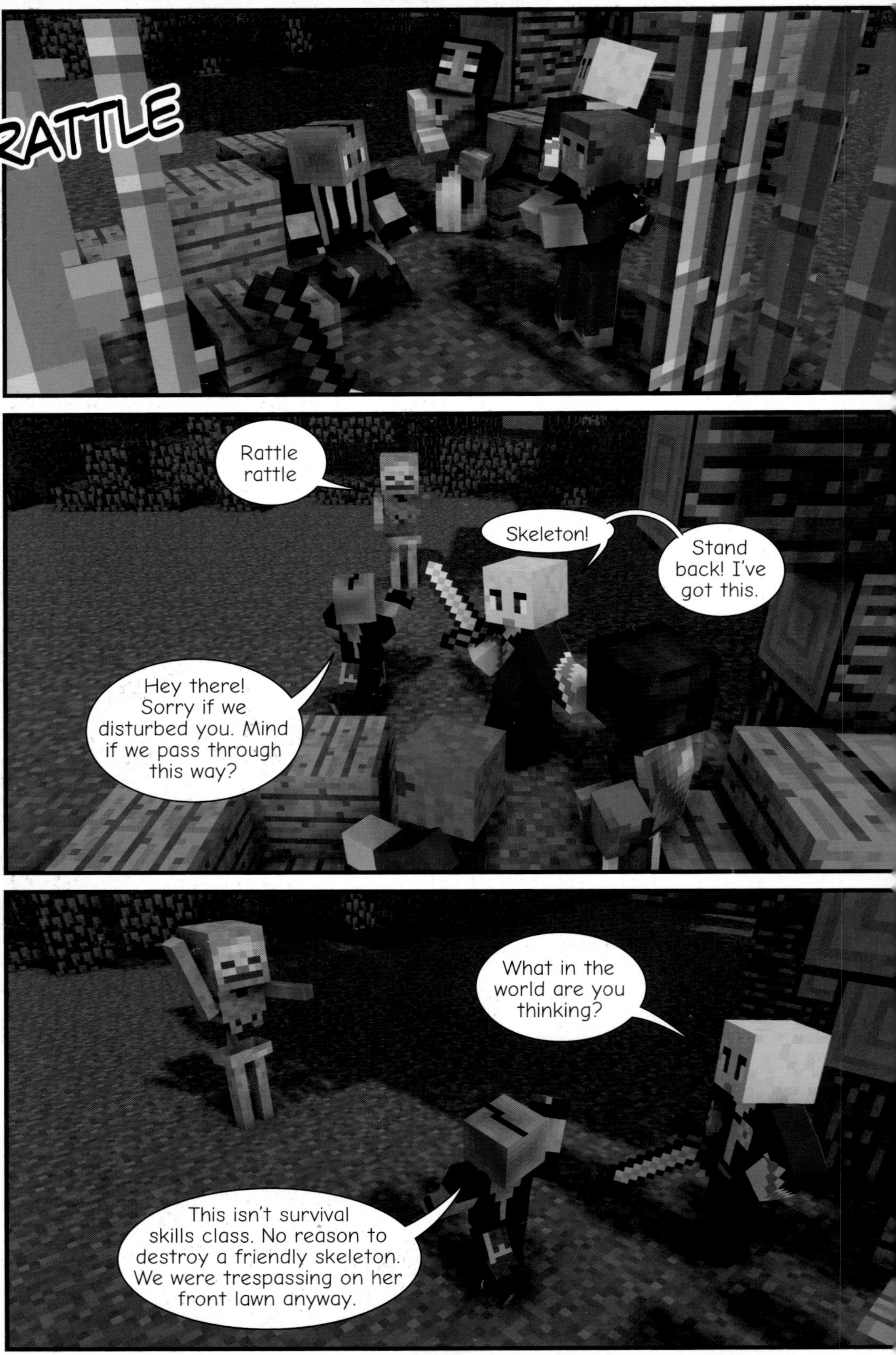
RATTLE
Rattle rattle
Skeleton!
Stand back! I've got this.
Hey there! Sorry if we disturbed you. Mind if we pass through this way?
What in the world are you thinking?
This isn't survival skills class. No reason to destroy a friendly skeleton. We were trespassing on her front lawn anyway.

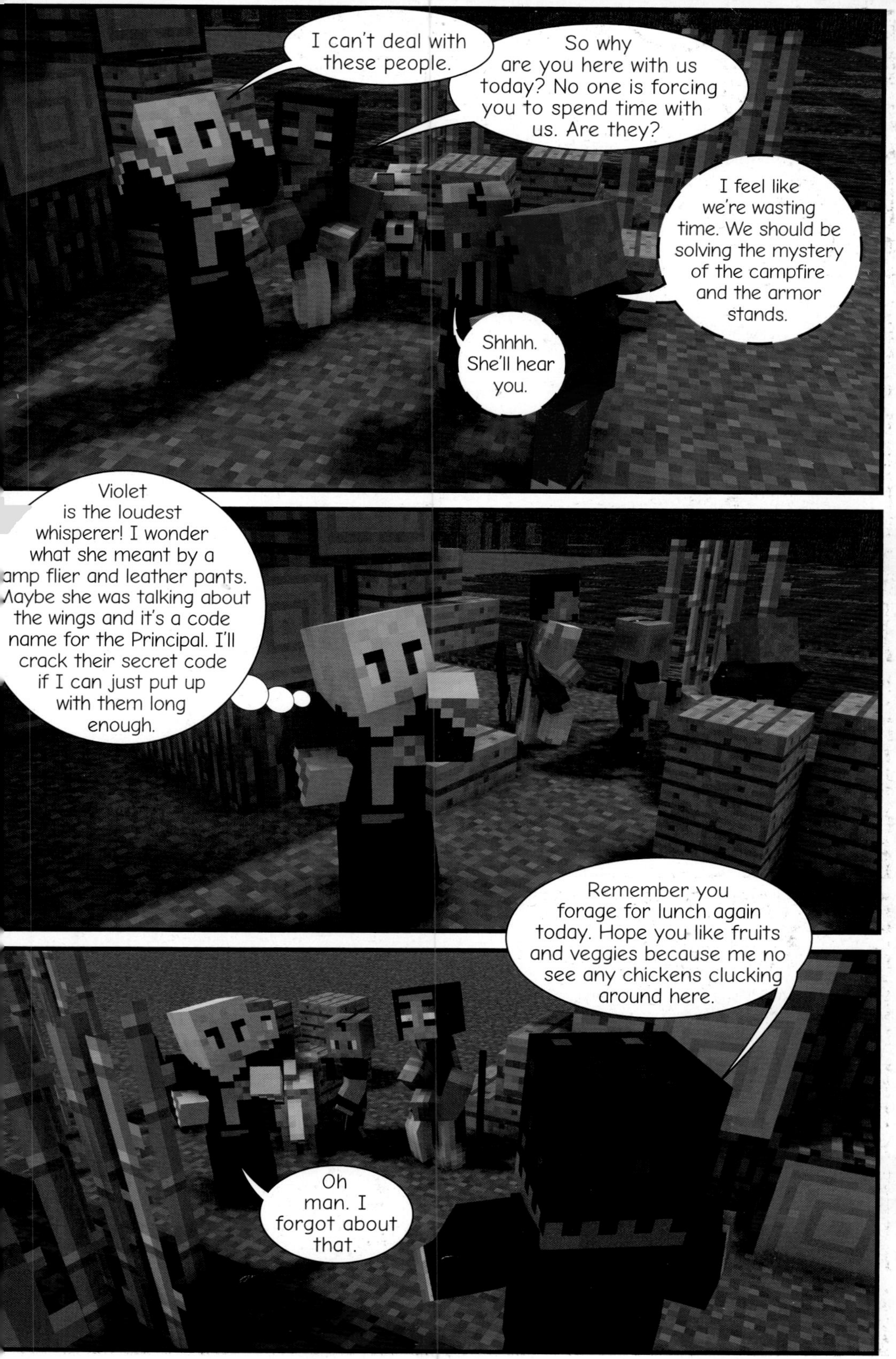
I can't deal with these people.
So why are you here with us today? No one is forcing you to spend time with us. Are they?
I feel like we're wasting time. We should be solving the mystery of the campfire and the armor stands.
Shhhh. She'll hear you.
Violet is the loudest whisperer! I wonder what she meant by a amp flier and leather pants. Maybe she was talking about the wings and it's a code name for the Principal. I'll crack their secret code if I can just put up with them long enough.
Remember you forage for lunch again today. Hope you like fruits and veggies because me no see any chickens clucking around here.
Oh man. I forgot about that.

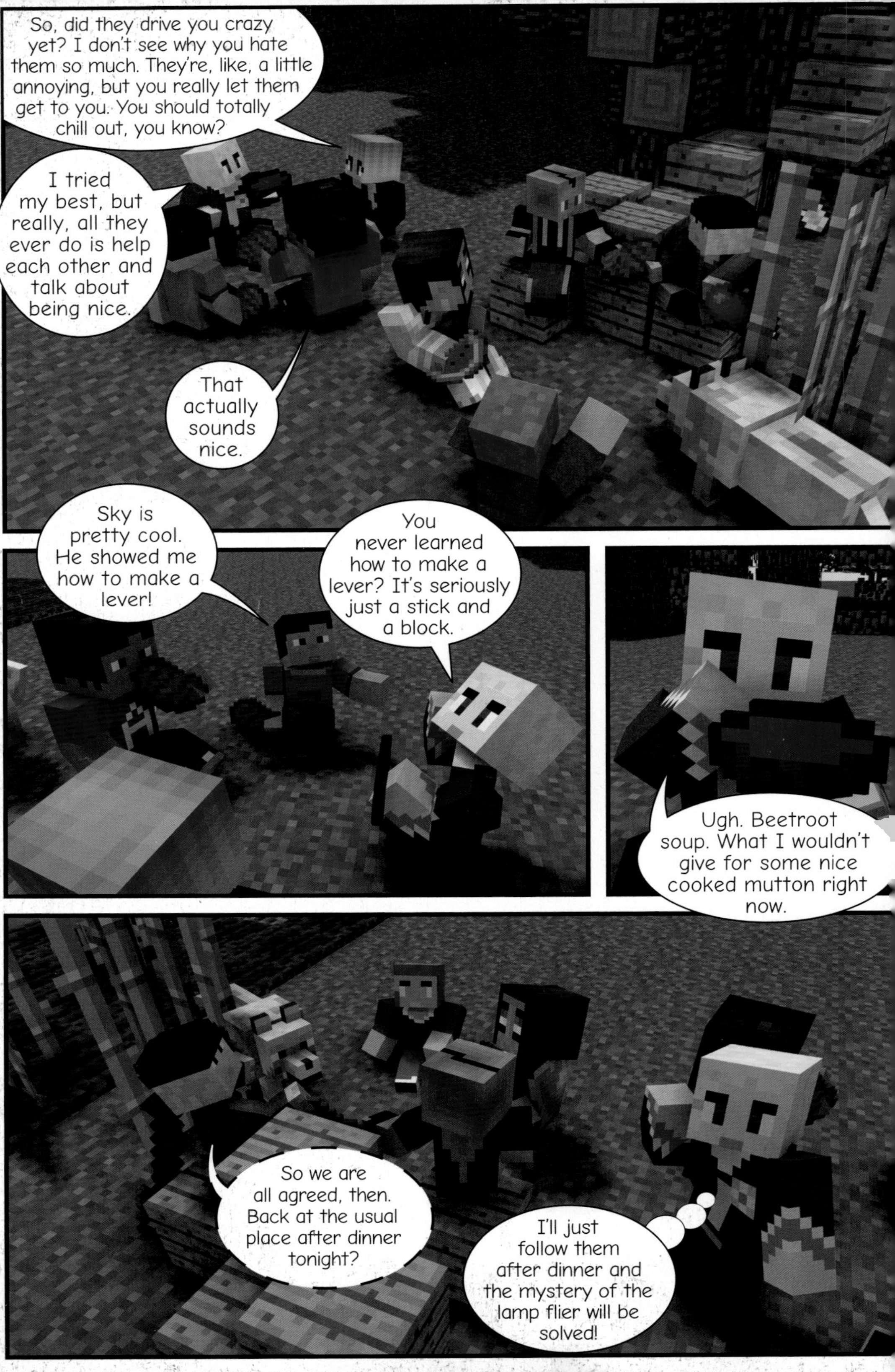
So, did they drive you crazy yet? I don't see why you hate them so much. They're, like, a little annoying, but you really let them get to you. You should totally chill out, you know?
I tried my best, but really, all they ever do is help each other and talk about being nice.
That actually sounds nice.
Sky is pretty cool. He showed me how to make a lever!
You never learned how to make a lever? It's seriously just a stick and a block.
Ugh. Beetroot soup. What I wouldn't give for some nice cooked mutton right now.
So we are all agreed, then. Back at the usual place after dinner tonight?
I'll just follow them after dinner and the mystery of the lamp flier will be solved!

CHAPTER 8

A COMMON ENEMY

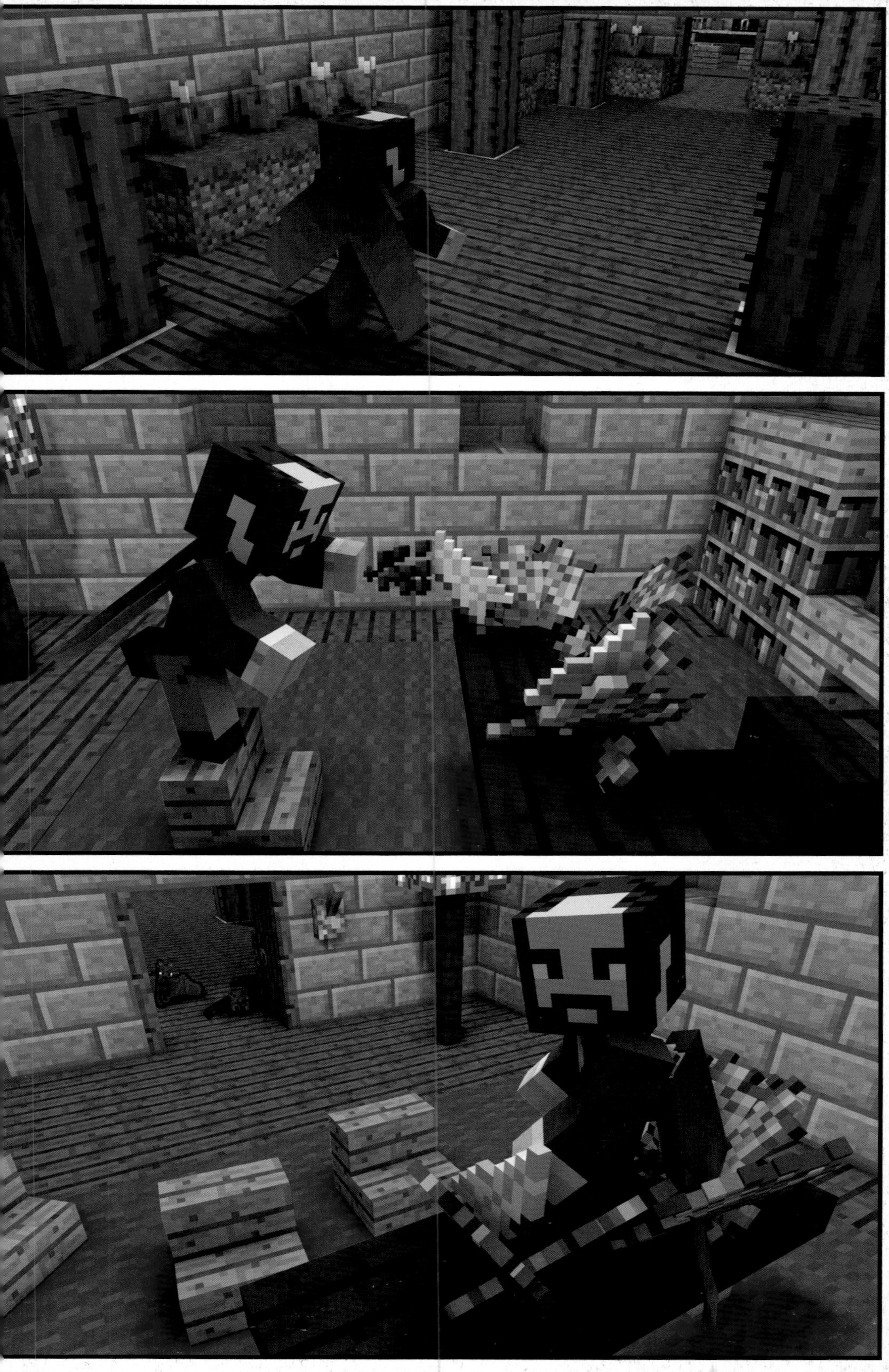

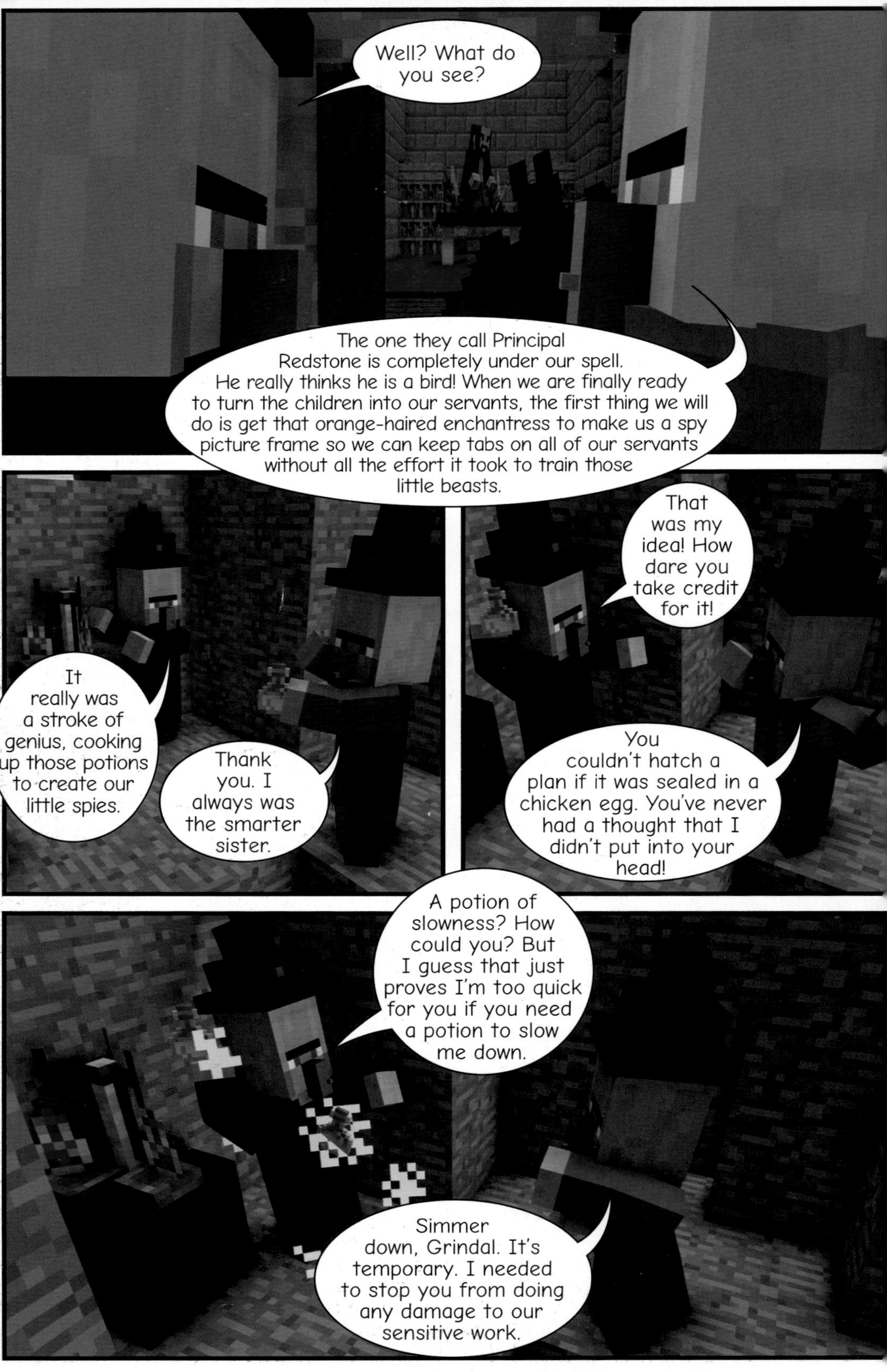
Well? What do you see?
The one they call Principal Redstone is completely under our spell. He really thinks he is a bird! When we are finally ready to turn the children into our servants, the first thing we will do is get that orange-haired enchantress to make us a spy picture frame so we can keep tabs on all of our servants without all the effort it took to train those little beasts.
It really was a stroke of genius, cooking up those potions to create our little spies.
Thank you. I always was the smarter sister.
That was my idea! How dare you take credit for it!
You couldn't hatch a plan if it was sealed in a chicken egg. You've never had a thought that I didn't put into your head!
A potion of slowness? How could you? But I guess that just proves I'm too quick for you if you need a potion to slow me down.
Simmer down, Grindal. It's temporary. I needed to stop you from doing any damage to our sensitive work.

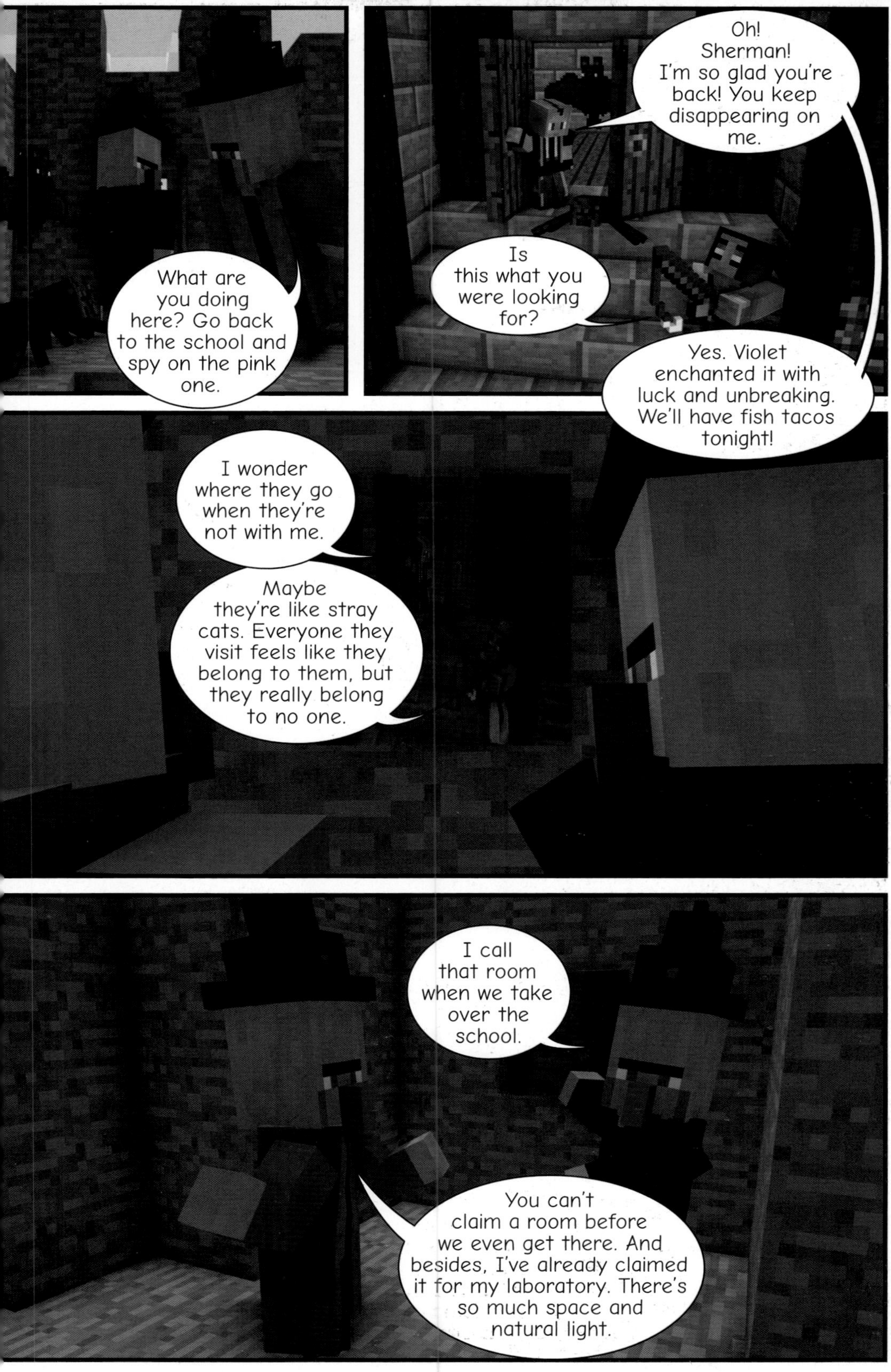
What are you doing here? Go back to the school and spy on the pink one.
Oh! Sherman! I'm so glad you're back! You keep disappearing on me.
Is this what you were looking for?
Yes. Violet enchanted it with luck and unbreaking. We'll have fish tacos tonight!
I wonder where they go when they're not with me.
Maybe they're like stray cats. Everyone they visit feels like they belong to them, but they really belong to no one.
I call that room when we take over the school.
You can't claim a room before we even get there. And besides, I've already claimed it for my laboratory. There's so much space and natural light.

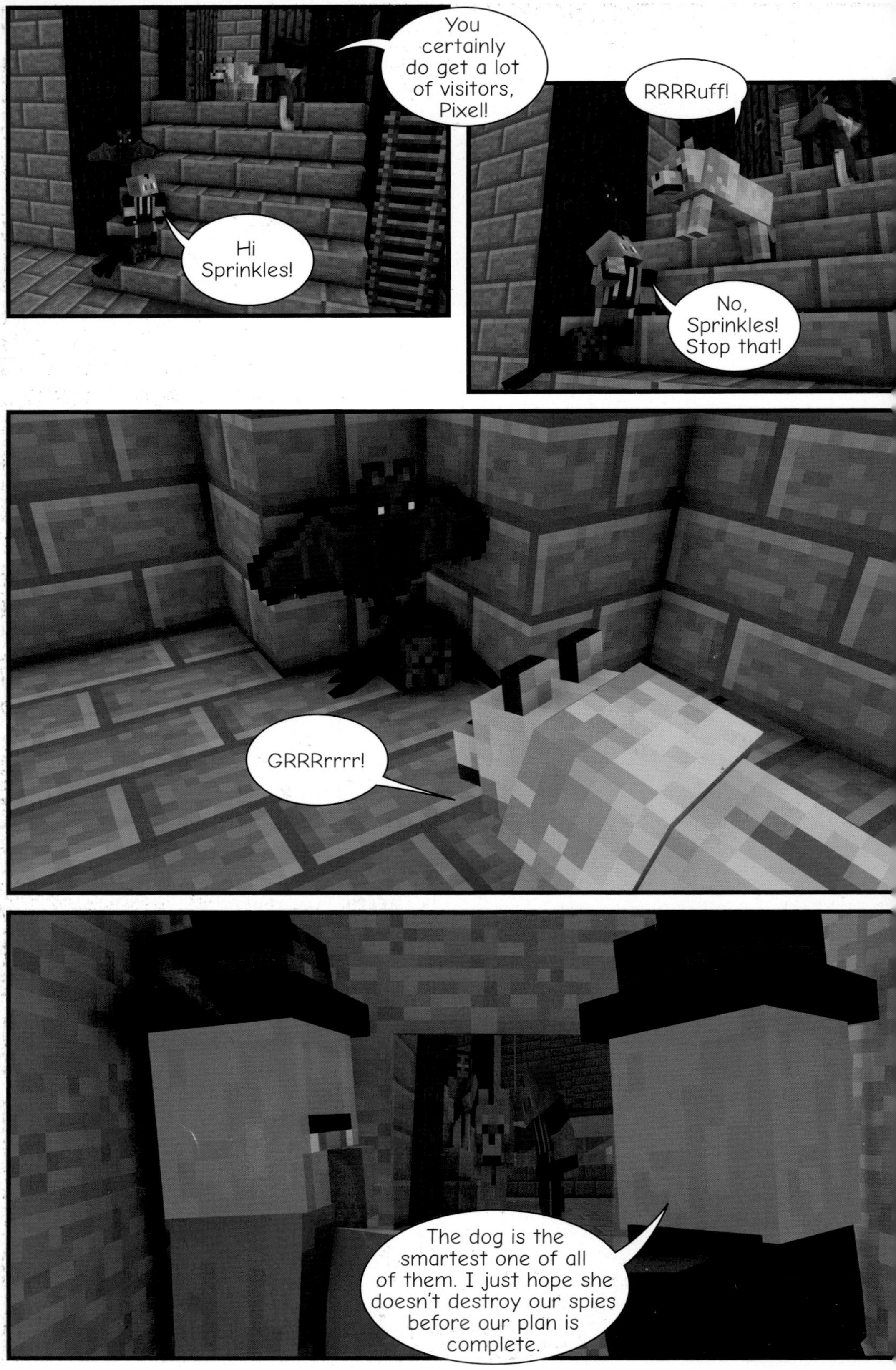
You certainly do get a lot of visitors, Pixel!
Hi Sprinkles!
RRRRuff!
No, Sprinkles! Stop that!
GRRRrrrr!
The dog is the smartest one of all of them. I just hope she doesn't destroy our spies before our plan is complete.

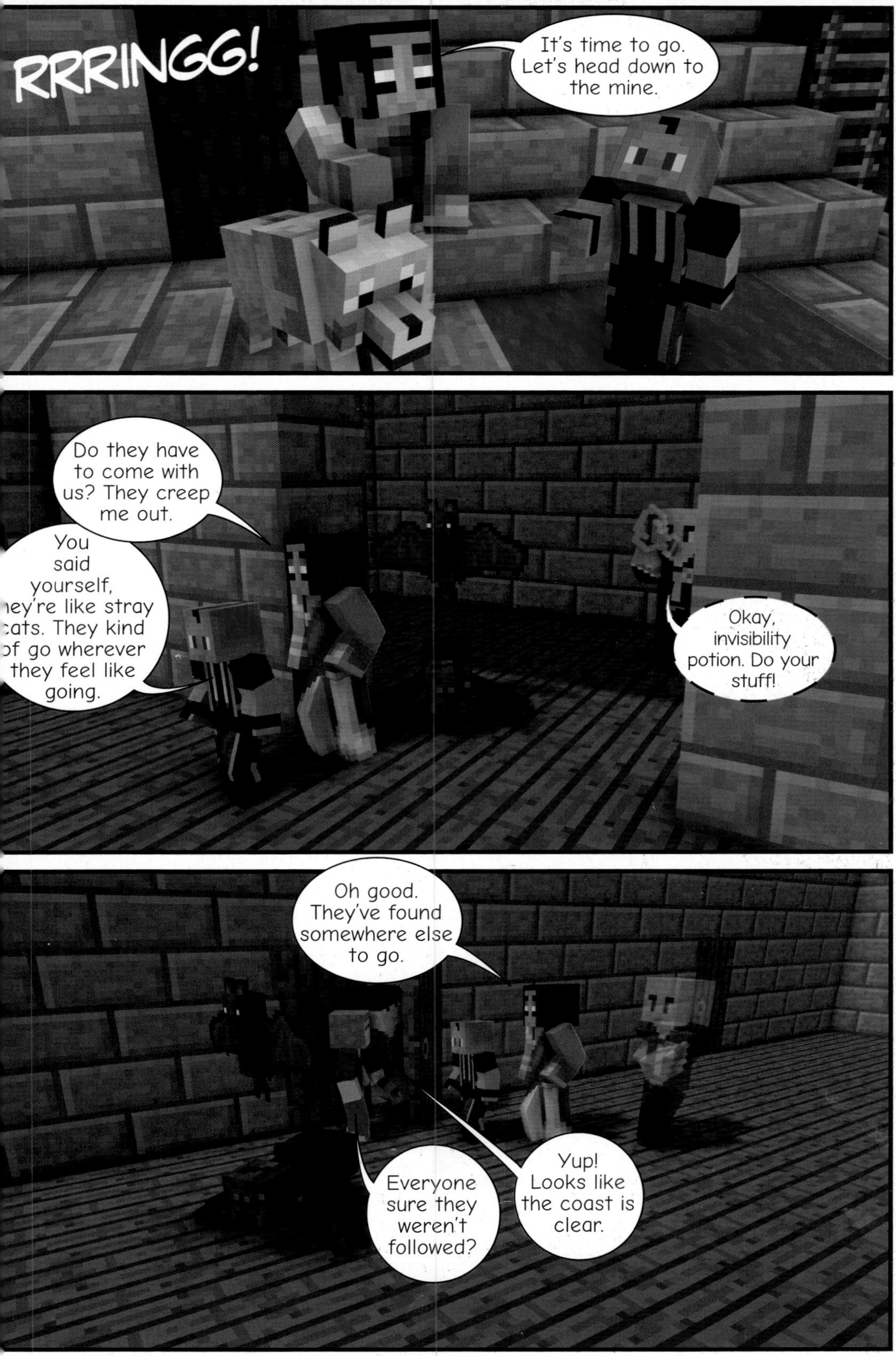
RRRINGG!
It's time to go. Let's head down to the mine.
Do they have to come with us? They creep me out.
You said yourself, ey're like stray ats. They kind f go wherever they feel like going.
Okay, invisibility potion. Do your stuff!
Oh good. They've found somewhere else to go.
Everyone sure they weren't followed?
Yup! Looks like the coast is clear.

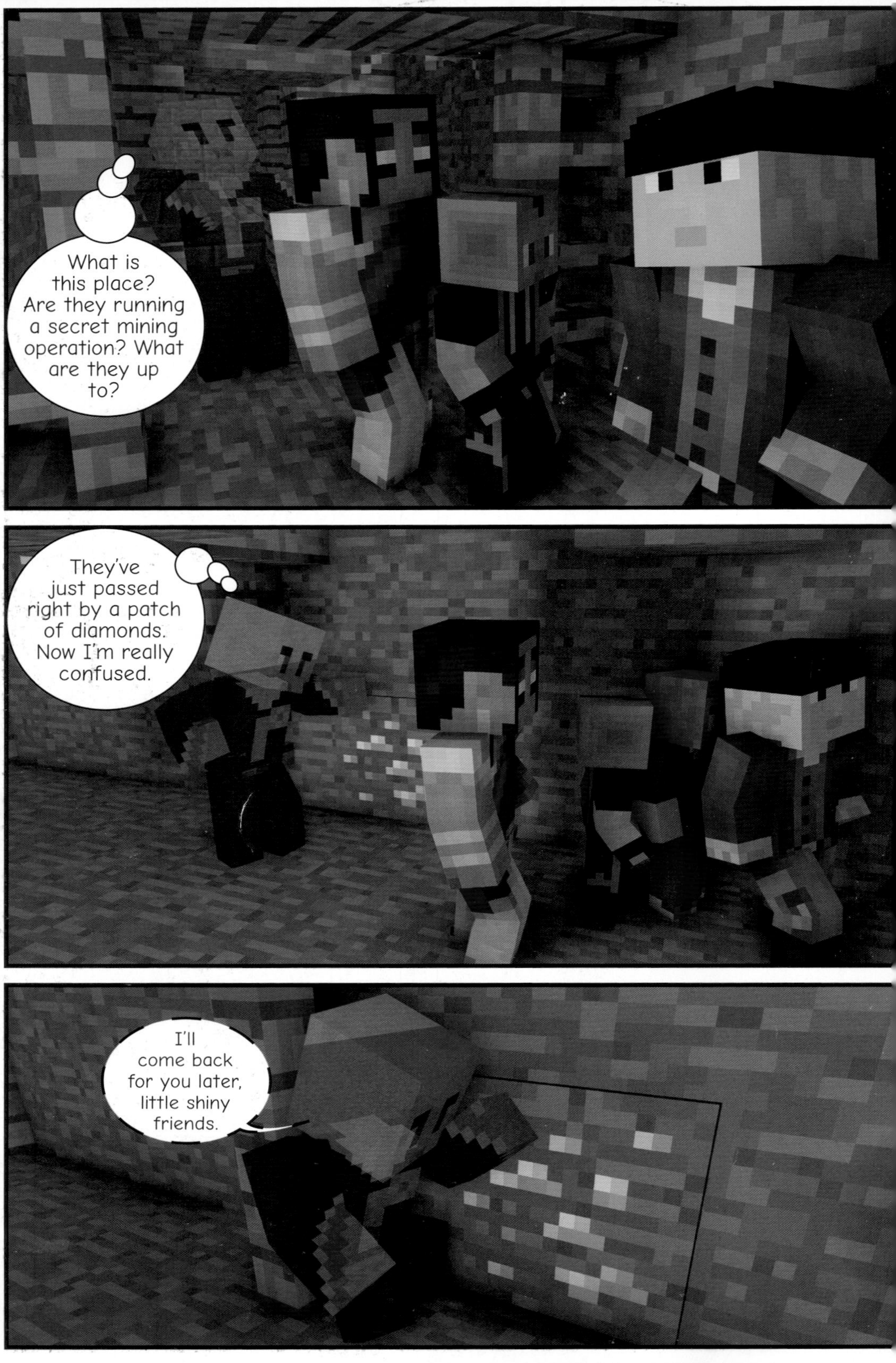
What is this place? Are they running a secret mining operation? What are they up to?
They've just passed right by a patch of diamonds. Now I'm really confused.
I'll come back for you later, little shiny friends.

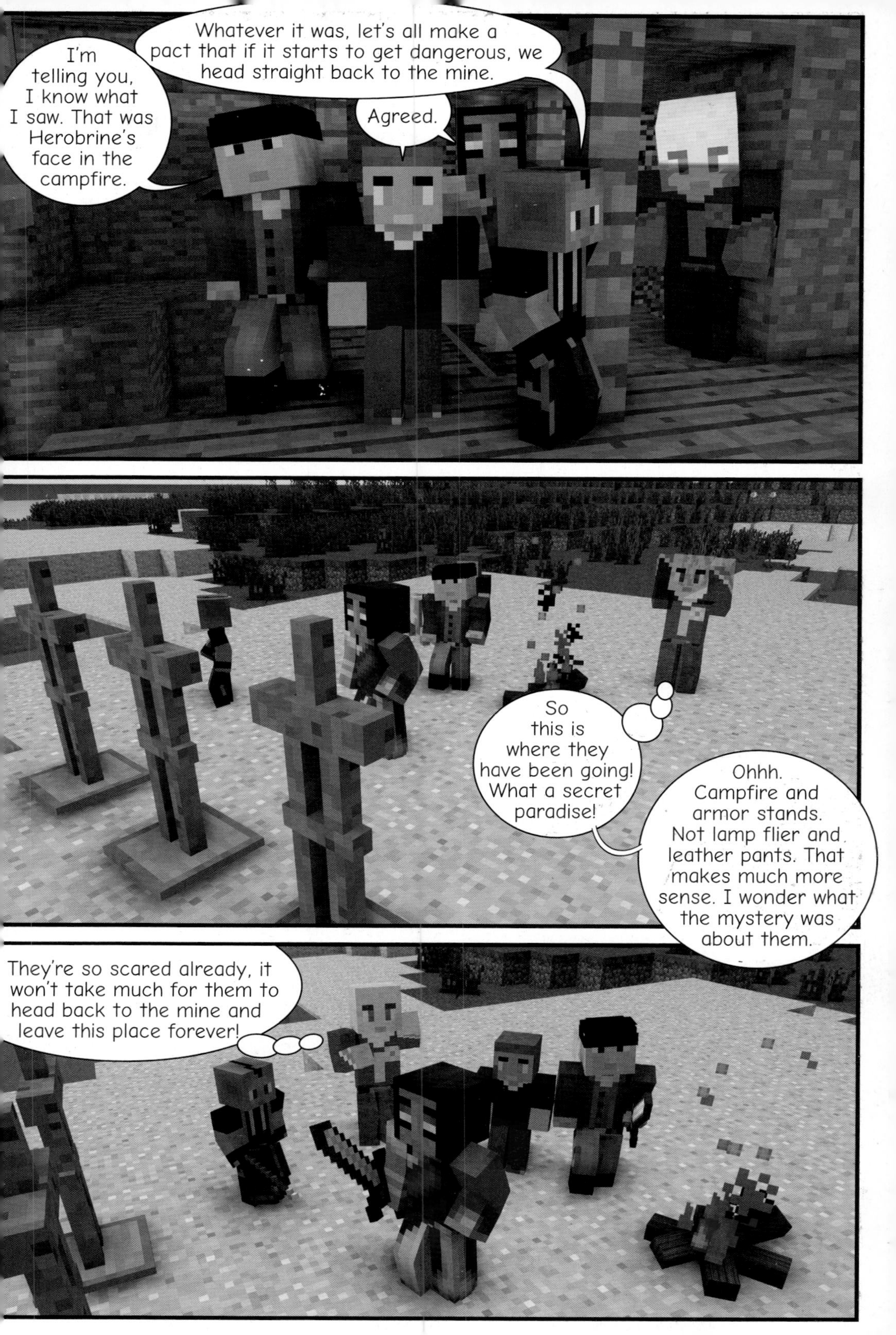
I'm telling you, I know what I saw. That was Herobrine's face in the campfire.
Whatever it was, let's all make a pact that if it starts to get dangerous, we head straight back to the mine.
Agreed.
So this is where they have been going! What a secret paradise!
Ohhh. Campfire and armor stands. Not lamp flier and leather pants. That makes much more sense. I wonder what the mystery was about them.
They're so scared already, it won't take much for them to head back to the mine and leave this place forever!

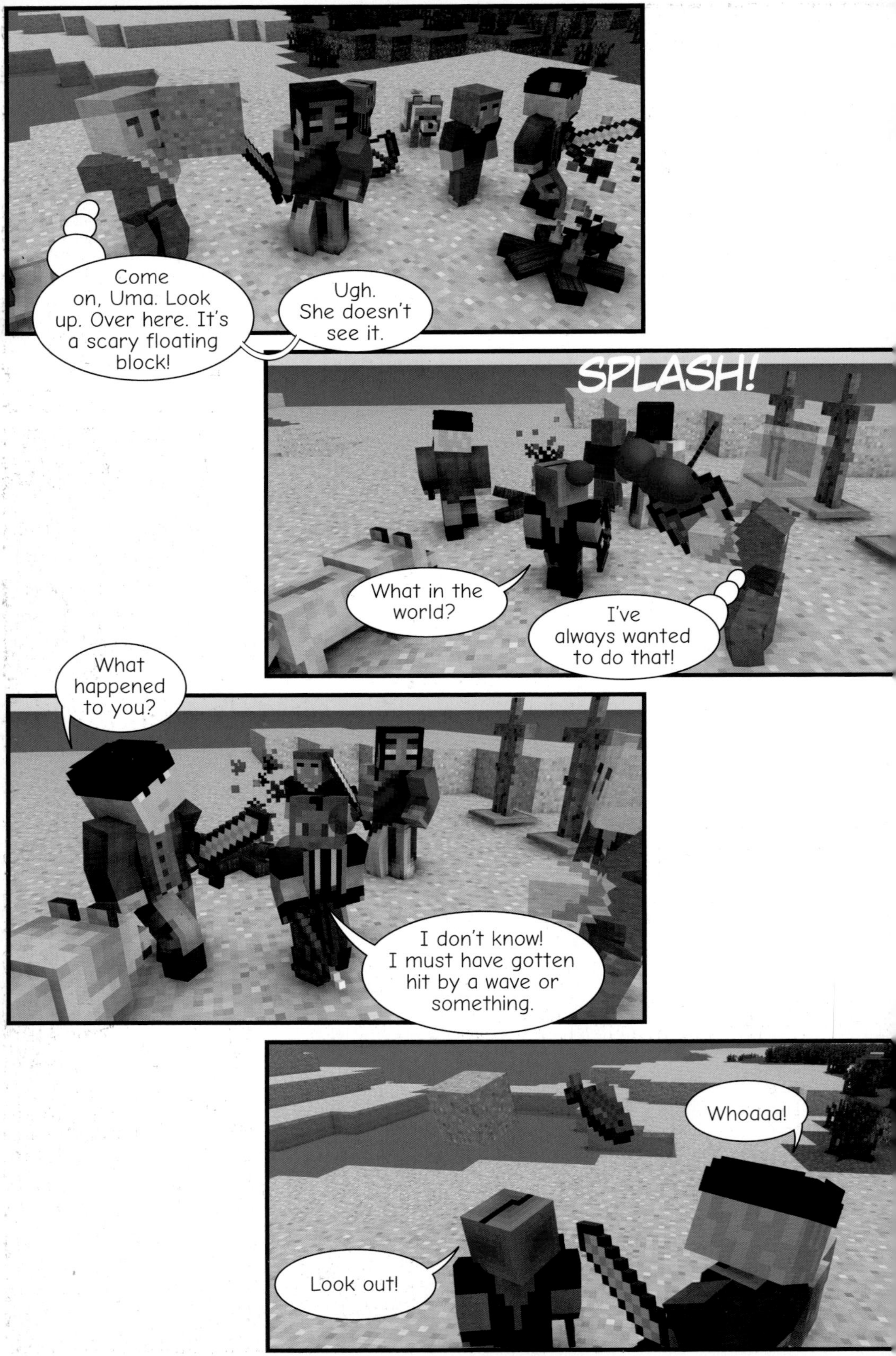

Come on, Uma. Look up. Over here. It's a scary floating block!
Ugh. She doesn't see it.
SPLASH!
What in the world?
I've always wanted to do that!
What happened to you?
I don't know! I must have gotten hit by a wave or something.
Whoaaa!
Look out!

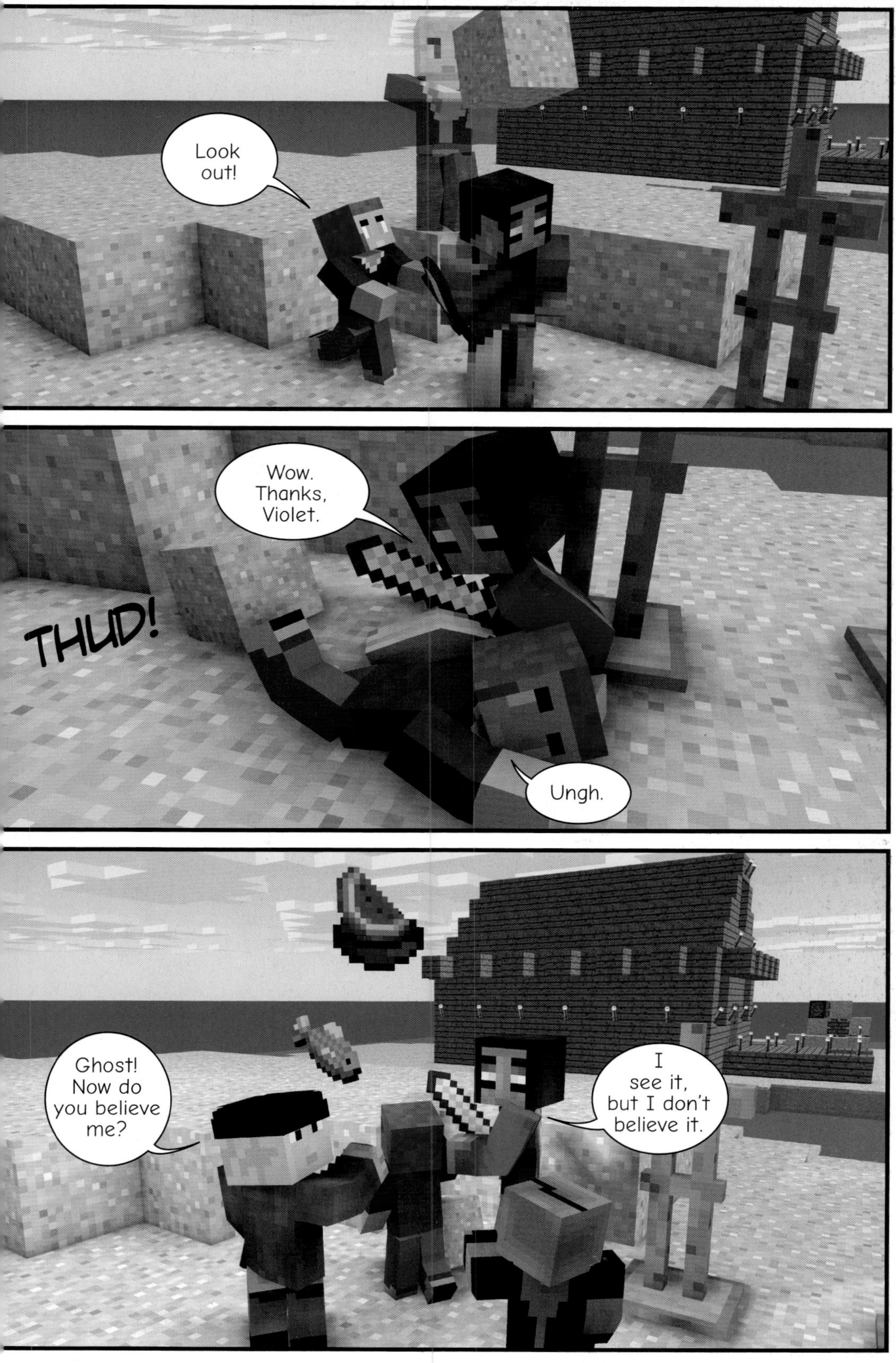

Look out!
Wow. Thanks, Violet.
THUD!
Ungh.
Ghost! Now do you believe me?
I see it, but I don't believe it.

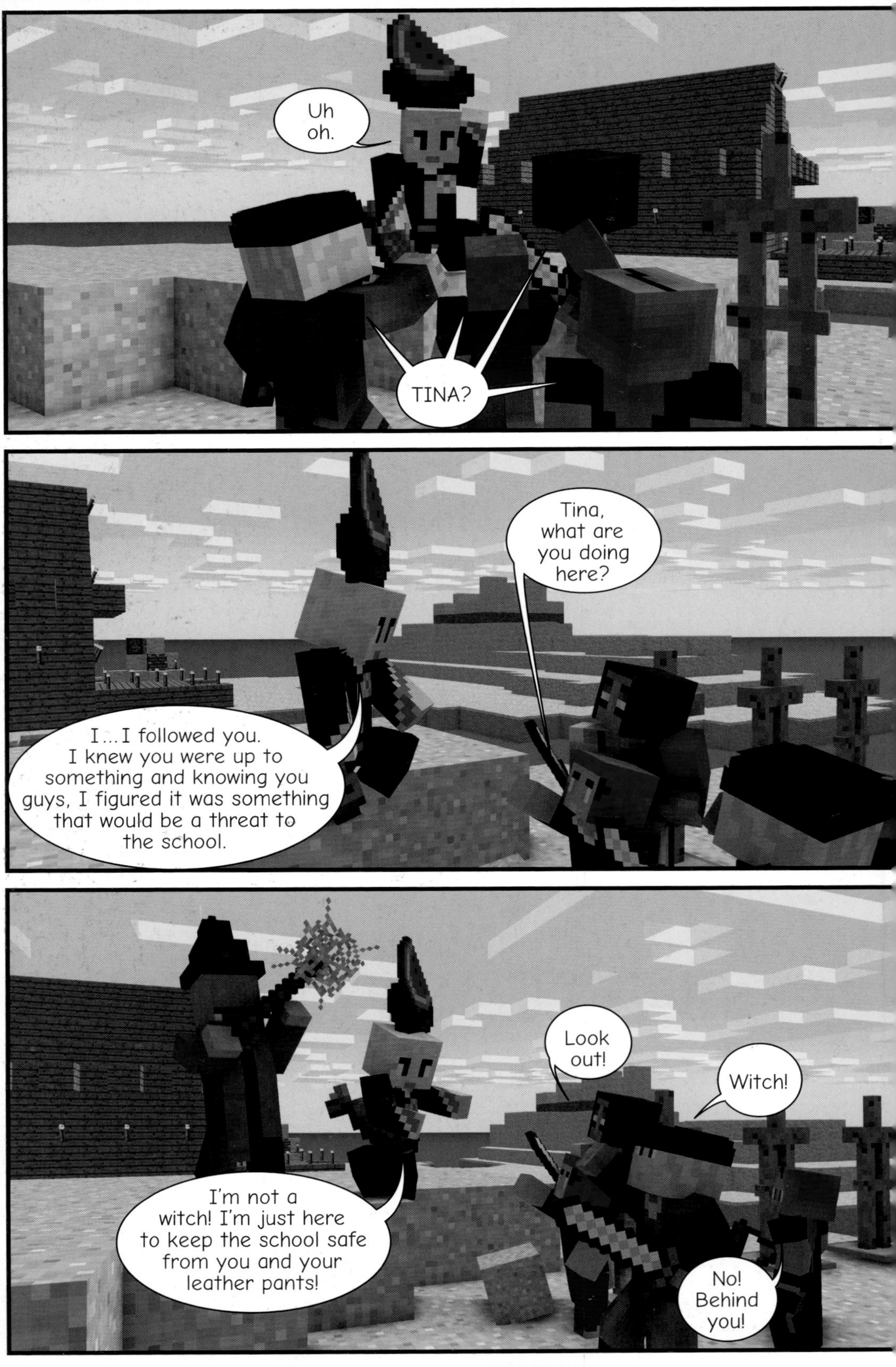
Uh oh.
TINA?
Tina, what are you doing here?
I...I followed you. I knew you were up to something and knowing you guys, I figured it was something that would be a threat to the school.
Look out!
Witch!
I'm not a witch! I'm just here to keep the school safe from you and your leather pants!
No! Behind you!

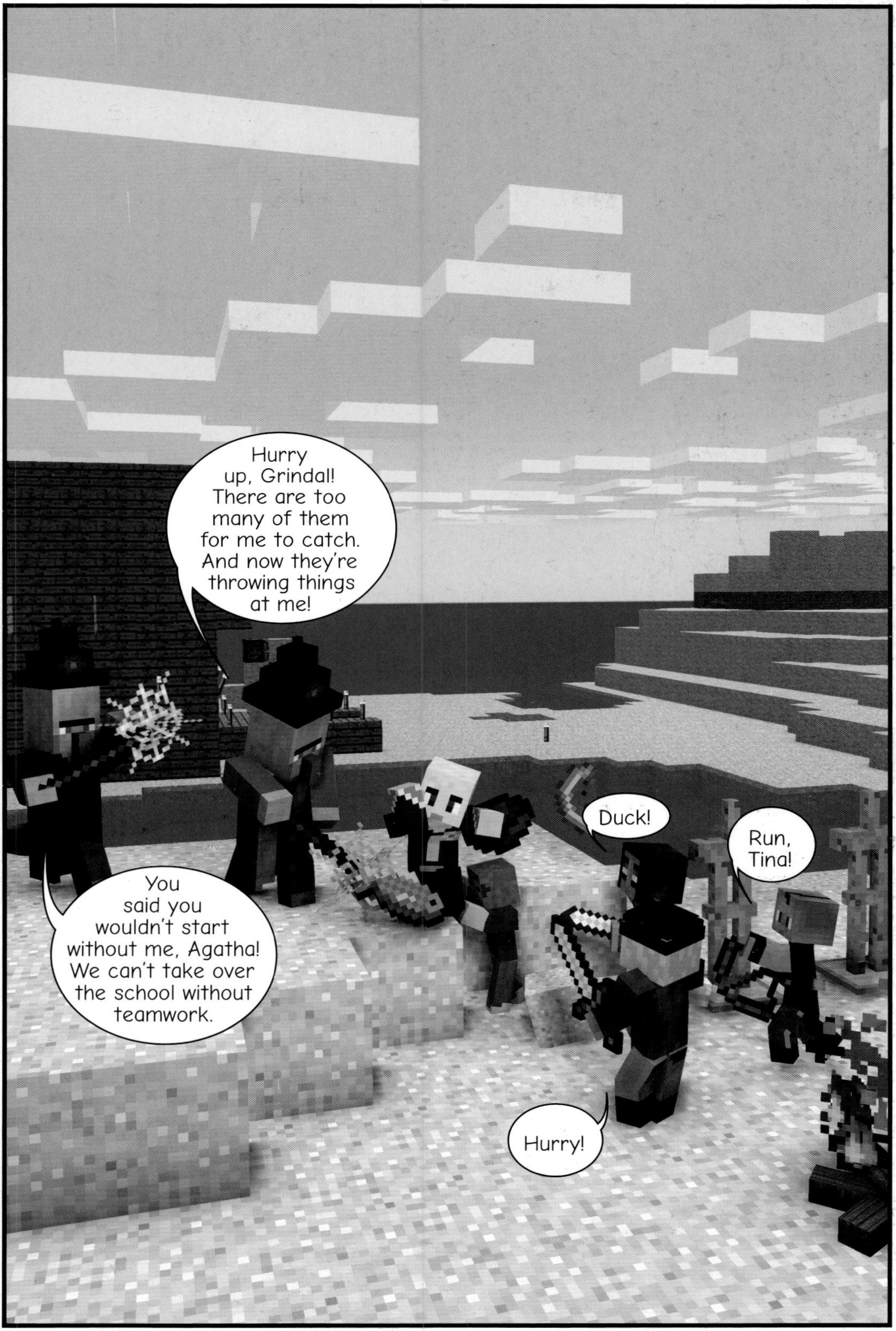
Hurry up, Grindal! There are too many of them for me to catch. And now they're throwing things at me!
You said you wouldn't start without me, Agatha! We can't take over the school without teamwork.
Duck!
Run, Tina!
Hurry!

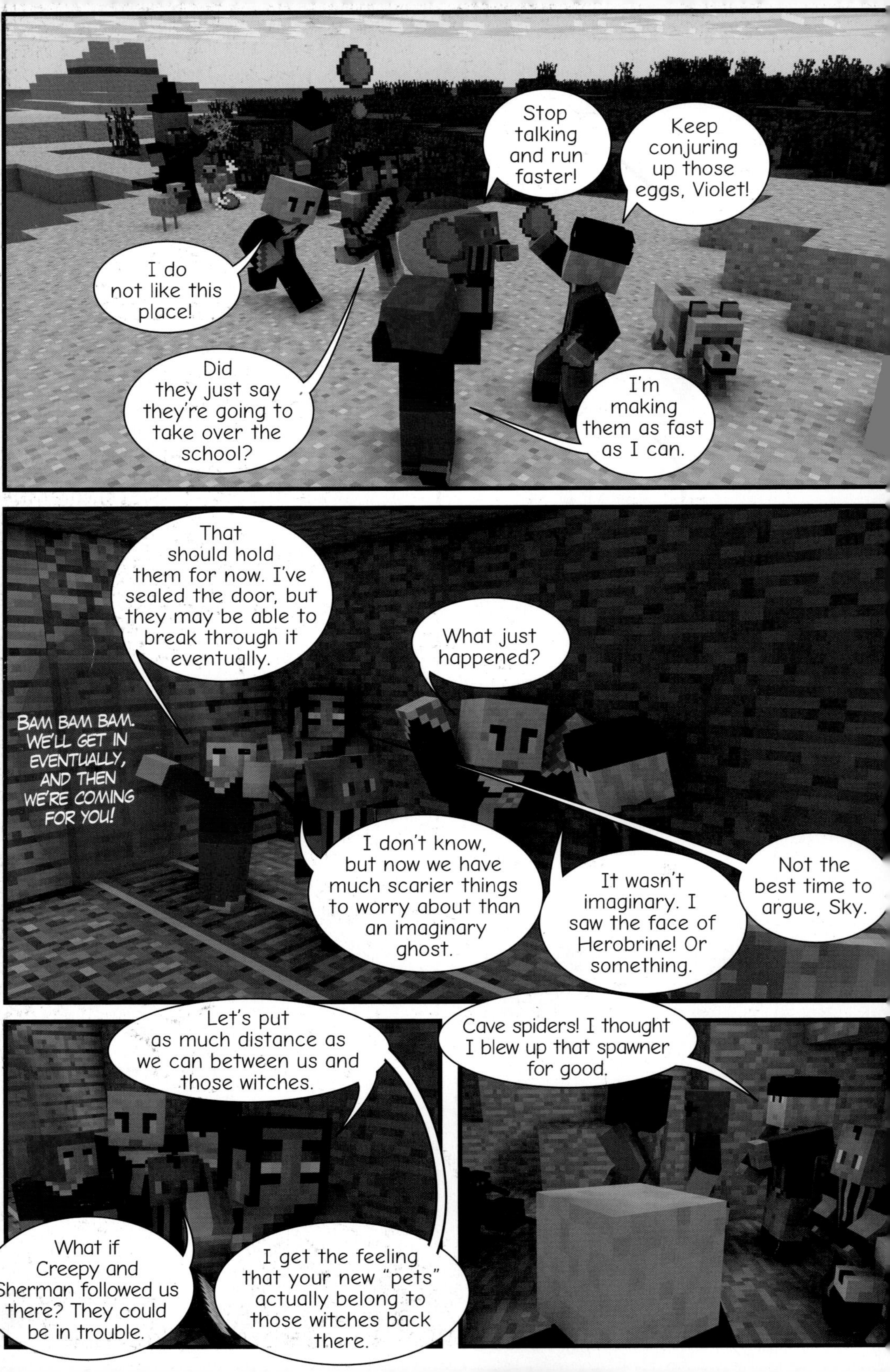
Stop talking and run faster!
Keep conjuring up those eggs, Violet!
I do not like this place!
Did they just say they're going to take over the school?
I'm making them as fast as I can.
That should hold them for now. I've sealed the door, but they may be able to break through it eventually.
What just happened?
BAM BAM BAM. WE'LL GET IN EVENTUALLY, AND THEN WE'RE COMING FOR YOU!
I don't know, but now we have much scarier things to worry about than an imaginary ghost.
It wasn't imaginary. I saw the face of Herobrine! Or something.
Not the best time to argue, Sky.
Let's put as much distance as we can between us and those witches.
What if Creepy and Sherman followed us there? They could be in trouble.
I get the feeling that your new "pets" actually belong to those witches back there.
Cave spiders! I thought I blew up that spawner for good.

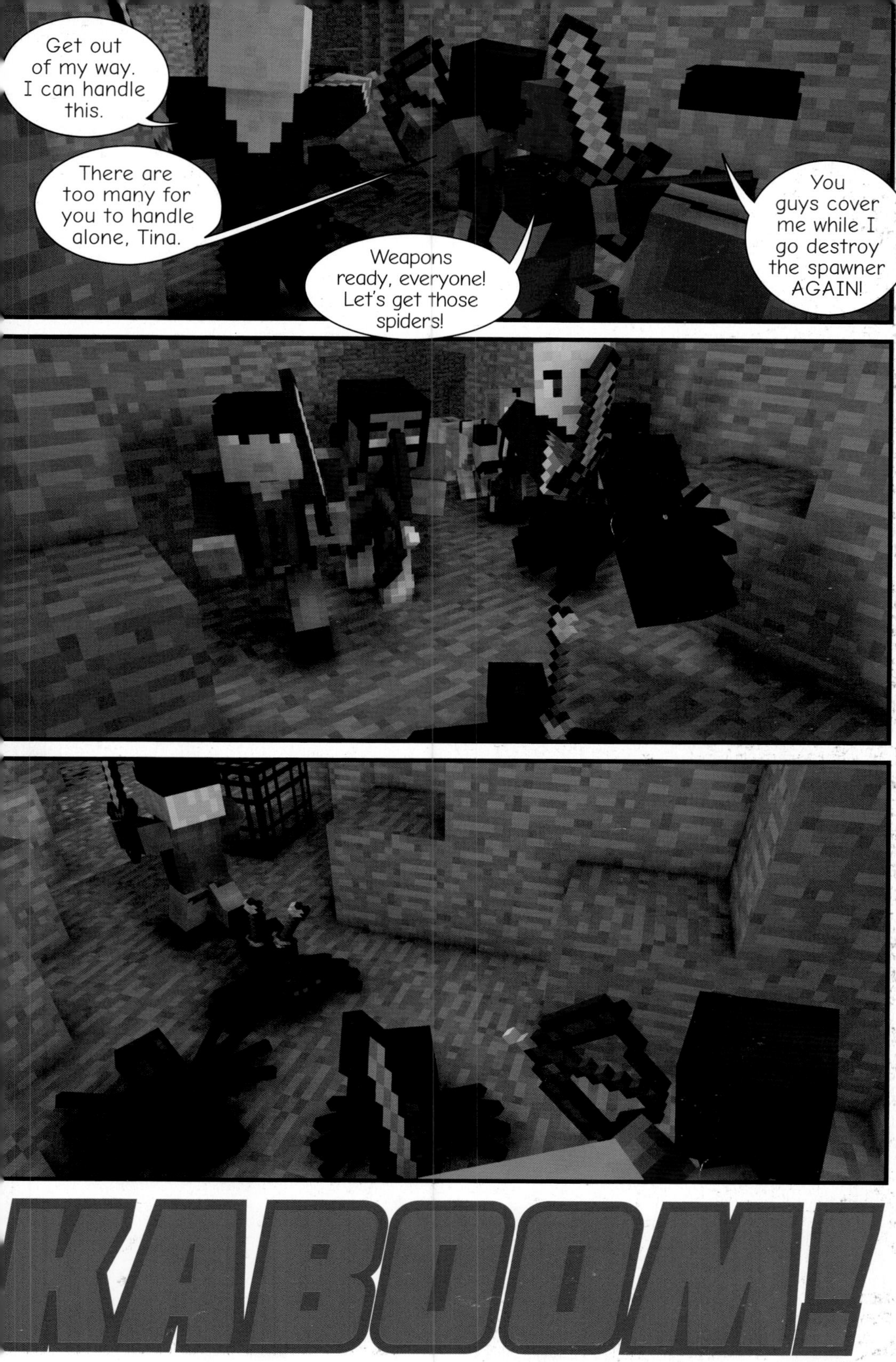
Get out of my way. I can handle this.
There are too many for you to handle alone, Tina.
Weapons ready, everyone! Let's get those spiders!
You guys cover me while I go destroy the spawner AGAIN!
KABOOM!

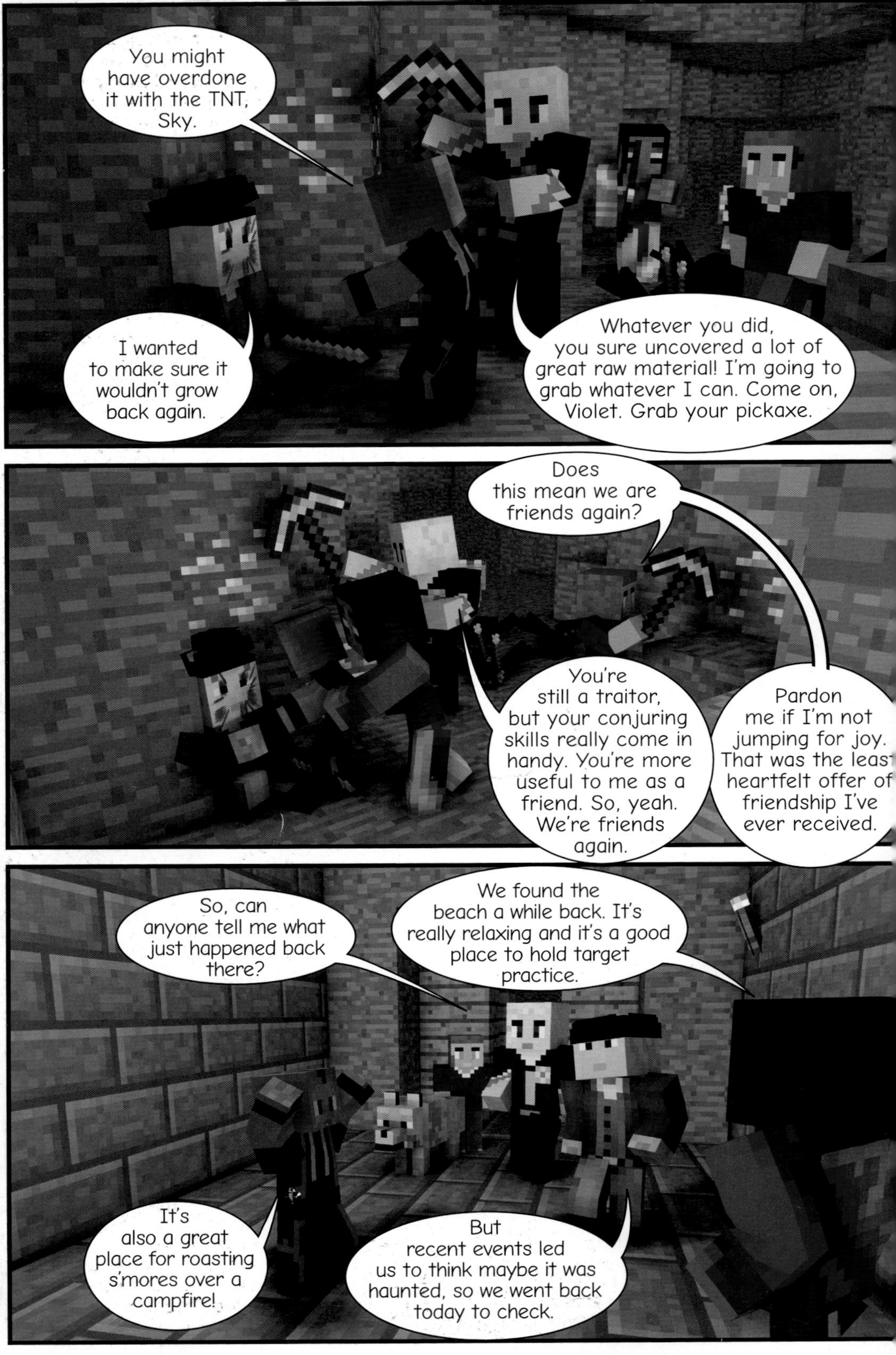
You might have overdone it with the TNT, Sky.
I wanted to make sure it wouldn't grow back again.
Whatever you did, you sure uncovered a lot of great raw material! I'm going to grab whatever I can. Come on, Violet. Grab your pickaxe.
Does this mean we are friends again?
You're still a traitor, but your conjuring skills really come in handy. You're more useful to me as a friend. So, yeah. We're friends again.
Pardon me if I'm not jumping for joy. That was the least heartfelt offer of friendship I've ever received.
So, can anyone tell me what just happened back there?
We found the beach a while back. It's really relaxing and it's a good place to hold target practice.
It's also a great place for roasting s'mores over a campfire!
But recent events led us to think maybe it was haunted, so we went back today to check.

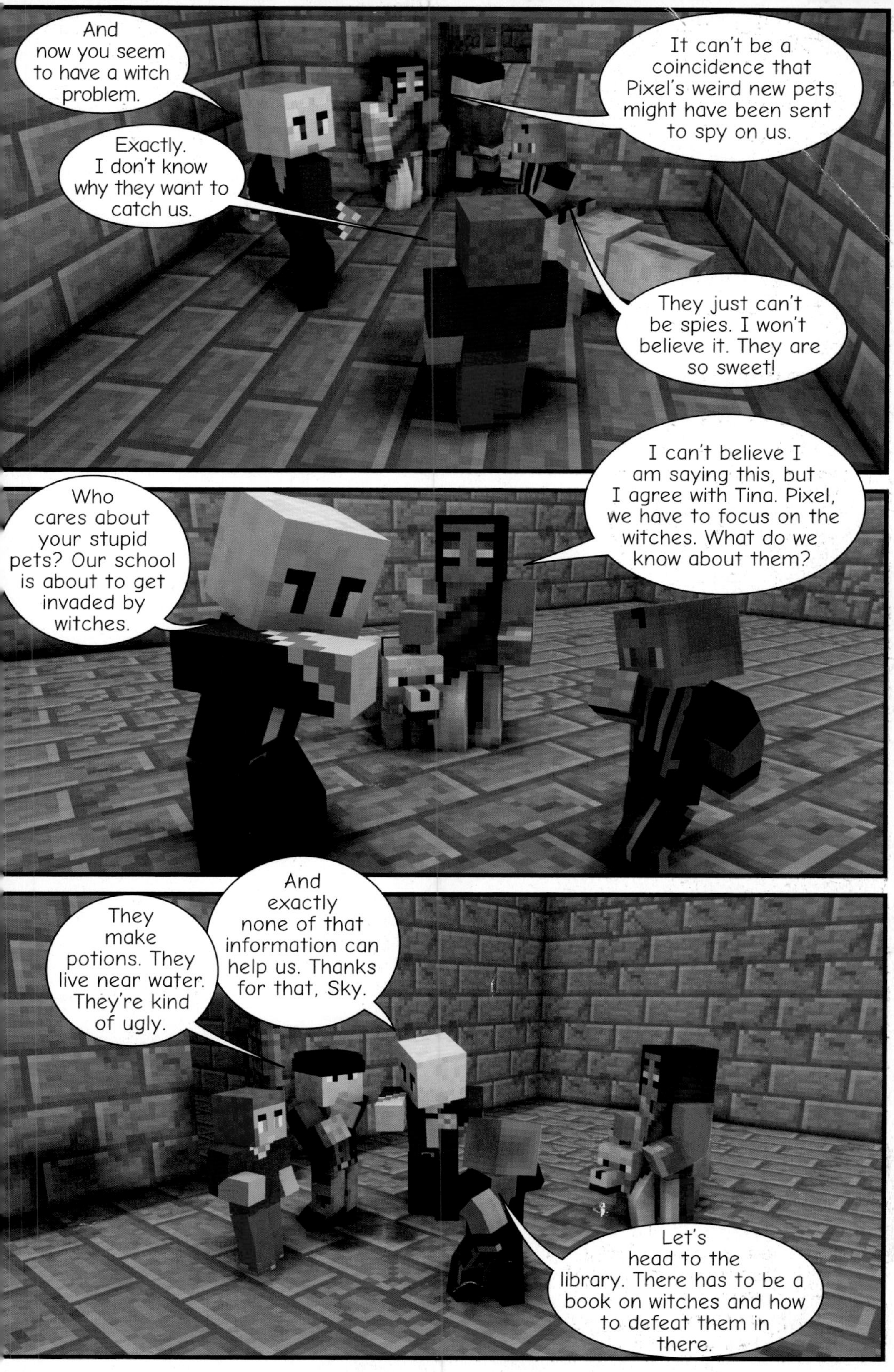
And now you seem to have a witch problem.
It can't be a coincidence that Pixel's weird new pets might have been sent to spy on us.
Exactly. I don't know why they want to catch us.
They just can't be spies. I won't believe it. They are so sweet!
Who cares about your stupid pets? Our school is about to get invaded by witches.
I can't believe I am saying this, but I agree with Tina. Pixel, we have to focus on the witches. What do we know about them?
They make potions. They live near water. They're kind of ugly.
And exactly none of that information can help us. Thanks for that, Sky.
Let's head to the library. There has to be a book on witches and how to defeat them in there.

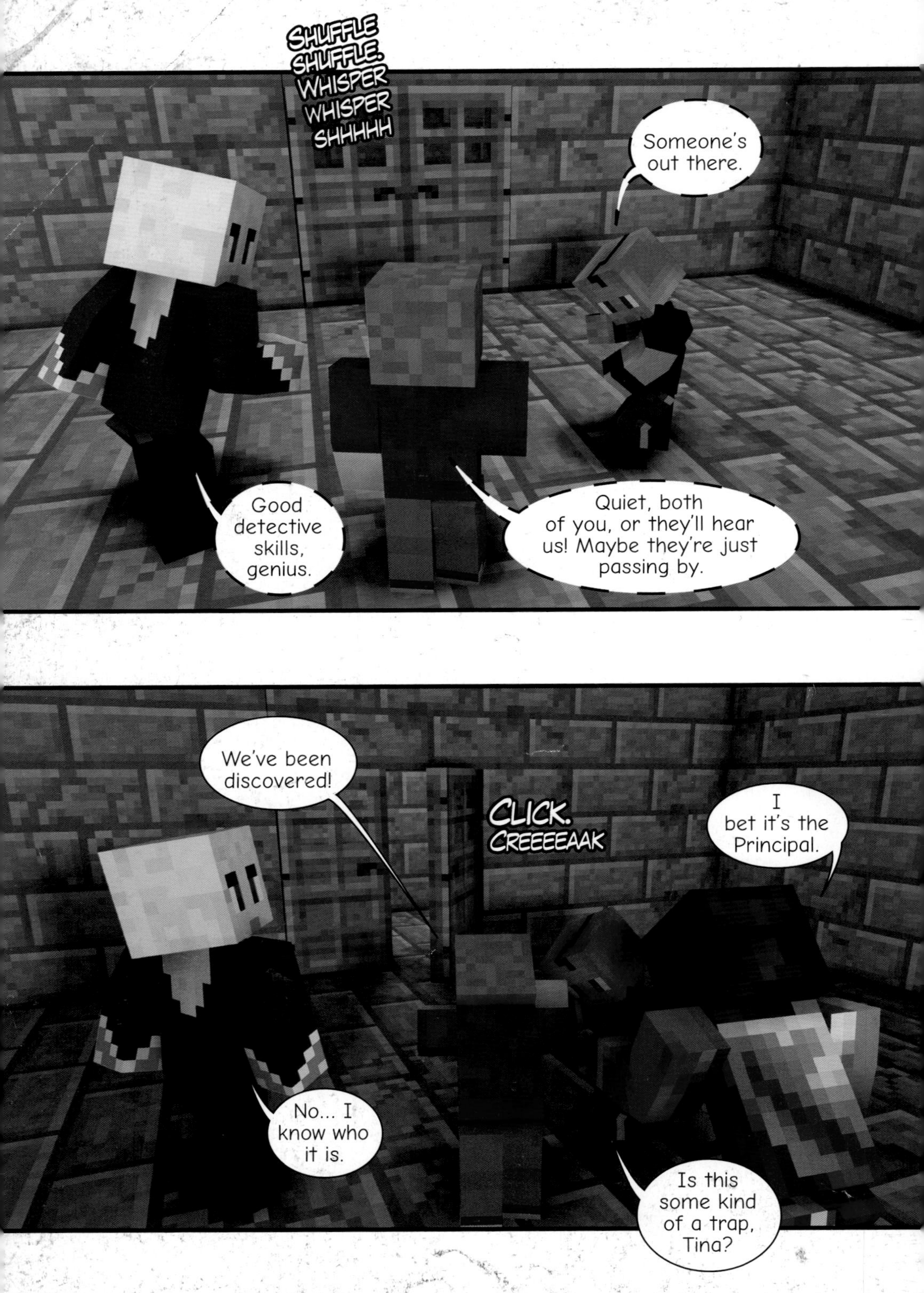
SHUFFLE SHUFFLE. WHISPER WHISPER SHHHHH
Someone's out there.
Good detective skills, genius.
Quiet, both of you, or they'll hear us! Maybe they're just passing by.
We've been discovered!
CLICK. CREEEEAAK
I bet it's the Principal.
No... I know who it is.
Is this some kind of a trap, Tina?

CHAPTER 9

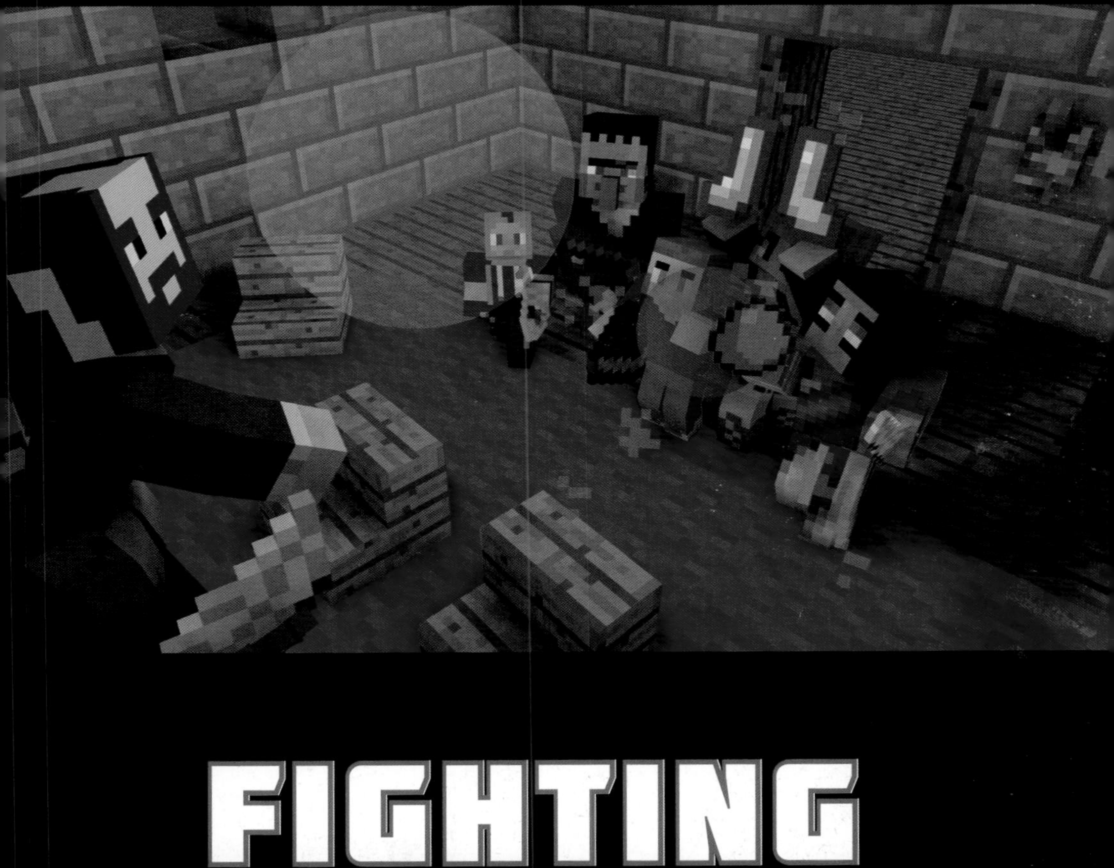

FIGHTING BACK

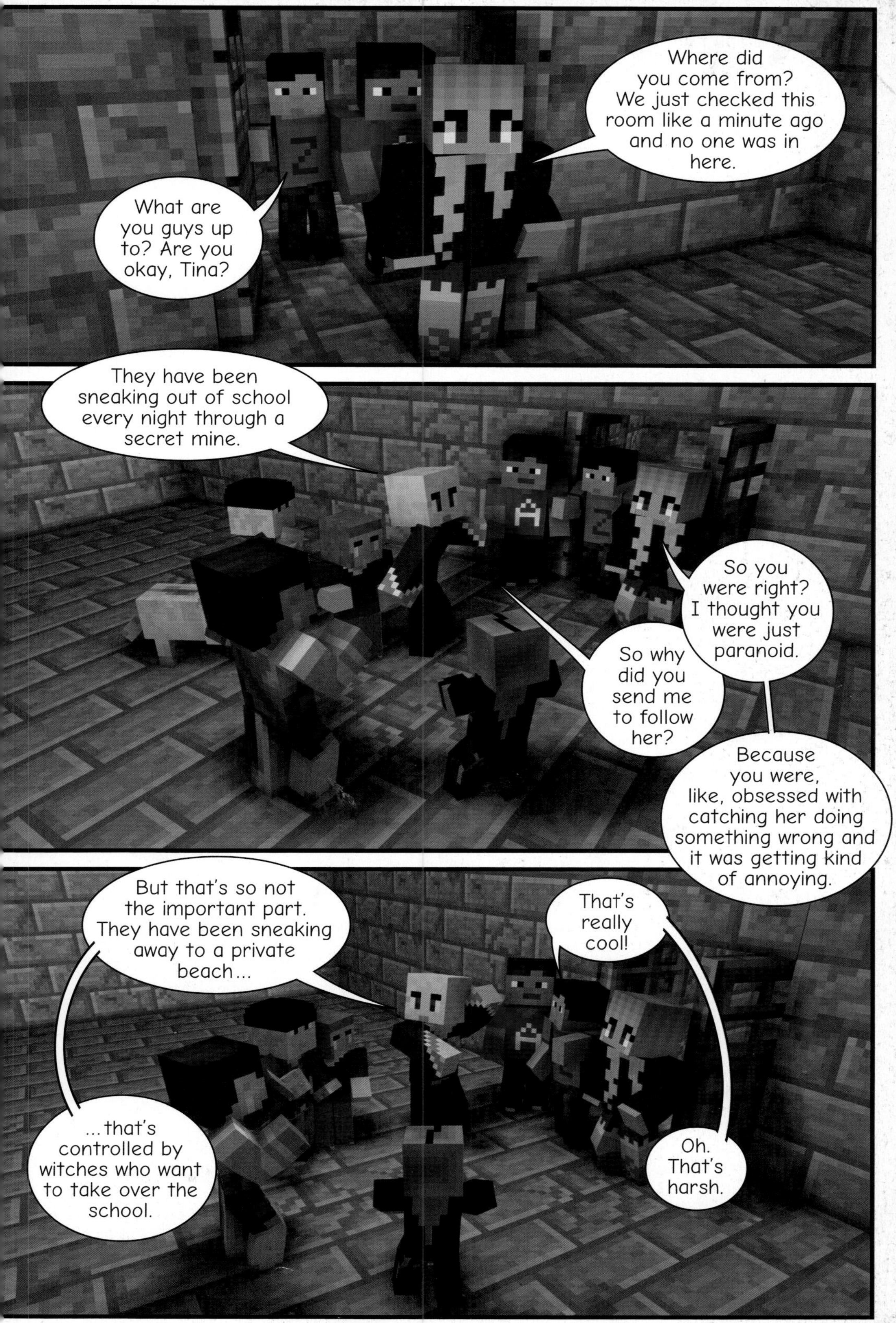

Where did you come from? We just checked this room like a minute ago and no one was in here.
What are you guys up to? Are you okay, Tina?
They have been sneaking out of school every night through a secret mine.
So you were right? I thought you were just paranoid.
So why did you send me to follow her?
Because you were, like, obsessed with catching her doing something wrong and it was getting kind of annoying.
But that's so not the important part. They have been sneaking away to a private beach...
That's really cool!
...that's controlled by witches who want to take over the school.
Oh. That's harsh.

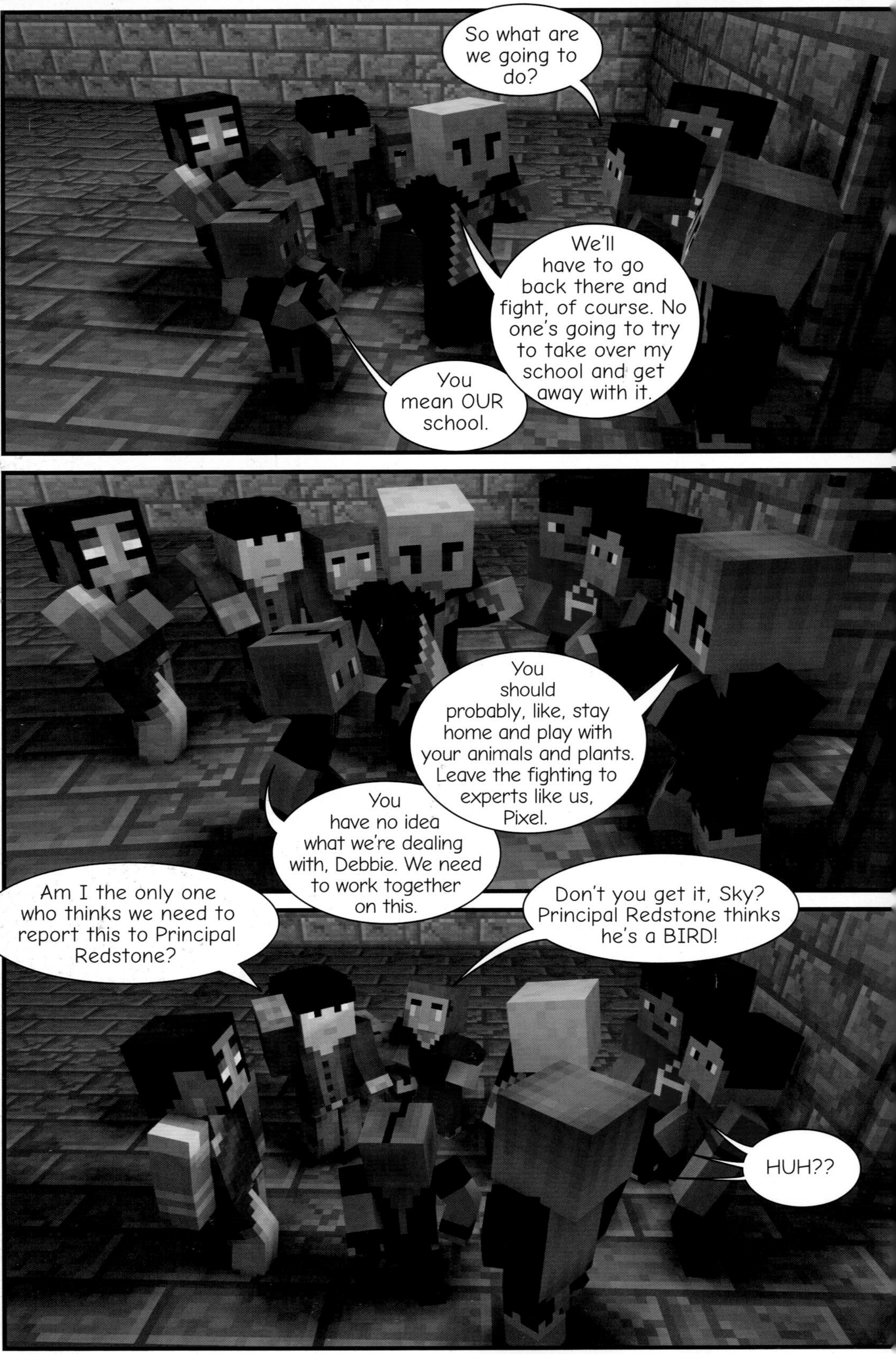
So what are we going to do?
We'll have to go back there and fight, of course. No one's going to try to take over my school and get away with it.
You mean OUR school.
You should probably, like, stay home and play with your animals and plants. Leave the fighting to experts like us, Pixel.
You have no idea what we're dealing with, Debbie. We need to work together on this.
Am I the only one who thinks we need to report this to Principal Redstone?
Don't you get it, Sky? Principal Redstone thinks he's a BIRD!
HUH??

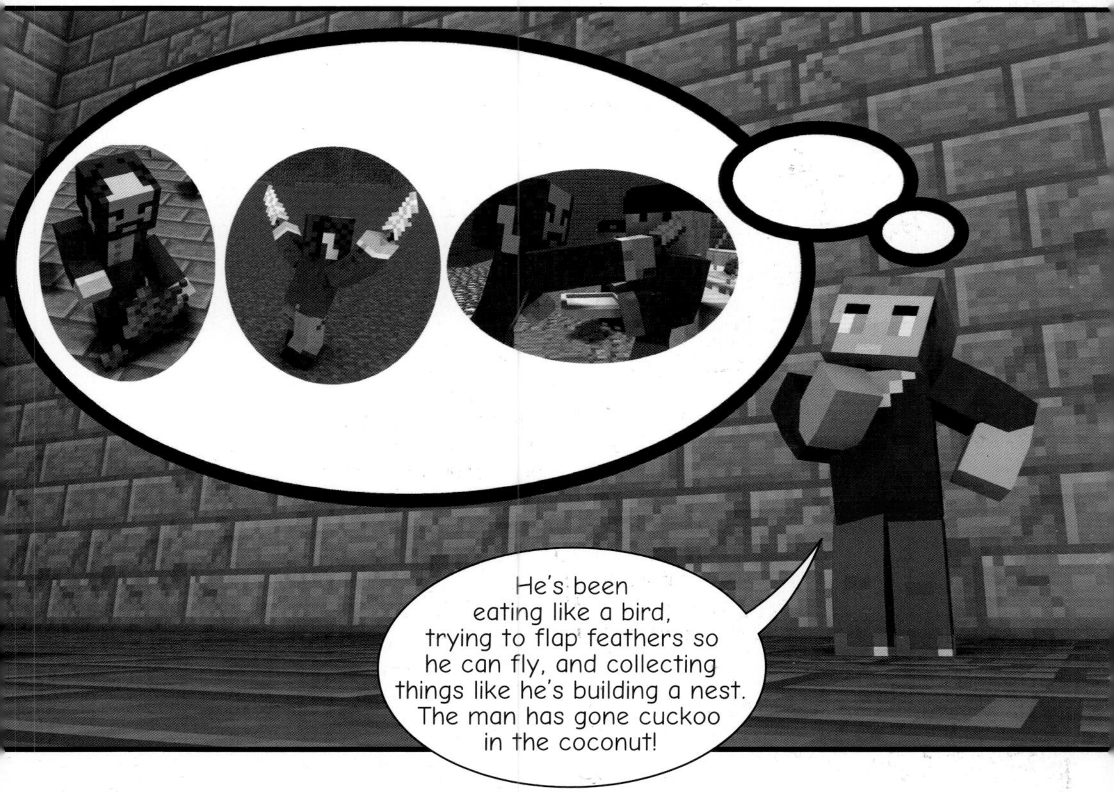
He's been eating like a bird, trying to flap feathers so he can fly, and collecting things like he's building a nest. The man has gone cuckoo in the coconut!

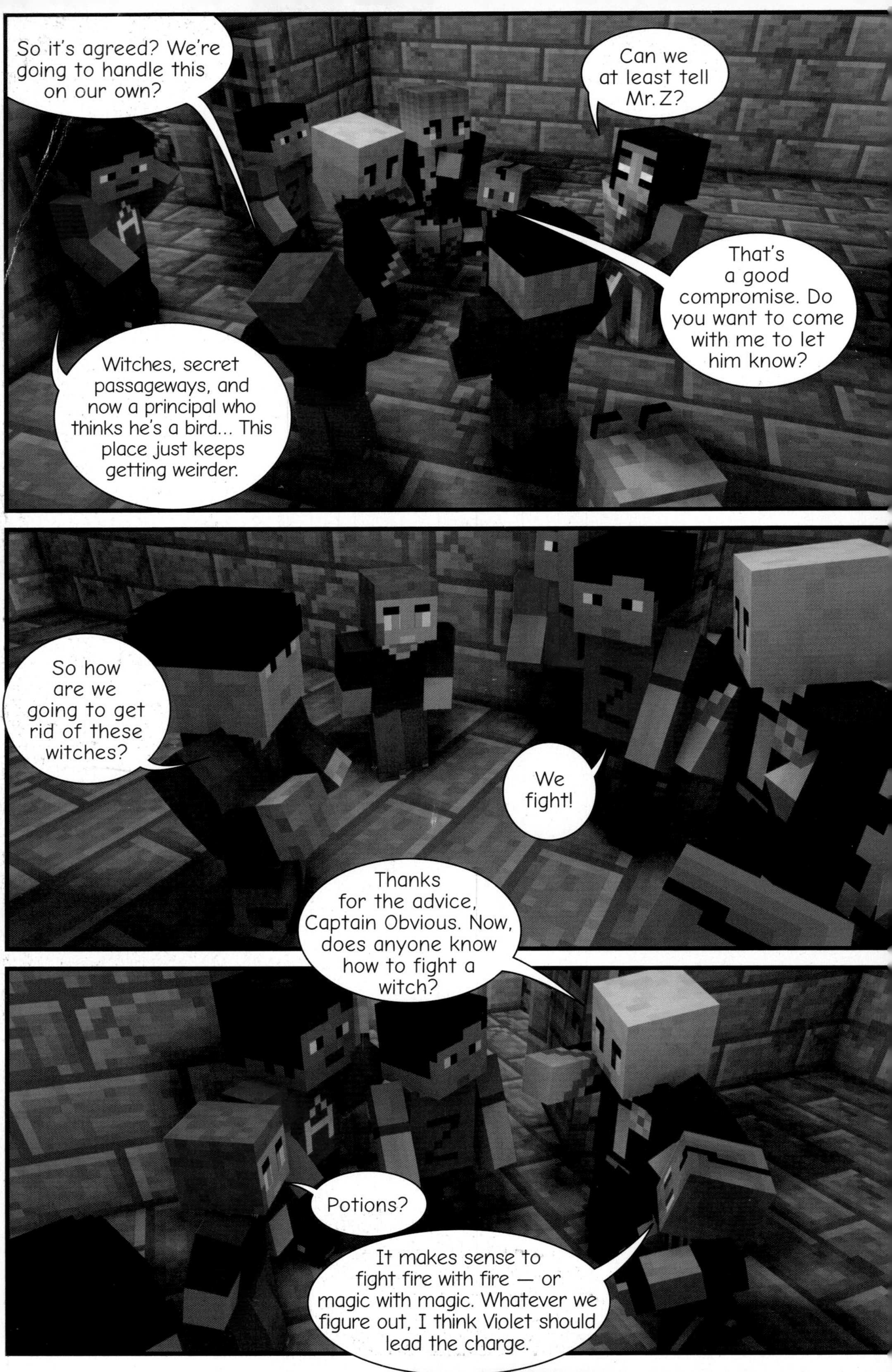

So it's agreed? We're going to handle this on our own?
Can we at least tell Mr. Z?
That's a good compromise. Do you want to come with me to let him know?
Witches, secret passageways, and now a principal who thinks he's a bird... This place just keeps getting weirder.
So how are we going to get rid of these witches?
We fight!
Thanks for the advice, Captain Obvious. Now, does anyone know how to fight a witch?
Potions?
It makes sense to fight fire with fire — or magic with magic. Whatever we figure out, I think Violet should lead the charge.

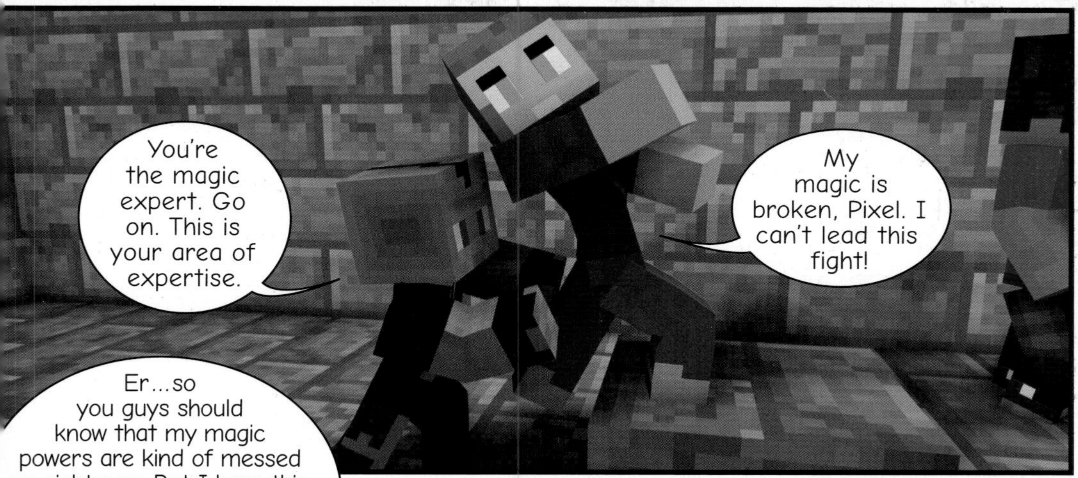
You're the magic expert. Go on. This is your area of expertise.
My magic is broken, Pixel. I can't lead this fight!

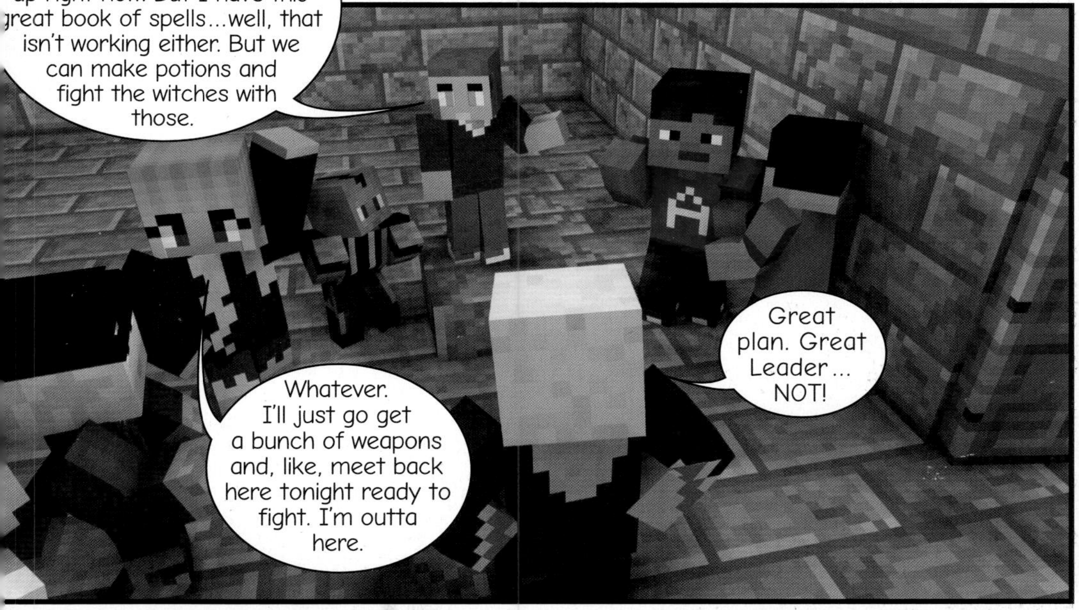
Er...so you guys should know that my magic powers are kind of messed up right now. But I have this great book of spells...well, that isn't working either. But we can make potions and fight the witches with those.
Whatever. I'll just go get a bunch of weapons and, like, meet back here tonight ready to fight. I'm outta here.
Great plan. Great Leader... NOT!

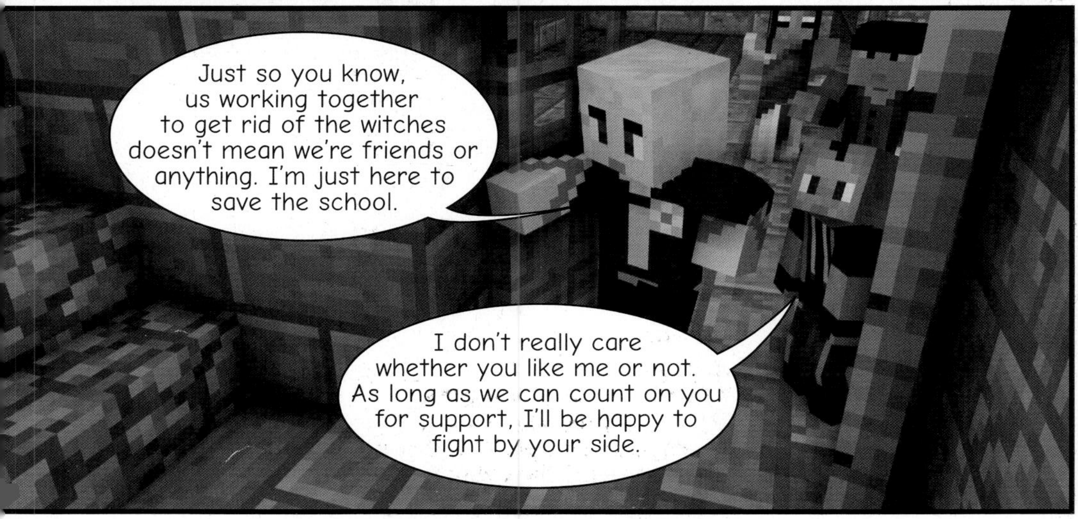
Just so you know, us working together to get rid of the witches doesn't mean we're friends or anything. I'm just here to save the school.
I don't really care whether you like me or not. As long as we can count on you for support, I'll be happy to fight by your side.

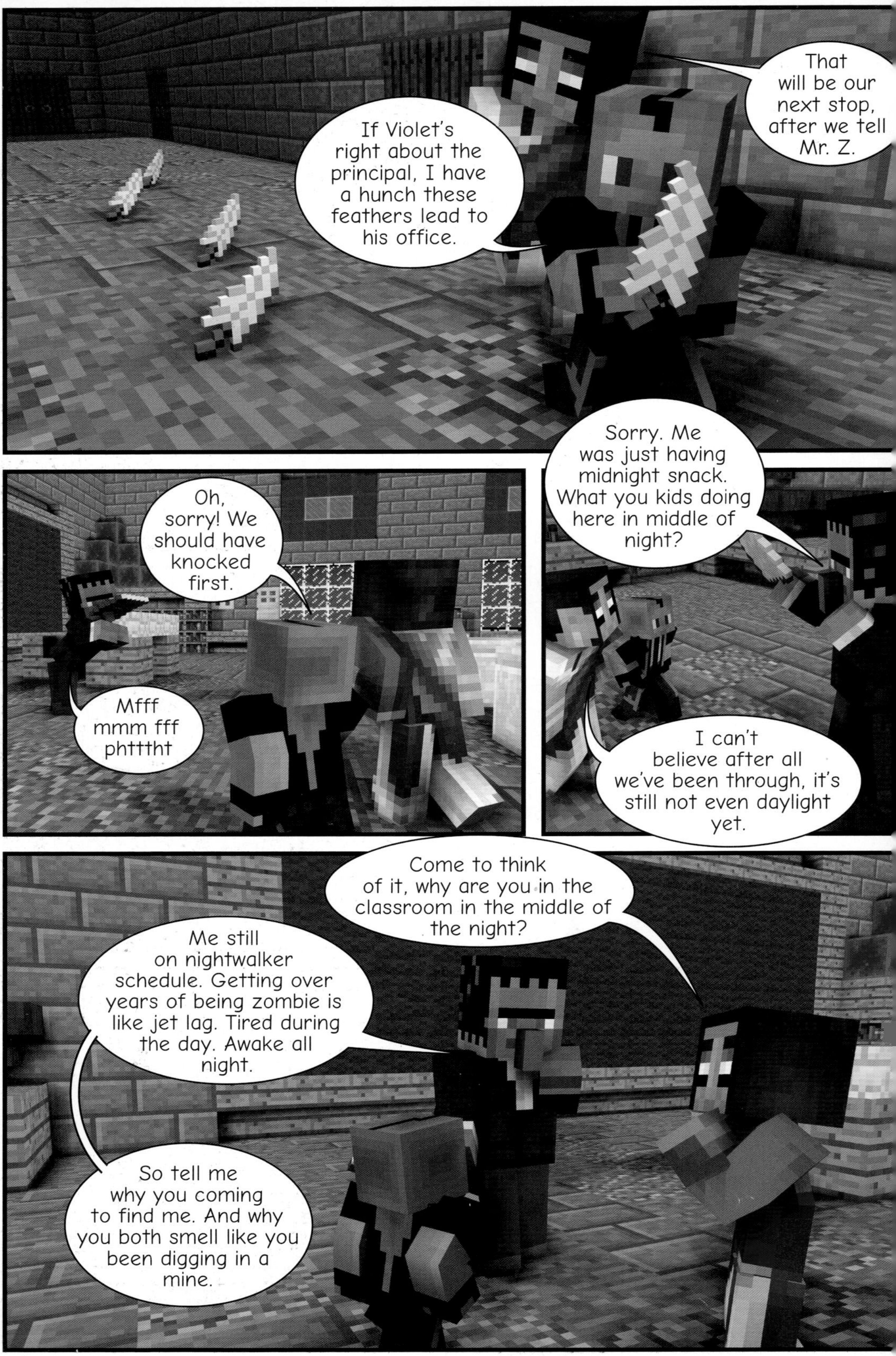
If Violet's right about the principal, I have a hunch these feathers lead to his office.
That will be our next stop, after we tell Mr. Z.
Oh, sorry! We should have knocked first.
Mfff mmm fff phtttht
Sorry. Me was just having midnight snack. What you kids doing here in middle of night?
I can't believe after all we've been through, it's still not even daylight yet.
Come to think of it, why are you in the classroom in the middle of the night?
Me still on nightwalker schedule. Getting over years of being zombie is like jet lag. Tired during the day. Awake all night.
So tell me why you coming to find me. And why you both smell like you been digging in a mine.

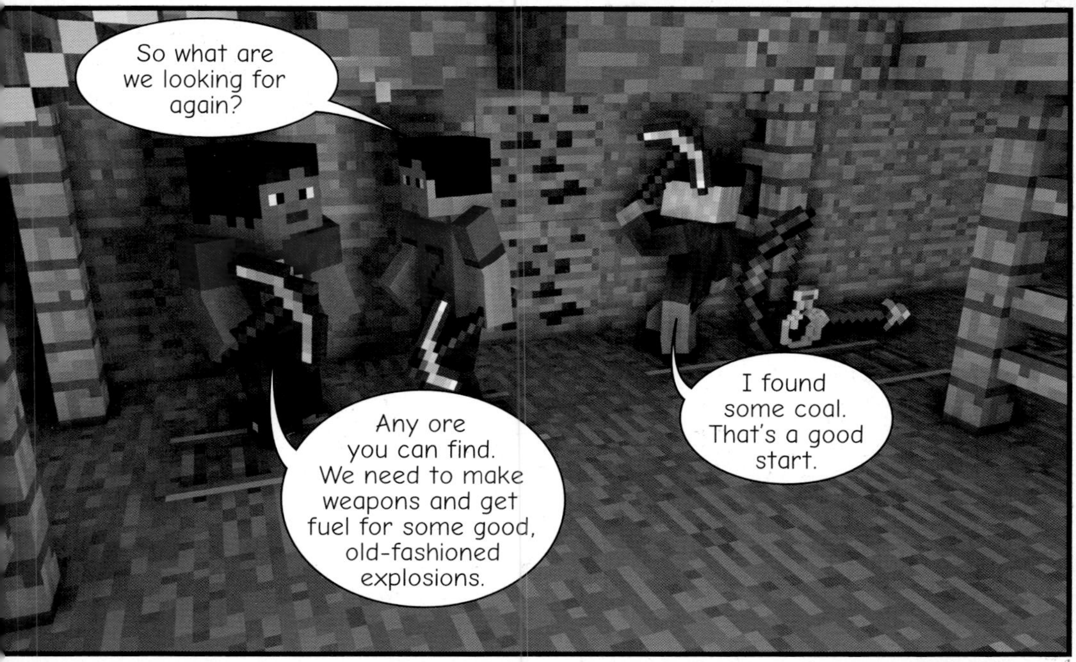
So what are we looking for again?
Any ore you can find. We need to make weapons and get fuel for some good, old-fashioned explosions.
I found some coal. That's a good start.

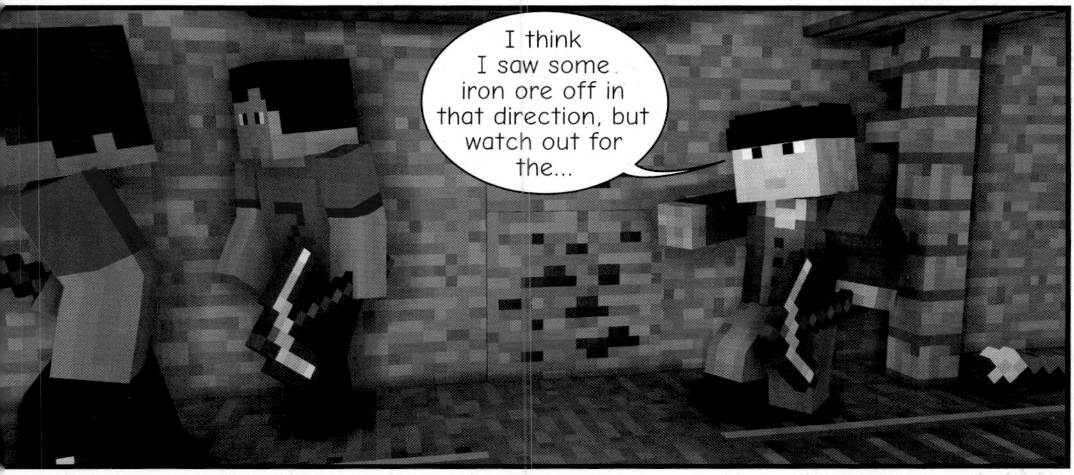
I think I saw some iron ore off in that direction, but watch out for the...

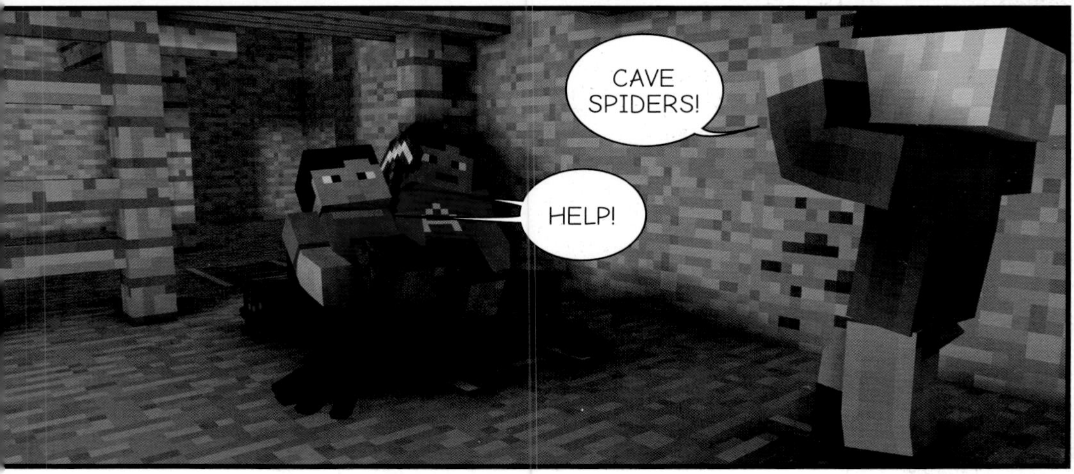
CAVE SPIDERS!
HELP!

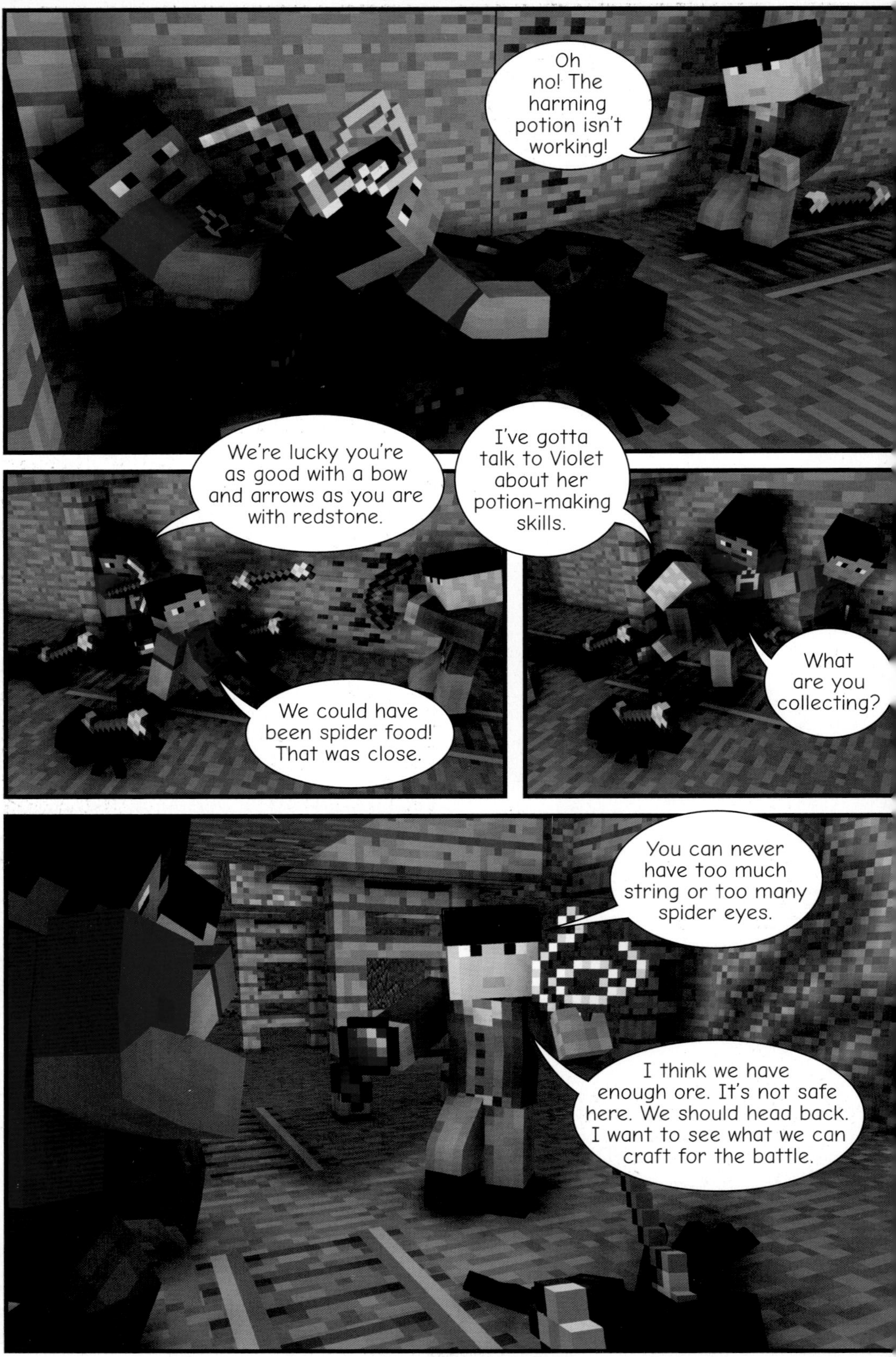
Oh no! The harming potion isn't working!
We're lucky you're as good with a bow and arrows as you are with redstone.
We could have been spider food! That was close.
I've gotta talk to Violet about her potion-making skills.
What are you collecting?
You can never have too much string or too many spider eyes.
I think we have enough ore. It's not safe here. We should head back. I want to see what we can craft for the battle.

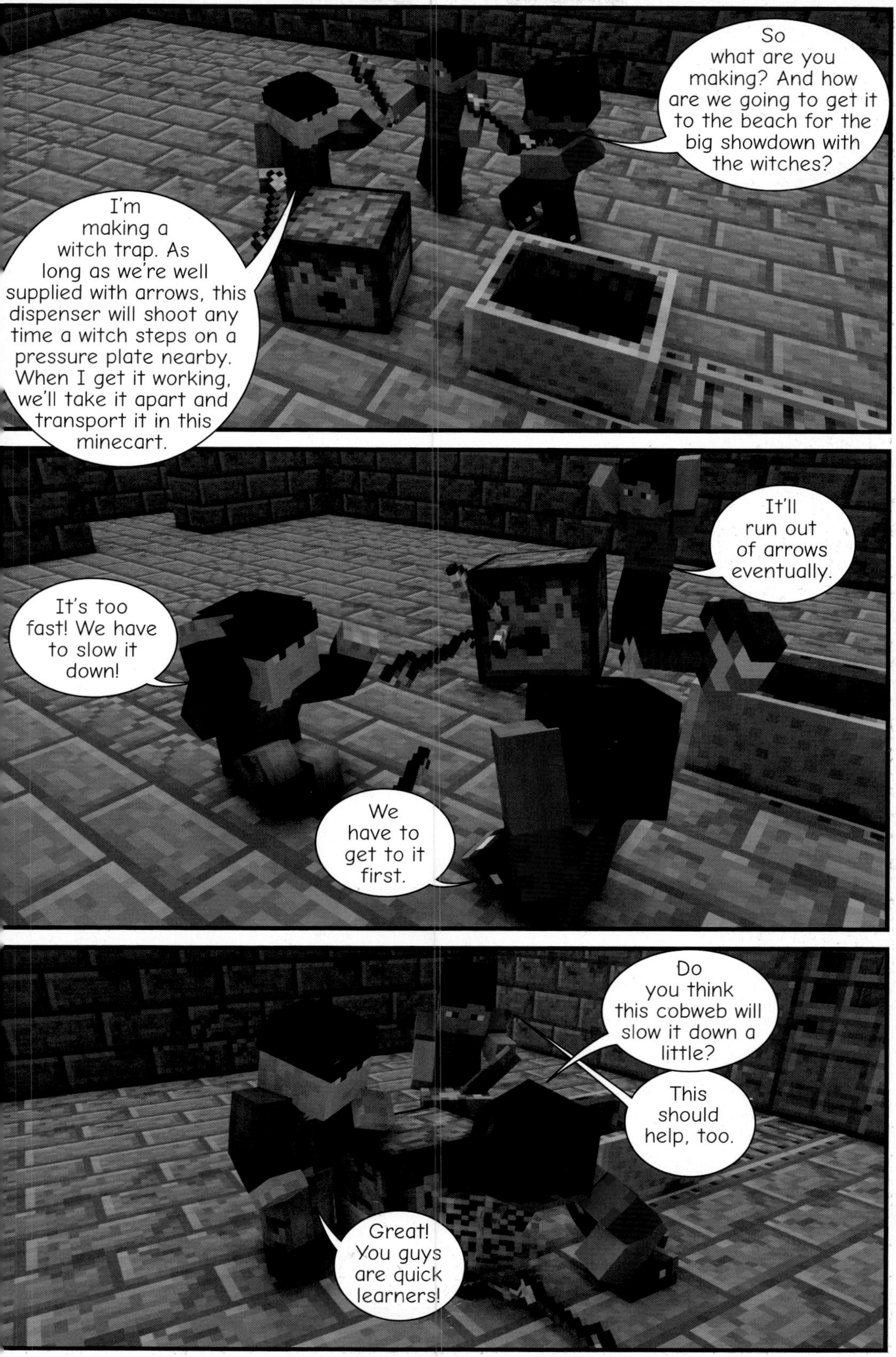

So what are you making? And how are we going to get it to the beach for the big showdown with the witches?
I'm making a witch trap. As long as we're well supplied with arrows, this dispenser will shoot any time a witch steps on a pressure plate nearby. When I get it working, we'll take it apart and transport it in this minecart.
It'll run out of arrows eventually.
It's too fast! We have to slow it down!
We have to get to it first.
Do you think this cobweb will slow it down a little?
This should help, too.
Great! You guys are quick learners!

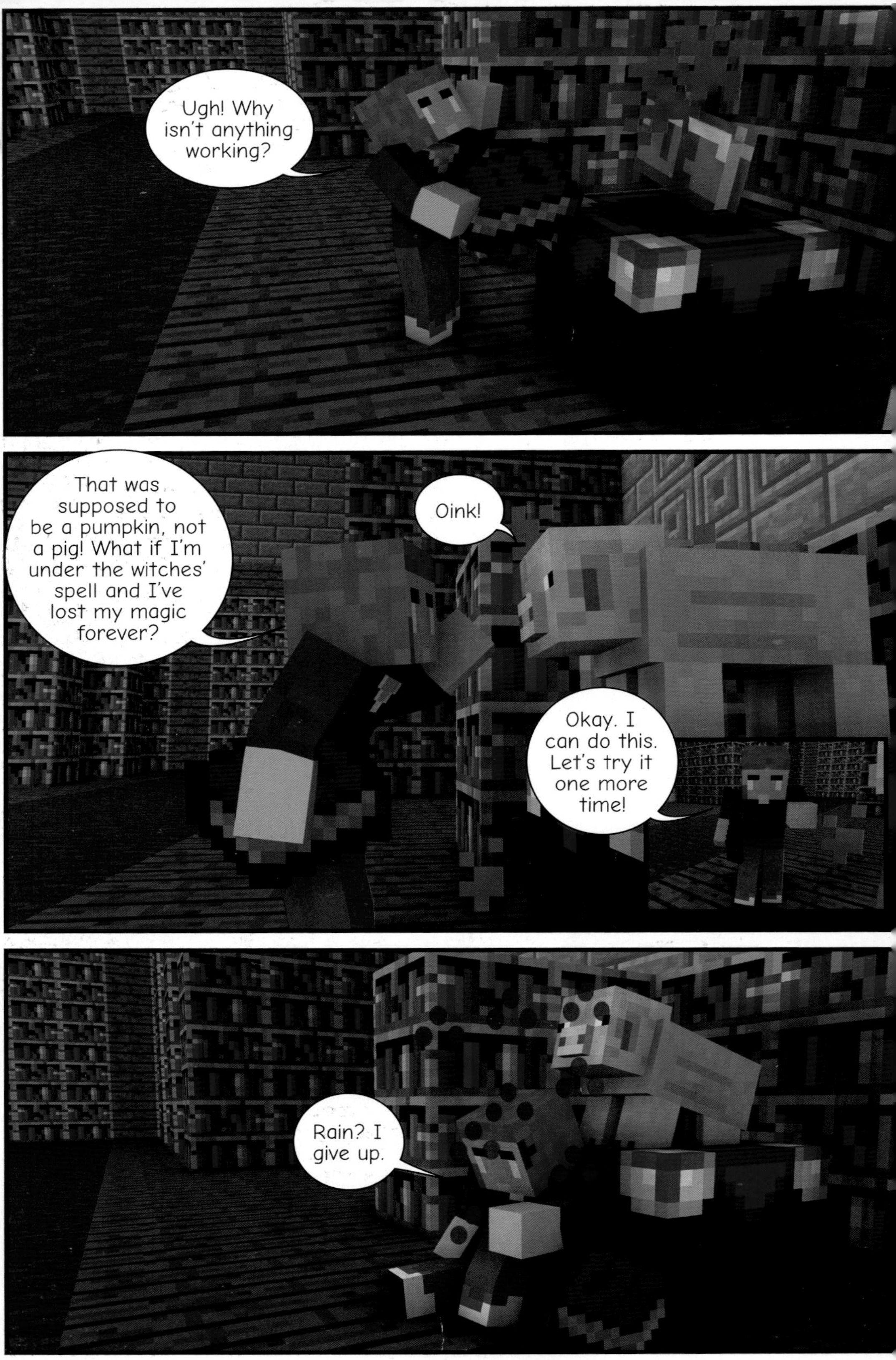
Ugh! Why isn't anything working?
That was supposed to be a pumpkin, not a pig! What if I'm under the witches' spell and I've lost my magic forever?
Oink!
Okay. I can do this. Let's try it one more time!
Rain? I give up.

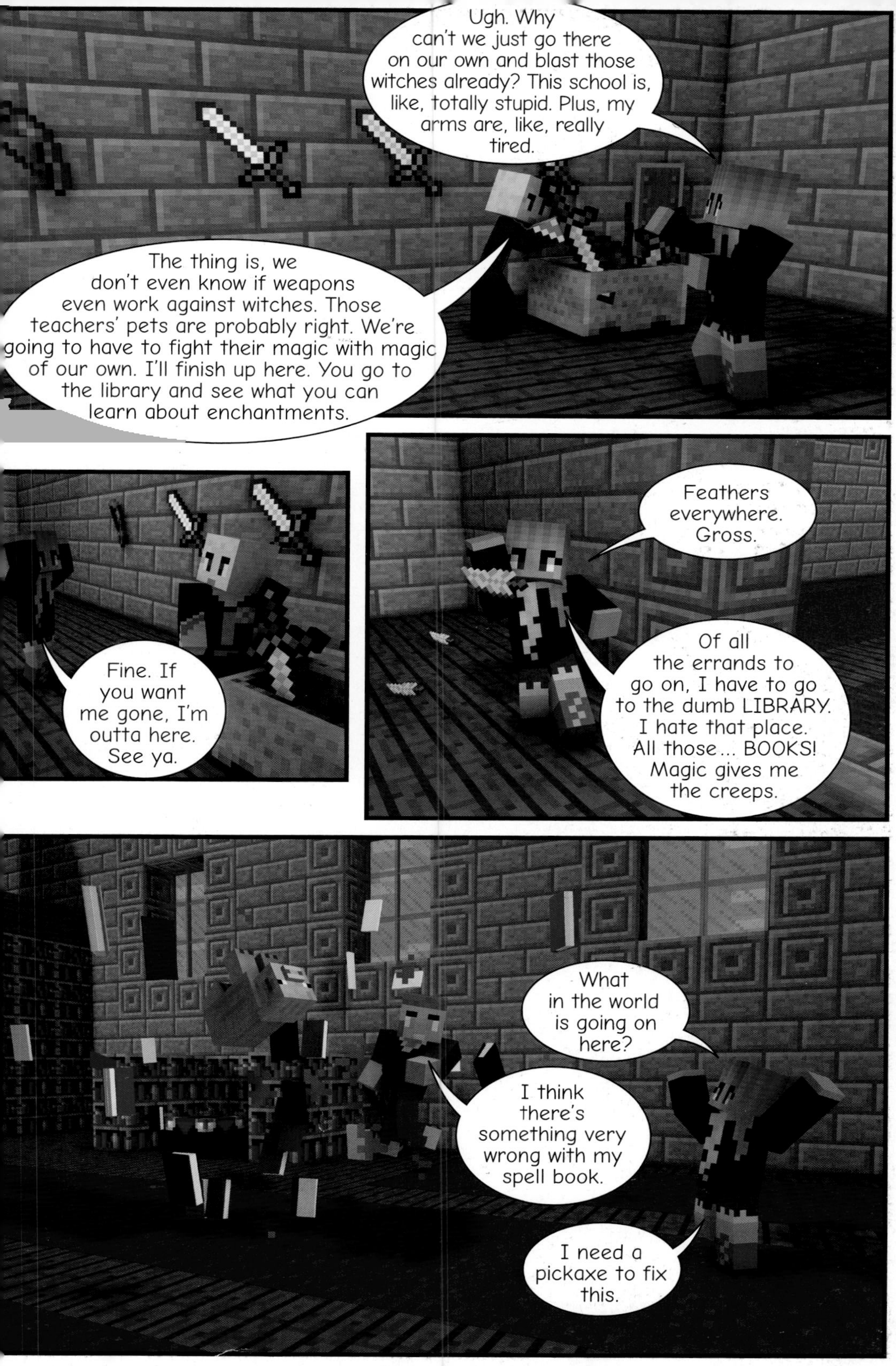
Ugh. Why can't we just go there on our own and blast those witches already? This school is, like, totally stupid. Plus, my arms are, like, really tired.
The thing is, we don't even know if weapons even work against witches. Those teachers' pets are probably right. We're going to have to fight their magic with magic of our own. I'll finish up here. You go to the library and see what you can learn about enchantments.
Fine. If you want me gone, I'm outta here. See ya.
Feathers everywhere. Gross.
Of all the errands to go on, I have to go to the dumb LIBRARY. I hate that place. All those... BOOKS! Magic gives me the creeps.
What in the world is going on here?
I think there's something very wrong with my spell book.
I need a pickaxe to fix this.

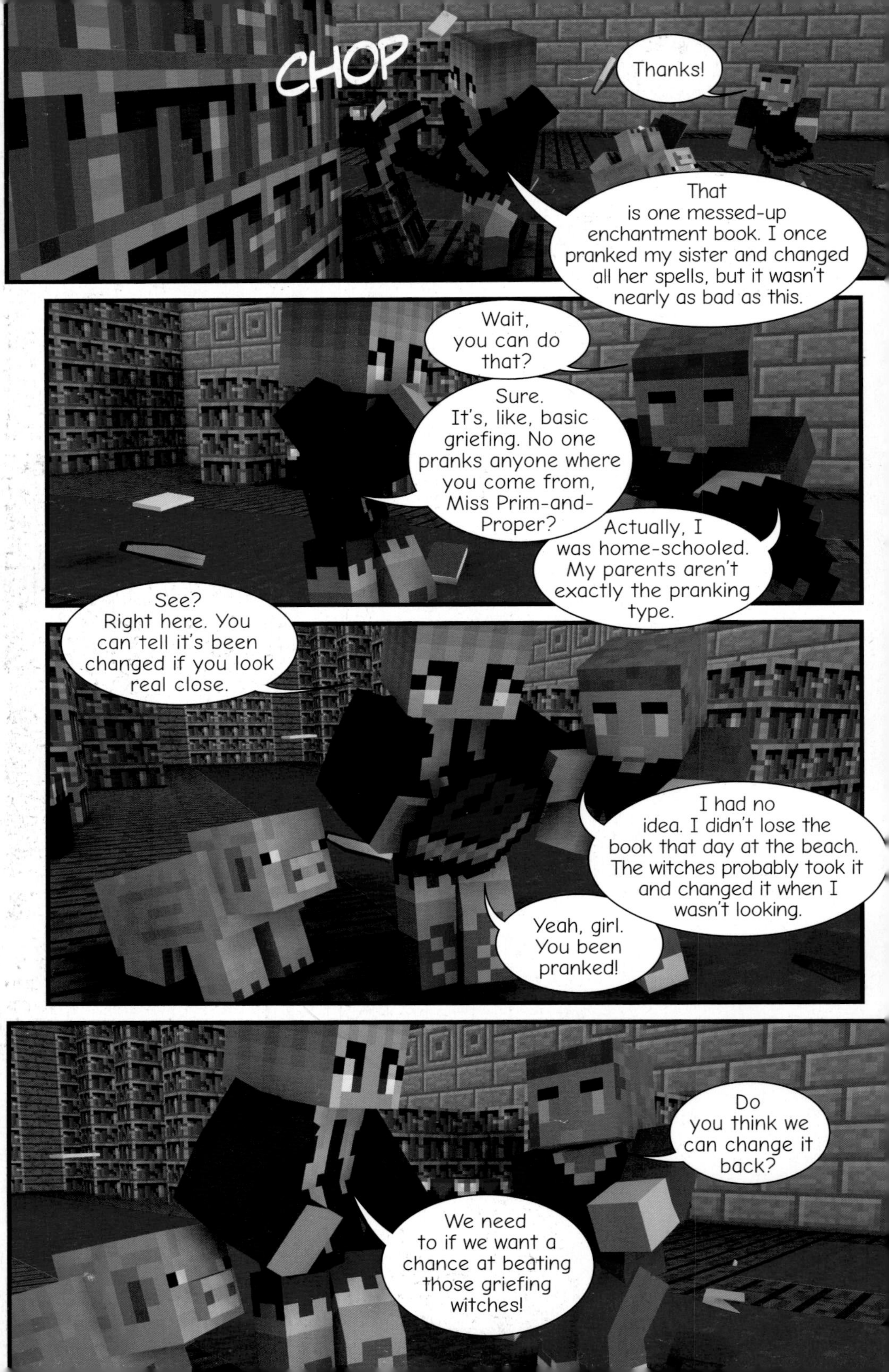
CHOP
Thanks!
That is one messed-up enchantment book. I once pranked my sister and changed all her spells, but it wasn't nearly as bad as this.
Wait, you can do that?
Sure. It's, like, basic griefing. No one pranks anyone where you come from, Miss Prim-and-Proper?
Actually, I was home-schooled. My parents aren't exactly the pranking type.
See? Right here. You can tell it's been changed if you look real close.
I had no idea. I didn't lose the book that day at the beach. The witches probably took it and changed it when I wasn't looking.
Yeah, girl. You been pranked!
Do you think we can change it back?
We need to if we want a chance at beating those griefing witches!

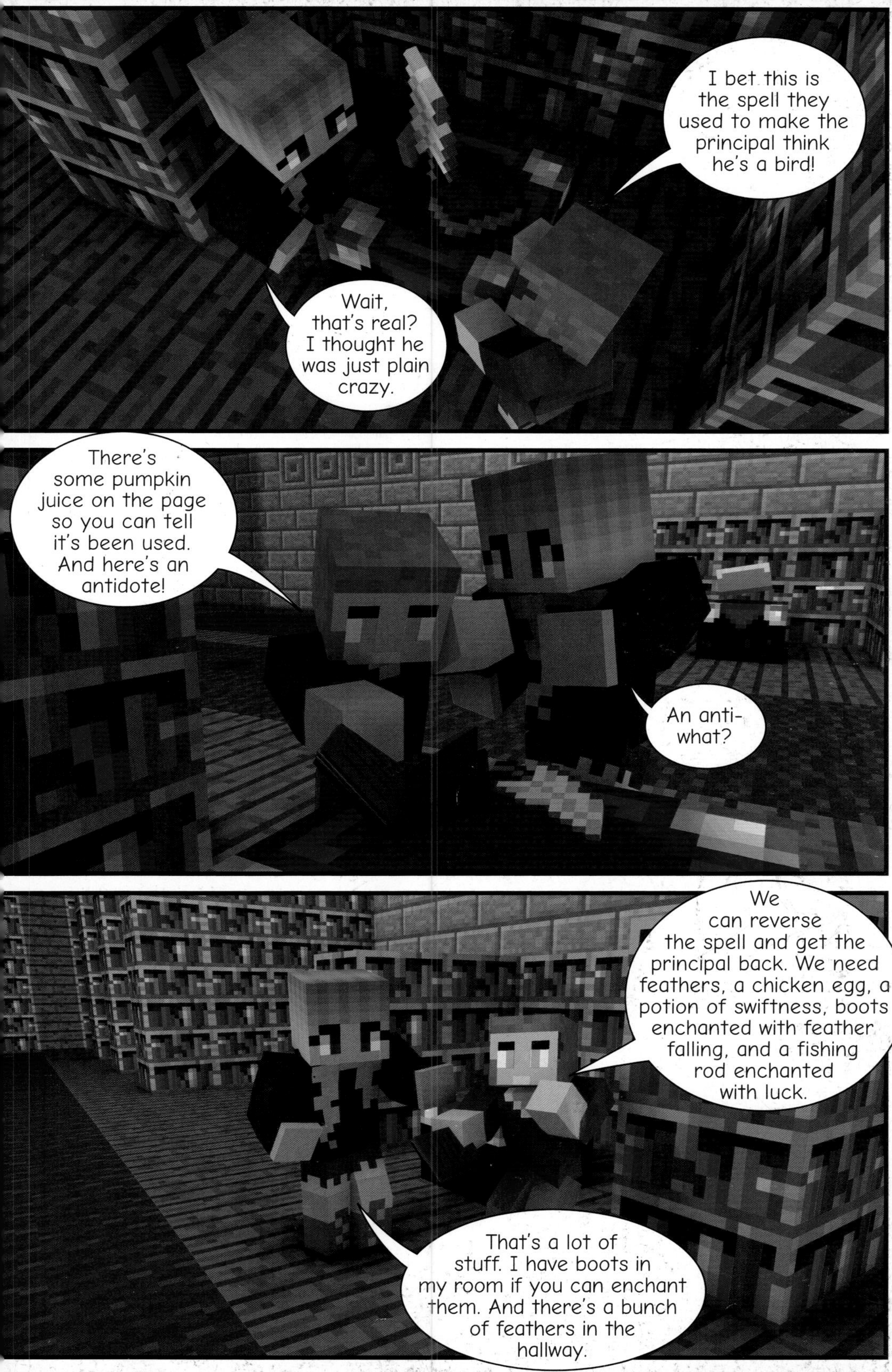
I bet this is the spell they used to make the principal think he's a bird!
Wait, that's real? I thought he was just plain crazy.
There's some pumpkin juice on the page so you can tell it's been used. And here's an antidote!
An anti-what?
We can reverse the spell and get the principal back. We need feathers, a chicken egg, a potion of swiftness, boots enchanted with feather falling, and a fishing rod enchanted with luck.
That's a lot of stuff. I have boots in my room if you can enchant them. And there's a bunch of feathers in the hallway.

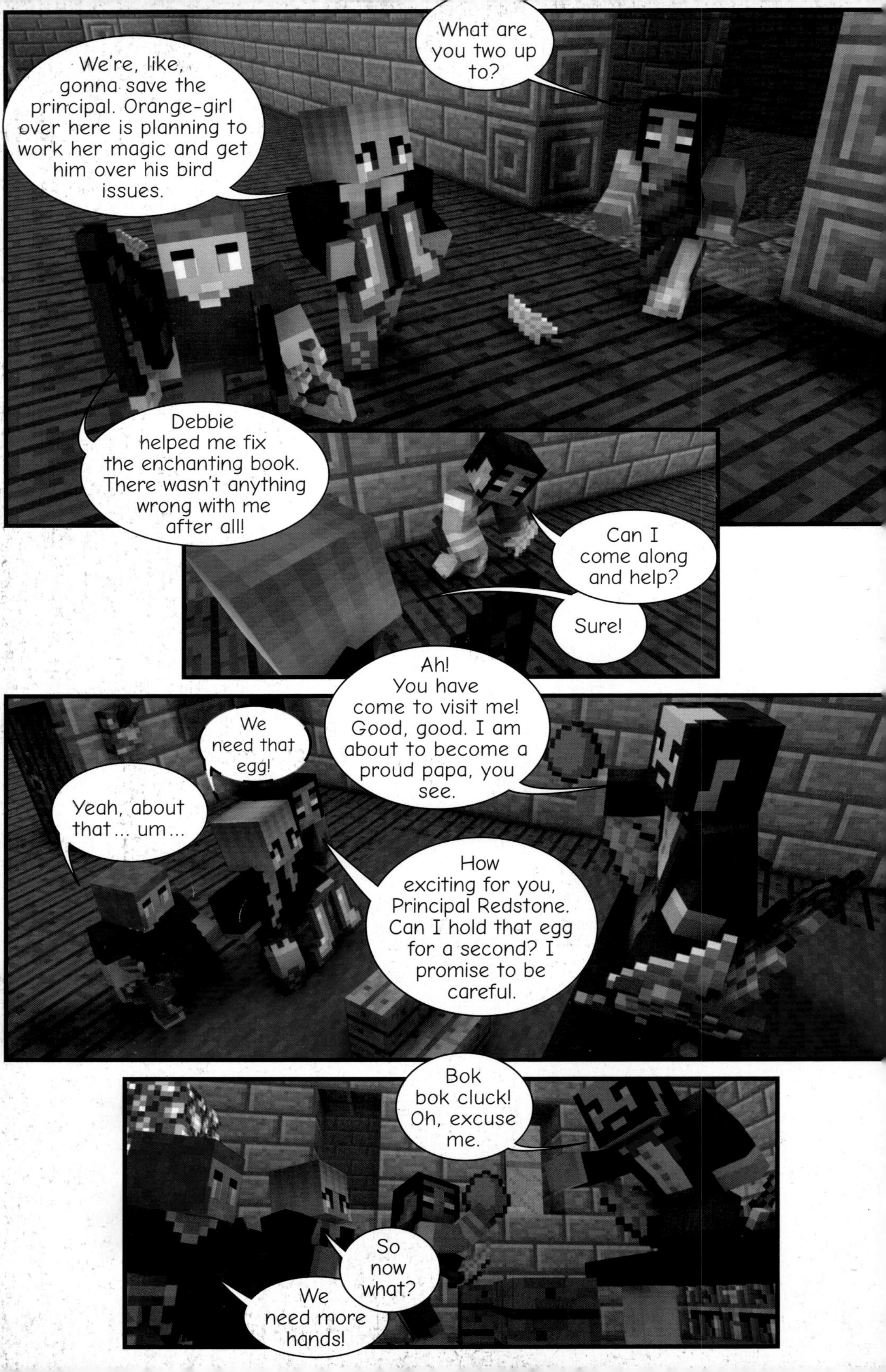

We're, like, gonna save the principal. Orange-girl over here is planning to work her magic and get him over his bird issues.
What are you two up to?
Debbie helped me fix the enchanting book. There wasn't anything wrong with me after all!
Can I come along and help?
Sure!
Ah! You have come to visit me! Good, good. I am about to become a proud papa, you see.
We need that egg!
Yeah, about that... um...
How exciting for you, Principal Redstone. Can I hold that egg for a second? I promise to be careful.
Bok bok cluck! Oh, excuse me.
So now what?
We need more hands!

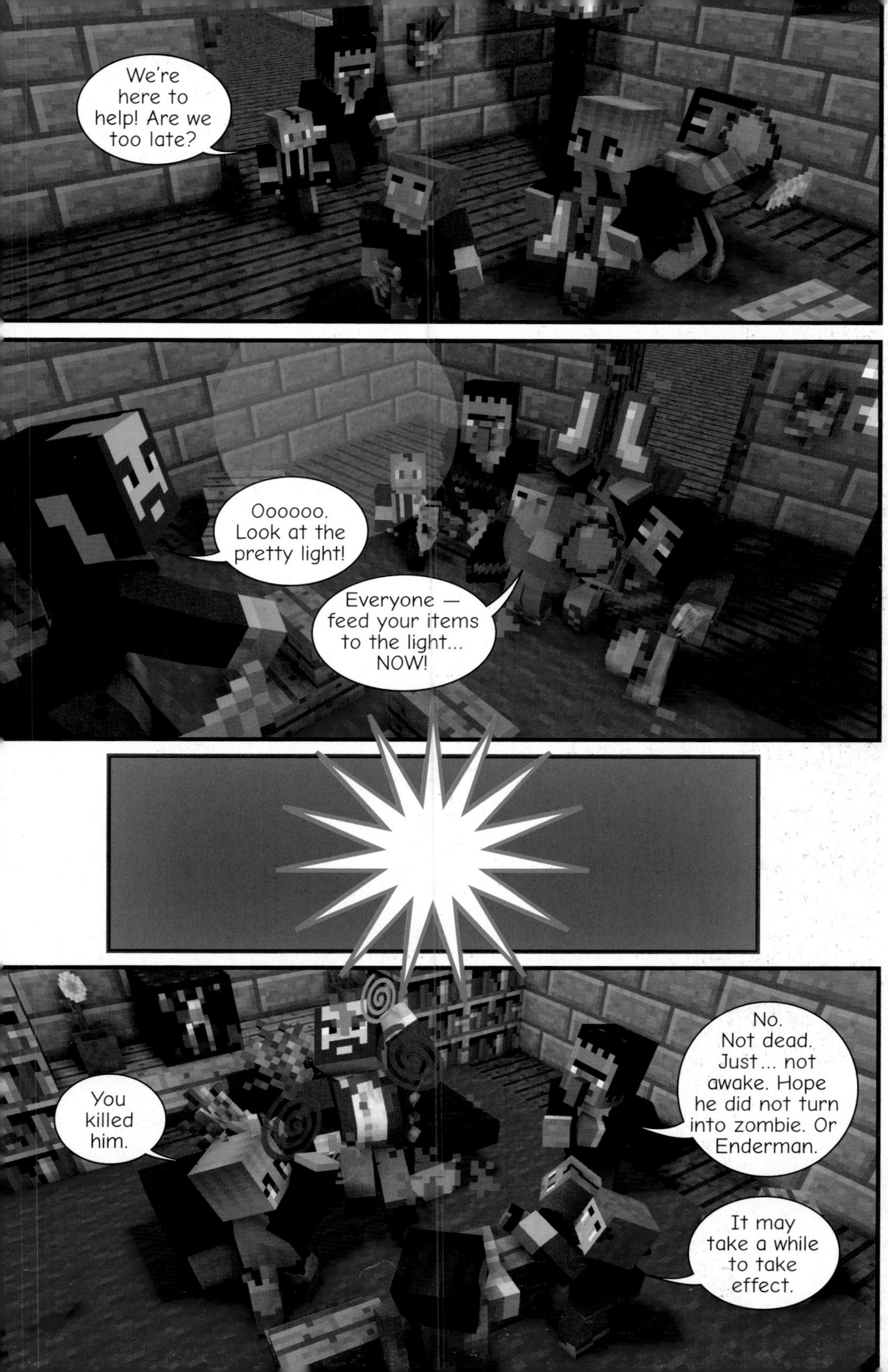
We're here to help! Are we too late?
Oooooo. Look at the pretty light!
Everyone — feed your items to the light... NOW!
You killed him.
No. Not dead. Just... not awake. Hope he did not turn into zombie. Or Enderman.
It may take a while to take effect.

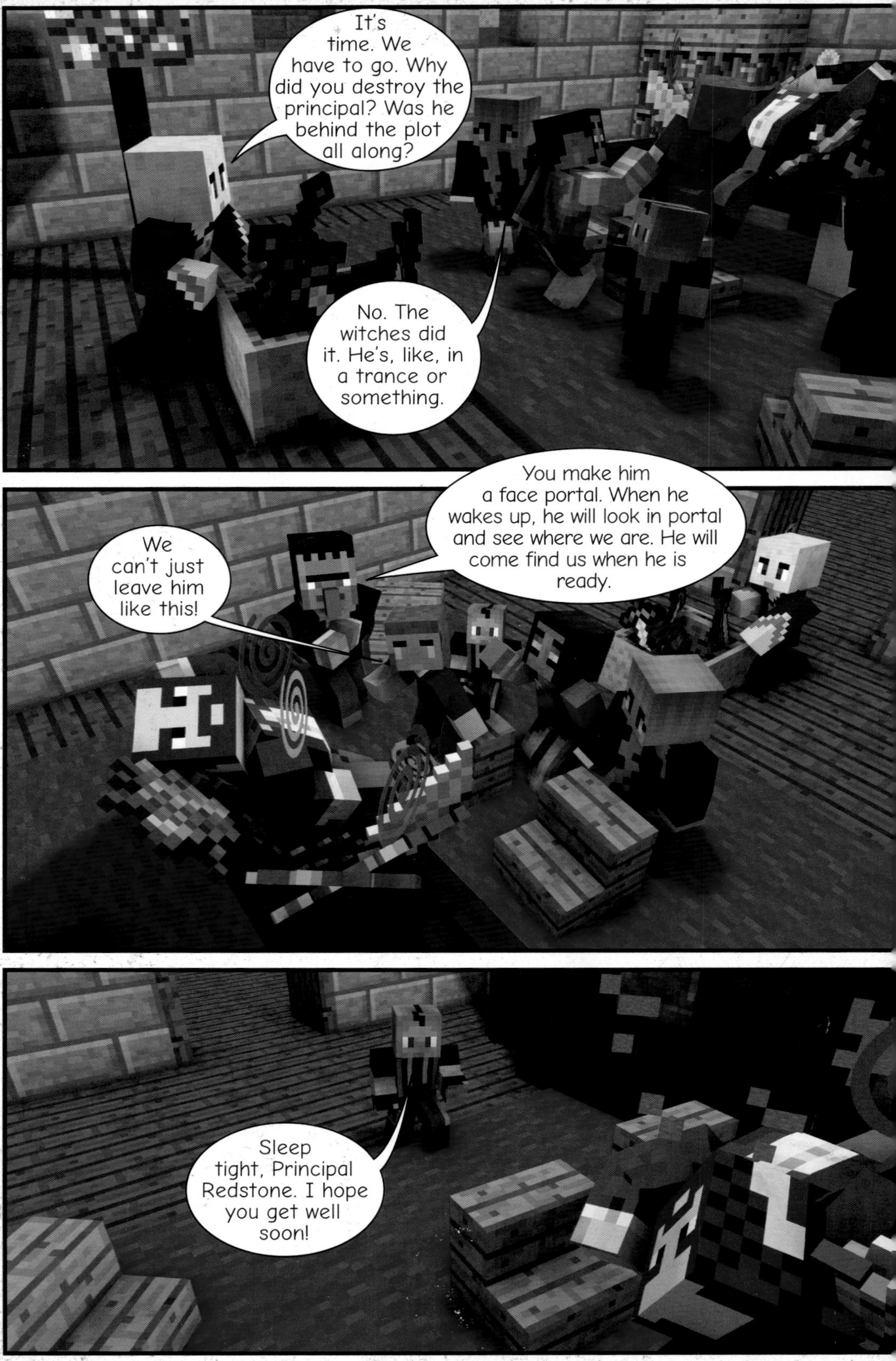
It's time. We have to go. Why did you destroy the principal? Was he behind the plot all along?
No. The witches did it. He's, like, in a trance or something.
We can't just leave him like this!
You make him a face portal. When he wakes up, he will look in portal and see where we are. He will come find us when he is ready.
Sleep tight, Principal Redstone. I hope you get well soon!

CHAPTER 10

BATTLE FOR THE BEACH

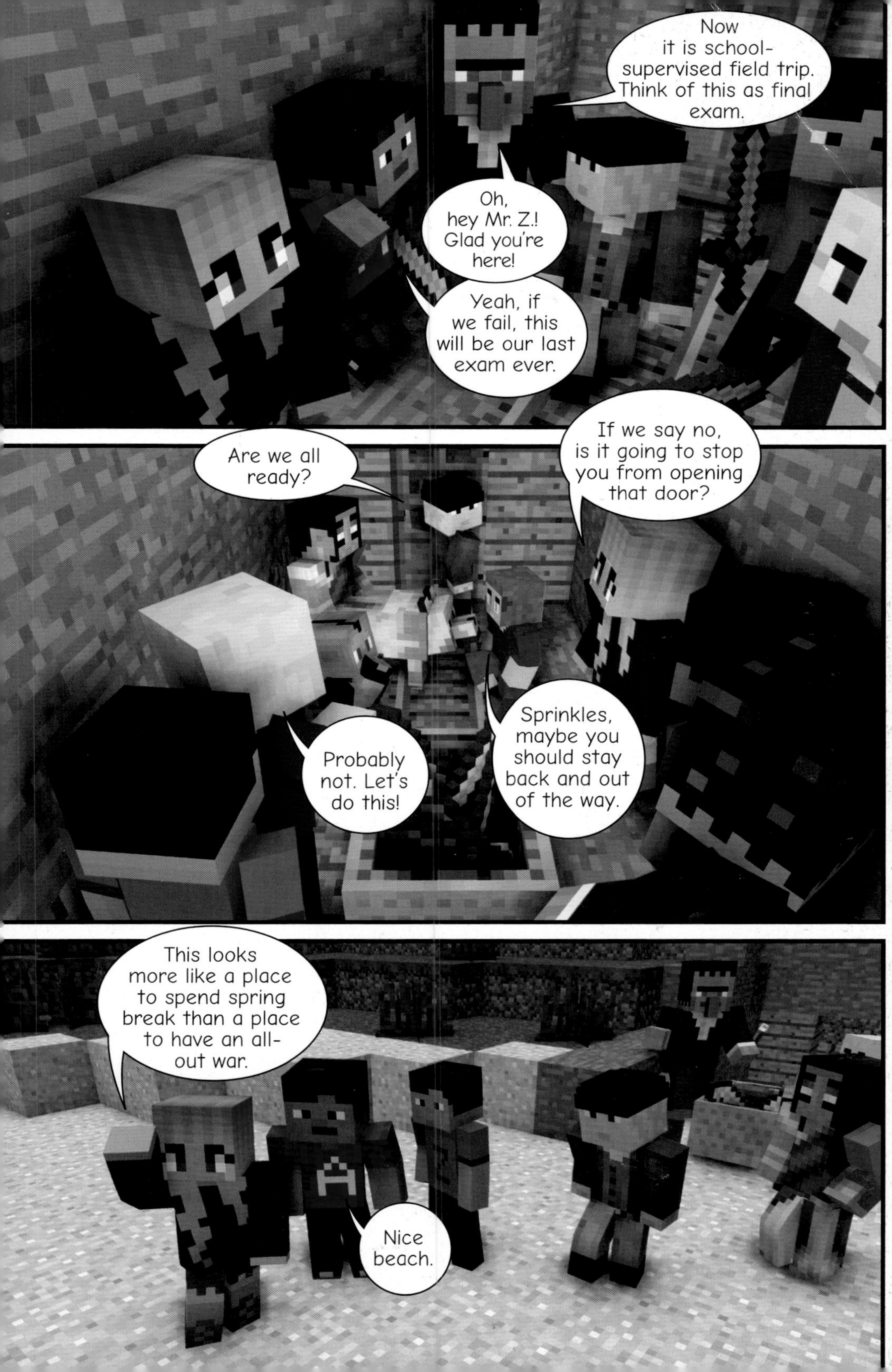
Now it is school-supervised field trip. Think of this as final exam.
Oh, hey Mr. Z.! Glad you're here!
Yeah, if we fail, this will be our last exam ever.
Are we all ready?
If we say no, is it going to stop you from opening that door?
Probably not. Let's do this!
Sprinkles, maybe you should stay back and out of the way.
This looks more like a place to spend spring break than a place to have an all-out war.
Nice beach.

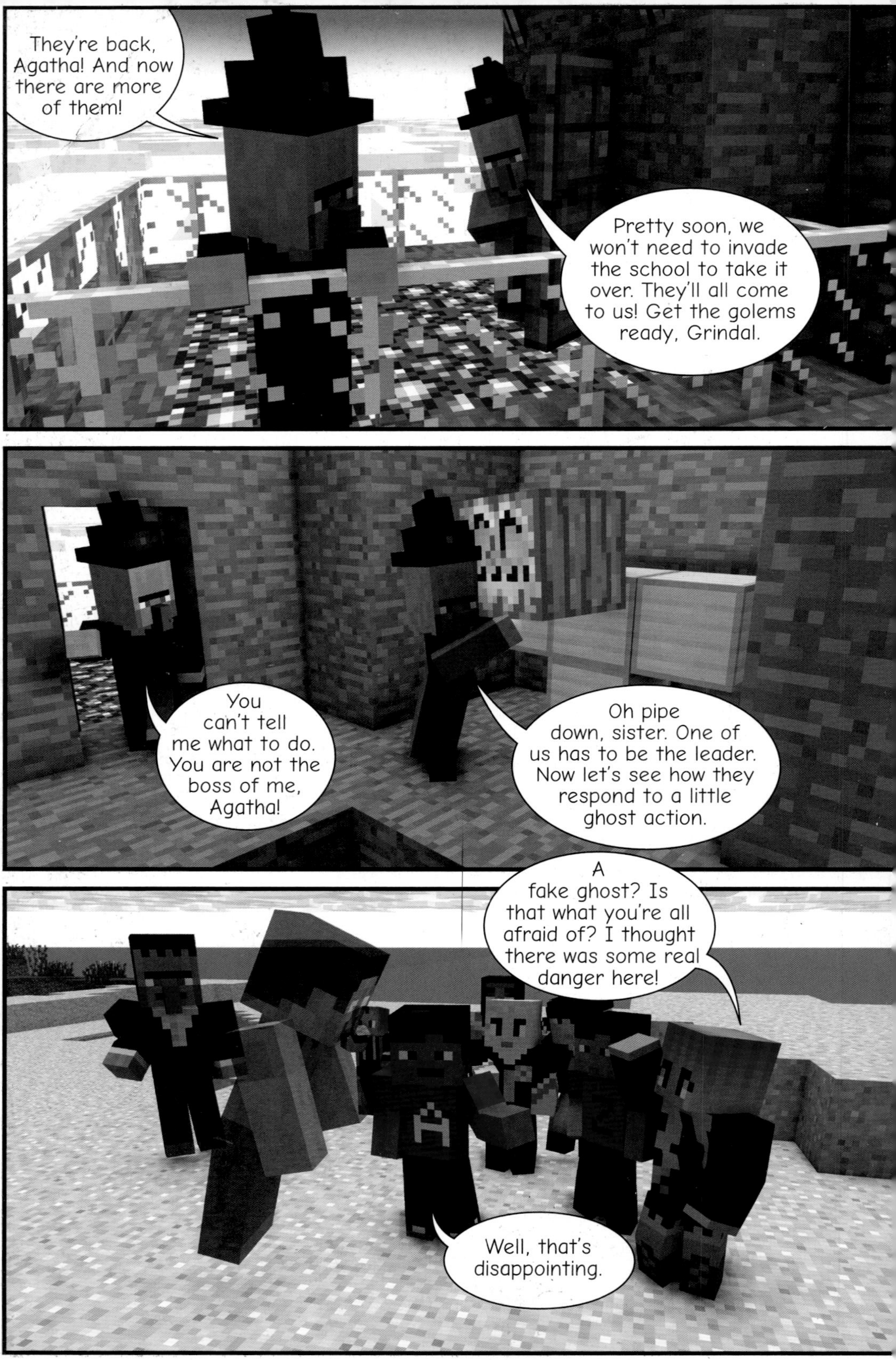
They're back, Agatha! And now there are more of them!
Pretty soon, we won't need to invade the school to take it over. They'll all come to us! Get the golems ready, Grindal.
You can't tell me what to do. You are not the boss of me, Agatha!
Oh pipe down, sister. One of us has to be the leader. Now let's see how they respond to a little ghost action.
A fake ghost? Is that what you're all afraid of? I thought there was some real danger here!
Well, that's disappointing.

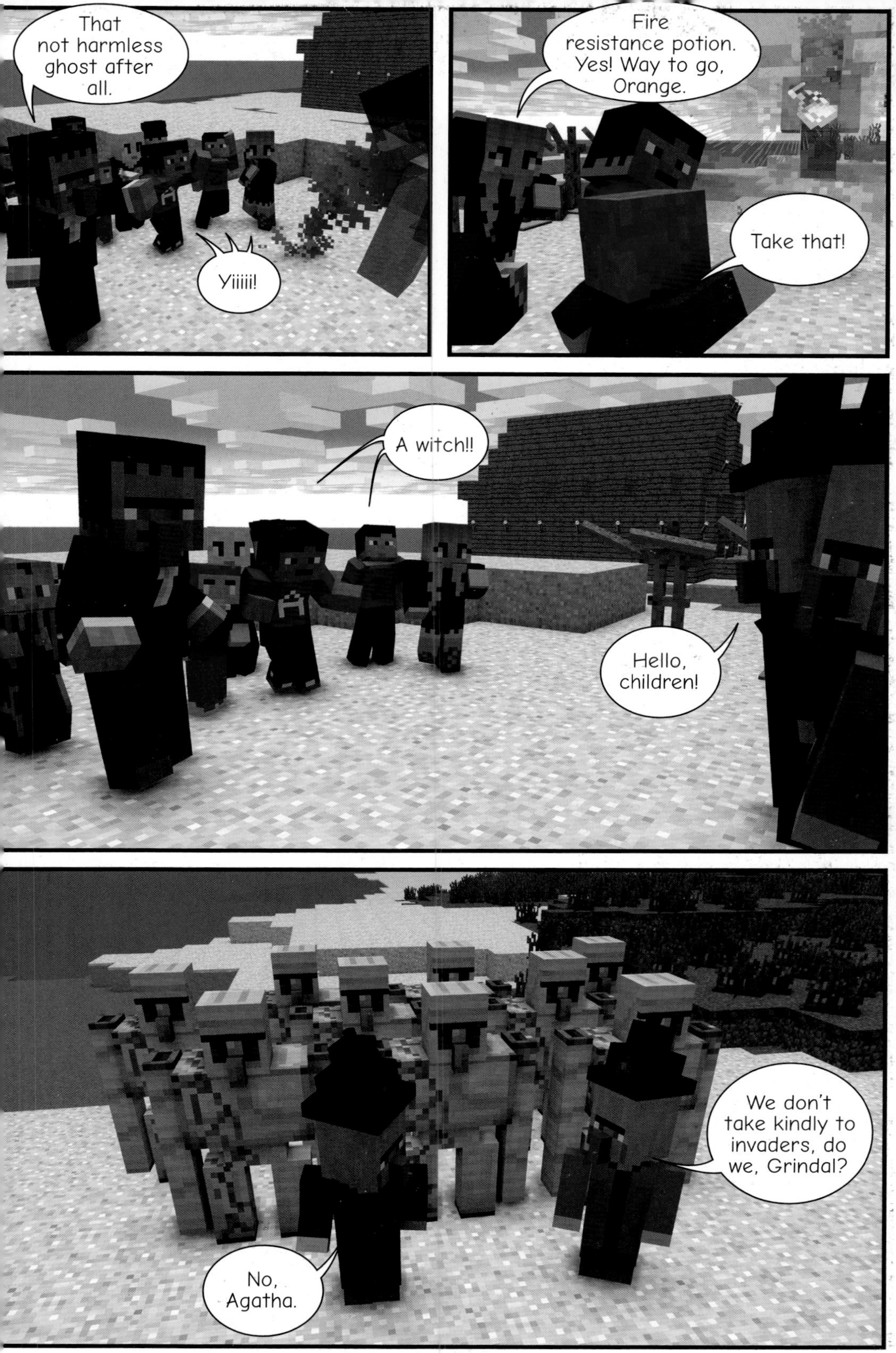
That not harmless ghost after all.
Yiiiii!
Fire resistance potion. Yes! Way to go, Orange.
Take that!
A witch!!
Hello, children!
We don't take kindly to invaders, do we, Grindal?
No, Agatha.

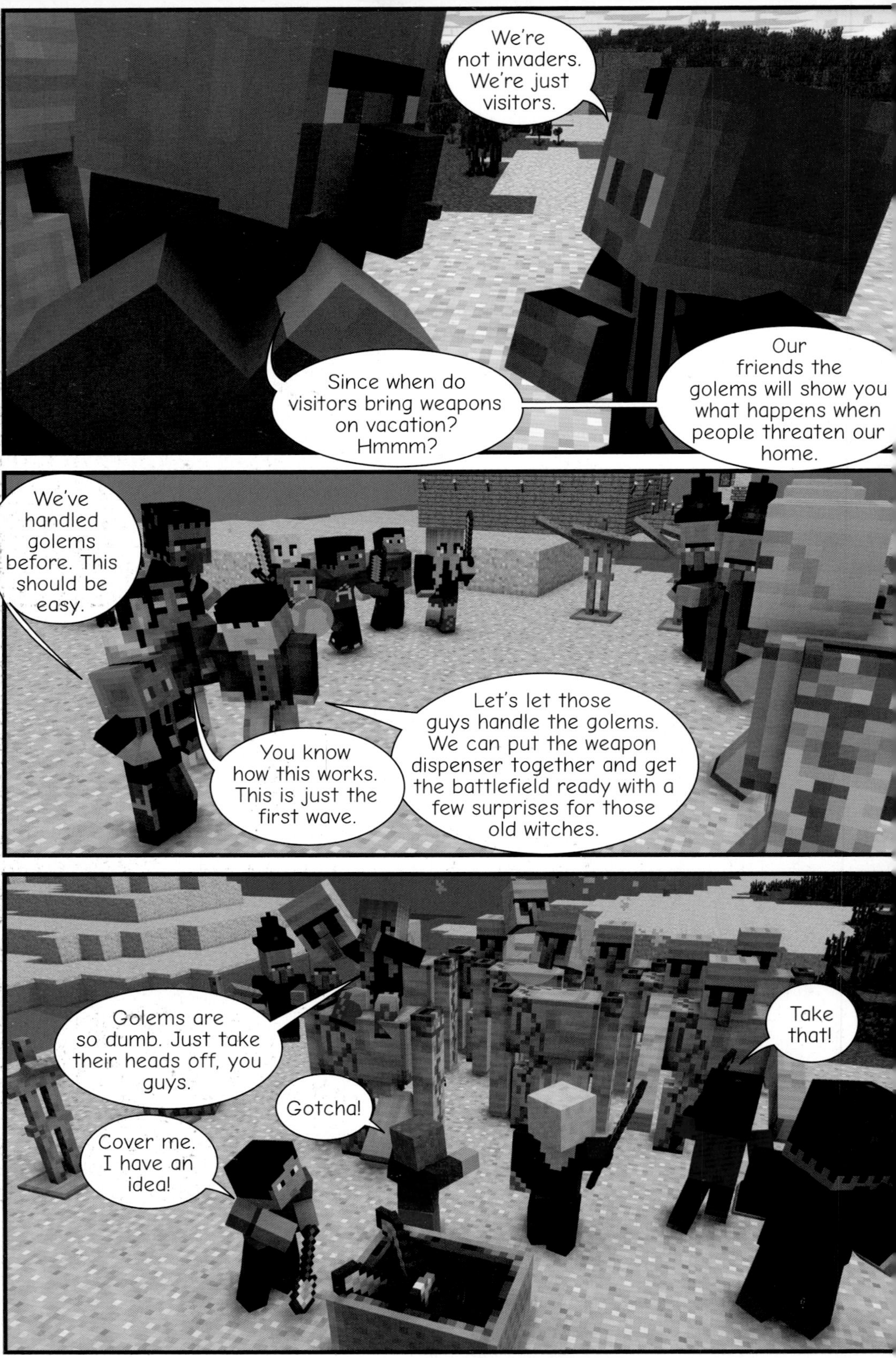
We're not invaders. We're just visitors.
Since when do visitors bring weapons on vacation? Hmmm?
Our friends the golems will show you what happens when people threaten our home.
We've handled golems before. This should be easy.
You know how this works. This is just the first wave.
Let's let those guys handle the golems. We can put the weapon dispenser together and get the battlefield ready with a few surprises for those old witches.
Golems are so dumb. Just take their heads off, you guys.
Take that!
Gotcha!
Cover me. I have an idea!

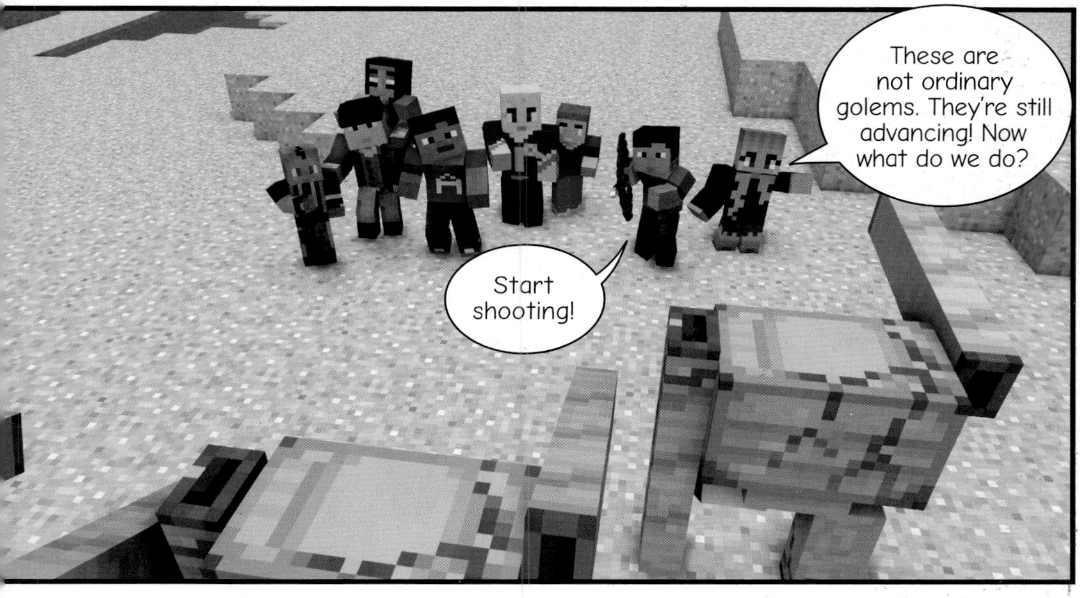
These are not ordinary golems. They're still advancing! Now what do we do?
Start shooting!

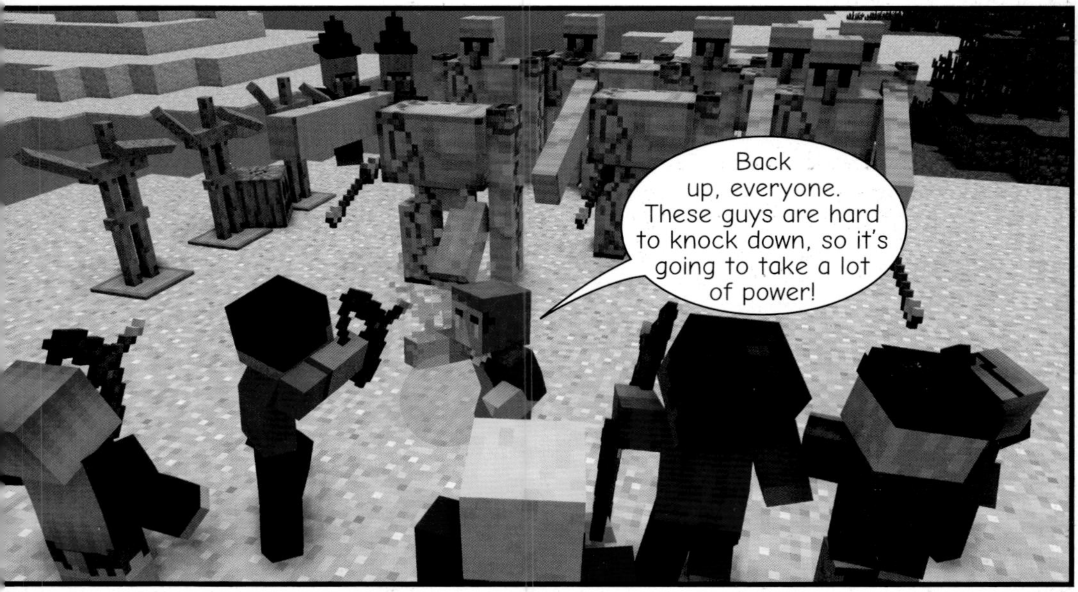
Back up, everyone. These guys are hard to knock down, so it's going to take a lot of power!

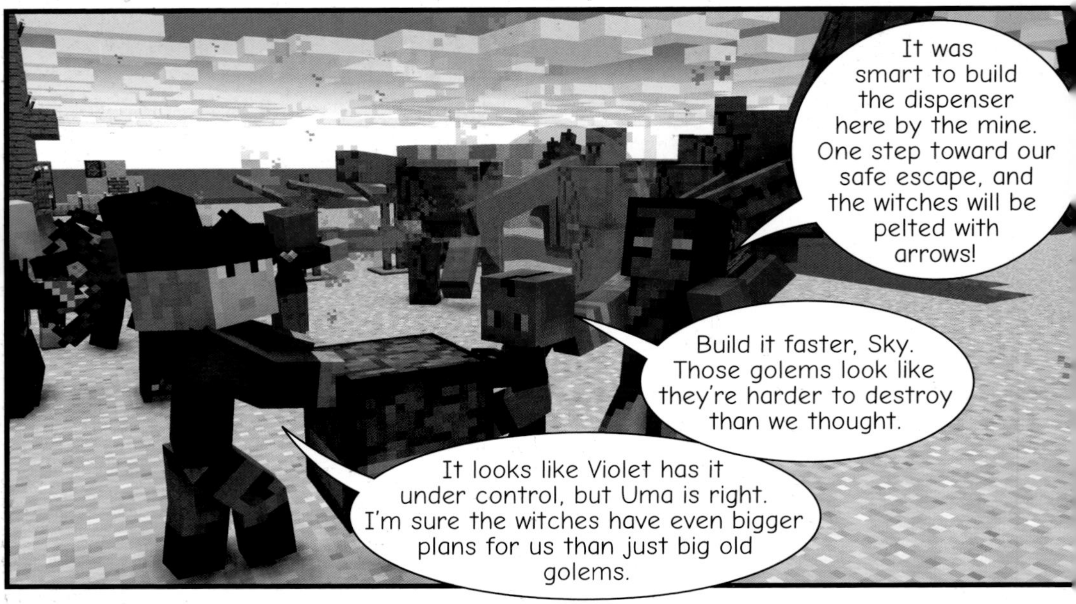
It was smart to build the dispenser here by the mine. One step toward our safe escape, and the witches will be pelted with arrows!
Build it faster, Sky. Those golems look like they're harder to destroy than we thought.
It looks like Violet has it under control, but Uma is right. I'm sure the witches have even bigger plans for us than just big old golems.

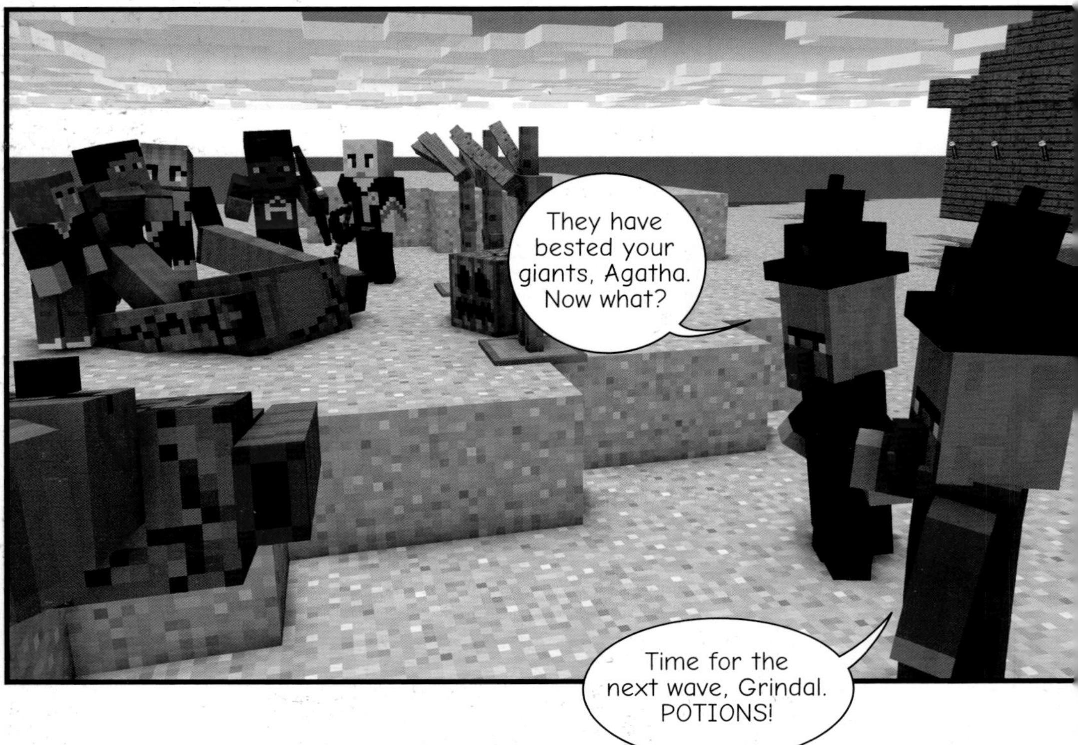
They have bested your giants, Agatha. Now what?
Time for the next wave, Grindal. POTIONS!

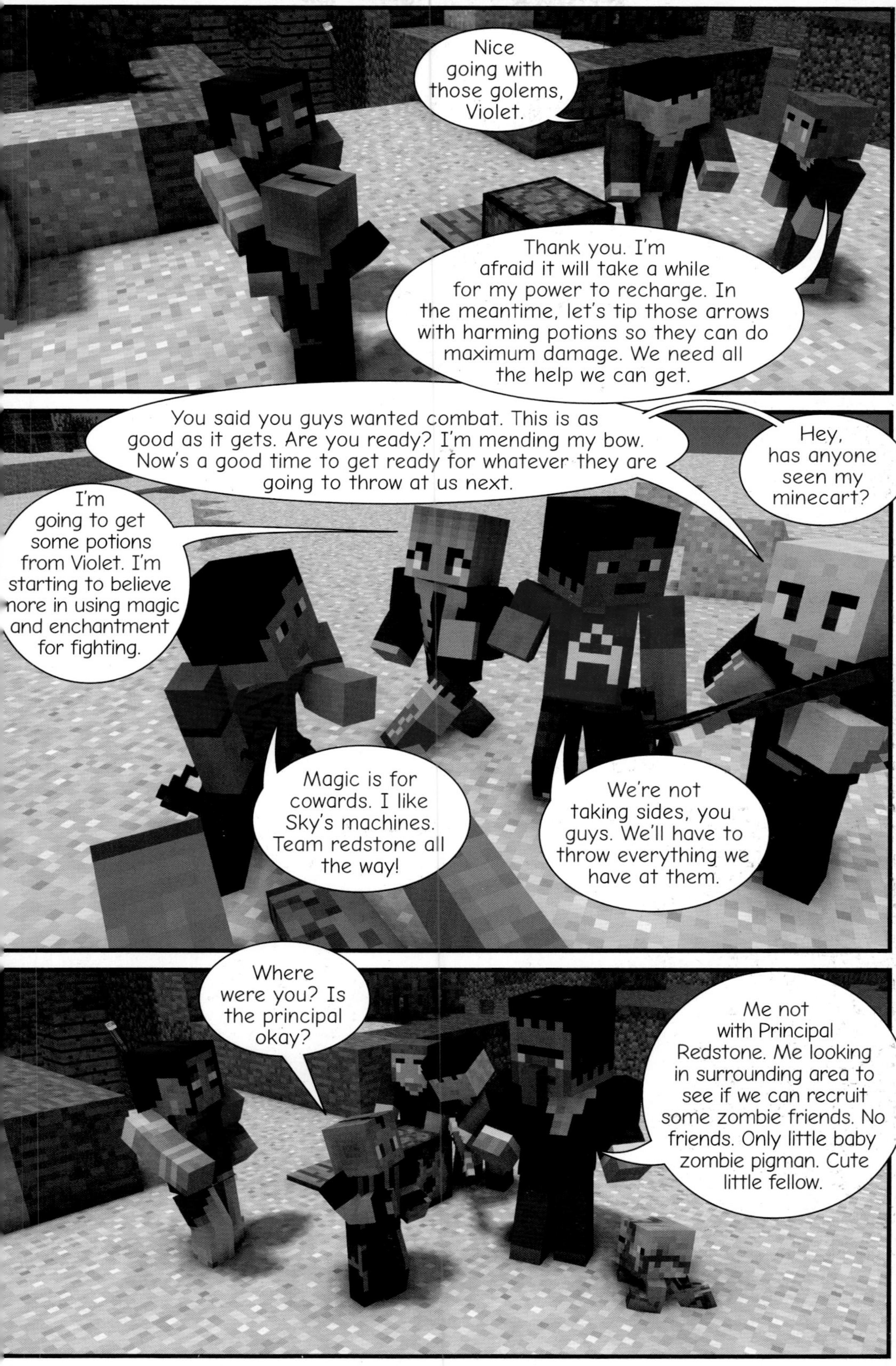
Nice going with those golems, Violet.
Thank you. I'm afraid it will take a while for my power to recharge. In the meantime, let's tip those arrows with harming potions so they can do maximum damage. We need all the help we can get.
You said you guys wanted combat. This is as good as it gets. Are you ready? I'm mending my bow. Now's a good time to get ready for whatever they are going to throw at us next.
Hey, has anyone seen my minecart?
I'm going to get some potions from Violet. I'm starting to believe nore in using magic and enchantment for fighting.
Magic is for cowards. I like Sky's machines. Team redstone all the way!
We're not taking sides, you guys. We'll have to throw everything we have at them.
Where were you? Is the principal okay?
Me not with Principal Redstone. Me looking in surrounding area to see if we can recruit some zombie friends. No friends. Only little baby zombie pigman. Cute little fellow.

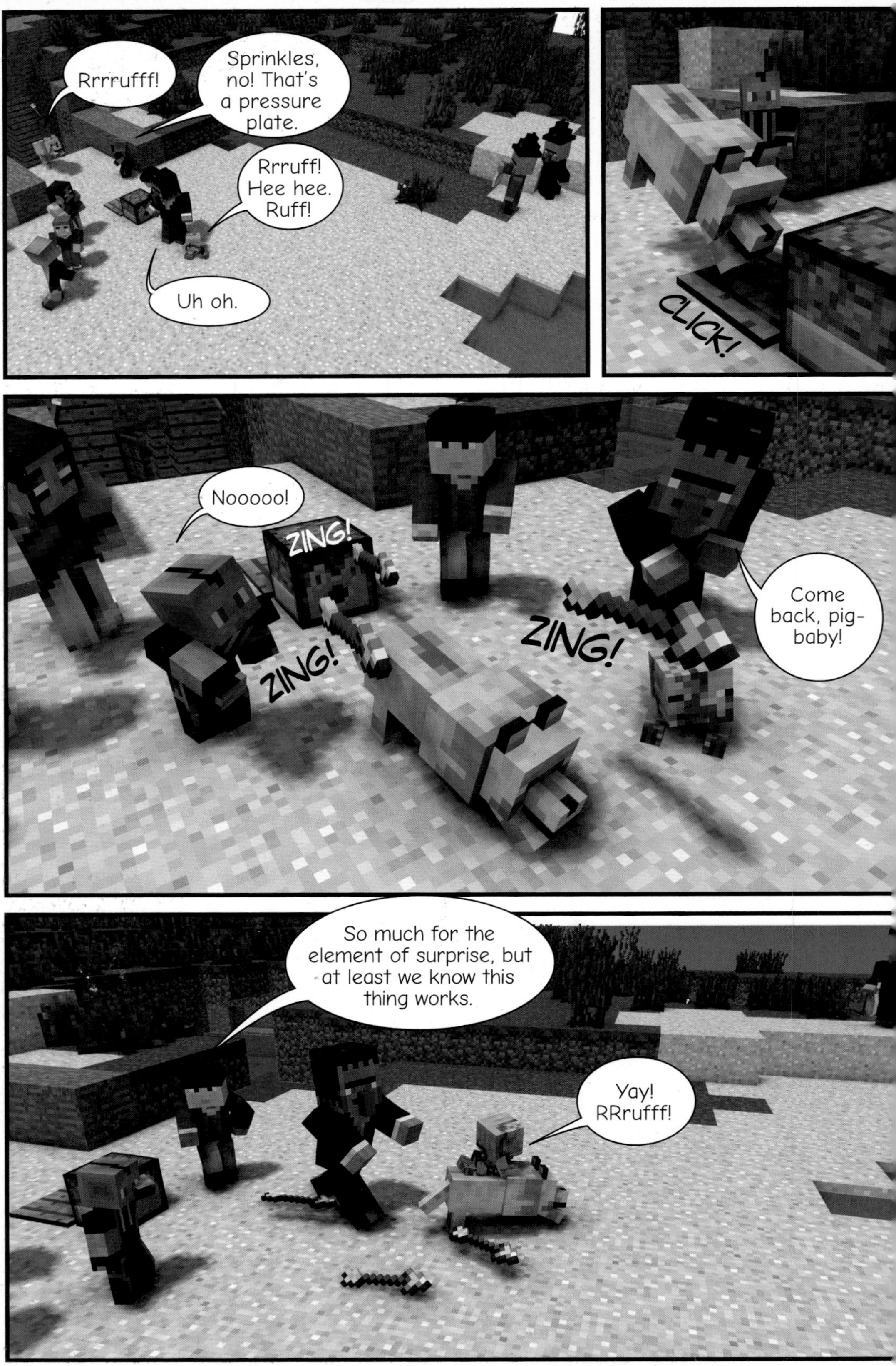
Rrrrufff!
Sprinkles, no! That's a pressure plate.
Rrruff! Hee hee. Ruff!
Uh oh.
CLICK!
Nooooo!
ZING!
ZING!
ZING!
Come back, pig-baby!
So much for the element of surprise, but at least we know this thing works.
Yay! RRrufff!

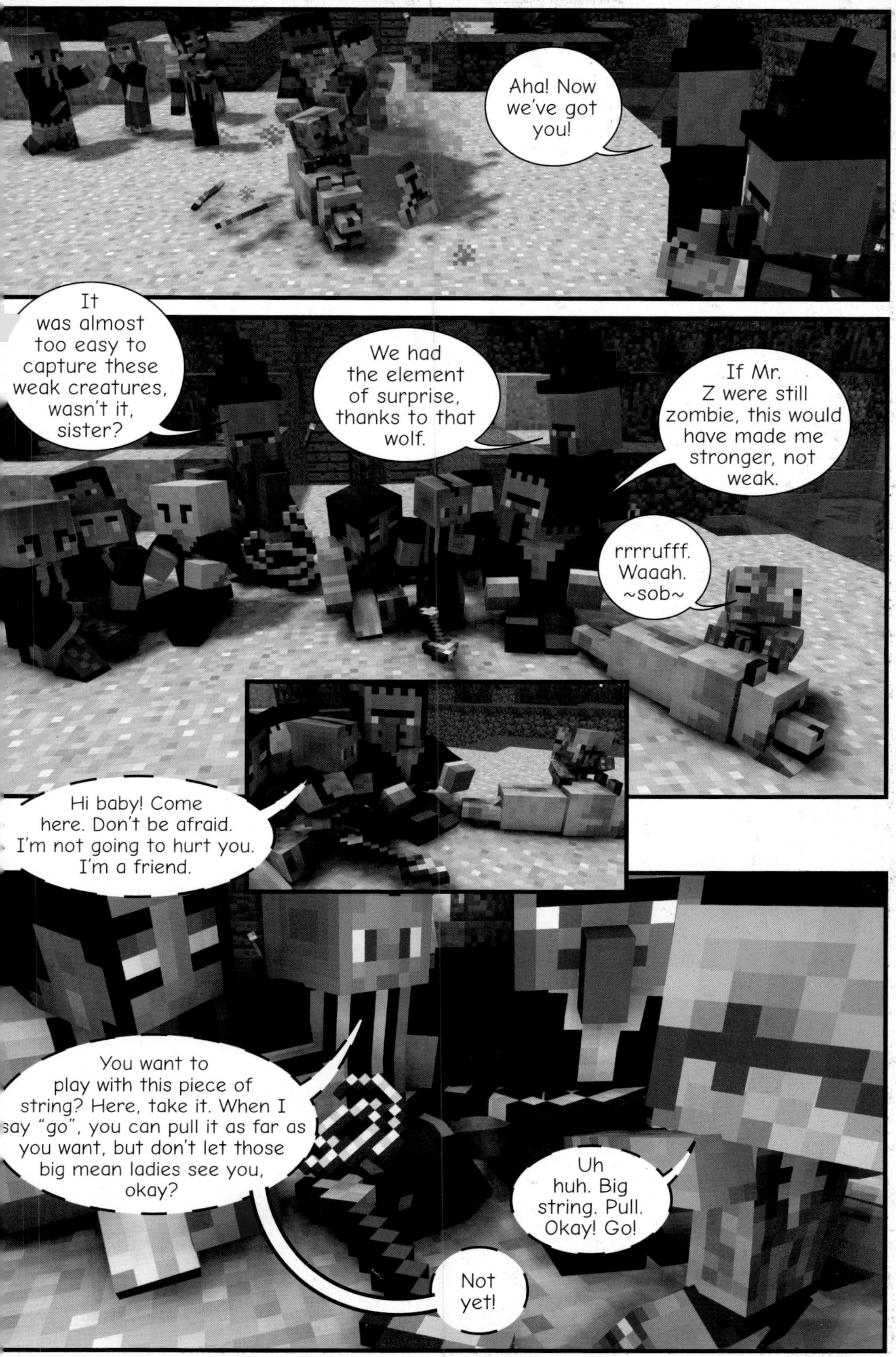
Aha! Now we've got you!
It was almost too easy to capture these weak creatures, wasn't it, sister?
We had the element of surprise, thanks to that wolf.
If Mr. Z were still zombie, this would have made me stronger, not weak.
rrrrufff. Waaah. ~sob~
Hi baby! Come here. Don't be afraid. I'm not going to hurt you. I'm a friend.
You want to play with this piece of string? Here, take it. When I say "go", you can pull it as far as you want, but don't let those big mean ladies see you, okay?
Uh huh. Big string. Pull. Okay! Go!
Not yet!

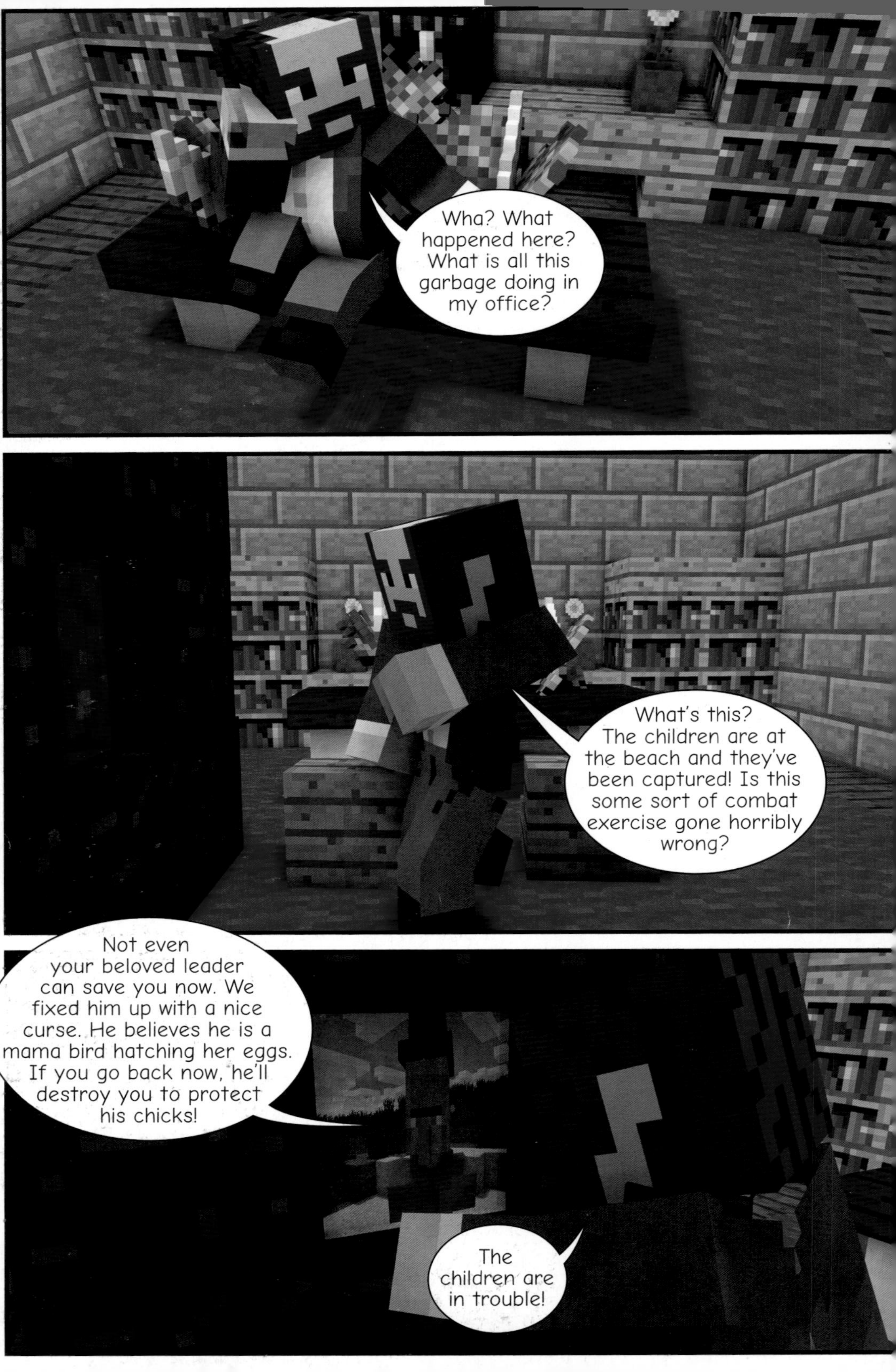
Wha? What happened here? What is all this garbage doing in my office?
What's this? The children are at the beach and they've been captured! Is this some sort of combat exercise gone horribly wrong?
Not even your beloved leader can save you now. We fixed him up with a nice curse. He believes he is a mama bird hatching her eggs. If you go back now, he'll destroy you to protect his chicks!
The children are in trouble!

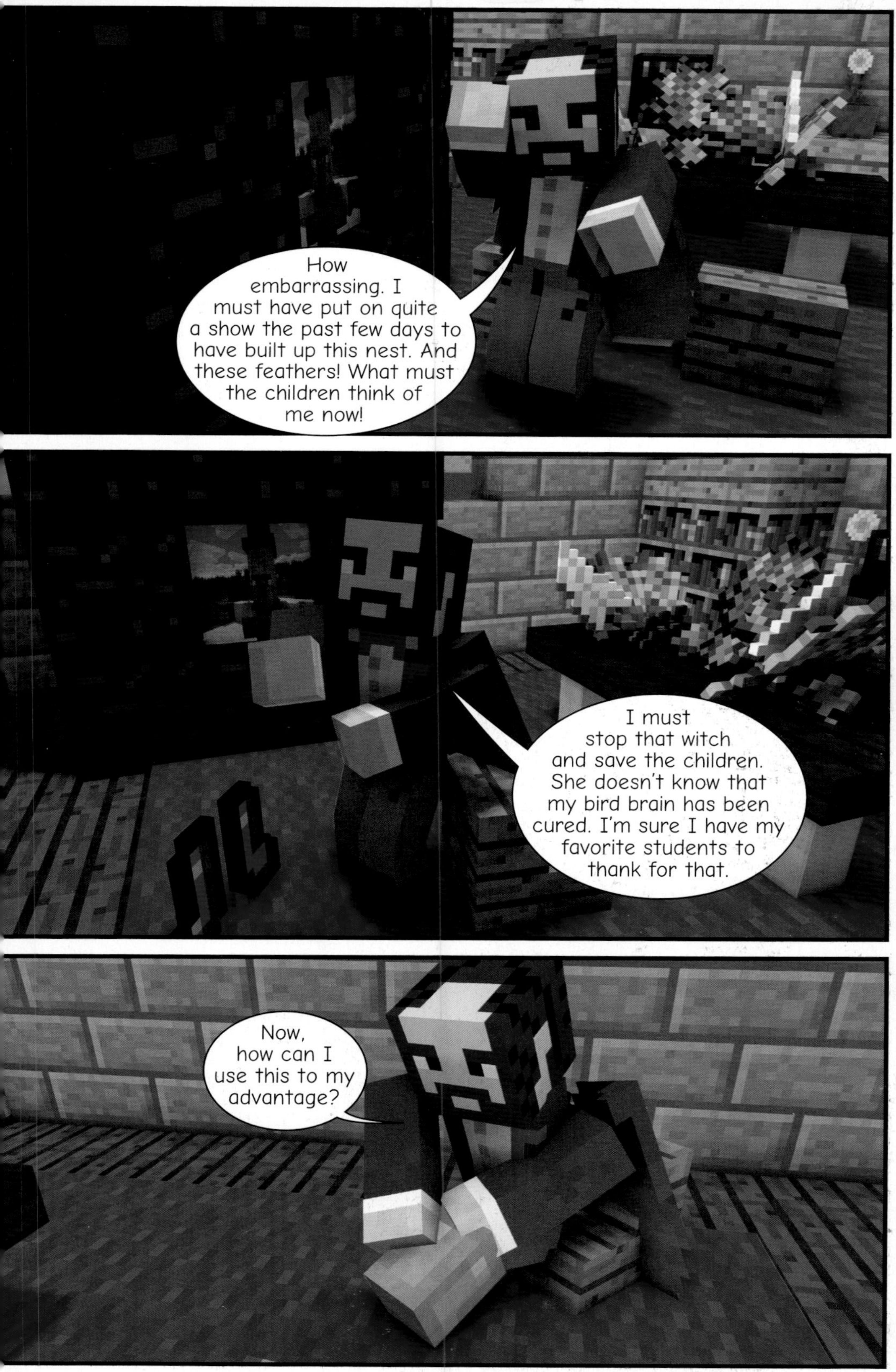
How embarrassing. I must have put on quite a show the past few days to have built up this nest. And these feathers! What must the children think of me now!
I must stop that witch and save the children. She doesn't know that my bird brain has been cured. I'm sure I have my favorite students to thank for that.
Now, how can I use this to my advantage?

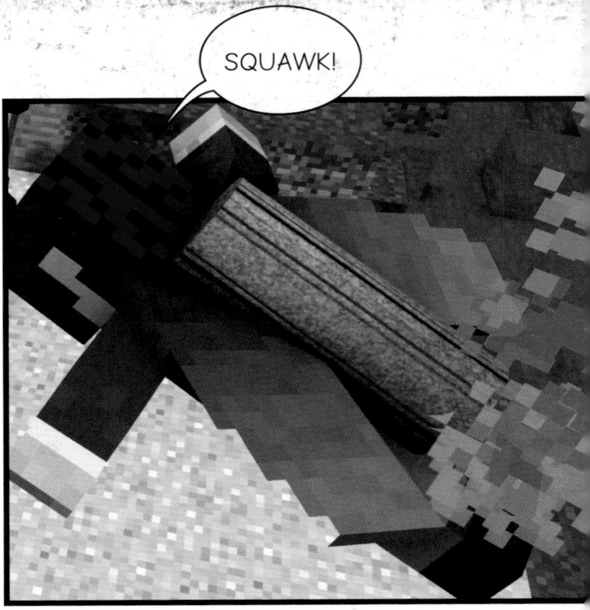
SQUAWK!

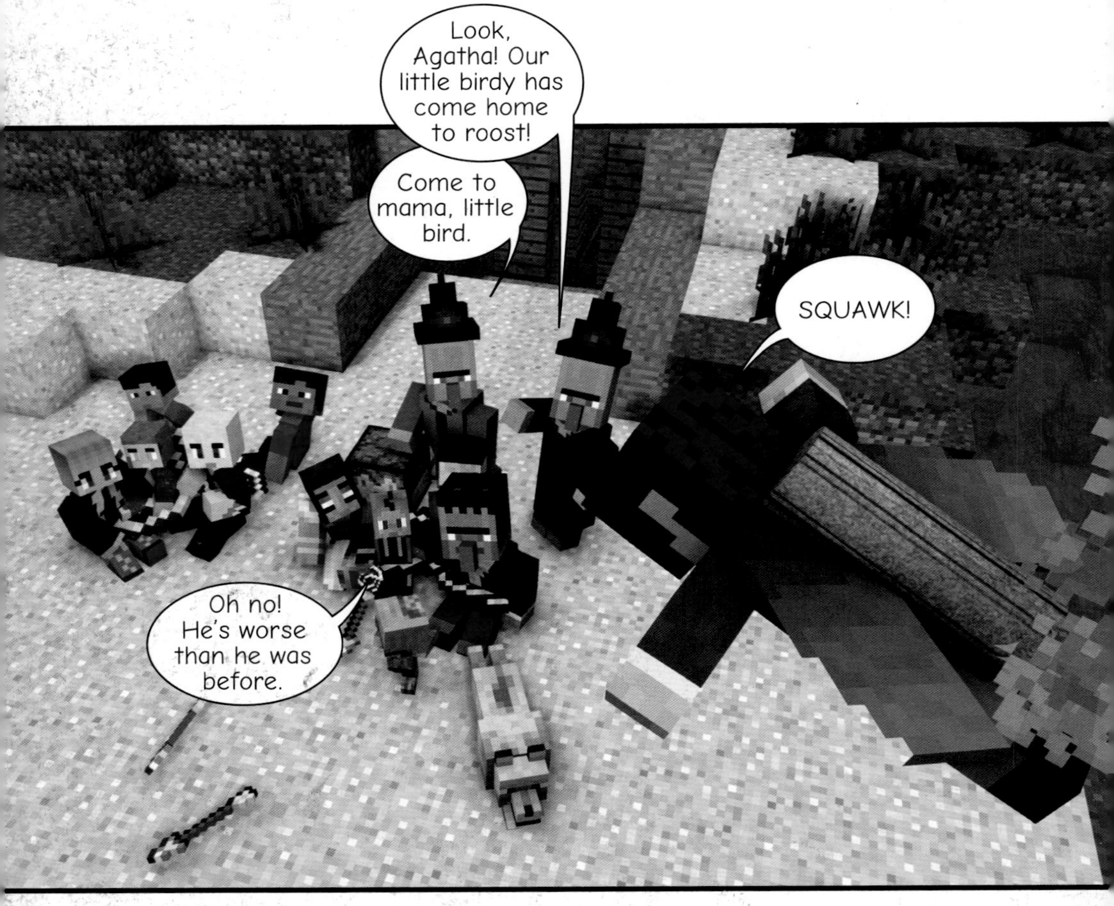
Look, Agatha! Our little birdy has come home to roost!
Come to mama, little bird.
SQUAWK!
Oh no! He's worse than he was before.

CHAPTER II

SURVIVAL
SKILLS
UNLEASHED

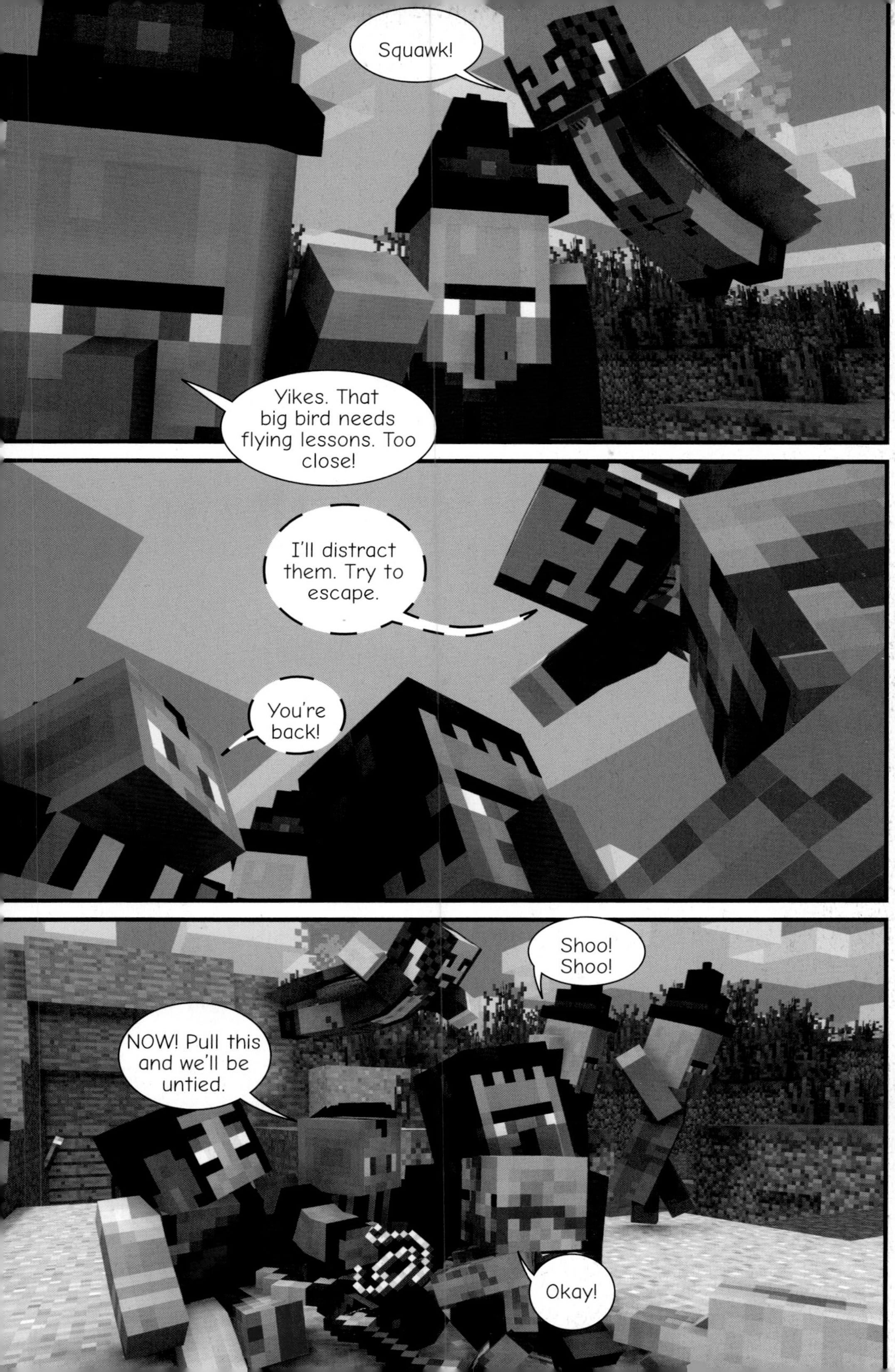
Squawk!
Yikes. That big bird needs flying lessons. Too close!
I'll distract them. Try to escape.
You're back!
Shoo! Shoo!
NOW! Pull this and we'll be untied.
Okay!

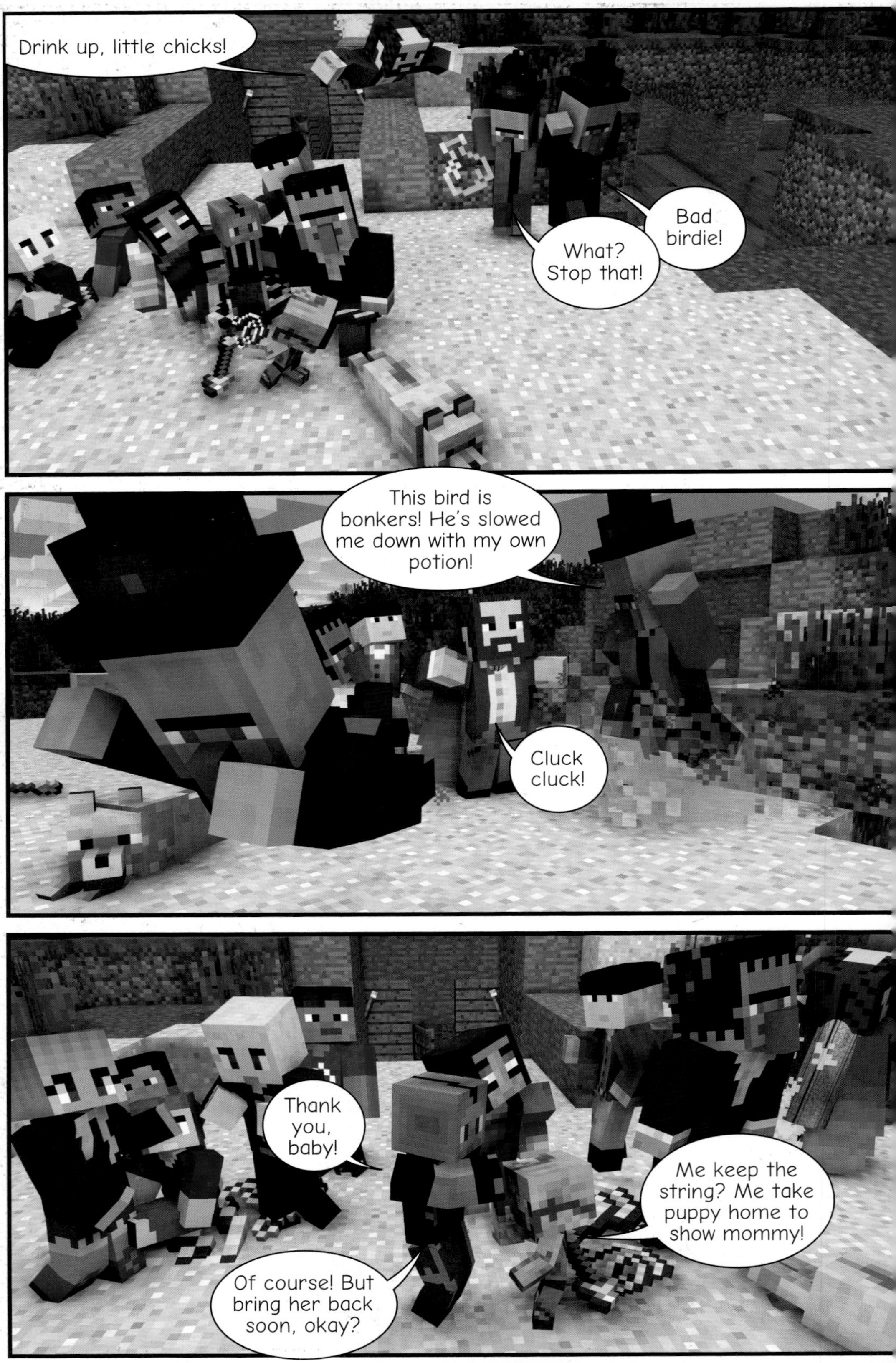
Drink up, little chicks!
Bad birdie!
What? Stop that!
This bird is bonkers! He's slowed me down with my own potion!
Cluck cluck!
Thank you, baby!
Me keep the string? Me take puppy home to show mommy!
Of course! But bring her back soon, okay?

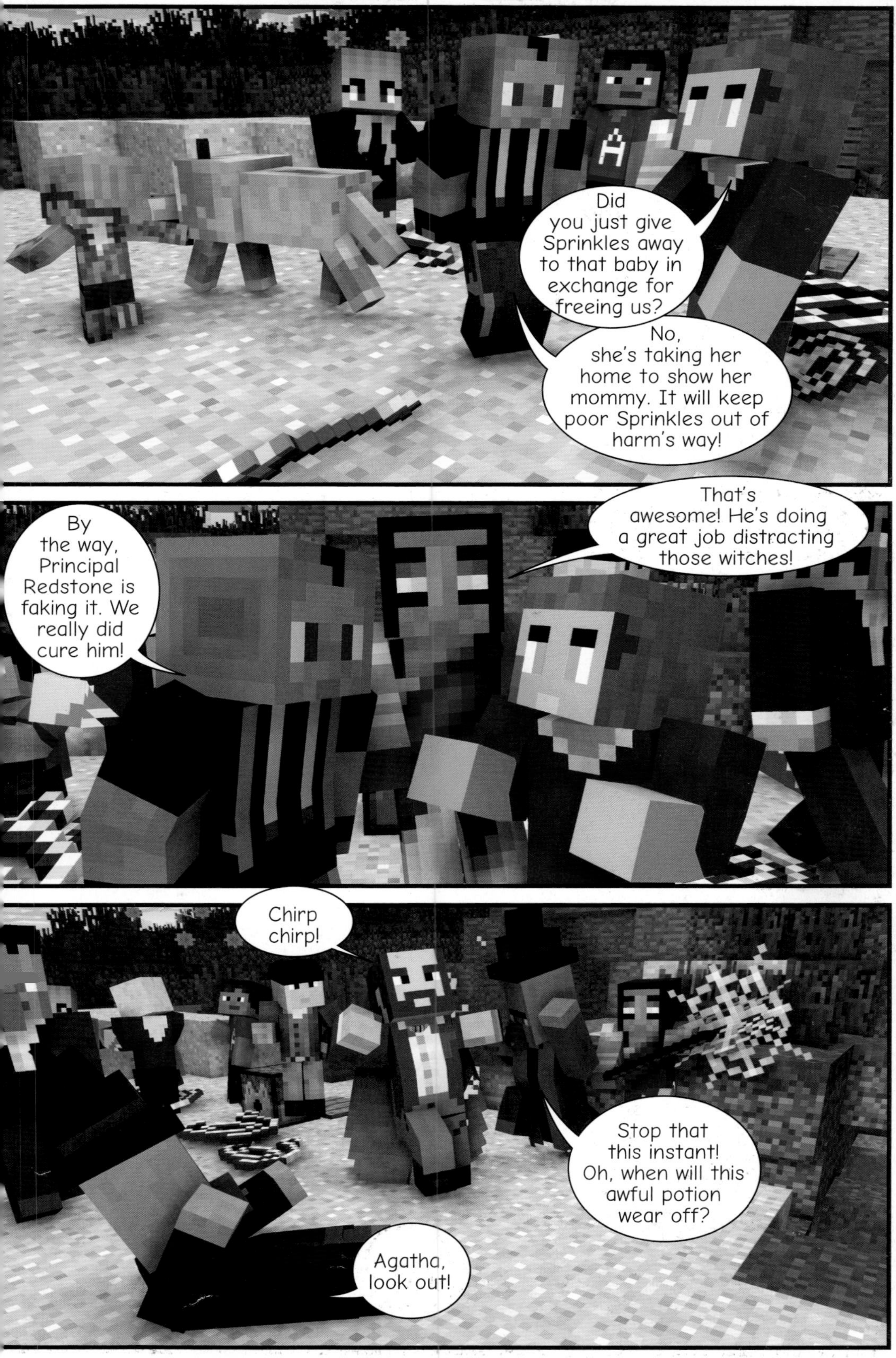
Did you just give Sprinkles away to that baby in exchange for freeing us?
No, she's taking her home to show her mommy. It will keep poor Sprinkles out of harm's way!
By the way, Principal Redstone is faking it. We really did cure him!
That's awesome! He's doing a great job distracting those witches!
Chirp chirp!
Stop that this instant! Oh, when will this awful potion wear off?
Agatha, look out!

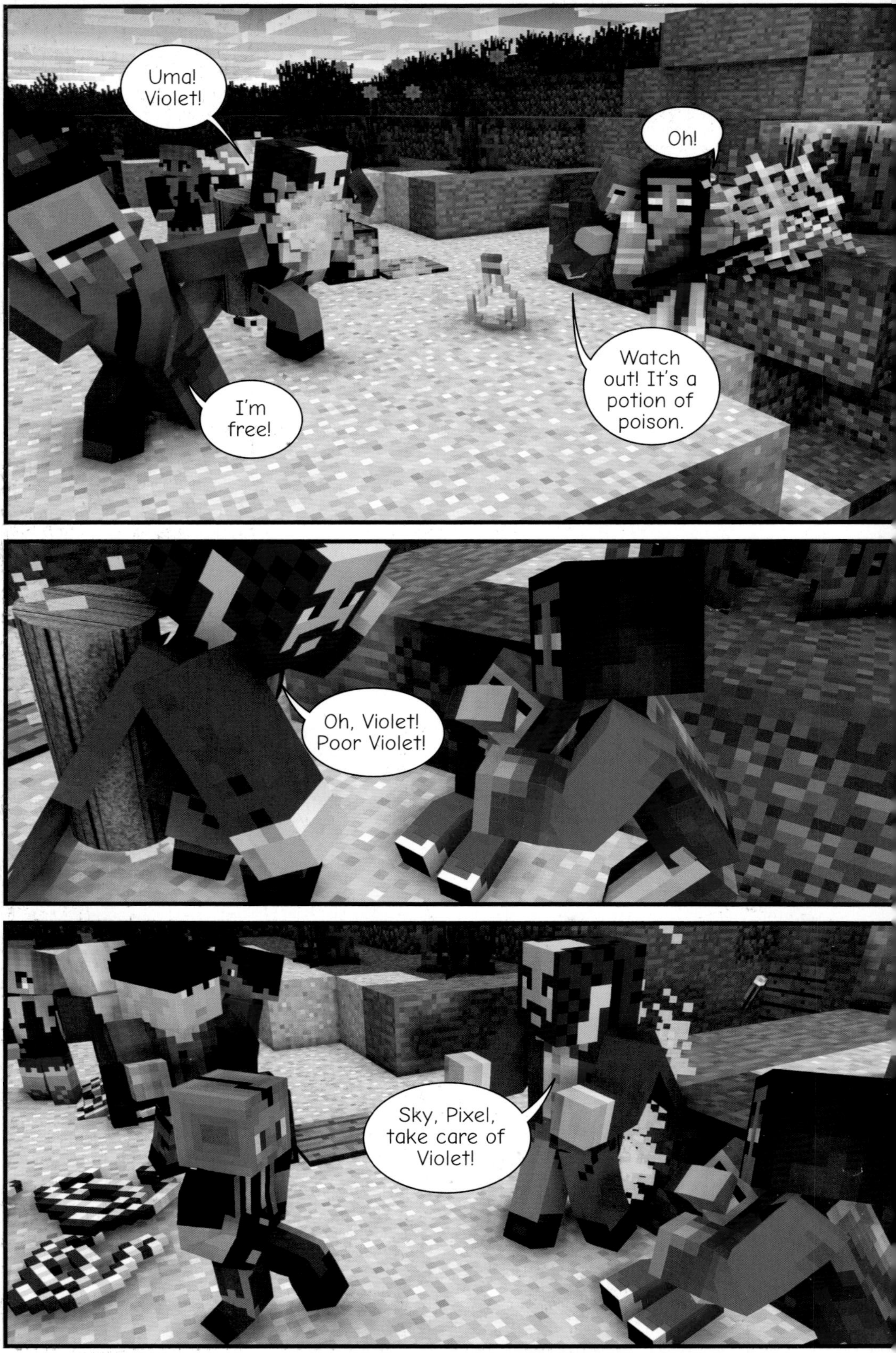
Uma!
Violet!
I'm
free!
Oh!
Watch out! It's a potion of poison.
Oh, Violet!
Poor Violet!
Sky, Pixel, take care of Violet!

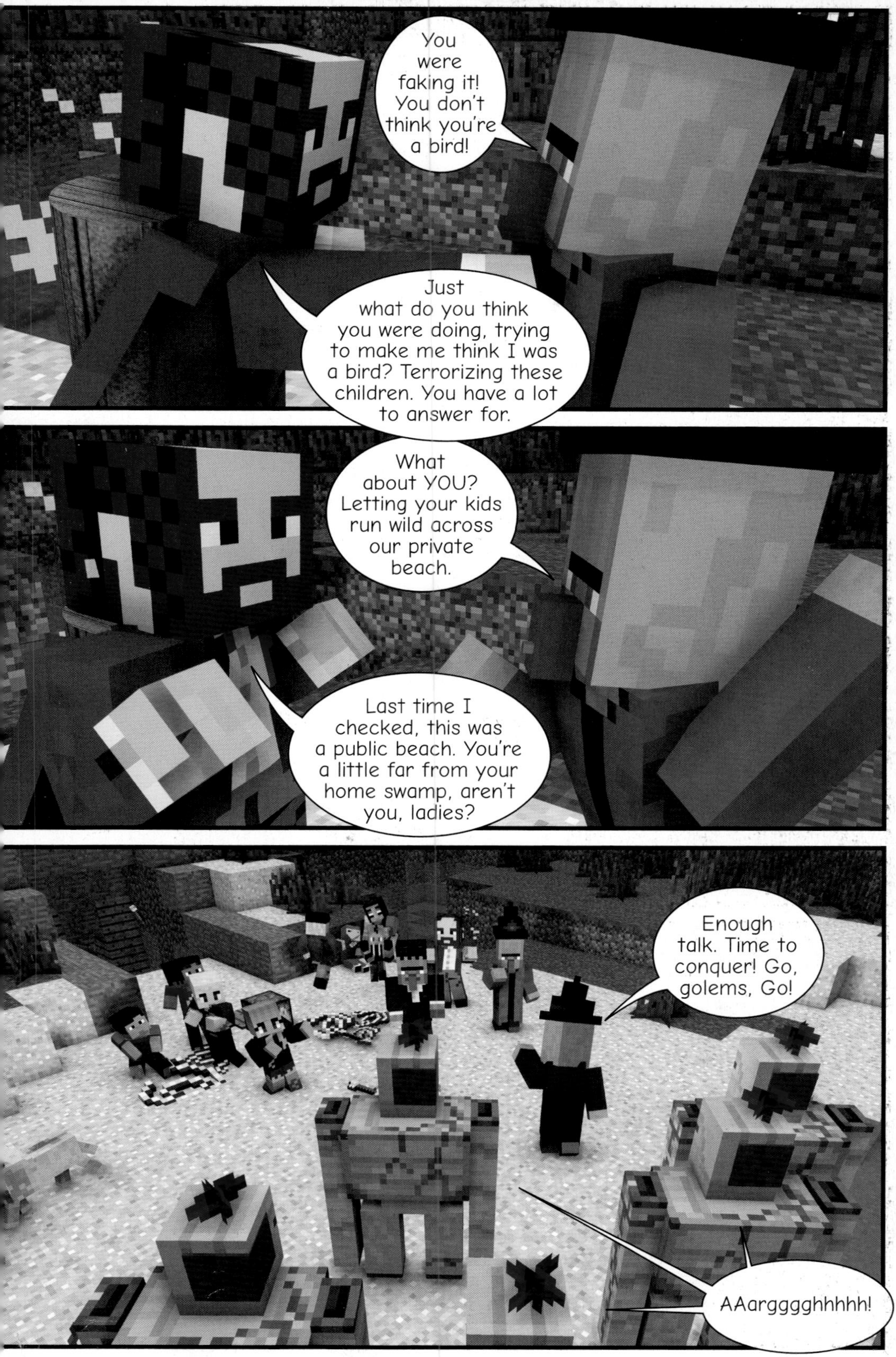
You were faking it! You don't think you're a bird!
Just what do you think you were doing, trying to make me think I was a bird? Terrorizing these children. You have a lot to answer for.
What about YOU? Letting your kids run wild across our private beach.
Last time I checked, this was a public beach. You're a little far from your home swamp, aren't you, ladies?
Enough talk. Time to conquer! Go, golems, Go!
AAargggghhhhh!

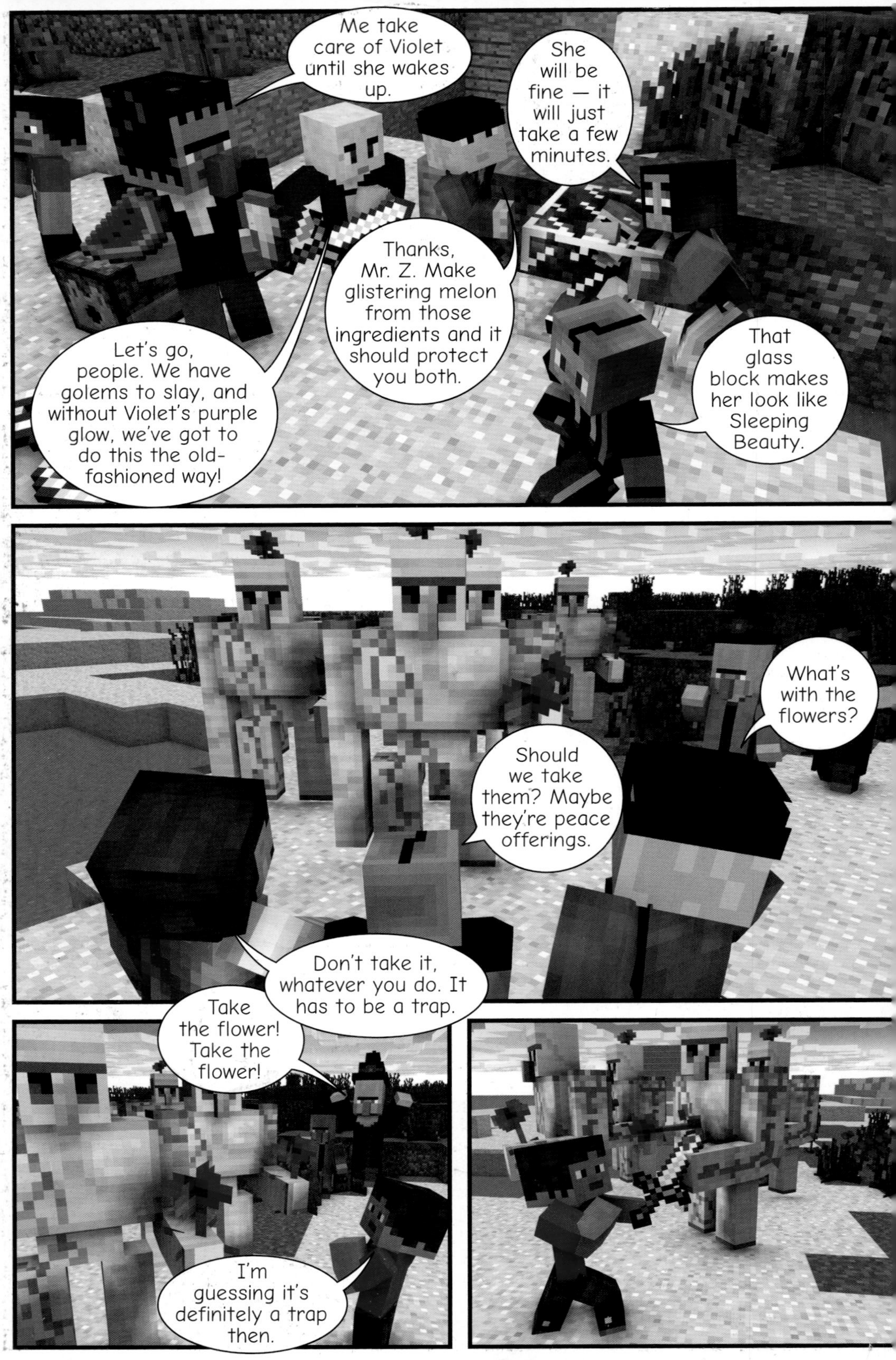
Me take care of Violet until she wakes up.
She will be fine — it will just take a few minutes.
Thanks, Mr. Z. Make glistering melon from those ingredients and it should protect you both.
Let's go, people. We have golems to slay, and without Violet's purple glow, we've got to do this the old-fashioned way!
That glass block makes her look like Sleeping Beauty.
What's with the flowers?
Should we take them? Maybe they're peace offerings.
Don't take it, whatever you do. It has to be a trap.
Take the flower! Take the flower!
I'm guessing it's definitely a trap then.

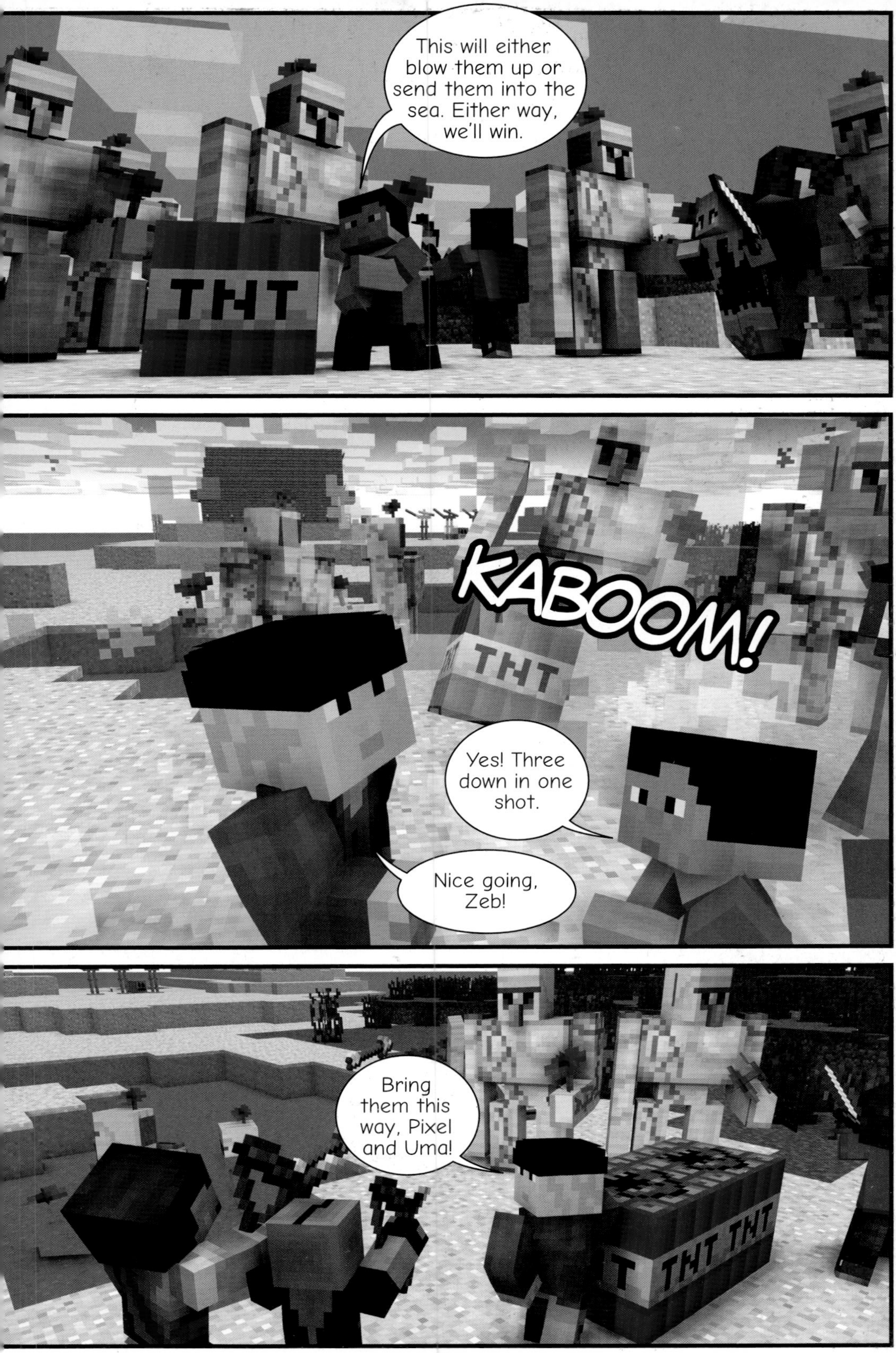

This will either blow them up or send them into the sea. Either way, we'll win.
KABOOM!
TNT
Yes! Three down in one shot.
Nice going, Zeb!
Bring them this way, Pixel and Uma!

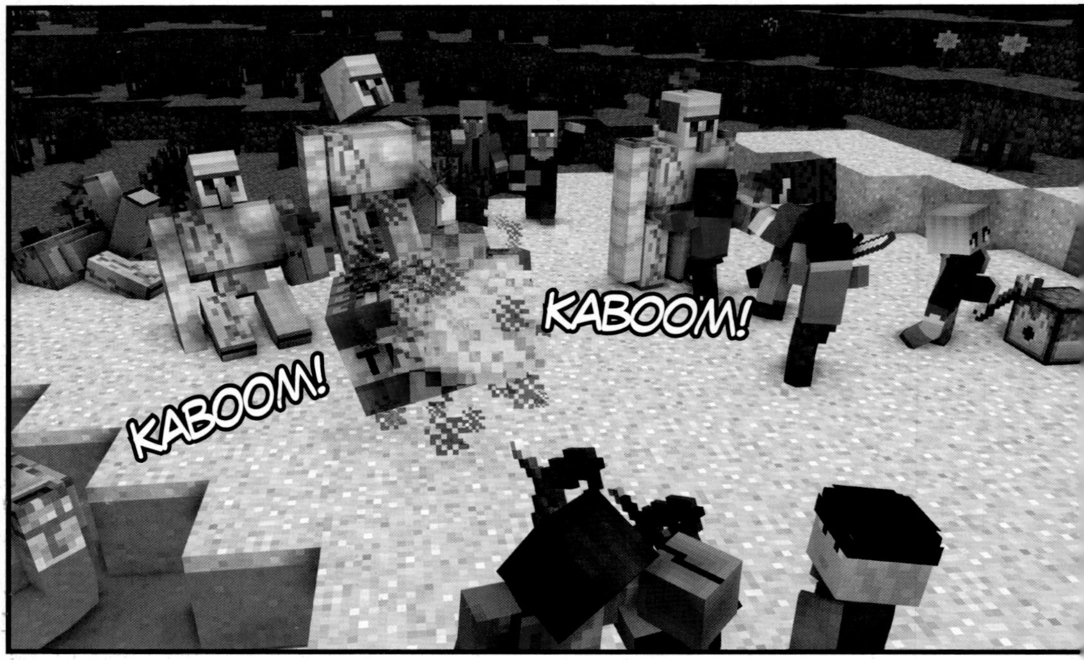
KABOOM!
KABOOM!

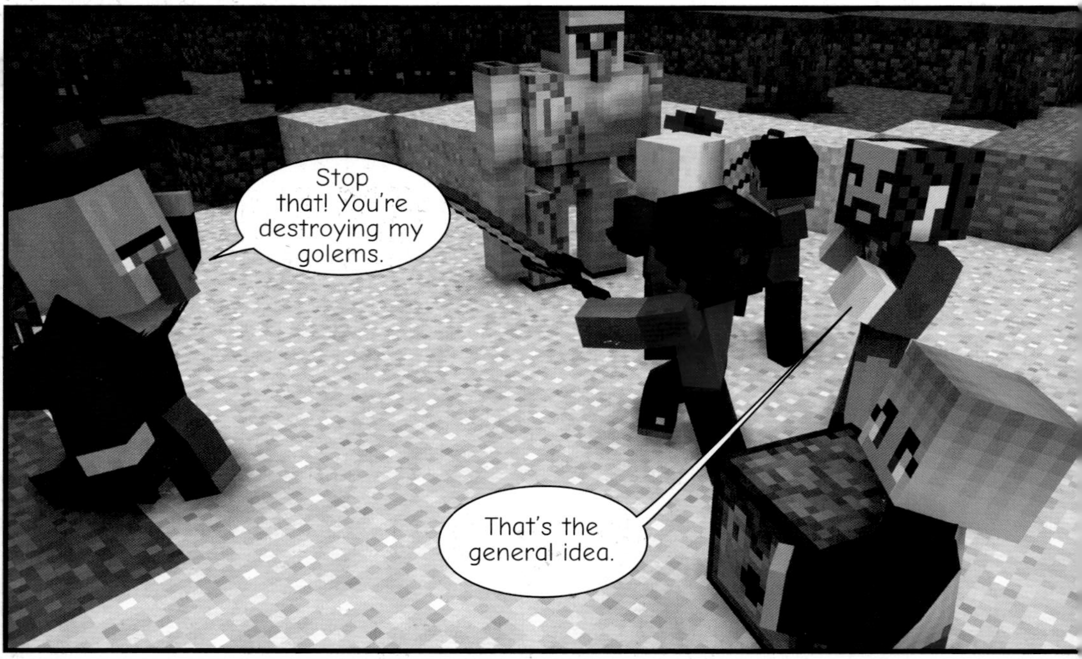
Stop that! You're destroying my golems.
That's the general idea.

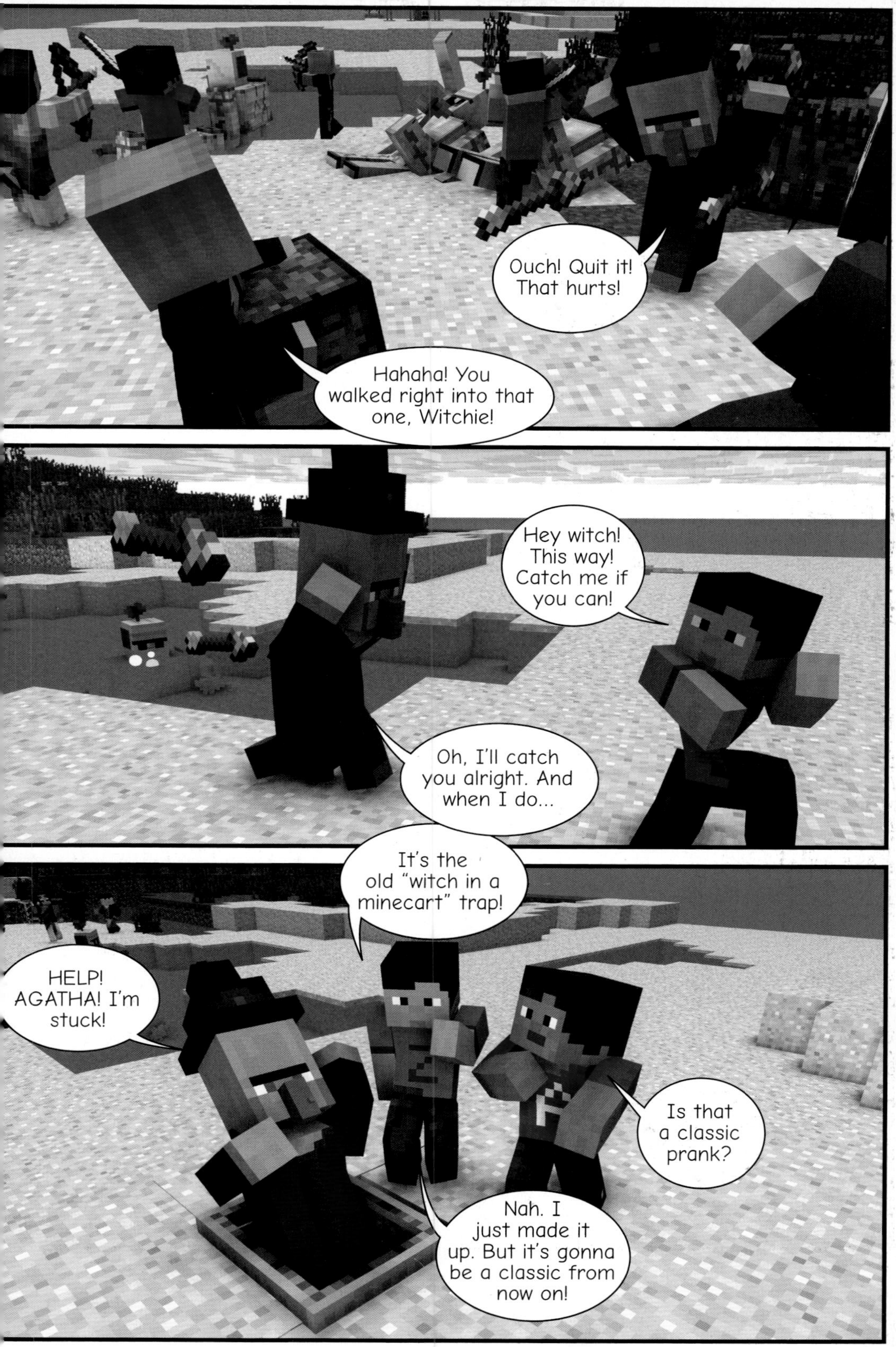
Ouch! Quit it! That hurts!
Hahaha! You walked right into that one, Witchie!
Hey witch! This way! Catch me if you can!
Oh, I'll catch you alright. And when I do...
It's the old "witch in a minecart" trap!
HELP! AGATHA! I'm stuck!
Is that a classic prank?
Nah. I just made it up. But it's gonna be a classic from now on!

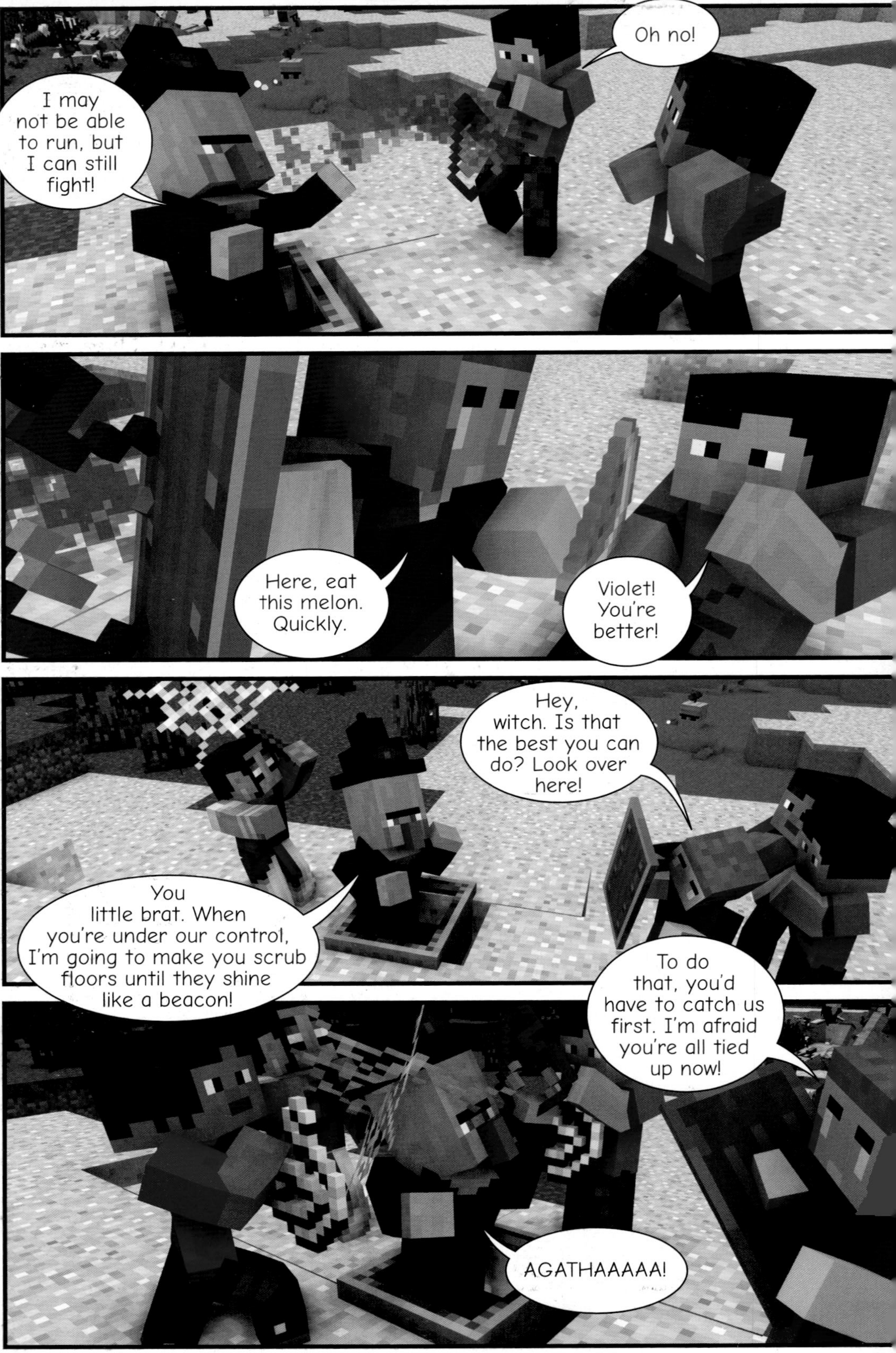
Oh no!
I may not be able to run, but I can still fight!
Here, eat this melon. Quickly.
Violet! You're better!
Hey, witch. Is that the best you can do? Look over here!
You little brat. When you're under our control, I'm going to make you scrub floors until they shine like a beacon!
To do that, you'd have to catch us first. I'm afraid you're all tied up now!
AGATHAAAAA!

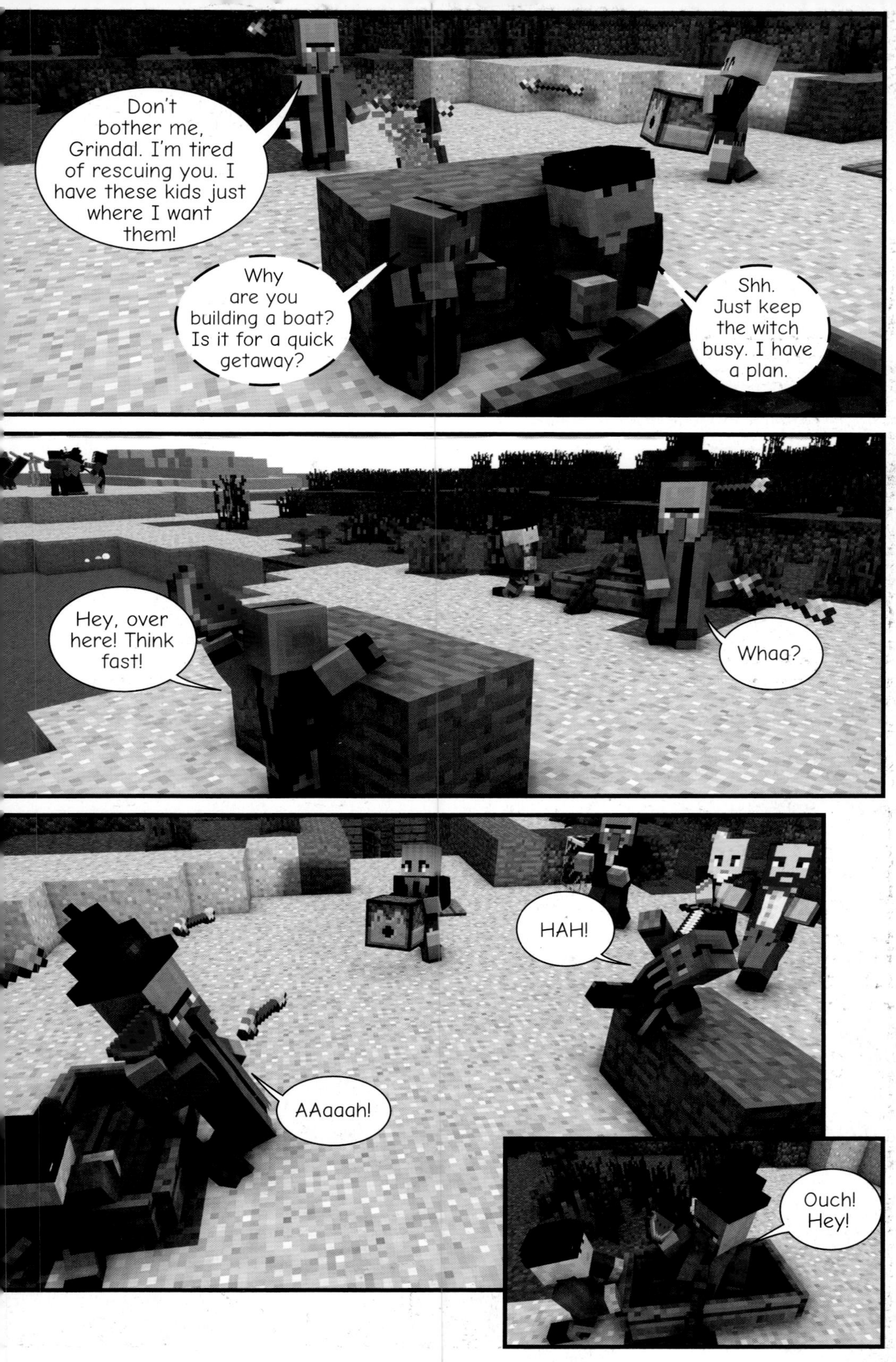
Don't bother me, Grindal. I'm tired of rescuing you. I have these kids just where I want them!
Why are you building a boat? Is it for a quick getaway?
Shh. Just keep the witch busy. I have a plan.
Hey, over here! Think fast!
Whaa?
HAH!
AAaaah!
Ouch! Hey!

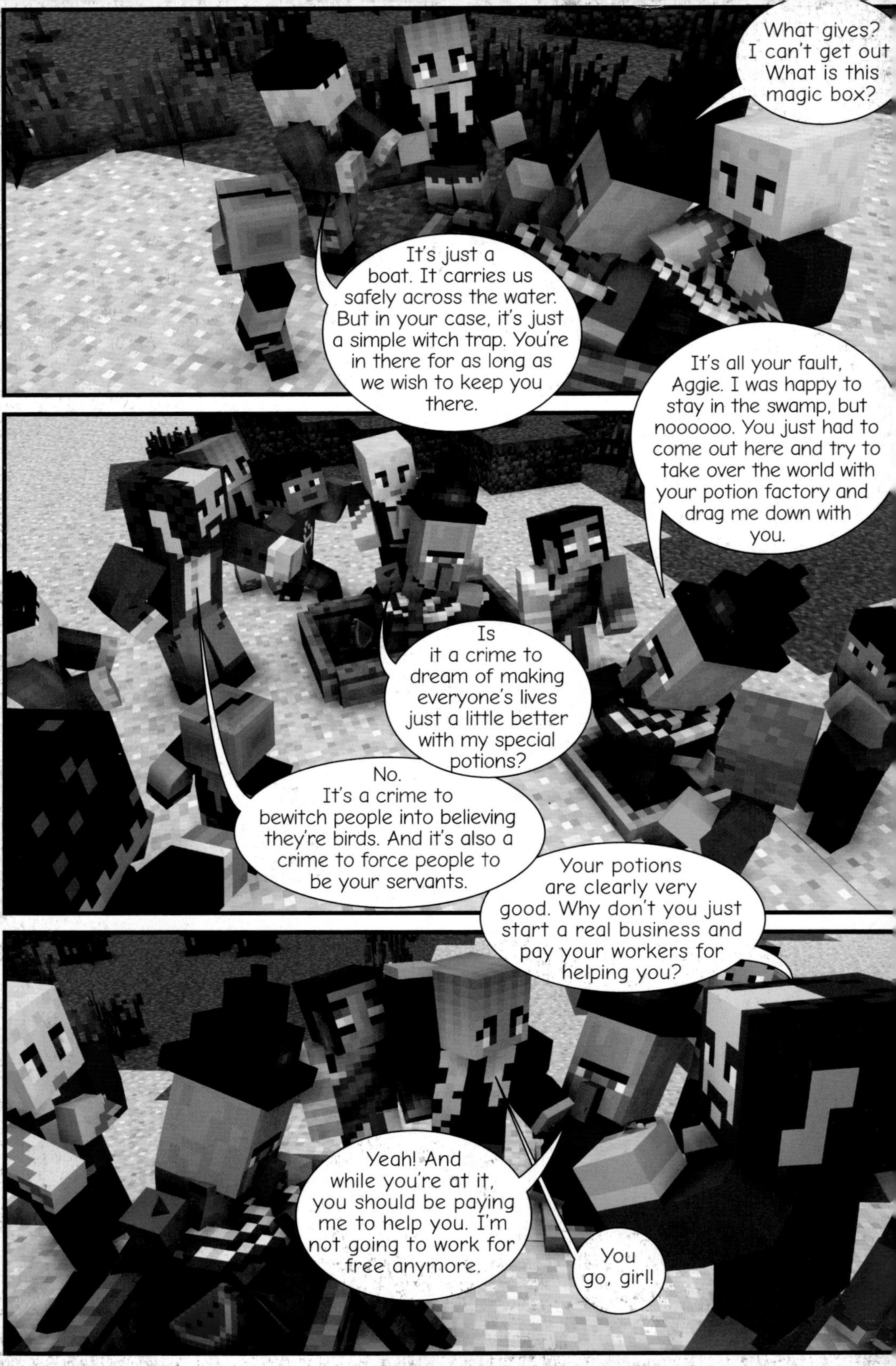
What gives? I can't get out What is this magic box?
It's just a boat. It carries us safely across the water. But in your case, it's just a simple witch trap. You're in there for as long as we wish to keep you there.
It's all your fault, Aggie. I was happy to stay in the swamp, but noooooo. You just had to come out here and try to take over the world with your potion factory and drag me down with you.
Is it a crime to dream of making everyone's lives just a little better with my special potions?
No. It's a crime to bewitch people into believing they're birds. And it's also a crime to force people to be your servants.
Your potions are clearly very good. Why don't you just start a real business and pay your workers for helping you?
Yeah! And while you're at it, you should be paying me to help you. I'm not going to work for free anymore.
You go, girl!

CHAPTER 12

FIRESIDE FEAST

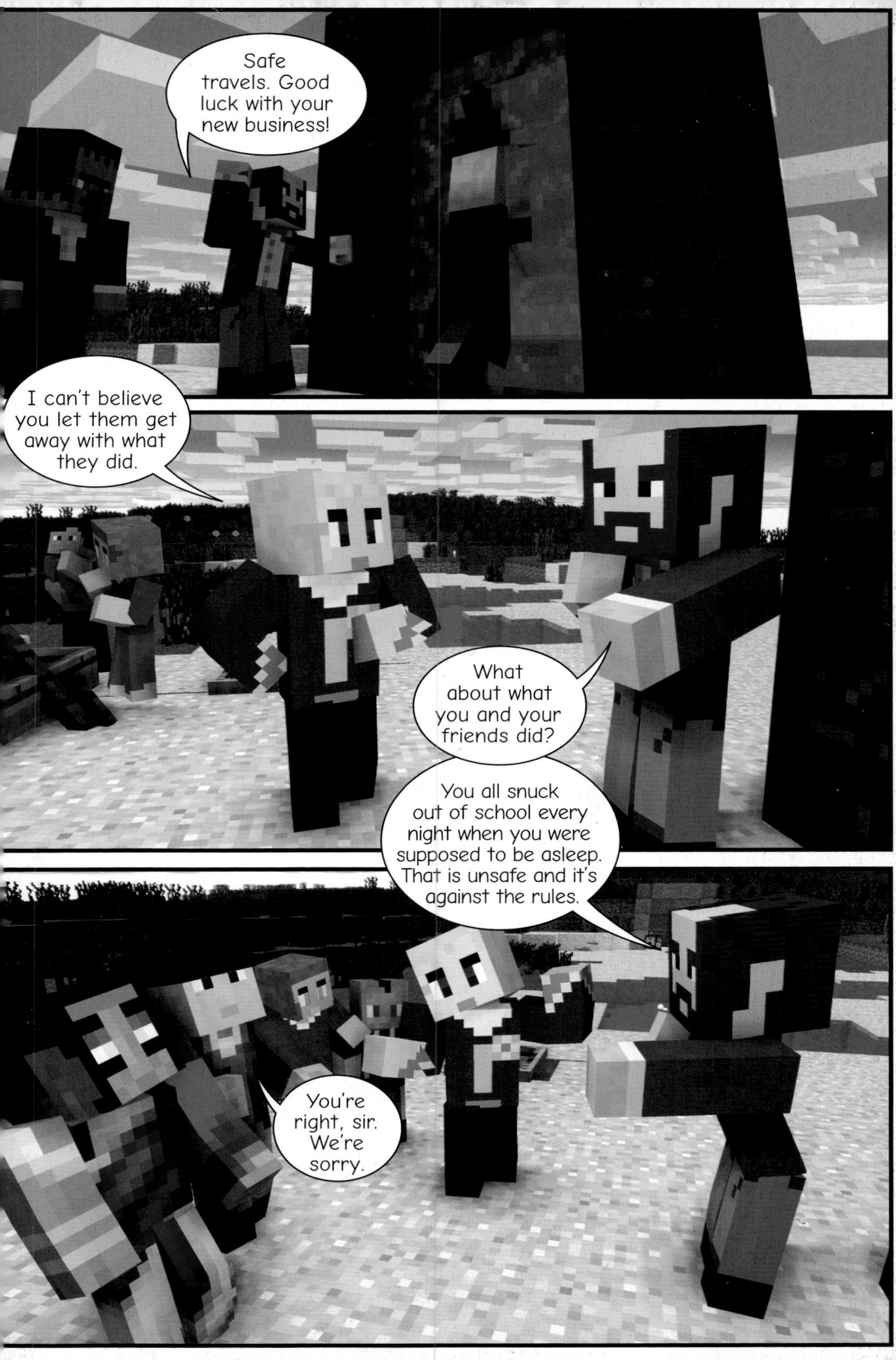
Safe travels. Good luck with your new business!
I can't believe you let them get away with what they did.
What about what you and your friends did?
You all snuck out of school every night when you were supposed to be asleep. That is unsafe and it's against the rules.
You're right, sir. We're sorry.

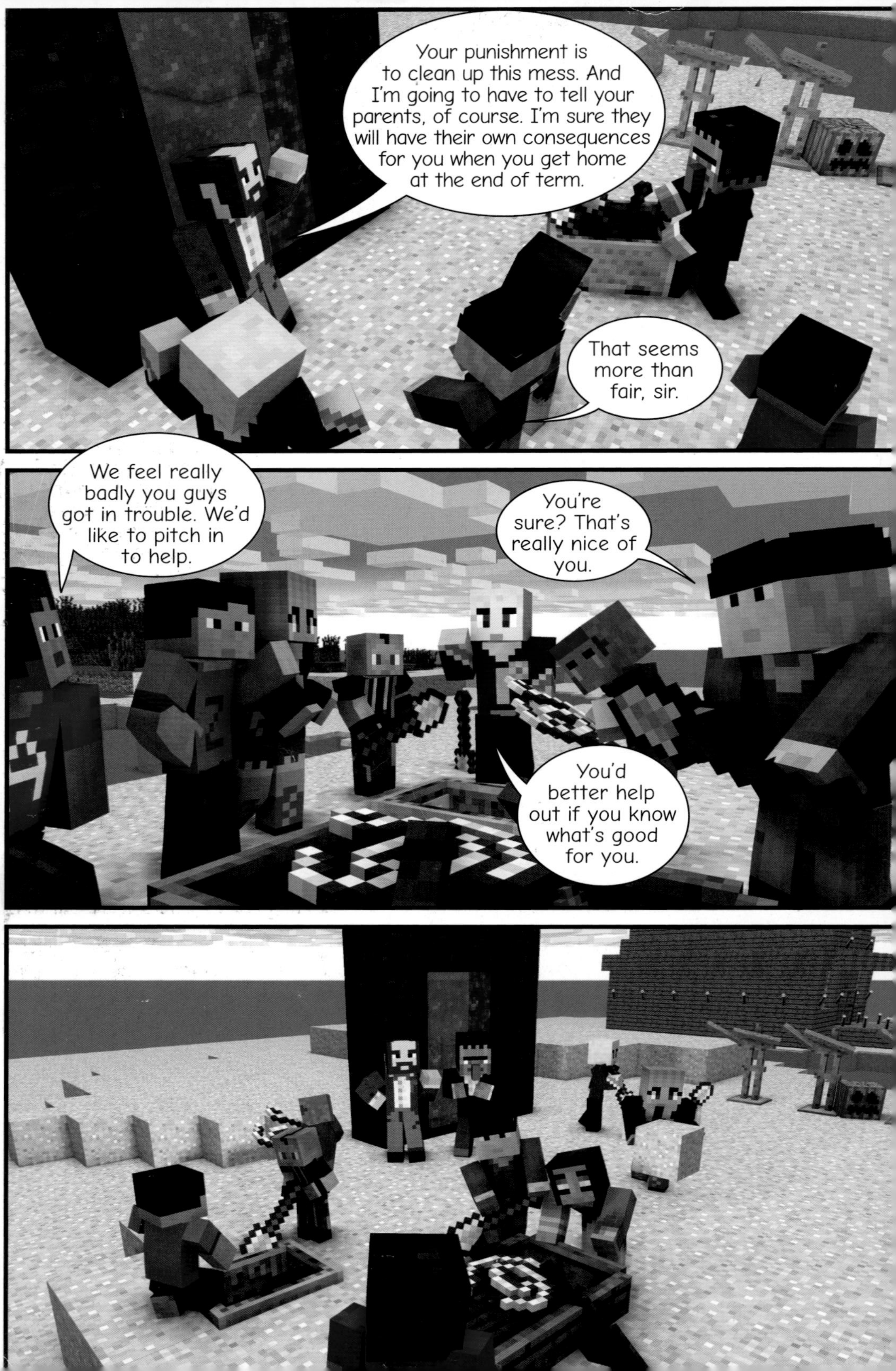
Your punishment is to clean up this mess. And I'm going to have to tell your parents, of course. I'm sure they will have their own consequences for you when you get home at the end of term.
That seems more than fair, sir.
We feel really badly you guys got in trouble. We'd like to pitch in to help.
You're sure? That's really nice of you.
You'd better help out if you know what's good for you.

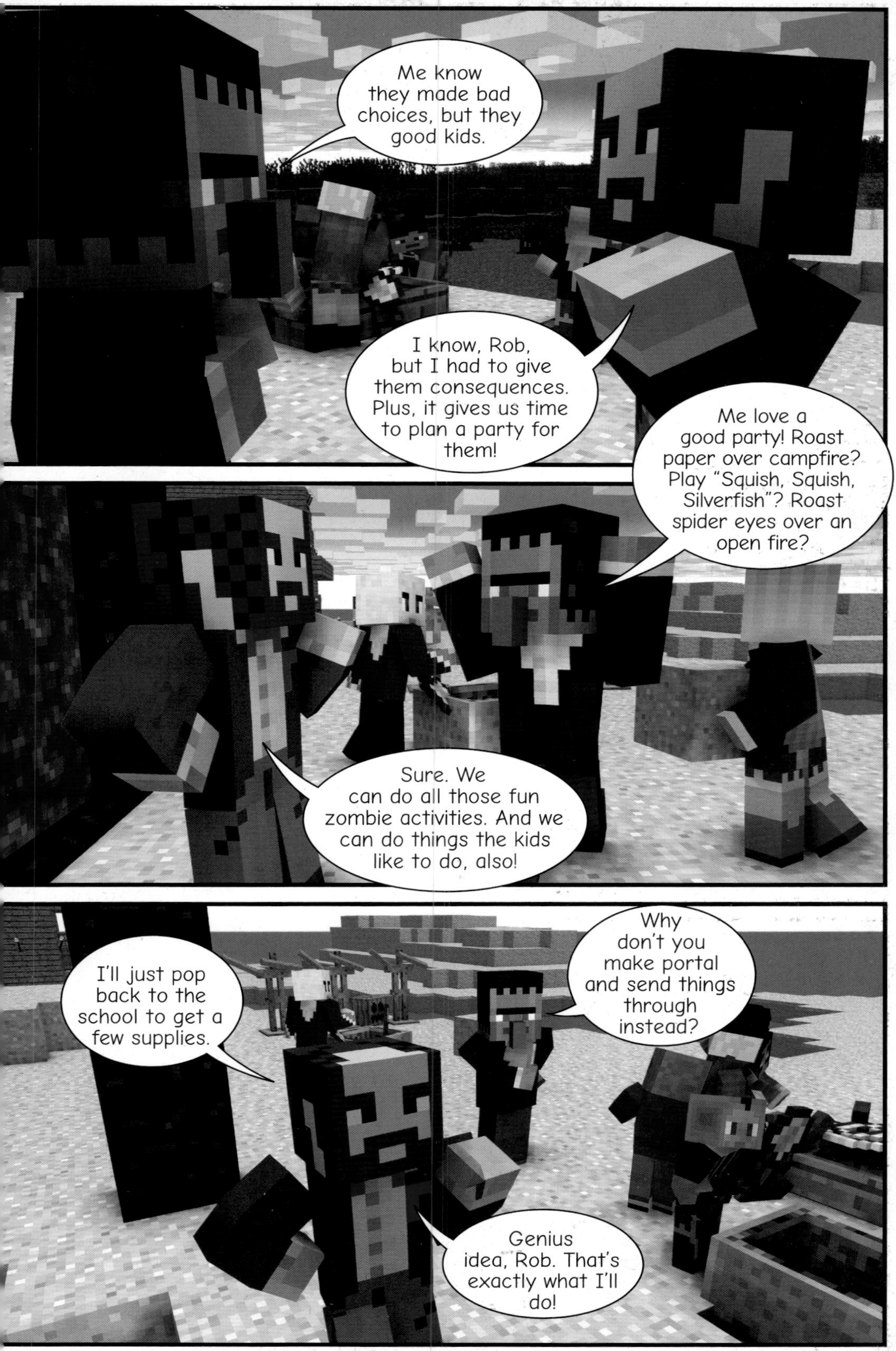

Me know they made bad choices, but they good kids.
I know, Rob, but I had to give them consequences. Plus, it gives us time to plan a party for them!
Me love a good party! Roast paper over campfire? Play "Squish, Squish, Silverfish"? Roast spider eyes over an open fire?
Sure. We can do all those fun zombie activities. And we can do things the kids like to do, also!
I'll just pop back to the school to get a few supplies.
Why don't you make portal and send things through instead?
Genius idea, Rob. That's exactly what I'll do!

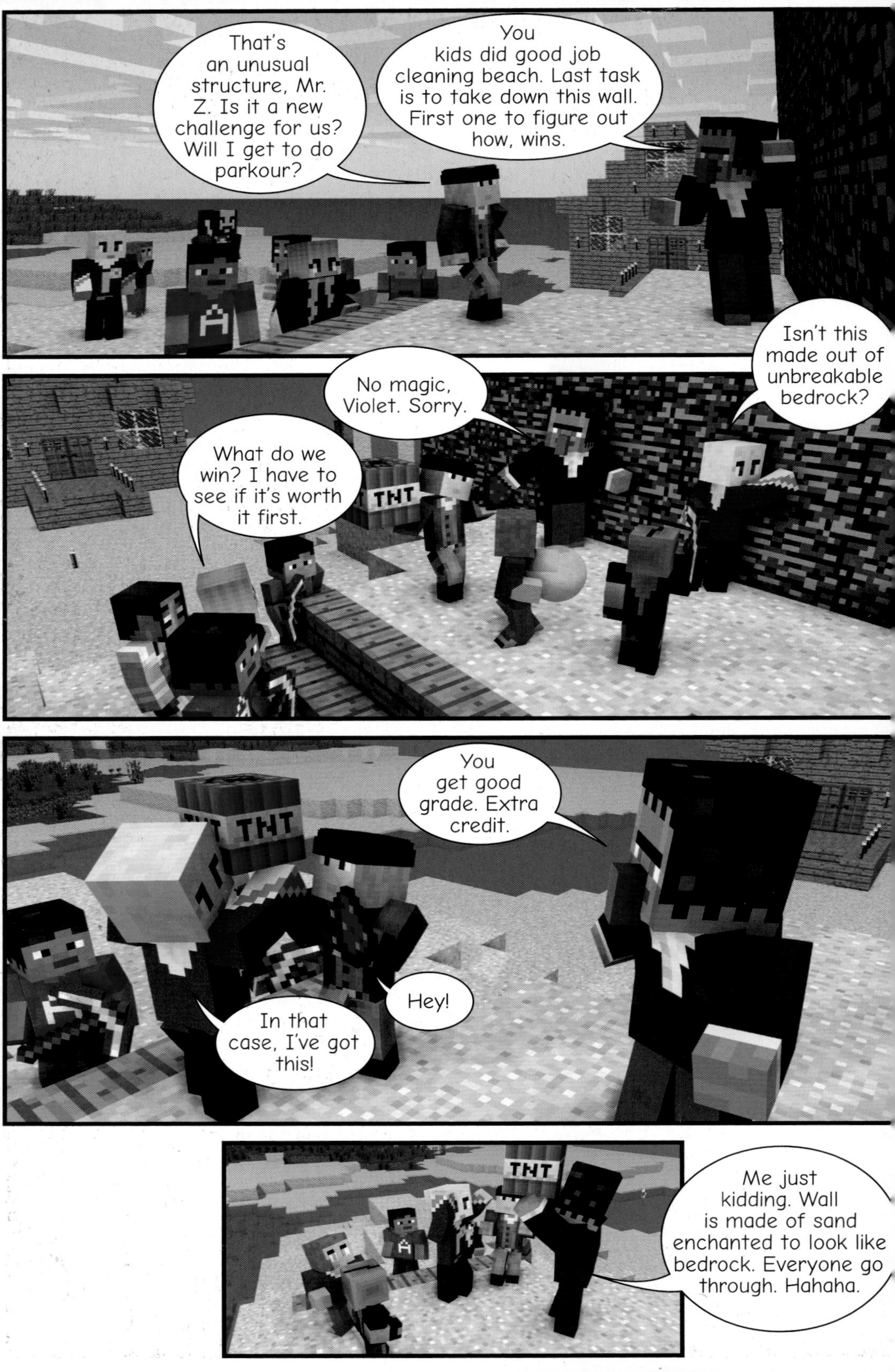
That's an unusual structure, Mr. Z. Is it a new challenge for us? Will I get to do parkour?
You kids did good job cleaning beach. Last task is to take down this wall. First one to figure out how, wins.
Isn't this made out of unbreakable bedrock?
No magic, Violet. Sorry.
What do we win? I have to see if it's worth it first.
TNT
You get good grade. Extra credit.
TNT
TNT
In that case, I've got this!
Hey!
TNT
Me just kidding. Wall is made of sand enchanted to look like bedrock. Everyone go through. Hahaha.

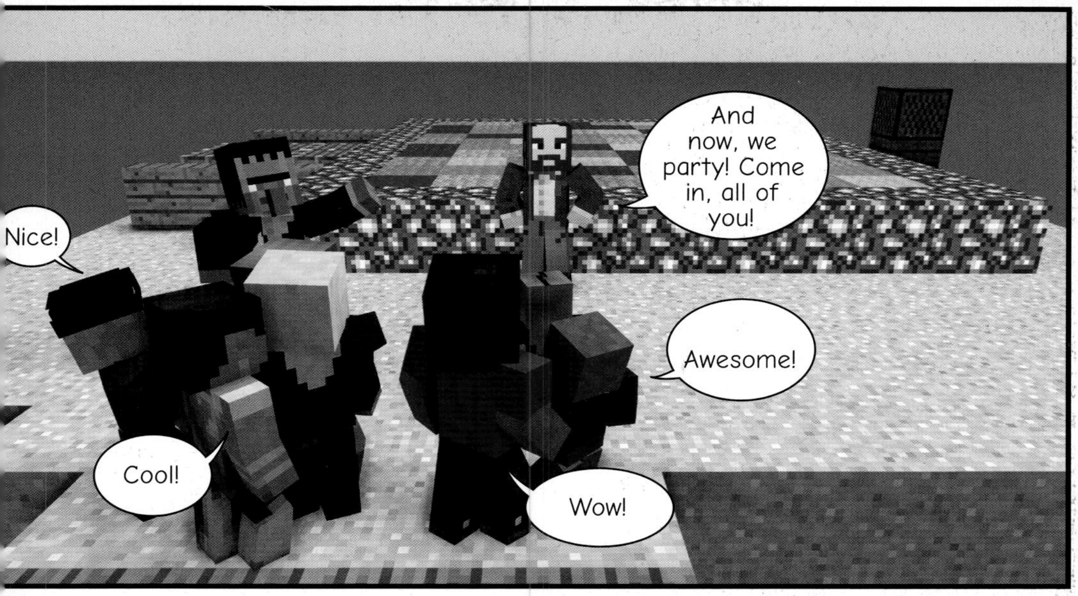
And now, we party! Come in, all of you!
Nice!
Awesome!
Cool!
Wow!

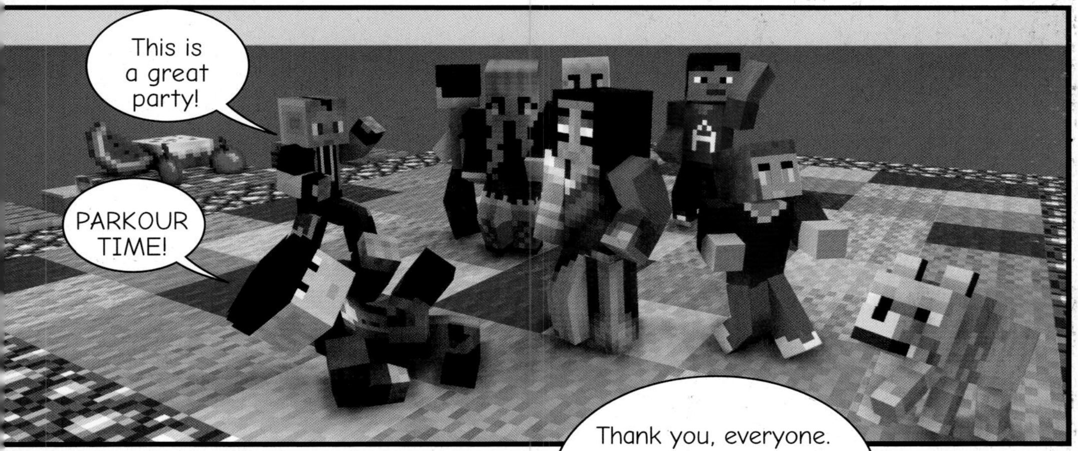
This is a great party!
PARKOUR TIME!

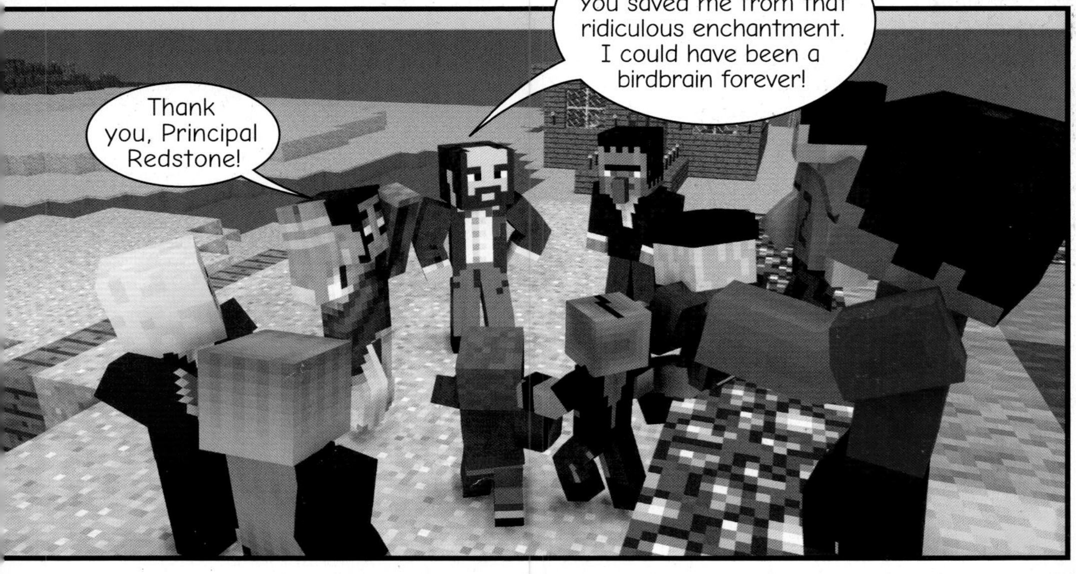
Thank you, everyone. You saved me from that ridiculous enchantment. I could have been a birdbrain forever!
Thank you, Principal Redstone!

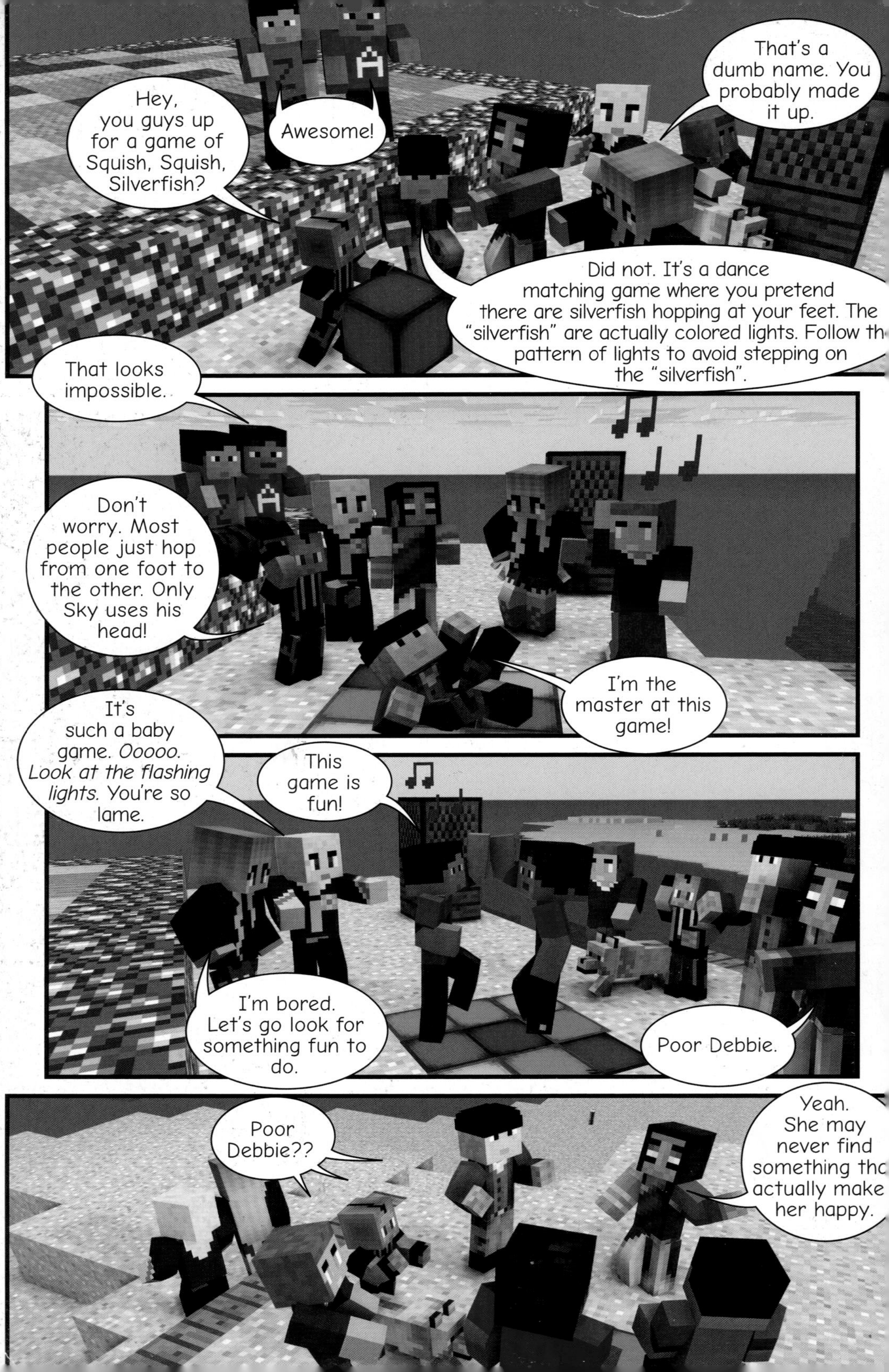
Hey, you guys up for a game of Squish, Squish, Silverfish?
Awesome!
That's a dumb name. You probably made it up.
Did not. It's a dance matching game where you pretend there are silverfish hopping at your feet. The "silverfish" are actually colored lights. Follow th pattern of lights to avoid stepping on the "silverfish".
That looks impossible.
Don't worry. Most people just hop from one foot to the other. Only Sky uses his head!
I'm the master at this game!
It's such a baby game. *Ooooo. Look at the flashing lights.* You're so lame.
This game is fun!
I'm bored. Let's go look for something fun to do.
Poor Debbie.
Poor Debbie??
Yeah. She may never find something tha actually make her happy.

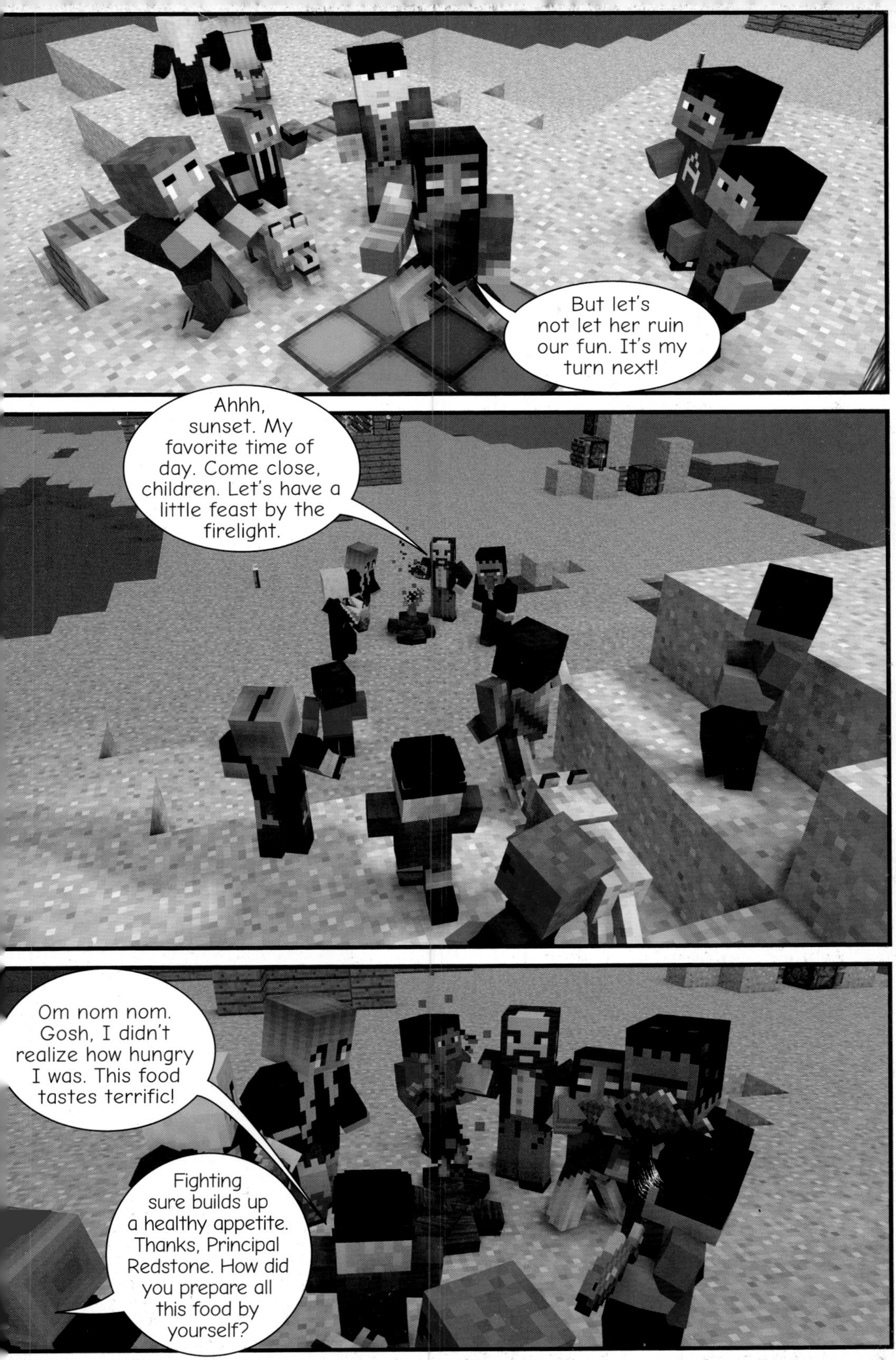
But let's not let her ruin our fun. It's my turn next!
Ahhh, sunset. My favorite time of day. Come close, children. Let's have a little feast by the firelight.
Om nom nom. Gosh, I didn't realize how hungry I was. This food tastes terrific!
Fighting sure builds up a healthy appetite. Thanks, Principal Redstone. How did you prepare all this food by yourself?

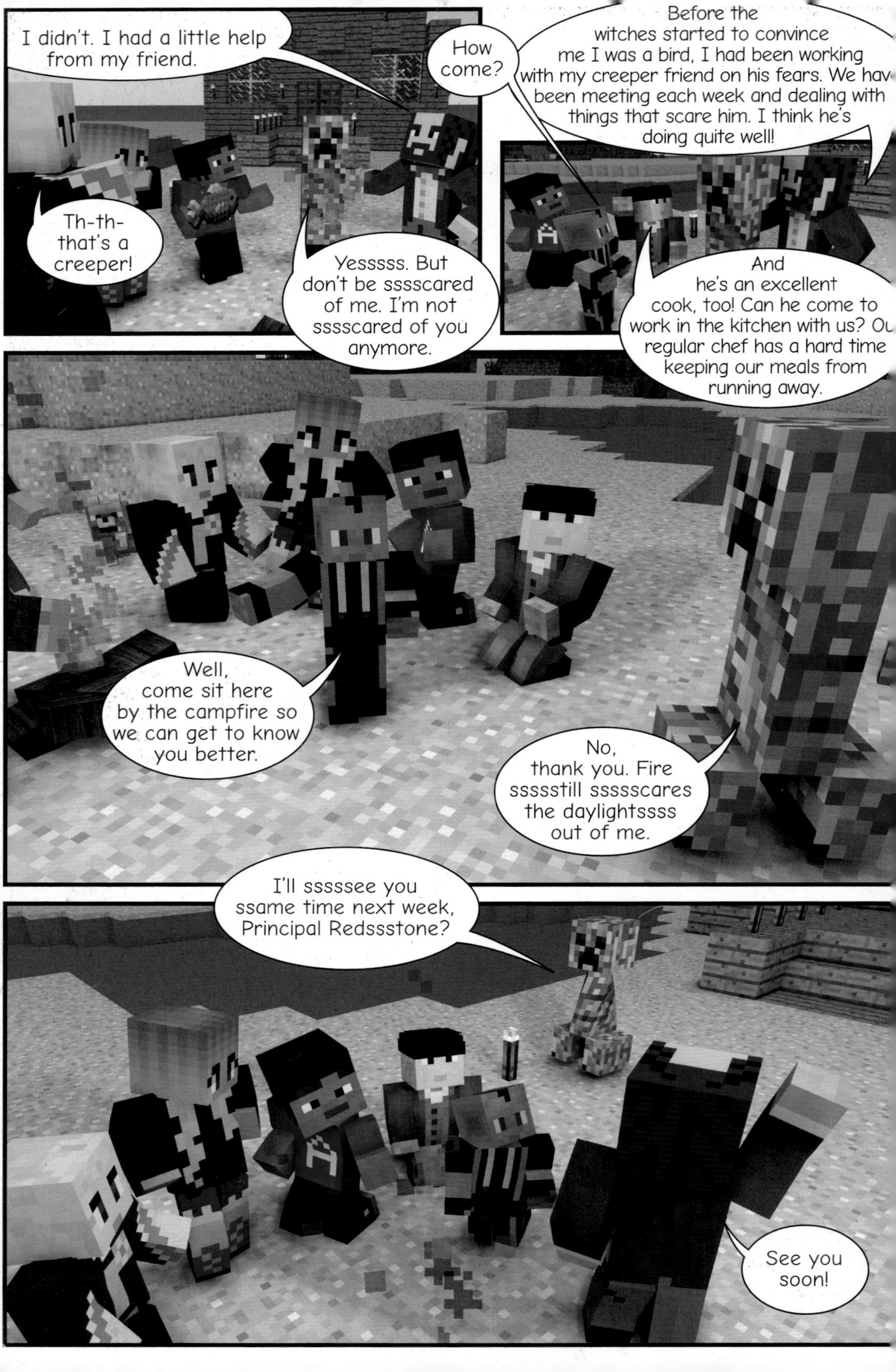
I didn't. I had a little help from my friend.
How come?
Before the witches started to convince me I was a bird, I had been working with my creeper friend on his fears. We hav been meeting each week and dealing with things that scare him. I think he's doing quite well!
Th-th-that's a creeper!
Yesssss. But don't be sssscared of me. I'm not sssscared of you anymore.
And he's an excellent cook, too! Can he come to work in the kitchen with us? Ou regular chef has a hard time keeping our meals from running away.
Well, come sit here by the campfire so we can get to know you better.
No, thank you. Fire ssssstill ssssscares the daylightssss out of me.
I'll sssssee you ssame time next week, Principal Redssstone?
See you soon!

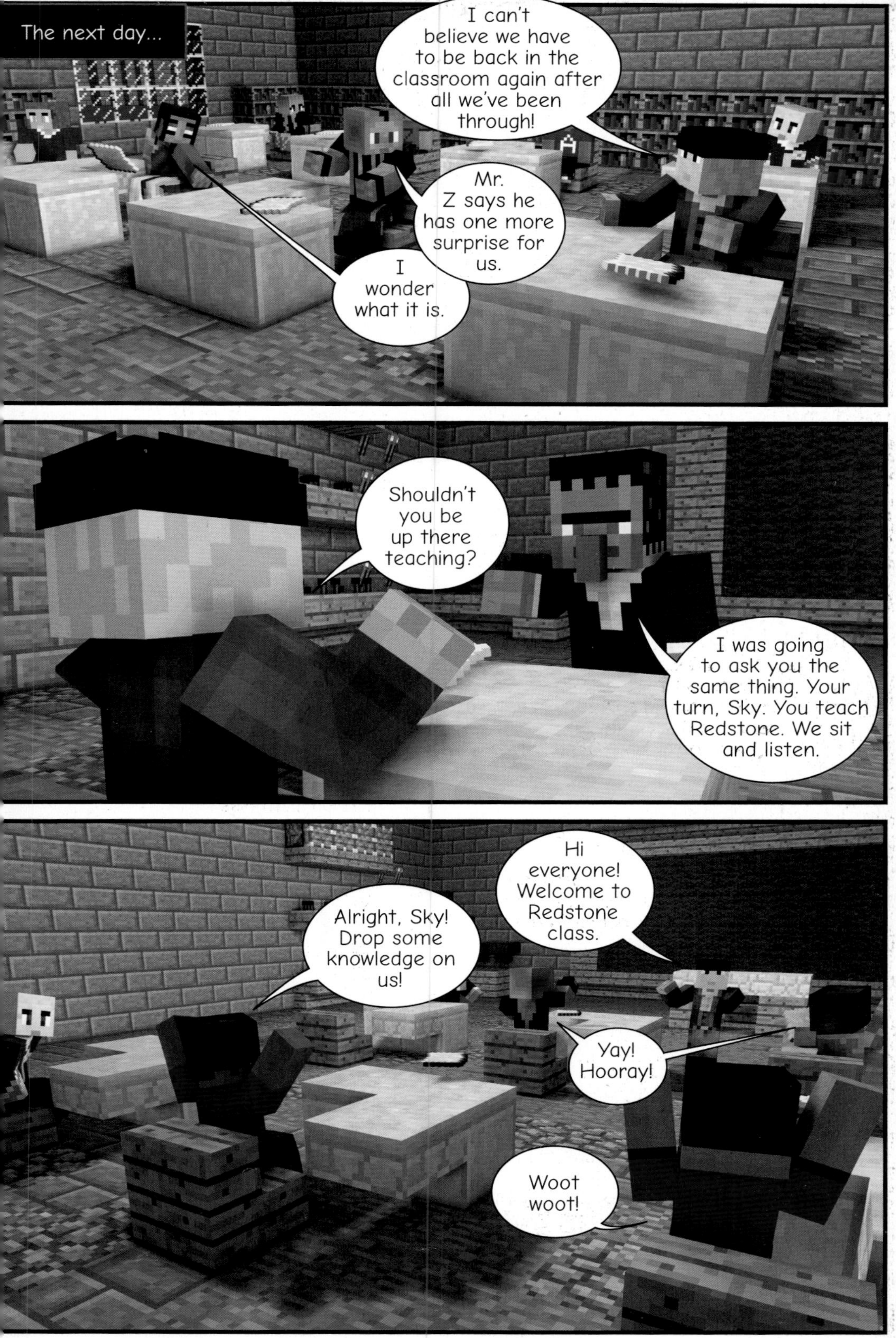

The next day...
I can't believe we have to be back in the classroom again after all we've been through!
Mr. Z says he has one more surprise for us.
I wonder what it is.
Shouldn't you be up there teaching?
I was going to ask you the same thing. Your turn, Sky. You teach Redstone. We sit and listen.
Hi everyone! Welcome to Redstone class.
Alright, Sky! Drop some knowledge on us!
Yay! Hooray!
Woot woot!

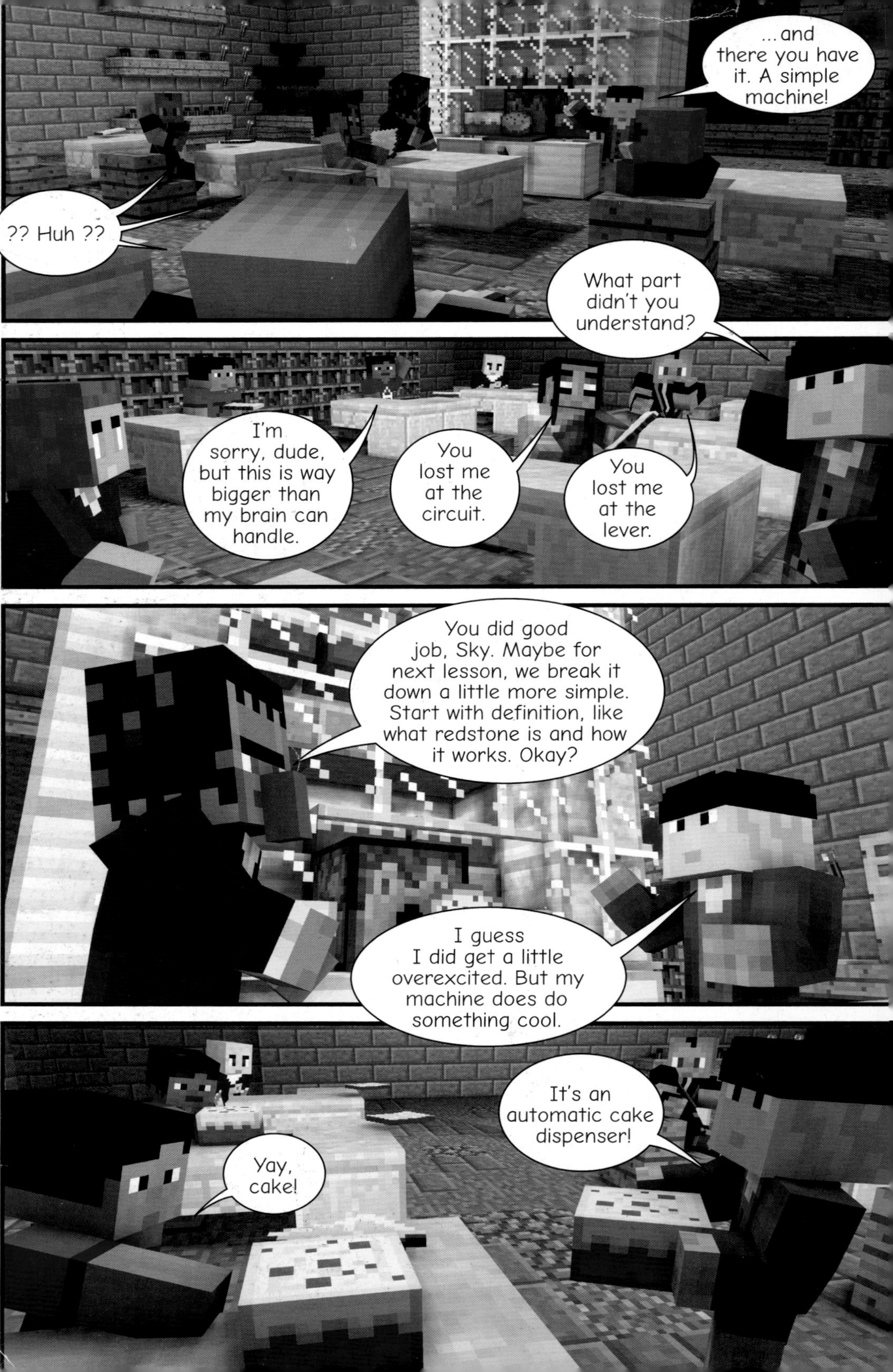
...and there you have it. A simple machine!
?? Huh ??
What part didn't you understand?
I'm sorry, dude, but this is way bigger than my brain can handle.
You lost me at the circuit.
You lost me at the lever.
You did good job, Sky. Maybe for next lesson, we break it down a little more simple. Start with definition, like what redstone is and how it works. Okay?
I guess I did get a little overexcited. But my machine does do something cool.
It's an automatic cake dispenser!
Yay, cake!

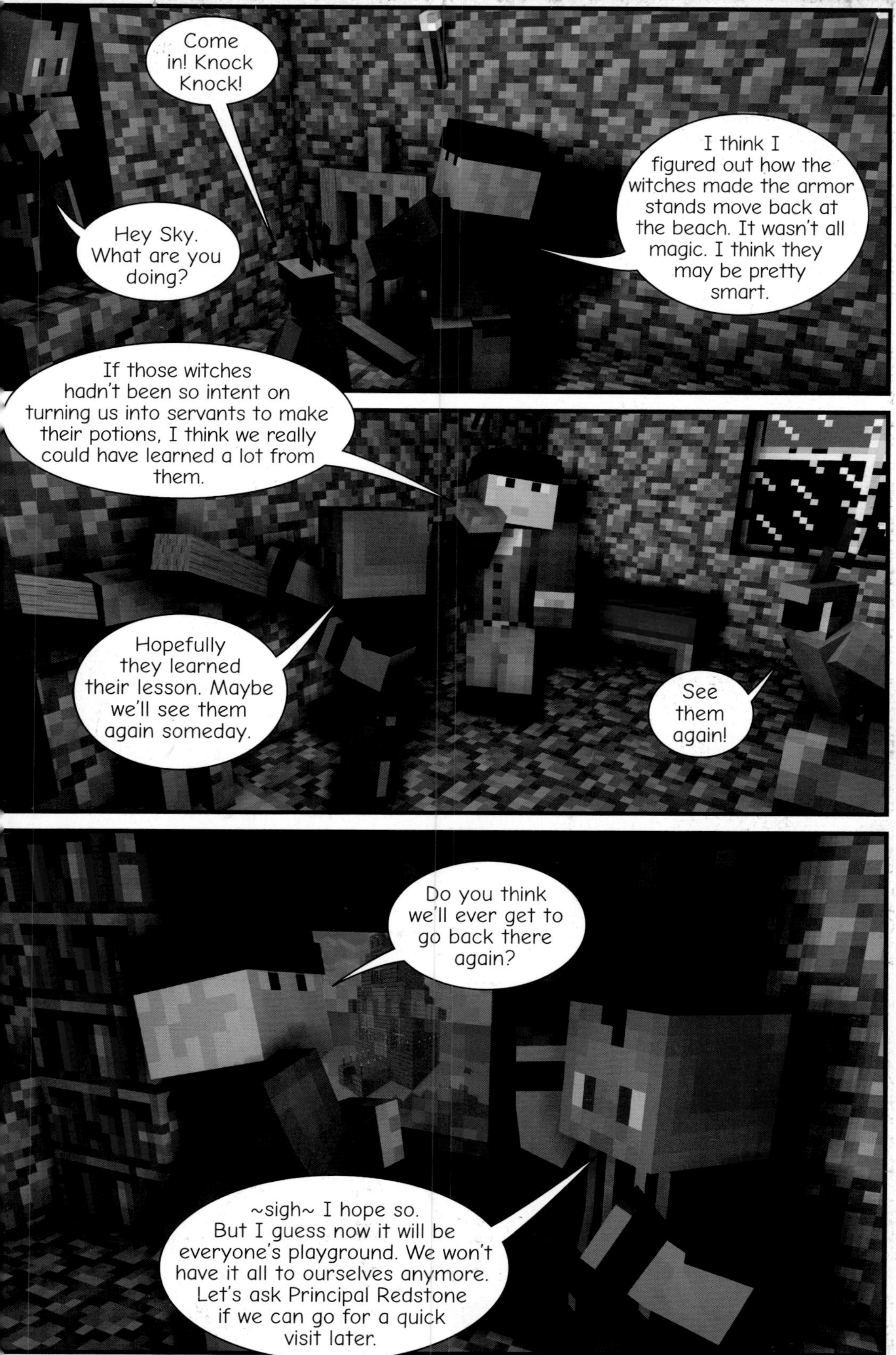
Hey Sky. What are you doing?
Come in! Knock Knock!
I think I figured out how the witches made the armor stands move back at the beach. It wasn't all magic. I think they may be pretty smart.
If those witches hadn't been so intent on turning us into servants to make their potions, I think we really could have learned a lot from them.
Hopefully they learned their lesson. Maybe we'll see them again someday.
See them again!
Do you think we'll ever get to go back there again?
~sigh~ I hope so. But I guess now it will be everyone's playground. We won't have it all to ourselves anymore. Let's ask Principal Redstone if we can go for a quick visit later.

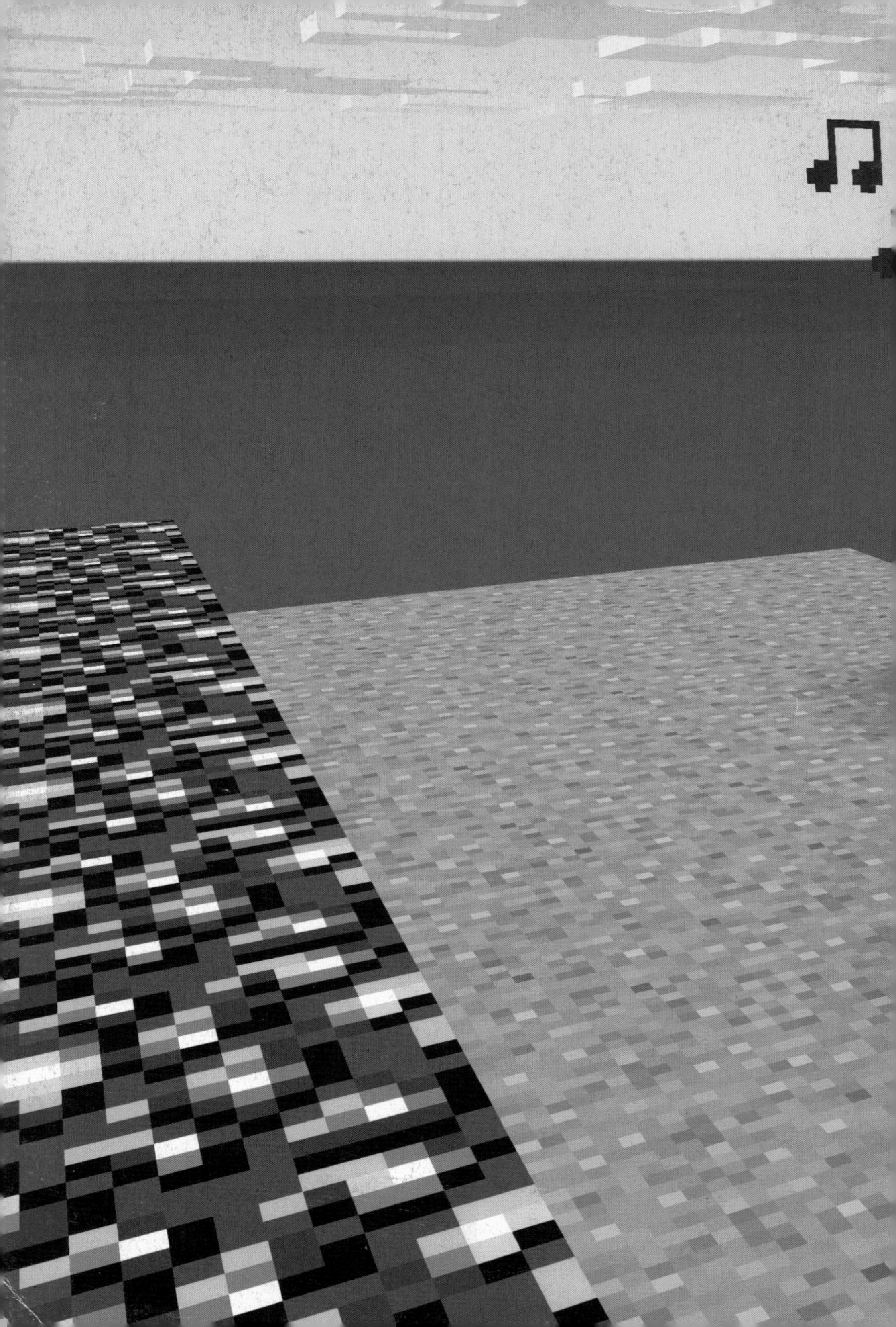

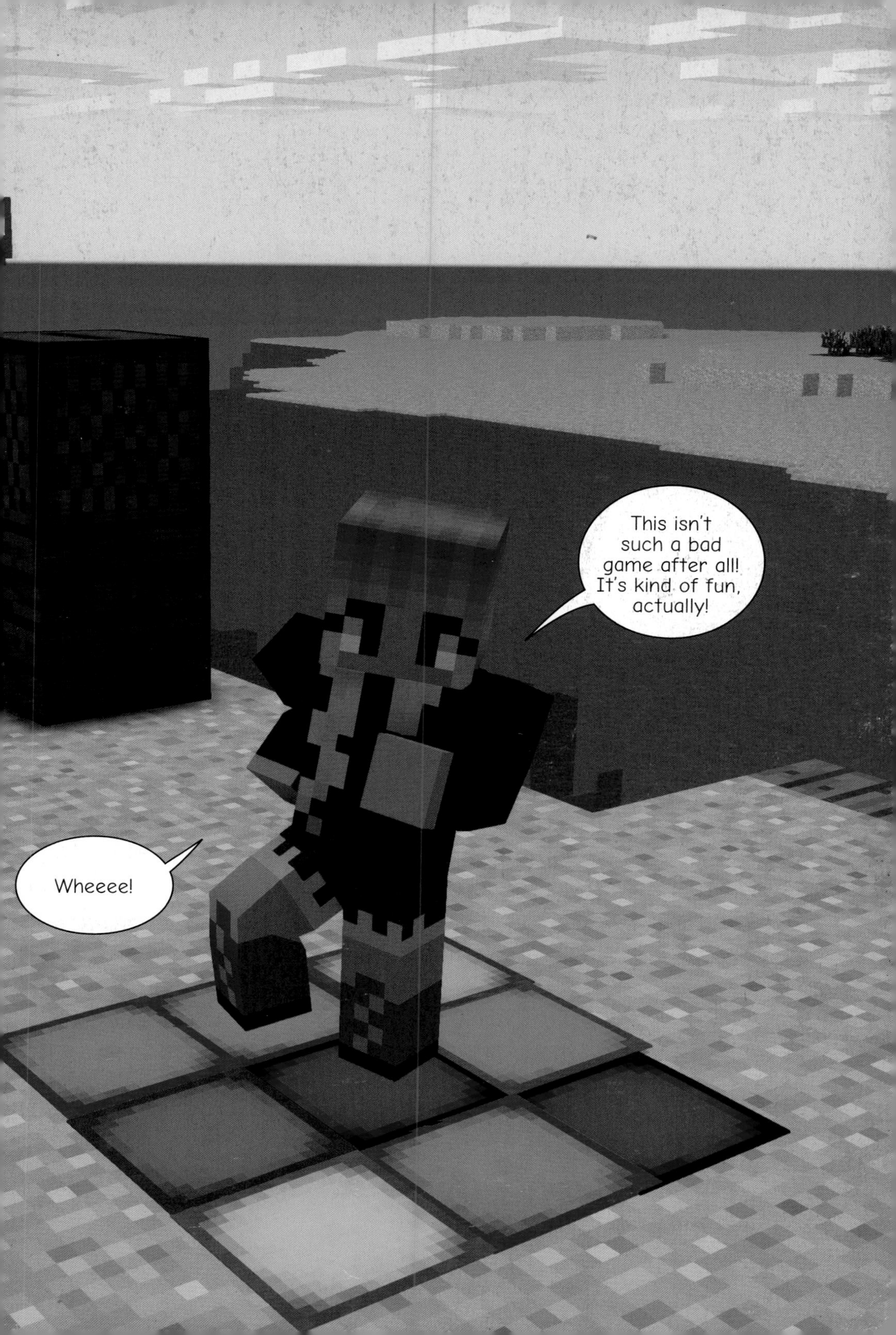
This isn't such a bad game after all! It's kind of fun, actually!
Wheeee!